THE ONCOMING STORM

Professionally Published Books by Christopher G. Nuttall

ELSEWHEN PRESS

The Royal Sorceress

The Royal Sorceress (Book I)
The Great Game (Book II)
Necropolis (Book III)

Bookworm

Bookworm
Bookworm II: The Very Ugly Duckling
Bookworm III: The Best Laid Plans

Inverse Shadows

Sufficiently Advanced Technology

Stand Alone

A Life Less Ordinary
The Mind's Eye

TWILIGHT TIMES BOOKS

Schooled in Magic

Schooled in Magic (Book I)
Lessons in Etiquette (Book II)
Study in Slaughter (Book III)
Work Experience (Book IV)
The School of Hard Knocks (Book V)
Love's Labor's Won (Book VI)
Trial By Fire (Book VII)

The Decline and Fall of the Galactic Empire

Barbarians at The Gates (Book I)
The Shadow of Cincinnatus (Book II)

HENCHMEN PRESS

First Strike

THE ONCOMING STORM

ANGEL IN THE WHIRLWIND

CHRISTOPHER G. NUTTALL

47NORTH

This is a work of fiction. Names, characters, organizations, places, events, and incidents are either products of the author's imagination or are used fictitiously.

Published by 47North, Seattle

www.apub.com

ISBN-13: 9781503947085
ISBN-10: 1503947084

Cover design by Ray Lundgren

Illustrated by Paul Youll

Printed in the United States of America

PROLOGUE

Admiral Junayd passed through the security field and stepped into the conference room, careful to remove his cap as he bowed to the First Speaker and the Lord Cleric. They nodded in return, pressing their hands together in greeting, then motioned him to a chair at the round table. Junayd sat down and composed himself, despite the growing excitement running through his mind. The greatest military operation in the Theocracy's history was about to begin. It was no time to allow his enthusiasm to overpower his common sense.

He looked up at the giant painting behind the First Speaker. Hundreds of men and women, some bound, others in chains, were making their way towards a giant starship that was sitting on the ground like a common aircraft. It was a lie, he knew, a fanciful depiction of a carefully planned exodus from Earth, but the essential truth shone through. The Believers had been forced into exile, forced to leave God's chosen world. Many of the exiles had lost the will to live in horror at what had been done to them.

But others had understood. God would not have allowed His faithful to be removed from their homeworld without a reason. It would be safer for them to be elsewhere. And now Earth was scorched rubble: the great cities of Rome, Jerusalem, and Mecca little more than blackened marks on a dead world. The religious leaders who had failed to realize their time was over were gone. And the United Nations, the force that had served as their enforcer, was gone too. The True Faith could begin its expansion into the galaxy—and no infidels would stand in its way.

He nodded in greeting as Inquisitor Samuilu stepped into the room, unable to avoid feeling a cold shiver running down his back as he met the man's eyes. Everyone was secretly guilty of something, the Inquisitors believed, and innocence was no defense if one caught their ever-roaming eye. Even a high-ranking admiral was not immune to suspicion. The Inquisitors spent most of their time rooting out heresy on the occupied worlds, but they had never relaxed their watch over the Believers.

And a word from them would be enough to condemn anyone to the stocks—or the gallows.

"Let us begin," the First Speaker said.

He spoke the words of a very old prayer, echoed by the other three men in the room, then looked up at Junayd. "Admiral," he said. "How fares our planning?"

Junayd took a long breath. "We will be ready to launch the offensive in six months, Your Holiness," he began. "Planning has been completed for a short, sharp campaign that will bring the infidel Commonwealth to its knees. We will trap and destroy their border fleets, then advance towards their homeworlds before they know what has hit them. Victory will be assured."

"Only God can assure one of victory," the Lord Cleric said.

That, Junayd knew, was true. Other religions, the shadows of the True Faith, had believed that God granted victory to his followers without forcing them to work for it. But the True Believers knew that God only helped those who helped themselves. What was the point of victory—or redemption—if it was just handed out on silver platters? But he dared not seem uncertain, not now. There was no shortage of others who would take his place if he ran afoul of his superiors.

"We have been watching their deployments to Cadiz ever since they annexed the border world," he said, instead. "Their readiness levels are at the lowest we have observed since we started monitoring them closely. The admiral in command spends most of his time on the planet, training and exercising schedules are not followed, and morale is incredibly low. We would not wish to wait long enough for the Commonwealth to appoint an *effective* commander to take Admiral Morrison's place."

The First Speaker smirked. "That would be inconvenient," he agreed.

"We have allies on the planet's surface," Junayd continued. "They will be ready to go on the offensive when our fleet arrives in the system. Cadiz will be cut off from the StarCom network, her command and control systems crippled, allowing us to score a decisive victory before the infidels can mobilize. Their long-term potential is staggering."

He kept his face impassive, refusing to admit how much that bothered him. The first conquests made by the Theocracy had been easy. They'd largely been primitive worlds, with no spacefaring capability at all. It had taken little more than a destroyer to crush formal resistance, then the Inquisitors had gone to work, digging out all who would dare to resist their place in the Theocracy. But the Commonwealth was different. It was a multisystem political entity with a growing trading fleet as well as a formidable military machine.

The Theocracy's industrial base was geared to support the colossal war machine they intended to use to conquer the settled galaxy. It was limited, more limited than Junayd cared to admit, yet they would never be able to relax some of the restrictions on economic and social development. It would give people ideas. But the Commonwealth didn't have that problem. Somehow, the infidels had created an economy that was growing by leaps and bounds. It presented a formidable threat as well as a challenge.

And it wasn't the only state to emerge from the ashes left by the Breakaway Wars. It was quite possible that the Commonwealth and the

Theocracy could batter each other to pieces, and then watch helplessly as another state moved in and took over. Or, for that matter, that the other states would block expansion of the True Faith. It could not be allowed.

"But nothing compared to ours," the Lord Cleric said.

The First Speaker smiled. "Six months," he mused. "Can you not attack earlier?"

"We would need to call up freighters to support the military offensive," Junayd said. "It will take several months to assemble them without damaging our economy too extensively."

Junayd paused. "Besides, we would also need to position our forces on our side of the border," he added. "And then place our agents in the right locations to do harm."

The First Speaker looked at the Lord Cleric, who nodded.

"You have permission to start assembling our forces," the First Speaker said, firmly. "And may God defend the right."

"I thank you," Junayd said. He stood, placing his hand on his heart. "And I pledge to you, Your Holiness, that the Commonwealth will be ours within a year."

CHAPTER ONE

"The Hotel Magnificent, My Lady," the shuttle pilot said. "I'll drop down on the roof?"

"Yes, please," Captain Lady Katherine Falcone said. She felt a tingle from her implants as security scanners swept the shuttle, confirming her presence. "I believe they should already have cleared us to land."

She looked down as the shuttle dropped towards the landing pad. It had been four years since she'd seen Tyre City from the air, but it never failed to impress. The designers had covered everything, from the Royal Palace to the military barracks and giant apartment blocks, in white marble, creating a glittering haze as aircars and shuttles flew overhead. Only the brooding presence of the giant planetary defense center, carved into a nearby mountain, spoiled the impression of a city out of fantasy. But then, the kings of Tyre had had the money to make their fantasies reality.

The shuttle touched down gently, allowing Kat to stand up and make her way through the hatch and out into the warm morning air. A pair of bodyguards stood there, their faces hidden behind black masks; her implants reported that she was being scanned, again, before the bodyguards stepped aside and allowed her to walk through the door into the hotel. She sighed inwardly as they followed her. They knew who she was. It was the paranoia of living in a goldfish bowl, among many other things, that had caused her to seek out her own career, as far from her family as possible.

She caught sight of her own reflection in a mirrored door before it opened and tried not to wince. Her family had the very best enhancements sequenced into their genes, ensuring that she had an estimated lifespan of over two hundred years, but she looked young, as if she were barely out of her teens. The long blond hair she had refused to cut, despite years on various starships, fell around her heart-shaped face, drawing attention from everyone who looked at her. The black uniform she wore, complete with the golden star on her shoulder that designated starship command, fitted her perfectly. But then, her body was perfect too.

At least I'm not Candy, she thought, thankfully. Her older sister spent most of her life aping fashion, even to the point of changing her body or gender completely, just to fit in with her friends. *But I could have turned out just like her.*

"My Lady," a voice said.

Kat looked up to see a thin, dark-skinned girl wearing a dress that left very little to the imagination. She sighed. One would have thought that the Hotel Magnificent could have dressed its maids and other staff in something more classy than a dress that wouldn't have been out of place in a pornographic VR sim. But she supposed the vast majority of the visitors probably appreciated the dresses. Besides, it was easy to underestimate someone who looked so harmless.

"Your father is waiting for you in the dining room," the maid said. She curtseyed. "If you would care to accompany me . . ."

"Of course," Kat said. Why would her father have chosen to meet her in the dining room? "I would be honored."

She saw the answer as soon as the maid led her into the giant room. It was immense, large enough for nearly fifty tables . . . and they were all completely empty, save one. Kat felt an odd mixture of embarrassment and shame as she saw her father, realizing that he'd spent millions of crowns merely to hire the room and ensure that everyone else who might have had a reservation was paid off. It was a display of power that she couldn't help but feel was a little vulgar. But one truth she'd learned as a child was that if you were rich enough, it didn't matter what sort of person you were. Everyone would want to be your friend.

Her father, Duke Lucas Falcone, rose to his feet as she approached. He was a tall man, his hair starting to go gray after years of serving as CEO of the Falcone Consortium. Kat didn't envy him his position, even though she knew there was almost no chance of her inheriting anything more than a trust account and some stocks and shares. She'd seen enough of how her older siblings had been prepared to take his place to know she didn't want it for herself.

"Father," she said, carefully. "Thank you for agreeing to meet with me."

"I was in the city," her father said gravely. "It was no hassle to see my youngest daughter."

He motioned for Kat to take a seat and then sat down facing her. Two maids appeared, as if from nowhere, each one carrying a menu in her delicate hands. Kat took one and placed it on the table, rolling her eyes at the sheer assortment of cutlery and glasses in front of her. The value of the knives and forks alone could have fed a poorer family for several weeks.

"Please tell me you don't roll your eyes like a teenager on your command deck," her father said, tiredly. "I don't think your crew would be very impressed."

Kat felt her face heat. She was twenty-nine years old and he *still* made her feel like a child the few times they met in person. He'd rarely had time for her or any of her nine siblings when they'd been children, leaving them in the care of the household staff. There were times when she understood precisely why Candy was intent on blowing through her trust fund as rapidly as possible. She wanted attention from her parents—and they'd only really paid attention when she'd done something shocking or scandalous. Kat had felt the same way as she'd grown into adulthood. But she'd joined the Navy instead of becoming a trust-fund brat.

"I imagine they wouldn't be," she said tartly. "I need to talk to you."

"Order your food first," her father advised. "This place does an excellent caviar and chutney . . ."

"Fish and chips, please," Kat said to the maid. Her father looked impassive, but she knew him well enough to tell he'd probably swallowed a disparaging comment. Fish and chips was a plebeian dish and they both knew it. "And a glass of water."

Her father ordered—something both expensive and unpronounceable—and then waited for the maids to leave before leaning forward to face her. "You wanted to talk to me," he said flatly. "Talk."

"I have been promoted to command a heavy cruiser," Kat said, tapping the golden badge on her shoulder. "What did you have to do with my promotion?"

"Congratulations would seem to be in order," her father mused. "Perhaps champagne . . ."

"*Father*!" Kat snapped. She took a breath, forcing herself to calm down. "I am too young and inexperienced to take command of a heavy cruiser," she said. "And there were at least forty other officers, some with previous command experience, ahead of me. I should not have been placed in command."

Her father smiled. "You doubt your own abilities? What happened to the girl who broke her arm climbing up the trees on the estate?"

Kat met his eyes, willing him to understand just how serious this was. "I should not have been offered command," she said. "Why did you pull strings to ensure I received the ship?"

"Because it was necessary," her father said.

"*Necessary*?" Kat repeated.

"Command of a heavy cruiser at such a young age," her father mused. "It will look good on your service record, won't it?"

Kat stared at him angrily. She'd been haunted by the Falcone name ever since she'd been old enough to realize that not everyone lived in a vast estate, nor had almost everything they desired as soon as they desired it. Going into the Royal Tyre Navy had seemed like a chance to escape her name, to earn fame and promotion on her own merits. But she was still followed by her family's name . . .

"Every single officer in the service will *know* you ensured I would get command," she said, finally. "I will never be taken seriously again."

"Correct me if I'm wrong," her father said, after a long moment, "but wasn't it you who was decorated for heroism when *raiders* attacked your ship?"

"It won't matter," Kat said. "I did well at Piker's Peak—and I didn't come first—but this is going to stink like Limburger."

Her father smiled. "You could always decline the command."

"You know I can't do that," Kat snapped. Declining promotion was technically permitted, within regulations, but it guaranteed that promotion would never be offered again. Her father should have understood . . . or perhaps he didn't. The corporate world was nothing like the military, no matter what management fads said. "Father . . ."

Her father, oddly, reached out and placed his hand on top of hers. It was a curiously intimate gesture from someone who had always been very reserved when he'd bothered to pay attention to her at all. The last time they'd spoken alone had been just after Kat had applied to join the Navy. He'd seen it, perhaps, as a cry for attention rather than a serious attempt to escape the family name.

"I understand how you feel," he said softly. "But I also know that the family needs you."

Kat felt her temper flare. "What do I owe the family?"

"Your life," her father said. He ticked points off on his fingers as he spoke. "Your expensive education. Your exclusive implants. Your looks and genetic legacy. And the safety bubble that protected you as you grew into adulthood."

He paused. "And are you going to *keep* acting like a teenager?"

Kat felt her face heat. What was it about her father that made her act like a child?

"There were reasons for my decision," he said when Kat said nothing. "And, if you will listen, I will enlighten you."

He paused as the maids returned, carrying two large plates of food. Kat wasn't surprised to see that the chef had done his best to make the fish and chips look expensive rather than the greasy food she remembered from the cafe near Piker's Peak. The senior cadets had gone there on weekend passes, just for the pleasure of eating something that wasn't Navy rations while having a drink or two with friends. And then most of the young men had headed to the brothel.

"Your ship is being assigned to Cadiz," her father said, once they'd eaten enough to satisfy the hunger pangs. "And I have some reason to believe the situation is dire."

Kat leaned forward, puzzled. "Father?"

"I haven't been able to find much hard evidence," her father confessed. "Even me, even with my connections; there's little evidence to find. But there are alarming whispers coming out of Cadiz Naval Base, while some of my . . . operations on Cadiz itself have been disrupted by the insurgency. And then there's the decision to appoint Admiral Morrison to command the 7th Fleet. Do you know him?"

"No," Kat said. It wasn't as if admirals made a habit of socializing with lesser beings, even those who happened to have aristocratic families. She made a mental note to read his file—the parts of it she could access, at any rate—as soon as possible. "I've never even heard of him."

"Probably for the best," her father said. "Admiral Morrison was a compromise choice, Katherine. The Hawks wanted someone more . . .

aggressive; the Doves wanted someone who wasn't inclined to make waves. Morrison seemed the best of a bad bunch. But, with war looming, choosing him to command the fleet might have been a deadly mistake."

Kat nodded. Everyone knew war was coming. Ever since the Commonwealth had encountered the Theocracy—and the first refugees had started streaming across the border—everyone had known that there would be war. Everyone . . . apart from a number of politicians who believed the galaxy was big enough for both the Commonwealth and the Theocracy. It sounded idiotic. Nothing anyone had seen had suggested the Theocracy was interested in peace.

"Local politics," her father said, when Kat voiced her thoughts. "The Opposition feels that the king and his loyalists pushed the Cadiz Annexation through on false pretenses. They're not inclined to pay much heed to suggestions that storm clouds are gathering on the horizon when Cadiz was such a costly disaster. But right now, their refusal to admit there may be war looming is costing us badly."

He took a breath and then sighed. "Admiral Morrison's position is almost impossible to assault right now," he added grimly. "We need hard evidence to propose to the Privy Council that the Inspectorate General be ordered to inspect Cadiz. But the only way to get that hard evidence is to send in the IG. Which we can't do without due cause . . ."

"Or a report from me," Kat said. "That's what you want, isn't it?"

"Among other things," her father said. "I believe you will have ample opportunity to observe Admiral Morrison at close range."

Kat didn't bother to hide her distaste. Naval tradition insisted that officers were not meant to criticize other officers to civilians, let alone spy on them. There was no shortage of officers who had been promoted through serving as someone's eyes and ears within the service, but she had never wanted to be one of them. The fact she'd been promoted so rapidly, she realized numbly, would convince a great many officers that that was precisely what she was.

"It gets worse," her father said. He didn't trouble himself with insincere condolences. "Are you aware that there's been an upswing in raider activity over the past four months?"

"No," Kat said, alarmed. "It's been covered up?"

"More or less," her father said. "Most of the media is owned by the big family corporations and none of them are eager to do anything that might drive confidence down and insurance rates up. Proportionally, losses are a small fraction of our overall merchant marine, but it's rapidly growing to alarming proportions. I believe the Admiralty is already assigning starships to serve as convoy escorts."

"Which reduces the number of hulls available for border patrol and screening duties," Kat said slowly. "I'd bet that isn't a coincidence."

"Me neither," her father said. "Raiders have been a problem since the Breakaway Wars, but this is on a considerably greater scale."

He took a breath. "And then there's trade with the Theocracy itself," he added. "They've layered whole new security precautions on our ships entering their space."

Kat gave him a sharp look. "You're trading with the enemy?"

"Certain . . . factions within the houses of Parliament believe that trade will eventually cause the Theocracy to moderate its territorial expansion and concentrate on economic growth," her father said. "Others think it's a good chance to gather intelligence. And still others believe that trade will convince the Theocracy that they don't have to be scared of us—and our expansion."

Kat couldn't help herself. She snorted.

"They're politicians," her father pointed out dryly. "A good grip on reality isn't part of the job description."

He shrugged. "Quite a few voters think the bastards have a point, though," he added. "If the Theocracy had been the ones to grab Cadiz, instead of us, wouldn't we be worried about what *they* would do with it?"

Kat considered it, reluctantly. She didn't want to admit it, but the politicians *did* have a point. The Commonwealth had expanded peacefully until Cadiz, when they'd annexed a world by force, even if they did have the best of intentions. It would be better for the locals to be part of the Commonwealth rather than the Theocracy, but it had cost the Commonwealth a great deal of goodwill among the other independent worlds. And was it worth it? By almost any measure, Cadiz was a net drain on the Commonwealth's resources.

Her father cleared his throat. "In any case, our crews have been completely isolated while their ships have been in Theocratic space," he said. "It doesn't bode well for the future."

"I see," Kat said.

"So we need you out there to report back to us," her father said. "We need an accurate report of just what is going on."

"Yes, sir," Kat said. "But if I see evidence that you're wrong, I won't hesitate to bring it to your attention."

Her father nodded, then reached into his pocket and retrieved a secure storage datachip, which he dropped on the table in front of her. "There's a contact code here that will allow you to access the StarCom," he said, "along with a number of personnel files and other pieces of information you might need. You should review it on your flight to Cadiz."

Kat nodded, wordlessly.

"Tell me," her father said, straightening up, "how is your relationship with Davidson?"

Kat felt her face turn bright red. One of the other reasons she'd been so quick to abandon her family estate was the simple lack of privacy. Everyone knew what she was doing almost all the time. She knew, just from listening to Candy's complaints, that the family security division vetted all of her friends and romantic entanglements, making sure that none of them posed any danger to the clan. There was no privacy at Piker's Peak either, but at least everyone was in the same boat.

"We're just friends," she said tartly. She shouldn't be surprised her father knew. She and Davidson had been lovers, once upon a time, but the call of duty had separated them, and so they'd parted platonically. "Why?"

"I'm having him assigned to your ship too," her father said. "If you need support, it will be good to have a marine you can trust behind you."

"Thank you," Kat said, icily. "And are you going to be making any other decisions for me today?"

"No," her father said.

He looked up, meeting her eyes. "I'd like to believe I'm wrong," he admitted. "Wars are chancy things—you would know better than I. But I don't think I'm wrong. And if the Theocracy *does* come over the border . . . you might have a chance to prove you belong in a command chair sooner than you might think."

Kat shivered.

CHAPTER TWO

"She's a child," Commander William McElney muttered.

Manfully, he resisted the temptation to throw the datapad across the compartment and into the bulkhead. It was a military-grade machine, capable of surviving an astonishing amount of abuse, but it still would have felt very satisfactory to try and smash it. Angrily, he pushed the impulse aside and reread the official notification for the second time. HMS *Lightning* had finally been assigned a commanding officer. And it wasn't him.

William clenched his teeth and then forced himself to relax. He'd hoped that he'd be appointed commander of *Lightning*, but he'd known it wasn't likely to happen. He hadn't been born on Tyre, after all, nor had he been born after Hebrides—his homeworld—had entered the Commonwealth. *Someone* like him would always lose out to a citizen of Tyre, even though the Navy's rapid expansion was opening up all kinds of possibilities for those born away from the capital and founder world. But discovering that his prospective CO was nothing more than a child . . .

He glowered down at the terminal and then keyed his access code into the device, accessing the naval datanet. Officially, he only had access to the bare bones of his new commander's file, but he'd been in the Navy long enough to learn a few tricks. Accessing the complete file—the one that would have been available to a captain or commodore—was relatively simple; indeed, he'd never understood why the Admiralty set out to classify such data in the first place. But it wasn't reassuring.

There was no aristocracy on Hebrides—or, at least, there hadn't been one until the Commonwealth had arrived. The planet had simply been too poor to support a ruling class, no matter the pretensions of some of the elected leaders. But he was familiar with the concept—he had thirty years in the Navy—and now, looking down at the file, he understood how his new commander had received her position. She was the daughter of one of the most powerful men in the Commonwealth, a man so staggeringly wealthy that he could buy an entire superdreadnought squadron out of pocket change. The nasty part of his mind wondered just how many superdreadnoughts the old man had bought just to ensure his daughter got a chance to sit in a command chair.

William skimmed through the rest of the file rapidly, noting—to his alarm—that it was surprisingly thin. Either she hadn't done anything worth mentioning or nothing had been written down—or, if it had, it had been classified well above top secret. He supposed that made a certain kind of sense. The aristocracy wouldn't be interested in having their dirty laundry aired for all to see, but they would need to know who was letting the side down or simply couldn't be trusted with any kind of real power. Kat Falcone, it seemed, wasn't considered a potential risk to the aristocracy's reputation.

Captain Kat Falcone, he reminded himself sternly. Resentment or no resentment, he was still a professional and he was damn well going to *act* professionally.

Shaking his head, he switched to the planetary datanet and ran a search. Hundreds of results popped up—it sometimes seemed the media had little better to do but report on the activities of young aristocrats—but Kat Falcone didn't seem to court scandal. Instead, the reports merely mentioned that she'd gone to Piker's Peak and then helped save a starship during a border tussle. That, at least, matched with the Navy file, although neither was very informative, suggesting that some of the details had been classified. It left an odd taste in his mouth.

A wider search revealed more about the Falcone family and corporation than he'd ever wanted to know. It was one of the original founding corporations that had moved operations to Tyre; it accounted for the planet's considerable economic growth before the Breakaway Wars had smashed humanity's fragile unity and created dozens of independent star systems, some on the brink of total collapse. The family had remained powerful through the economic crash, and then played a key role in organizing the Commonwealth and building up the Royal Tyre Navy. As aristocracies went, he had to admit, they were definitely enlightened.

So why, he asked himself, had the Duke ensured that his daughter received one of the most coveted command chairs in the Navy?

William knew she wasn't qualified. He'd looked it up. The youngest person to be appointed to command a heavy cruiser had been thirty-seven—eight years older than Captain Falcone. A handful of younger officers had taken command briefly, when their commanders were disabled, but only one of them had been allowed to keep the ship. That particular officer had been in line for a command of his own, according to the files, and the Admiralty had merely decided to leave him on the ship rather than transfer him elsewhere. And he'd been thirty-six.

William's wristcom bleeped. "Yes?"

"This is Ross," Lieutenant Linda Ross said. Her voice was, as always, calm and professional. "We have received a signal from groundside. Captain Falcone is on her way."

William gritted his teeth, unsurprised. It spoke well of her that she wanted to see her new command as soon as possible, he supposed, but *Lightning* was nowhere near ready to receive her. Half of the ship's personnel were assigned to urgent duties, while the remainder were scattered all over the ship. The Admiralty had been dragging its feet on assigning additional crewmen to *Lightning*, something that irked him more than he cared to admit. But a superdreadnought had required urgent crew replenishments in a hurry and *Lightning* wasn't scheduled to leave for another two weeks.

"Understood," he said.

"She specifically requests no greeting party," Lieutenant Ross added. "And she also wants readiness files transmitted to her at once."

William lifted an eyebrow. He'd served under five captains since joining the Navy and some of them had been egotistical enough to demand that their senior officers stop work and greet them whenever they returned to the ship. A greeting party was traditional, at least when the captain boarded for the first time, but it would be a headache at such short notice. The captain's appointment had only been confirmed nine hours ago, for crying out loud. But it spoke well of her too, that she didn't want a greeting party.

"Transmit the files," he ordered. Technically, they shouldn't be sent until after the captain had formally assumed command, but there was no point in withholding them. It would be petty, pointless spite. "Do we have an ETA?"

"Thirty minutes," Linda said, after a moment. "She's coming directly from the planet."

"I'll meet her at the shuttlebay," William said. He glanced down at the terminal once again, then returned it to his belt. "Pass the word to the other senior officers, Linda. The captain is about to come aboard."

He closed the channel and then looked around the Ready Room. It had been intended for the starship's commander, but he'd found himself using it during the desperate struggle to get *Lightning* worked up and ready for deployment. As always, the yard dogs had missed things that only experienced crewmembers would have noticed, while other items or problems simply didn't show themselves until the starship was run at full power for the first time. He looked at the pile of paperwork on his desk—the *captain's* desk—and sighed to himself. The room would have to be cleaned before the captain laid eyes on it . . .

No, he told himself. *There isn't anyone who can be spared from more important work.*

Leaving the office behind, he walked through Officer Country and into his own cabin. It was smaller than the captain's chambers, but it suited him, even though the bulkheads were still bare and utterly untouched by any paintings or moving images. A handful of old-fashioned paper books sat on a bookshelf, each one very well thumbed. They'd cost him a month's salary apiece, but they'd been worth it. There was something about a paper book that was never quite matched by anything on the datanet.

He stripped down rapidly, then pulled his white dress uniform over his underclothes and glanced at the mirror. His homeworld hadn't possessed any form of rejuvenation technology until after they had made contact with the Commonwealth and it showed. Naval personnel were offered rejuvenation treatments as a matter of course, but his hair was already starting to turn gray, even though he was only sixty. He had a good seventy years of life left in him, he knew, assuming he wasn't killed in the line of duty, yet he looked old. And he wasn't vain enough to use cosmetic surgery to make himself look young.

Besides, he thought, *looking old makes it easier to get younger crewmen to pay attention.*

He keyed his wristcom. "Inform me when the captain is five minutes from arrival," he ordered. "And then hold any calls for me unless they're priority one."

The thought made him smile. *Everything* was priority one right now, with yard dogs crawling over the cruiser's hull and countless problems popping up every day that only the CO could solve. Captain

Falcone was going to jump right into the deep end, as soon as she assumed command. But, as a good XO, he would take as much of the weight from her shoulders as he could.

"Aye, sir," Lieutenant Ross said.

♦ ♦ ♦

Kat felt, at times, as though she belonged in space far more than anywhere else. Space was simple, governed by a set of cold equations that even the most advanced technology in existence couldn't thrust aside completely. If one made a mistake, one died; it was far simpler than political or social struggles on the planet below. She pressed her face against the porthole as the shuttle rose out of the atmosphere, feeling nothing but relief as the planet fell away behind them. In space, she was free . . .

Or as free as I will ever be, she thought, sourly. Her father's influence followed her everywhere, ensuring that no one would ever think she'd earned something on her own merits. They might even be right. Her father didn't have to pull strings overtly to ensure that some toadying admiral would try to flatter or promote his daughter, all in hopes of pleasing Duke Falcone.

Maybe I should just run.

It was rare, she knew, for a member of the aristocracy to simply abandon her title and walk away, but it did happen. There were even legends of one particular aristocrat who had cashed in his trust fund, bought a handful of starships, and set out to build a trading empire of his own on the other side of the Dead Zone surrounding Earth. Others, more practically, found places to live on the other worlds and allowed the universe to pass them by. But Kat knew she was too ambitious to ever abandon her dreams and just walk away. Besides, she knew she'd done well at Piker's Peak. She was damned if she was throwing her achievement away because of a fit of pique.

"We're passing the StarCom now," the pilot called back. "Any last messages?"

Kat snorted, then turned to stare at the giant construction as it floated in high orbit around the planet. It looked crude, like a brick orbiting the planet, but she knew it was a technological marvel, allowing humanity to pulse messages through hyperspace without an open vortex. And yet she also knew that it was incredibly vulnerable. Dozens of automated Orbital Weapons Platforms surrounded the StarCom, while other orbital fortifications and gunboats were nearby, ready to protect it if necessary. Tyre was the only Commonwealth world that had more than one StarCom, but losing this one would be disastrous. They'd wind up dependent on starships to carry messages from star to star, crippling the speed of information as it flowed around the Commonwealth.

She shook her head and then allowed her gaze to drift towards lights orbiting the planet. It was hard to see much at this distance, at least with the naked eye, but she knew what they were: giant orbital industrial nodes, space habitats, and shipyards, some of them owned by her family. Few human minds could truly comprehend the sheer scale of industry surrounding the planet—and yet it was smaller than Earth's legendary asteroid belt. But Earth was gone now, the Sol System devastated by the Breakaway Wars. Tyre might be the single greatest industrial node remaining in human space.

Unless the Theocracy has a larger industrial base of its own, she thought, morbidly. No one knew anything about the internal layout of Theocratic space, at least nothing more detailed than they had known prior to the Breakaway Wars. Most of the worlds within their sphere had been stage-one colonies, barely capable of supporting themselves, but a handful had funded their own settlement and produced small industrial bases of their own. *How far had they progressed*, she asked herself, *under Theocratic rule?* There was no way to know.

She shook her head as they flew away from the planet, the twinkling lights blurring into the ever-present stars, then turned her attention to the files her father had given her. Much of the data was, as she'd expected, drawn from naval databases, but some came from independent civilian analysts. Naval officers tended to scorn; Kat, who had seen some of the analysts who worked for her father, knew better. Civilians often had a different—and sometimes illuminating—way of looking at the universe. It was, at the very least, an alternate point of view.

The first file tabulated shipping losses along the border. Kat worked her way through it and slowly realized that her father had, if anything, underestimated the situation. The losses were tiny in absolute terms, but they were steadily gnawing away at the Commonwealth's merchant marine. It would be years before the big corporations were undermined fatally by their losses, yet the smaller companies and the independents were in big trouble. She was astonished that the problem hadn't made the mainstream media, no matter what the bigger corporations said. But then, it would be a brave editor who went against the will of his ultimate superior.

If the losses are made public, insurance rates will soar, Kat thought. She could see why her father and the other CEOs wanted the matter to remain quiet. *But sooner or later, someone is going to notice anyway. Or are we compensating the colonies for destroyed ships out of our own pockets?*

The next file detailed other problems along the border. It wasn't easy to mine large tracts of hyperspace—energy storms and gravity waves ensured the mines wouldn't stay in place for very long—but the Theocracy had been doing it, showing an astonishing persistence and a great deal of paranoia. Kat couldn't help agreeing with the analyst's conclusion: no one, not even the most bloody-minded state in human history, would expend so many resources on mining hyperspace unless they had something to hide.

Or perhaps they don't want us to spread ideas about freedom into their space, Kat thought, remembering a handful of refugees she'd met during border patrol. They'd stolen a starship and made it out of the Theocracy, placing their lives in the Commonwealth's hands rather than stay one moment longer under oppressive rule. Their stories had been horrifying. The Theocracy gave lip service to the idea of religious freedom, but those who didn't accept the True Faith suffered all kinds of legal penalties. It was, apparently, incentive to convert.

The third file consisted of a detailed political briefing, written by yet another independent analyst. Kat felt her eyes glazing over as she tried to follow the jargon—it seemed that jargon changed every year, depending on who was sitting in the houses of Parliament—and eventually skipped to the executive summary. Kat had to read through it twice to understand what her father had been trying to tell her. The Commonwealth was enduring a political deadlock; the War Hawks demanding preparations for war, perhaps even a first strike, while the Doves were skeptical of any real threat from the Theocracy. After all, the Commonwealth was much larger than any other state the Theocracy had overwhelmed.

"Captain," the pilot said, "we're entering final approach now."

Kat nodded, returned the datachip to her uniform pocket, and then scrambled forward into the empty co-pilot's chair. Outside, a cluster of lights was slowly coming into view, a mobile spacedock surrounding a starship. She leaned forward, her breath catching in her throat, as HMS *Lightning* took shape and form. *Her* command, she told herself, forgetting her anger at her father for pulling strings on her behalf. *Lightning* was *her* command.

The vessel was longer than Kat had expected, she noted, although she'd reviewed the files on the *Uncanny*-class heavy cruisers when she'd received the first notification. *Lightning* resembled a flattened cone, her white hull bristling with shield generators, missile tubes, weapons mounts, and sensor blisters. Her name was prominently blazed on her hull, drawing Kat's attention to the drives at the rear of the ship. If the files were to be believed, *Lightning* enjoyed a higher realspace velocity than anything larger than a destroyer or frigate.

But she still won't have a hope of outrunning a gunboat swarm, she thought. A gunboat was tiny, able to outrace almost anything. And they were hard to hit. *Or a missile.*

The thought was chilling. No one had fought a real conflict since the Breakaway Wars—and that hadn't really included formal fleet actions. Who knew how well doctrine would hold up when the Navy was tested in a real fight? Like it or not, she knew, there would be a steep learning curve as soon as the war began. *If* the war began . . .

She shook her head. She knew that was wishful thinking.

"Take us in," Kat ordered, unable to hide the excitement in her voice. "Put us down as quickly as possible."

CHAPTER THREE

William watched, keeping his face impassive, as the shuttle passed through the force field holding the atmosphere inside the shuttlebay and settled down on the deck with an audible *clunk*. He'd known captains who would be annoyed with the pilot for such a rough landing, which he suspected proved the captains had never been in actual combat. Landing in a combat zone was always far rougher than landing onboard a peaceful starship. But he pushed the thought aside as the hatch opened with a *hiss*, revealing his new commanding officer.

She *was* young, he realized, the part of him that had been raised on a world without rejuvenation technology mentally classing Captain Falcone as a teenager. Even knowing she was twenty-nine, almost thirty, it was hard to escape the emotional reaction to her apparent age. He knew there were midshipwomen on *Lightning* who looked about the same age, and indeed *were* the same age, but they certainly didn't have pretensions to command.

He kept his face under strict control as Captain Falcone stepped onto the deck, then saluted the flag painted on the bulkhead. By tradition, he couldn't formally greet her until after she had made her salute.

He drew in a breath as she turned to face him. She was pretty, he had to admit, too pretty to be quite natural. Cosmetic surgery and genetic programming had been nonexistent on Hebrides until after the Commonwealth had rediscovered his homeworld, but Tyre had never lost the technology. His captain looked like a perfectly proportioned young woman, attractive enough to set hormones raging throughout the ship. Even her uniform was perfectly tailored to draw attention to her beauty. He had to call on all of his years of discipline to remember that she was his captain, as well as a fellow officer.

And if that doesn't prove that the Commonwealth is decadent, he thought sourly, *what will?*

She lifted her elegant eyebrows. "Permission to come aboard?"

"Permission granted," he said, and then saluted. "I'm Commander McElney, your XO."

"Thank you," she said, returning his salute and then extending her hand for him to shake. "I'm Captain Falcone."

William nodded as he shook her hand. Her voice seemed to lack an aristocratic accent, although four years at Piker's Peak and then several more years as a serving officer would have probably helped it to fade away. And her salute was perfect, something that really shouldn't have been a surprise. Young cadets were drilled in saluting until they could do it in their sleep. She still looked absurdly young, but she was a graduate of Piker's Peak. It was only experience she lacked.

"I took the liberty of preparing a tour of the vessel," William said. "We're still working up for departure, but most of the officers and crew are in place."

Her eyes narrowed. "*Most* of the officers and crew?"

William was mildly impressed. He'd known captains who wouldn't have picked up on his words. But then, she'd served as an XO too. And being an XO was good experience for understanding the difference between what someone said and what they actually *meant.*

"Yes, Captain," he said. "We're short around forty crewmen. The Admiralty needed to assign additional crew to *Thundercloud* and tapped the men who were supposed to be assigned to us. We've been promised replacements within a week."

"Failing that, we might have to draft some of the Yard Dogs," Captain Falcone said. She didn't sound as though she was joking. "Overall, Commander, what is our status?"

William smiled. He'd taken the liberty of preparing a set of detailed briefing notes too.

"We ran full-power tests last week, then replaced several components and ran the tests again," he said. "Drives, life support, shields, and weapons are all at optimal readiness, apart from long-range shipkiller missiles. The Admiralty has promised us a resupply within the week. Overall, we're at roughly ninety percent readiness right now. I expect we will meet our scheduled departure date."

"Unless they choose to move it forward," Captain Falcone said.

"Yes, Captain," William said. He'd been expecting a message telling him precisely that for several weeks, ever since *Lightning* had been formally commissioned into the Navy. Ninety percent readiness was hardly *bad*. They could fly, fight, and generally give a good account of themselves if they ran into hostiles. "It's a very real possibility."

The captain smiled. It was sweet, but he thought he detected an air of cool calculation behind it. "I think you'd better give me the tour now, before I formally assume command on the bridge," she said. "I want to see everything for myself."

"Certainly," William said, with the private thought that it spoke well of her. "If you'll follow me . . . ?"

He half expected her to grow bored within minutes of the tour beginning, but Captain Falcone managed to surprise him by keeping herself awake and attentive as they moved from department to department. Sickbay, Main Engineering, and Tactical were all at full readiness, thankfully. The captain listened to the various departmental heads as they outlined their current status, then watched a tactical simulation as the crews worked on their consoles, trying to practice for every conceivable encounter with the enemy. But far too much of it, William knew, was guesswork. There was little hard data on the warships developed and deployed by the Theocracy.

"We've seen destroyers and frigates, but nothing heavier," he explained when the captain finally asked. "Some of the ships have even been UN designs, probably refugees from the Breakaway Wars. All extensively modified and refitted, of course, but nothing to show us the cutting edge of their technology. But then, they wouldn't need to be more advanced than the UN to overwhelm the worlds closest to Ahura Mazda."

The thought was a bitter one. If the Commonwealth had been a hair less expansionist, Hebrides might have been discovered by the Theocracy and brought under its rule. There would have been resistance, of course, but with an enemy controlling the high orbitals the outcome would never have been in doubt. If all the horror stories were true, the Theocracy was quite prepared to engage in mass slaughter as well as shipping in hundreds of thousands of settlers to ensure the demographic balance turned in their favor. The Commonwealth might be biased in favor of Tyre, but its member worlds still had local independence. There was no way the Theocracy would offer the same deal to its captive worlds.

"So we need to try to project what they might have developed on their own," Captain Falcone mused, bringing him back to the here and now. "Or stolen from us."

"They had an industrial plant with them when they were booted off Earth," William reminded her. The UN had been fond of exiling small groups from Earth, officially for their own good, although it also made it easier to work towards total planetary unity. "They should have been as advanced as the UN before the Breakaway Wars."

"We've advanced," the captain said. "Have they?"

William said nothing. Instead, he led her into Main Engineering, where they were greeted by Chief Engineer Zack Lynn. Like William himself, he wasn't a native of Tyre, although he had followed the engineering track rather than command track. It was, William suspected, rather more fulfilling than command track, at least for the moment. A good engineer couldn't be passed over for someone with poorer qualifications but the right birthplace.

"Captain," Zack said, gruffly. If he had any doubts about the captain's appearance, he kept them to himself. "It's a pleasure to meet you at last."

"Thank you," Captain Falcone said. "And are we ready for departure?"

"We can leave whenever you give the order," Lynn said. He nodded towards the large status display in front of Fusion One. "Our stockpile of spare parts has been badly reduced, thanks to the components that failed during full-power tests, but we should have them replaced within the week. Overall, however, we have had far fewer problems than *Uncanny*."

William saw the captain wince and nodded in agreement. HMS *Uncanny* had been intended to serve as the first starship in her class, but her construction and commissioning had been plagued by design faults and problems that had delayed her completion for nearly a year. By the time she had finally entered service, she had gained a reputation as an unlucky starship—wags even called her HMS *Unlucky*—and hardly anyone wanted to serve onboard her. Hell, her first CO had even died in an accident when an airlock seal broke at the worst possible time.

"I'm glad to hear it," she said. "Please keep me informed of your status."

"Full reports are in the message buffer in your office," William said. "I have reviewed them and believe they are suitable."

The captain looked briefly embarrassed. She'd been an XO until her promotion, William knew, and it would take time to break her of the habits of being an XO, including reviewing status reports in order to save the captain from having to do it herself. But at least she was well aware of her responsibilities to the crew.

"Thank you," the captain said finally. "And now I believe I should see the bridge."

♦ ♦ ♦

Kat couldn't help feeling a little out of her depth as they rode the intership car towards the bridge. *Lightning* was smaller than *Thunderous*, the battle cruiser she'd served on as XO, but *Thunderous* had been in service for several years before she'd assumed her post. The responsibilities of serving as a starship's first commanding officer were different, she knew, from merely taking over command from a previous captain. If nothing else, there was no prior history for her to study.

Her XO was definitely older than she was, she knew. According to a very brief skim of his files through her implant—it was rude to access implants in polite company, let alone use them in conversation—he was old enough to be her father, maybe even her grandfather if he started early. *That* wasn't a surprise—her real father was older still—but there was something about him that suggested age. He'd clearly not had the rejuvenation treatments from a very early age, she noted, instead deliberately trying to look old and distinguished. There wouldn't be anything wrong with his general fitness, she was sure, but he was mentally old.

And he didn't seem to like her.

Kat had grown up in a sheltered estate, but she wasn't naive. She had learned, from a very early age, that there were people who would suck up to her purely because of her family connections while hiding their contempt behind bland smiles. One of the very few practical lessons Kat had had from her mother was how to determine what someone *really* felt about her, a harder task than it seemed. Anyone who was anyone on Tyre had implants to help disguise their emotions if they feared revealing more than they wanted in front of prying eyes. It took careful perception to tell when someone was trying to hide their feelings—and that, she had learned, suggested that they had something to hide.

The XO seemed . . . distrusting, almost disdainful. His attempt to hide it was good, but not good enough. Kat wondered, bitterly, just what he felt about her. Had he thought he would win command for himself . . . or had he thought Kat was far too inexperienced to take command of a heavy cruiser? He would be right, she had to admit, if he thought the latter. She knew she wasn't ready to take command of anything larger than a destroyer, not yet . . .

There was a *ding* as the hatch opened, revealing the bridge. Kat stopped and stared, allowing her gaze to move from station to station. The captain's chair sat in the center of the compartment, surrounded by a semitranslucent orbital display that showed the shipyard surrounding *Lightning*. Only half of the consoles were staffed, she noted, which didn't surprise her. No one expected to be attacked here, in the heart of the Commonwealth's defenses. Tyre was surrounded by enough firepower to make even fanatics think twice about risking an attack.

But we can't take that for granted, she reminded herself. *The Theocracy is a whole multi–star system of fanatics.*

Kat kept her face impassive as she took a closer look. Several of the unmanned consoles were clearly not installed yet, a handful of technicians working frantically to link them into the starship's datanet. The private console beside the captain's chair was blank. It looked as though the bridge was far from ready for action. She made a mental note to review all the reports closely, despite knowing they should be left for the XO. She needed to know what was going on. Surprises, in the military, were rarely *nice.*

"Captain on the bridge," the XO said.

There was a rustle as the crew stood and saluted. For a long moment, Kat enjoyed the sensation, knowing that she would never step onto her bridge for the first time again. And then she reached for the piece of paper in her uniform jacket, slowly pulling it out and unfurling it. That too, she knew, was part of the ceremony. She couldn't take another step onto the bridge without asserting her authority.

"Captain Katherine Falcone," she read. She had memorized the words already, but she had to appear to read from the parchment. "You are ordered to assume command of HMS *Lightning* and serve as her Captain, Mistress under God. Fail in this charge at your peril. By order of Grand Admiral Tobias Vaughn, First Space Lord."

There was a long pause. She allowed the moment to stretch out, then turned to her XO.

"Mr. XO," she said, "I assume command."

The XO's face remained impassive. "I stand relieved," he said.

Kat let out a long breath she hadn't realized she'd been holding. There was only ever one source of authority onboard a starship, one person who held command. As long as he'd been the senior officer, William McElney had been the acknowledged commander of the starship, even once Kat had come onboard. But now . . . she was the commanding officer. The final responsibility was hers. She felt the full weight of command settling around her shoulders and fought to keep her face impassive. Independent command was the ambition of every commissioned officer in the Navy, but it could also break her. The buck would stop with her.

"Thank you," she said. "Please make a note in the log of the date and time I assumed command."

He nodded and then saluted. That too was tradition.

Kat felt her cheeks heat up as a smattering of applause ran through the bridge.

She took a breath. Some officers wrote speeches for when they assumed command. Kat hadn't bothered, as she had honestly never expected to be granted her own command for at least another five years, if she were lucky. Besides, the speeches had always struck her as pretentious. The crew would have more than enough opportunity to formulate an opinion of their commander without being forced to sit through a tedious address.

"Return to your duties," she ordered.

She watched them sit down, their backs a little straighter now they knew their captain was watching them. The memory of her first days as a commissioned officer warmed her as she walked over to the command chair, passing through the insubstantial hologram, and sat down. It felt good, soft enough for her to relax, hard enough to ensure she wouldn't fall asleep. *That* wasn't a shooting offense, but any junior officer unlucky enough to fall asleep while on watch would rapidly start wishing it *was*.

Her XO stood behind Kat as she touched her console with a finger, activating the system and linking directly into the starship's datanet. The automated command systems buzzed around her, displaying the *Lightning*'s current location and plotting courses automatically to prospective destinations. Not, she knew, that she would trust the systems completely. One rule of AI was that *true* AIs always went insane shortly after being brought to life, and nothing lesser could hope to replace the human element from starship command. But without the automated systems, the ship's efficiency would be cut in half.

She resisted the temptation to play with the system any further. Instead, she rose to her feet and passed command to the tactical officer, Lieutenant Commander Christopher John Roach. He was a young man, younger than she was, but a nasty scar ran down the left side of his face, and he'd chosen to shave his head completely as well. Kat made a mental note to review his file too, and then motioned for her XO to follow her into her Ready Room. Inside, she stopped dead. The compartment was dirty as hell, the deck covered in pieces of paper, datapads, and several coffee mugs. It didn't look remotely ready for *any* commanding officer.

"I've been using it as an office," the XO admitted. "There was no time to clean up."

Kat felt an odd flash of irritation, which she forced down sharply. The XO was entirely correct. He needed to stay near the bridge and he needed an office, a place to work without disturbing the bridge crew. Using the Ready Room—*her* Ready Room—was the logical solution. But it still gnawed at her.

"Don't worry about it," she said. She hesitated, then said what she knew she had to say. "Keep using it until we are ready for deployment."

"I believe a steward has been assigned to you," the XO said. "She will clean the room once she arrives."

Kat nodded, reluctantly. A steward was something she'd managed to avoid, even though she was entitled to one as an aristocrat. But there was no point in declining one now.

She picked a pile of datapads off a chair, wondering why anyone needed so many, then placed them on the desk and sat down.

"So," she said, once her XO had found a place to sit, "tell me about my starship."

CHAPTER FOUR

"Come," Kat ordered as the door bleeped.

She barely looked up from her datapad until she heard someone clearing his throat in front of her. The sound made her look up to see a short, bald man standing there, wearing the gray shipboard uniform of the Royal Marine Corps. Kat found herself smiling openly as she rose to her feet and walked around the desk to envelop him in a hug. It had been far too long since she'd seen her old friend and former lover.

"It's good to see you again," she said, remembering when they'd first met. "Time and the Marine Corps have been good to you."

Captain Patrick James Davidson—he would be given a courtesy promotion to colonel while onboard ship—hugged her back, then let her go. Kat understood, even though it hurt a little; they were no longer lovers, while he was—technically—her subordinate. Marines had a great deal of independence, but not from their starship's commander.

"I was promoted, eventually," Davidson said. He grinned toothily. One of his front teeth had been knocked out on deployment and he'd never bothered to have it replaced. "They must have grown sick of scraping the barrel for officers to promote ahead of me."

"Something always rises to the top," Kat agreed. She walked back the table and sat down, then smiled at him. "Thank you for accepting this posting."

"Ah, it was a choice between this ship or another hellworld," Davidson said. He suddenly stood to attention. "Colonel Patrick James Davidson and crew reporting for duty, *Captain*!"

"Welcome onboard," Kat said dryly. She waved at the seat behind him. "Take a seat, Pat, and put off the formality."

Davidson sat, but still remained ramrod straight. Kat smiled to herself. Even when they'd been on shore leave, free of all other demands on their time, he had been unmistakably a marine. She had half expected him to loosen up with the promotion and added responsibility, but he still seemed as tough and determined as ever. But then marines were only ever promoted from the ranks. None of them graduated from OCS without experience as an infantryman first.

"It's been years," she said. "What have you been doing?"

"Spent a great deal of time on MacKinnon's World," Davidson said. "The locals voted for annexation and they're generally happy, but there's a small bunch of resistors who have been making everyone else miserable. They could have had an island of their own, if that was what they wanted, but instead they started to attack settlements and so-called collaborators."

Kat nodded, unsurprised. "And you managed to hunt them down?"

"Gave them a damn good thrashing, the one time they fought a pitched battle," Davidson said. "We ensured the local security forces got enough breathing space to make certain they had time to rebuild, train, and take the offensive. But it will be years before all support for the insurgents fades away into nothingness."

He shrugged and then met her eyes. "Did you pull strings to get me onboard?"

Kat didn't want to admit to anything, but she knew she couldn't lie to him. "My father pulled strings," she admitted. "Far too many strings."

"I was due to assume command of a company anyway," Davidson assured her. "I'm not too disappointed by the way things have turned out."

And few people know we were lovers, Kat thought. None of the crew from HMS *Thomas* had been assigned to *Lightning*. As far as anyone knew, she and Davidson might have crossed paths, but they were hardly *close*. But if someone had good reason to think strings had been pulled, they might deduce the truth. And then who knew what they would think?

She looked up, meeting his eyes. "Can we talk freely?"

"Of course," Davidson said.

Kat nodded. Captains couldn't talk to anyone about their doubts or fears, not when it was important never to show weakness in front of their junior officers. The only person on the ship who came close to them in terms of authority and position was the Marine commander, who had similar tasks and responsibilities. They could talk to each other openly, if they developed a good working relationship. By that standard, she knew, Davidson and herself were probably far *too* close. They'd been lovers, after all.

He'd seen her naked and vulnerable. He wouldn't put her on a pedestal.

"I don't think some of my officers like or trust me," she said, reluctantly. It had taken her time to unbend enough to really talk to new friends once she'd joined the Navy. Back home, anything said was almost certain to be used against her at some later date. "And I feel overwhelmed."

She waved a hand at the datapads on the desk. Three days after her arrival, the compartment had been cleaned, but there were still an enormous amount of files to read and paperwork to sign. Normally, a commanding officer would have much more lead time before assuming her post, enough time to read the files for herself and decide how she wanted to proceed. *Kat* had the uncomfortable feeling that she was falling behind, no matter what she did. It was one hell of a struggle to force herself to read just one more file . . . and then another . . . and then another.

"You are young for your post," Davidson pointed out. His eyes sharpened. "Did you pull strings to gain promotion?

"My father did," Kat said. She'd liked Davidson from the start because he'd never treated her any differently, even after learning who her father was. But then, marines from the aristocracy tended to assume false names when they entered boot camp. Everyone started at the bottom and worked their way up. "He has . . . *concerns*."

She hadn't really wanted to talk about it, but the whole story came tumbling out. Davidson listened, carefully, as she outlined her father's fears, then the steps he was taking to try to obtain some hard data. By the time she was finished, Davidson was frowning, an expression she knew meant trouble. He'd only looked like that once before in her presence, after one of his fellow marines had screwed up badly. It was a fearsome sight.

"I have heard . . . rumors, through Marine Intelligence, that things are *not good* along the border," he said slowly. "But only rumors."

Kat felt her eyes narrow. The Marine Corps had a separate intelligence section, something that irked both the Office of Naval Intelligence and the civilian External Intelligence Agency. It was normally geared around local intelligence collection to support Marine deployments, but it did tend to collect tactical and strategic intelligence as well. Sometimes, it even picked up on something the larger intelligence services had missed.

"I see," she said carefully. "What did they say?"

"Nothing *concrete*," Davidson admitted. "Mostly, there were concerns about the growing insurgency on Cadiz and the certainty that *something* is supplying the insurgents with heavy weapons from offworld. The wretched planet is sucking in too many of our cadre of Marines, not to mention the Army and forces from Commonwealth planets. Hell, the latter are growing increasingly reluctant to send any further forces to Cadiz, citing the Commonwealth Charter. Overall, Marine Intelligence thinks that Cadiz isn't the only world that has received attention from the Theocracy. Those missionaries might have done more than try to spread the good word."

Kat grimaced. The Commonwealth had total religious freedom—and total separation of church and state. There had been no choice. The Commonwealth couldn't afford to exclude potential member states because of their religions, as long as they adhered to the Commonwealth Charter. If someone wanted to worship Satan, or accept a subordinate position because of gender, there was no law prohibiting it . . .

. . . which made it hard to deal with missionaries from the Theocracy. Kat suspected—and she knew that most of her fellow officers shared her suspicions—that the missionaries were nothing more than spies. But they couldn't be barred from any member planet, not without breaking the Commonwealth's laws. All the intelligence services could do was keep an eye on them and watch for signs they had something else in mind.

"All along the border," she mused. "And those insurgent groups might be receiving help too."

"Not on the same scale as Cadiz," Davidson said. "But every other world voted for annexation. Cadiz . . . did not."

And that, Kat knew, was the core of the political struggle that had deadlocked the houses of Parliament. Cadiz had been, for all intents and purposes, invaded and conquered, without even the benefit of a great many people willing to welcome the Commonwealth. Peace was needed to start investments on the surface, investments that would pay off handsomely in the long run, but the locals weren't interested in peace. All they wanted was to get the outsiders off their world, which would leave them hopelessly vulnerable when the Theocracy came calling.

Other resistance groups could be handled. They could be fended off until the newly annexed world was ready to take responsibility for its own security . . . and the economic boom undermined whatever support the resistance had from the population. But Cadiz . . . Kat suspected that there were members of Parliament who would vote for unilateral withdrawal tomorrow if the issue were put to a vote. And that would be costly too.

Davidson cleared his throat. "It does look like war is looming," he said. "Many of the readiness reports from Cadiz are not good either."

Kat looked up at him, sharply. "You have evidence?"

"Just funny little reports from Marine detachments," Davidson said. "You do realize that there are very few Bootnecks on 7th Fleet?"

Kat blinked. Davidson commanded a full company of marines, one hundred in all. A superdreadnought rated at least four companies of marines. In total, Admiral Morrison should have had around three *thousand* marines assigned to his fleet. Marines didn't just kill people and break things. They served as everything from shipboard police to damage-control officers and emergency manpower.

"They've been assigned to the planet, largely," Davidson explained, answering her unspoken question. "The report wasn't too clear, but it looks as though the only ships that still have Marine complements are starships on escort or border patrol duty. Now . . . what does that tell us about the situation on the ground?"

"That it's poor," Kat said. It wasn't a guess. The Commonwealth had assigned nearly a *million* soldiers and marines to Cadiz, but they were garrisoning an entire *planet*. If they needed to strip marines from their starships, she suspected, the local commander clearly felt he needed them. "And that there's hardly anyone to provide support services for the fleet."

She looked down at the desk. "Who's providing onboard security?"

"Shore Patrol, I suspect," Davidson said. "If there's anyone providing it at all."

Kat fought down the urge to start screaming. The Shore Patrol was universally loathed among spacers, being neither spacers themselves nor civilian law enforcement. Their normal role was nothing more than patrolling spaceports, pulling drunken spacers out of bars, and providing first responders for certain emergencies. It was far from uncommon for isolated Shore Patrolmen to be beaten by drunken spacers, who would then slip away to their starships and swear innocence when the senior chiefs demanded answers. If Shore Patrolmen were providing boarding parties . . .

She shook her head in disbelief. Boarding a starship, even if the crew had surrendered, was a tricky job at the best of times. The Shore Patrol weren't even trained as junior crewmen, let along experienced spacers. There was a reason such tasks were normally left to the Marines.

"I think that's something that should be relayed to my father," she said, although she wasn't sure what—if anything—could be done with it. Any half-decent PR flack could come up with a dozen excuses that would sound plausible, at least to a civilian. "But . . ."

She looked up, meeting his gray eyes. "I don't think my XO trusts me."

"So you said," Davidson replied. "You must be rattled. It's not like you to jump around."

Kat nodded wordlessly. He knew her well.

Davidson placed his hands on her table, then leaned forward. "You *are* too young and too inexperienced to be formally assigned command of this ship," he said. "Your XO—and your other officers—will be aware of it. As your family name is rather well known . . ."

Kat snorted, rudely. There wasn't a person in the Commonwealth who hadn't heard of the Falcone family.

". . . they will suspect that strings were pulled to get you command," Davidson continued. He paused, significantly. "No. They will *know* that strings were pulled to get you command—a command you didn't earn. They will be *very* worried about your competence and well they should be. For all they know, your previous successes came about because of your family name too."

"They should have seen me at Piker's Peak," Kat said ruefully. "I didn't flunk out, but . . . I didn't exactly win any awards."

"I don't think that would reassure them," Davidson said. "Whenever someone new takes command, even in the Marines, there is a period when everything is out of shape and nothing feels quite right. No one quite trusts the newcomer, particularly if they haven't served with her or him before. Hell, things change even when the new CO is promoted from the ranks of those already serving within the unit. In your case, it's worse because you have far less experience than anyone else."

Kat nodded. "Even a marine who was promoted as soon as it was legally possible would have the experience of being an infantryman," she mused. "I didn't come up from the ranks."

"No, you didn't," Davidson said. "And your XO did. I don't blame him for having a chip on his shoulder."

"I know," Kat said. She'd reviewed personnel files until she'd felt her eyes glazing over, starting with William McElney. "He wasn't even born as a Commonwealth citizen."

"That's a problem that will probably come back to bite us," Davidson said. "We treat people like him as second-class citizens, no matter their competence."

Kat sighed, remembering lessons from a series of tutors. The idea of creating the Commonwealth had caused an almighty struggle in the houses of Parliament, with some families contemplating a whole new series of markets for their goods while others feared the dilution of their power base in the wake of an influx of newcomers. In the end, a compromise had been hammered out, ensuring the current balance of power was maintained while the newcomers were allowed to enter the aristocracy. Given time, the projections had maintained, the newcomers would become part of High Society.

They might be right, she thought. *But that does no good for anyone born before their world joined the Commonwealth. They'll never rise as high as they could.*

"My advice," Davidson said, "is to be the best captain you can be."

Kat glowered at him. "And I couldn't have thought of that for myself?"

"Sometimes the only way out is through," Davidson said, unabashed. "You will have to work hard to convince them that you deserved to be promoted. Think of yourself as a version of Labelle Jones."

"Oh," Kat said. Her lips twitched, humorlessly. "That isn't the most reassuring thing you could say."

She remembered. The story had been taught at Piker's Peak as a cautionary tale, although no one had been quite sure if it was a warning about the dangers of favoritism or how people could jump to the wrong conclusions. A young officer, assigned to a remote station, had been promoted several times, simply because the bureaucracy insisted that someone higher in rank had to be in command. But when the screwup had finally been noticed by the Inspectorate General, no one had been willing to believe it was just a clerical error. The poor officer's next set of superiors had assumed the worst, that she'd been the beneficiary of an absurd degree of favoritism and piled work on her until she'd nearly collapsed.

"I'm not trying to be reassuring," Davidson said. "I'm trying to tell you that earning the respect and trust of your subordinates isn't going to be easy."

"I know," Kat said. She looked down at her hands for a long moment and then looked up. "And how are your marines?"

"Settling in," Davidson said. "We *would* like the use of the main corridor, if you don't mind."

"Once it's clear of junk," Kat said. At least the crew was making rapid progress now. "And . . ."

She shook her head, dismissing the thought. Part of her had wanted to ask if he was seeing someone. His file had said he wasn't married, but marines rarely married until they left the service or became combat lifers. But he might still have a girlfriend on Tyre or one of the other ships . . . God knew she hadn't exactly been chaste since they'd split up and gone their separate ways.

". . . I'll expect you to handle your men," she said, instead. Their relationship could never be the same, no matter what she wanted. And she was being stupid even considering the possibility, not when she was his commanding officer. "And I'll see you at dinner tonight."

Davidson lifted an eyebrow. "Dinner?"

Kat smirked but then tried to hide it. Perhaps he'd had the same thought too.

"You're the last officer to board the ship," she said, instead. "I was waiting for you before hosting a formal dinner."

"I look forward to it," Davidson said stiffly. He rose to his feet. "With your permission, Captain, I will return to Marine Country. I have training exercises to plan."

"Me too," Kat said. They couldn't fly into battle, not yet, but they could run exercises to make sure they made all the obvious mistakes before actually facing a real enemy. "I'll see you tonight."

She watched him go, then turned back to her terminal, feeling an odd tinge of regret. She missed what they'd shared, more than she cared to admit . . .

But at least, she told herself firmly, there was one person she could trust on her ship.

CHAPTER FIVE

All things considered, Commander William McElney conceded reluctantly, it could have been worse.

The captain was inexperienced, at least when it came to being a commanding officer. She had a tendency to do too much of the work that should have been left to her XO, a common trait in newly promoted captains. But at least she wasn't a tyrant or a whiny brat in a naval uniform. He'd served under both kinds of commanding officers in his long career. But he was still worried about the first time *Lightning* went into battle. Who knew how the captain would react?

He pushed the thought to one side as he stepped into the conference room and glanced around the table, silently gratified to note that all of the senior officers had made it. They'd spent the last two days finalizing preparations for departure, something that had worn them out and made him urge the captain to ensure they had a day or two of rest before they actually departed the system. There was no time for shore leave, even to the orbital Intercourse and Intoxication station, but at least they could have stood down for a day. But the captain had warned that it would depend on their orders from the Admiralty.

The conference room seemed smaller than he remembered, now that it was actually serving its designated role. A large holographic image of the starship hung over the table, which was surrounded by comfortable chairs and a handful of consoles. A coffee maker sat against one bulkhead, with several officers glancing wistfully towards the machine. William sighed and then motioned for the steward to begin serving coffee. There were days when he knew the Navy practically *ran* on coffee. He took his seat, beside the captain's chair at the head of the table, and waited. Captain Falcone entered the compartment moments later.

She looked tired but happy, he noted as he rose to his feet in greeting. Somehow, actually working so closely with her made it easier to ignore the fact she looked too young to be on a starship, let alone sitting in the command chair. He had a feeling, judging from her expression, that the Admiralty had finally gotten around to cutting the starship her orders. No captain, not even the most rule-abiding commanding officer, would be entirely happy drifting in orbit near Tyre. It would be far too easy for the Admiralty to interfere with the smooth running of their starship.

He sighed at the thought. The new crewmen had arrived, as promised, and some of them were going to be trouble. He would have rejected them, if there had been time, but the missives from the Admiralty insisting that they move up their departure date had grown more frequent and more ominous. Instead, all he could do was ride herd on the potential troublemakers and make sure the senior chiefs did the same. It was possible that careful supervision would turn them into valuable crewmen. Or at least keep them out of trouble.

"Please be seated," the captain said as she took her seat at the end of the table. There was a rustle as the officers sat down, then a pause as the steward served the captain a mug of coffee. "I would like to start by saying that you have all worked very hard to prepare this ship for departure and I am very proud of you."

You would like to say? William thought, dryly.

He dismissed the thought a moment later; he'd had some commanding officers who indulged themselves with word games, but Captain Falcone didn't seem to be one of them. Instead, it was just a clumsy choice of words.

"We have finally received our orders from the Admiralty," Captain Falcone continued. "We will be departing for Cadiz in two days. Unfortunately, we will also be escorting a convoy of nine civilian merchantmen. It will not be an easy task."

That was an understatement, William knew. Merchantmen didn't tend to have the inherent flexibility of military starships, not when their contracts specified that deliveries had to be made by a specific date or penalty clauses would come into effect. One of the bigger shipping firms would hardly be inconvenienced by having to pay out compensation for late delivery, but it could literally ruin a smaller firm—or an independent shipper. Indeed, he would have expected the latter to run through hyperspace on their own, relying on the energy storms to cloak their presence.

The holographic image changed. This time it showed nine bulk freighters, all Rhesus-class. The Rhesus was an old design, dating all the way back to the era before the Breakaway Wars, but it was known for being reliable and—more importantly—easy to refurbish as technology grew more advanced. William would have bet half his monthly paycheck that none of the freighters in the convoy still had anything from their original configuration, apart from their hulls. Even civilian-grade sensors had advanced immensely since the days of the UN.

"It's four weeks to Cadiz," the captain continued. "During that time, we will both be handling escort duties and running constant exercises. It is my intention to have this ship ready for battle by the time we arrive at Cadiz. We do not know when war will break out, but it *will*. We have to be ready."

William couldn't disagree. Scuttlebutt around the fleet suggested the Admiralty expected war to break out within the year, although cynics wondered if the whole collection of rumors was an attempt to justify the latest military budget as it fought its way through Parliament. It was true enough that the Royal Navy had claimed a larger share of the budget ever since the Commonwealth had come into existence, but it didn't take superdreadnoughts to provide convoy protection and hunt down pirate bases. *That* was a task for frigates or destroyers.

"The latest weather report suggests the presence of a storm moving towards us in hyperspace," Lieutenant Nicola Robertson said. The navigator looked uncommonly nervous, although that wasn't too surprising. Predicting the course and duration of energy storms in hyperspace was more a matter of lucky guessing and consulting tea leaves rather than good, reliable science. "We may have to add an extra week to our journey to avoid brushing up against its edges."

William held his breath, wondering how Kat would respond. Some captains would have understood the point, others would have snapped at the impudent officer who had dared to question their arrangements. Which one, he asked himself, was Captain Falcone?

"Better to take a week longer to reach our destination than try to fly through a storm," Captain Falcone said simply. She gave Lieutenant Robertson a reassuring smile. "I would prefer not to test the ship's hull *that* violently."

Thank God, William thought. In theory, a low-level storm could be navigated through as easily as an aircar would fly through turbulence in a planetary atmosphere. But in practice hardly anyone would take the risk if it could be avoided. And a high-level storm would rip the ship apart so thoroughly that no one would ever find any wreckage, not even a few stray atoms. Captain Falcone, at least, understood the basic realities of travel through hyperspace, unlike some of William's former commanding officers. *They* had seemed to think that their will bent the laws of time and space themselves.

He nodded at Nicola, who looked relieved. She was young—like most navigators, she had learned her trade at Bendix Base, rather than

Piker's Peak—and had little grasp of military formality. Technically, she wasn't even in the line of command. William had a private suspicion that her informality would get her into trouble one day, although he intended to ensure it didn't happen on his watch. And she was pretty enough to get into a different kind of trouble on shore leave.

Lieutenant Commander Roach cleared his throat. "Captain," he said carefully, "are any other warships being assigned to the convoy?"

The captain's face darkened. "No," she said. "The freighters have a handful of weapons mounts apiece, but we're the only true warship."

William nodded to himself in approval. Captain Falcone understood the implications. Judging from the level of communications traffic between *Lightning* and Naval HQ, she'd also tried to argue with her superiors, requesting additional support. But she'd clearly failed.

Roach put it into words. "Captain," he said, "we can't guarantee security for nine freighters in hyperspace."

"I know," the captain said. Her mouth twisted, as though she had bitten into a lemon. "We might lose one of our ships in a distortion zone and never realize it."

She was right, William knew. Hyperspace played merry hell with sensors, particularly long-range sensors. It was quite possible for a pirate ship to shadow the convoy, satisfy itself that it could pick off one of the freighters, then attack during an energy distortion that would make it impossible to tell that something had gone wrong. It would be hours before the freighter failed to check in, at which point it would be countless light years away, being looted by the pirates. The crew would be in for a fate worse than death.

He rather doubted their weapons would make any difference. The big corporations could afford weapons licenses, cramming as many armaments into their freighter hulls as they liked, but it wouldn't make them effective warships. Freighters wallowed like pigs in mud, their sensors and shields rarely military-grade . . . hell, there were restrictions on selling military-grade technology to civilians, even for the big corporations. There was just too great a chance of it falling into *very* unfriendly hands.

And it was starting to look as though someone had set the captain up to fail.

"We cannot hope to hide the convoy," Captain Falcone said. "The scheduled departure date cannot be put back any further. Anyone with eyes on the system will be able to track our numbers, course, and speed, then make a rough estimate of our location. And ten ships are easier to locate in hyperspace than one."

She took a breath. It was easy to see she was nervous. "I plan to turn our weakness into a strength," she continued. "Standard doctrine places the escorting warship at the prow of the convoy. I intend to place us at the rear. We will pose as a freighter."

There was a long pause. No one spoke.

William evaluated it rapidly. It was risky, he had to admit; if they ran into an ambush, the first freighters would be hammered before *Lightning* even realized they were under attack. But few pirates would dare to take on a heavy cruiser, even if they thought they had the firepower advantage—and few pirate groups had anything larger than a frigate under their command. It was much more likely that they would try to pick off the freighter at the rear of the convoy, rather than challenge a warship directly . . .

And, if the Captain's plan worked, they would run right into a heavy cruiser instead.

"Workable," William said. "Do you intend to use drones to ensure that any observers see us at the prow of the convoy?"

"One of the freighters carries a modified Electronic Countermeasures package," the captain said briskly. "*Mother's Milk* will pose as *Lightning*. She wouldn't fool anyone in normal space, but in hyperspace sensors are unreliable enough to create reasonable doubt."

She smiled coldly. "Maybe next time we can have *all* the freighters posing as warships," she added. "Make them guess which of us is the *real* contender."

"The odds would favor them," William pointed out.

"We could run a pair of drones forward, if we mounted a control station on *Mother's Milk*," Roach offered. "Their sensors would give us some additional warning if anyone took up position in front of us."

"Costly," William pointed out. Drones configured to work in hyperspace cost a cool five million crowns apiece. The bean counters would be furious, even if the drones were recovered and recycled. "They might garnish your wages to pay for them."

"But worthwhile," Captain Falcone said. "See to it."

William made a note of it on his terminal, thinking hard. The captain was from an aristocratic family. She would, if the scandal pages were accurate, have a trust fund, a share in the family's wealth for her to use as she pleased. Was hers large enough to afford a five-million-crown drone? It was unlikely she *needed* her monthly paycheck to live a life of reasonable luxury . . . He felt a flicker of envy. Growing up on Hebrides had been far from easy. If his brother hadn't . . .

He shook his head, forcing the thought to one side. Memories of his brother and what he'd done to feed the family still brought stabs of pain and guilt. Thirty years in the Royal Navy had never quite healed the scars.

"We could also follow a more evasive course," Lieutenant Robertson suggested. "If we went off the normal shipping lanes . . ."

"Too great a risk of losing one of the freighters," the captain said, so quickly that it was clear she'd already considered the possibility. "We couldn't take the chance."

"They would have real problems picking up the navigational beacons," William agreed. "Not every ship has a skilled navigator."

Robertson blushed, as he'd hoped she would, rather than looking crushed.

The captain cleared her throat. "I will not shed any tears for a destroyed raider," she said firmly. "However, I intend to capture a raider intact if possible, along with her crew. I have"—her face twisted in disgust—"authority to offer them life on a penal world if they surrender once we have them at gunpoint."

William shared her feelings. Pirates were the scum of the universe as far as any naval officer was concerned, and the Royal Navy had legal authority to simply execute captured pirates on the spot. In some ways, it was counterproductive—there was rarely any attempt to interrogate prisoners before shoving them out the airlock—but few pirates actually knew anything useful. Their senior officers, well aware of what fate awaited them, often fought to the death.

"There has been a considerable upsurge in raider activity recently," Captain Falcone continued before anyone could muster an objection. "We need to know if a foreign power"—there could be no doubt which one she meant—"has been supporting the raiders for reasons of their own. Prisoners may be the only way to obtain hard evidence."

There was a long silence. Roach finally broke it.

"Captain," he said, "what will *happen* to the prisoners if they're not going to be spaced?"

"They will be held in the brig, then transported to Nightmare," the captain said flatly. "Once they're on the surface, they can work or die."

Roach looked pleased, William noted. Nightmare was a marginally habitable planet, its original settlers fighting a losing battle to survive when they'd been rediscovered. The Commonwealth had transported most of the settlers to another world, then turned Nightmare into a penal colony. It was possible that the prisoners could master their new world, the government had argued at the time, eventually creating another member world for the Commonwealth. And if they killed each other there . . . well, they wouldn't be hurting innocents. Everyone who was exiled to Nightmare thoroughly deserved it.

The captain gave them a moment to assimilate what she'd said, then went on. "We will take tomorrow as downtime," she said, "then prepare for departure. There's no time for shore leave, I'm afraid, but there will be reduced duty hours for almost all of the crew. Please don't overindulge in the still I'm not supposed to know about."

William concealed his amusement with an effort. There was *always* a semi-legal still on a naval vessel, producing alcohol that was barely suitable for human consumption. It was tolerated as long as the operators didn't do anything stupid, but it was generally the XO's responsibility to keep an eye on it. The captain was not meant to know anything—officially—about the still. But she'd been an XO herself not too long ago.

Captain Falcone rose to her feet. "Dismissed," she said as her officers rose. "Mr. XO, please remain a moment."

She waited until the conference room was empty, then turned to face him. "I want you to take some rest too," she said firmly. "You've been pulling double duty since you were assigned to *Lightning*."

"It's part of the job," William said.

"I know," the captain pointed out. "But you're working yourself to death."

William shrugged, expressively. A few days of leave would be enough to go to the I&I station, or perhaps a more expensive holiday on Tyre if he'd felt like stretching his legs. Or he could have gotten a hotel room and just slept for several days, or found someone young, female, and willing to share his bed. But a day wasn't enough to do anything, apart from relaxing in his cabin or watching entertainment flicks. He hadn't been brought up to be lazy.

"If that's an order," he said, "I will obey. But . . ."

"It *is* an order," Captain Falcone said. There was a thin smile on her face. She'd probably been very like him when she'd been an XO. "Get some rest, Bill. You need it."

"Bill," William repeated. The nickname brought back bad memories. His brother had always called him Bill—or worse. "Please just call me William, Captain."

The captain gave him a sharp look, but nodded. "Get some rest, William," she repeated. "I think there will be little time for resting when we're on our way."

William saluted, then left the compartment. The hatch hissed closed behind him.

Outside, he stopped and considered, briefly. He'd worried about the captain. He knew he had good reason to worry about the captain. But perhaps he'd been wrong. Perhaps it wouldn't be so bad after all.

CHAPTER SIX

The bridge looked and felt different as Kat stepped through the hatch and walked towards her command chair. All of the consoles were manned this time; each one installed, then checked and checked again until the engineers were absolutely certain they were working perfectly. She felt the hum of the starship's drives, a constant background noise ever since the fusion plants had been activated for the first time, grow stronger as the chief engineer ran his final checks. *Lightning* was finally ready to separate herself from the shipyard and head into deep space.

Kat settled back in her command chair, trying to control the mounting excitement within her heart. This was *her* ship. She'd sat in command chairs before, stood watches, and even held command for days at a time, but none of those ships were *hers*. *Lightning* was *her* ship and she was finally ready to leave. She forced herself to calm down as she keyed the console and then looked up at the display. *Lightning* still sat in the midst of the independent shipyard, like a baby attached to her mother. That was about to change.

Bracing herself, she activated the internal communicator. "Mr. Lynn," she said, formally. "Status report."

"All systems are green, Captain," the chief engineer said. She'd had a dozen meetings with him since they'd first met and he'd impressed her with his competence. At least he didn't seem to be one of the engineers who inflated his estimated repair times to make himself look like a miracle worker. "Our fusion plants are online, drive harmonics are nominal, and the vortex generator is at optimal readiness."

"Good," Kat said. She looked up at Commander McElney. "Mr. XO?"

"All stations report ready," her XO said. His face was impassive, but she thought she detected a hint of concern. No one could forget just how much bad luck had struck *Lightning*'s predecessor. "We are ready to separate from the shipyard."

Kat took a long breath. "Check the tubes, then seal all airlocks," she ordered. No one would be in the tubes now, not after the alert had sounded, but they had to take precautions anyway, just in case. Besides, overlooking safety precautions was a bad habit. "And then prepare to cut the power lines."

Minutes ticked away before the XO spoke again. "Captain," he said formally, "all tubes are cleared. The airlocks are sealed."

"Cut the power lines," Kat ordered. Previously, her ship had drawn its power from the shipyard's fusion cores. Now, *Lightning* would be completely reliant on her own reactors for power. "Engineering?"

"These beauties took the strain without even dimming the lights," Lynn pronounced. "All power cores are functioning optimally. Battery power is held in reserve."

Kat had to smile. Keeping the lights on was hardly a significant demand, not compared to the ship's drives or weapons. They could have operated the lights through batteries alone for days, if necessary. But it was good to know there hadn't been any minor problems.

"Disengage from the tubes," she ordered softly. "And then prepare to take us out of the yard."

"Maneuvering thrusters online," Lieutenant Samuel Weiberg reported.

The helmsman looked disgustingly confident in his skills, but he had reason to be. "Drive field generators standing by."

A faint shiver ran through the hull, so faint that Kat wondered if she'd imagined it.

"Tubes disengaged," her XO said. "We will be clear to depart in five minutes."

Kat felt her heartbeat racing in her chest, thumping so loudly that it was a wonder no one else could hear it. Her ship was finally ready to depart . . . She braced herself, mentally counting down the seconds. Suddenly, she just couldn't wait.

"The shipyard just signaled us," Linda Ross reported. The communications officer looked up from her console, her gaze meeting Kat's. "We are cleared to depart."

"Take us out," Kat ordered.

A dull quiver ran through the vessel as the maneuvering thrusters fired, slowly pushing *Lightning* out of the shipyard and into open space. The quivering grew stronger as the helmsman checked and rechecked his systems, knowing that a single mistake could have disastrous consequences if he didn't catch it in time. Drive fields were so much simpler, Kat knew as she watched him work, but bringing a drive field up within a shipyard would tear the complex apart. They would have to wait until they were in open space before powering up the drives and leaving the system behind.

She watched the display until they were outside the shipyard and then keyed her console. "Mr. Lynn?"

"Drive nodes are online," the engineer said. "You may bring the drives to full power at will."

Kat smiled. "Bring up the drive," she ordered. "And then run a full cycle of tests before we go anyway."

"Aye, aye, Captain," the helmsman said. Another quiver, stronger this time, ran through *Lightning*. The background noise deepened for a long moment, then returned to the steady thrumming that had pervaded the entire ship since the fusion cores were activated. "Drive online . . . field active in twenty seconds."

Kat held her breath. This, she remembered, was where *Uncanny* had suffered her first major systems failure. Her drive nodes had proved utterly unequal to the strain placed on them and blew, one by one, leaving the starship tumbling helplessly through space. After that, she had been mildly surprised the Navy had kept the ship in commission, let alone built a second cruiser to the same—if somewhat modified—specifications. She felt tension rise on the bridge as *Lightning* quivered, a faint sensation spreading through the hull, then settling down.

"Drive field active, seventy percent power," Weiberg informed her. "All systems appear to be handling the strain."

The XO looked relieved. Kat didn't blame him. Apart from the potential for disaster, a repeat of the *Uncanny* debacle would probably have destroyed both of their careers. The last she'd heard, almost everyone who had served on *Uncanny* as senior officers had left the Navy, although not all of their careers had been blighted. Some had no longer felt like pushing their luck.

"Good," Kat said. She took a breath, then leaned forward. "Bring us up to one hundred percent power."

The quivering grew stronger as the ship shook herself down, but the status lights remained green. *Lightning* wanted to *move*, Kat realized; she'd been in the shipyard far too long. And now she was in open space.

"Take us towards the convoy," she ordered. Briefly, she wondered what the Admiralty would have told the merchantmen if *Lightning* had been unable to escort them. Probably would have detached a cruiser from Home Fleet to do the honors. "Mr. XO?"

"All stations report full readiness," the XO said. "No problems detected."

Kat smiled and sat back in her command chair as her ship sliced through the vacuum of space, heading towards the gathering convoy.

The quivering was almost completely gone now, even though the starship was operating at full power. She glanced down at the constant stream of updates from the datanet and felt a wave of relief as she realized that most of the bugs that had crippled *Uncanny* had been removed. At least the Navy had learned from the disaster, she noted. She'd always had the impression the Navy was slow to learn, let alone incorporate changes into later generations of starships.

But Uncanny lost power in front of a horde of dignitaries, she reminded herself. King Hadrian himself had been there. *No one could be allowed to sweep such a balls-up under the table.*

She leaned back and studied the long-range sensors as they came to life, feeding data into her personal display. Tyre was one of the most heavily industrialized star systems in the known galaxy and it showed. Her sensors tracked asteroid miners, remote industrial nodes, cloudscoops for mining helium-3 from the gas giants, and thousands of spacecraft or starships making their way to and from high orbit. Tyre itself was surrounded with orbital defenses, including thirteen massive battle stations and countless remote platforms. It all looked so safe and impregnable.

Earth felt the same way, she thought, feeling cold ice running down her spine. At Piker's Peak, she'd studied the Breakaway Wars. *Who knows what will happen when the system comes under attack?*

She shivered. Before the Breakaway Wars, the UN had believed humanity's homeworld to be untouchable. They'd found out the hard way they were wrong and they hadn't lived long enough to correct their error. And now, all that was left of the once-proud Sol System was a handful of asteroid settlements, struggling to survive against the odds. The UN and most of the worlds that had taken the lead in fighting it's control were long gone.

"Approaching convoy waypoint," Weiberg reported. On the display, the nine freighters were coming into view, grouped around a small trade station. There was a faint hint of amusement in his voice. "Request permission to slow down."

"Granted," Kat said. Had she ever been that young? She looked towards Lieutenant Ross. "Contact the convoy master. If they're ready to depart, we might as well leave the system at once."

She waited for the response, silently regretting the lack of a formal launching ceremony. *Lightning* had been commissioned weeks ago, of course, but it would still have been nice to have a dedication. But the *Uncanny* disaster had ensured that her sister would have a far less public launch and departure. There had been so many questions asked in Parliament that the Navy had bent over backwards to avoid publicity this time around. Kat didn't mind—there would have been questions about her qualifications she would have found hard to avoid—but her crew deserved better.

"The convoy master reports that his ships will be ready to depart in twenty minutes," Lieutenant Ross said. "They have to bring up their own drives."

Idiot, Kat told herself sharply. A freighter—even one of the most modern freighters in the galaxy—could hardly afford to keep its drive field active at all times. The wear and tear on the drive nodes would cost them thousands of crowns to fix, if the drives didn't fail completely while they were in hyperspace. *You should know better.*

She turned to look at the tactical officer. "Raise shields," she ordered. "Cycle the weapons systems; bring us to full tactical alert."

Alarms howled through the ship as the crew raced to combat stations. They'd run endless drills while they were in the shipyard, but this was different. Kat watched as the starship's shields snapped into existence, silently relieved that the Navy designers had indulged their usual desire for multiple redundancy. *Lightning* could take a great deal of damage and still maintain her shields. But she wished there was more time for a live-fire exercise.

"Shields and weapons at one hundred percent efficiency," Roach reported after several minutes had passed. "Long-range tactical sensors active; passive sensors active. Running tracking exercises now."

Kat allowed herself a moment of relief.

"Good," she said. "Stand down from combat stations, then devise a set of exercises for when we reach Cadiz. There should be some harmless asteroids in the system we can use for target practice."

"There should be drones too," the XO put in.

His voice was impassive, but Kat thought she sensed doubt in his tone. Cadiz Naval Base was on the front lines of the war everyone *knew* was coming. Seventh Fleet should be training every day, running live-fire exercises constantly, despite the cost. But she'd checked the shipping manifests and noted that Admiral Morrison hadn't requested any replacement drones from Naval HQ. It was just possible, she supposed, that his techs had managed to salvage all the drones, but she wouldn't have put money on it. No matter how good the techs were, one or two drones per exercise were always a write-off.

She gritted her teeth. It was far more likely Admiral Morrison wasn't running any training exercises—and that was absurd. Didn't he know there was a war on its way?

Lieutenant Ross cleared her throat. "Captain, the convoy master reports that his ships are ready for departure," she said. "He would like to know if we intend to open a vortex for the merchantmen."

Kat tapped her console. "Engineering, this is the captain," she said. She wasn't surprised by the request. Each use of a vortex generator cut its lifespan by several months . . . and they were staggeringly expensive. She didn't blame the civilians for wanting to rely on a military ship to open the pathway into hyperspace. "Can we hold a vortex open long enough for the merchantmen to enter hyperspace?"

"Yes, Captain," Lynn assured her. "We should have more than enough power to hold the gate open for ten minutes, if necessary."

Kat nodded, then closed the channel and turned back to the helmsman. "Plot the gate coordinates, then pass them to the convoy," she ordered. "We'll follow them into hyperspace, closing the gate behind us."

"Aye, aye, Captain," Weiberg said. He worked his console for a long moment, designating a location several thousand kilometers from the station. Opening a gate close to a large structure was asking for trouble. "Gate coordinates set."

"Take us there," Kat ordered. *Lightning* started to move, followed by her nine charges. Kat had to wince as she saw what passed for a formation among the civilians, and she shook her head ruefully. This wasn't a parade. "Lieutenant Ross?"

Ross turned to look at her. "Captain?"

"Transmit a formal departure notification to System Command," Kat ordered. It was unlikely that System Command would object to their departure, not after they'd received orders to leave as quickly as possible, but the signal had to be sent. "Attach a full copy of our readiness status and the test results from our final trials."

And let them know the ghost of Uncanny *didn't put in an appearance*, she thought. It wasn't something she could attach to an official communication. She'd send a private note to the Admiralty later. *They should have sent someone to give us a proper farewell, no matter what I wanted. The crew deserved better.*

"We are in position, Captain," Weiberg informed her. "Vortex generator is online; coordinates locked."

Kat looked up and met her XO's eyes, then looked back at the display. "Open the vortex," she ordered. It was time to leave. "And hold it open as long as possible."

Space seemed to twist in front of the starship, a blaze of light rapidly spinning into a tear in the fabric of existence. She saw the eerie lights of hyperspace peeking through, like something from a very different universe, then forced herself to relax as the first of the freighters went through the vortex. There were members of her crew who refused to watch as the ships passed through, claiming the vortex was actually a giant mouth waiting to swallow them, but she'd never had that problem. All she felt was relief at getting underway and leaving Tyre far behind.

"The last of the freighters has passed through," Roach reported. The tactical officer sounded amused. "They're heading towards the first waypoint now."

"Take us through," Kat ordered.

There was a faint sensation of . . . *wrongness* as they passed through the vortex, which rapidly faded away to nothingness. A handful of people had problems in hyperspace, but none of them joined the Navy. They stayed firmly on the ground or made the trip in stasis. "Status report?"

"The vortex generator performed splendidly," Lynn stated. The engineer sounded pleased with himself. "We didn't need to activate any of the secondary power systems at all."

"Excellent," Kat said. She watched as the vortex faded away into nothingness, leaving them in hyperspace. Her sensors insisted that there was no one close enough to follow her ships, let alone pick up on her deployments. "Communications, pass the deployment plan to the convoy master."

"Aye, aye, Captain," Ross said.

Kat turned to the XO. "Have the shuttle launched," she added. They'd loaded the shuttle with command and control systems for the drones prior to leaving the shipyard, but she hadn't risked informing the convoy master of what she had planned. "Once the equipment is mounted, launch two drones to provide additional sensor coverage."

"Aye, Captain," the XO said.

Kat watched him leave and then turned her attention to the display. Hyperspace was always relatively calm near a star, as only an idiot or a suicidal fool would try to fly through the area of hyperspace that corresponded to the location of a star in the real world. It would get much worse as they headed away from Tyre, she knew; even short-range communications would become erratic. And who knew who might be following them, relying on hyperspace to cloak their presence? The pirates just had to get lucky once to secure a hard lock on her hulls.

"The convoy master . . . ah, sounds a little astonished," Ross reported. No amount of control could hide the nervousness in her voice. It *was* her first posting as communications officer, after all. "But he says he will comply."

Doubts my sanity, Kat translated to herself. She had a feeling his response had been rude, too rude for any officer to dare repeating. God knew she'd done the same as a junior officer. *But as long as he does as he is told, it doesn't matter.*

"Take us to our position," she ordered. The freighters were already forming up, although their formation was, if anything, even less orderly than their formation in real space. "And then we can start our journey to Cadiz."

And see what comes crawling out after us, she added, mentally.

CHAPTER SEVEN

"You seem to have forgotten how to fight," Davidson said. "How *terrible*."

Kat lay on her back on the mat, wondering if it was worth getting up. Davidson had taught her how to spar, years ago, but she'd never had the time to become one of the navy's martial artists. Indeed, being able to kill a man with a single blow wasn't a valued skill on the bridge of a starship. It did build confidence, she had to admit, but little else.

"It's been too long," she muttered as she sat upright. Her entire body was covered in sweat while her muscles ached in pain. "I should have sparred more."

"*That* is evident," Davidson said. He stuck out a hand to help her to her feet. "You've really let yourself go."

Kat glowered at him as she stood upright. Her body, thanks to genetic engineering, didn't decay as far or as fast as a baseline human, but she still needed to exercise regularly just to keep herself in shape. She rather suspected that the engineers had been more interested in designing her for beauty than endurance, although the former was often a matter of taste while the latter required far more extensive enhancement. But she'd refrained from looking into their files, fearful of what she might find. She loved her father dearly, at least when he wasn't interfering with her life, yet she had no illusions about his ruthlessness.

"You should have more practice sessions," Davidson warned as he let go of her hand and reached for a towel. "What would you do if we were boarded by a bunch of scurvy pirates?"

"Shoot them with my pistol," Kat said. "Have you ever fought hand-to-hand on a pirate ship?"

"I had a sucker come at me with an axe once," Davidson said. He passed her the towel and reached for another one for himself. "I don't know *what* era he thought he was living in."

Kat dried the sweat off her body, then looked around, silently grateful that Davidson had picked a private sparring chamber for their exercise. She didn't want to show any form of weakness in front of the crew, even though cold logic suggested that anyone who had endured boot camp should be able to handle someone who hadn't. Besides, she had a feeling that Davidson hadn't wanted his marines to see either. Their relationship was closer than it should have been.

"He was probably drunk or drugged," she said as she walked through the hatch and into the shower. Water cascaded down from high overhead as she pulled off her exercise clothes, dropping them into the cleaning bin. "Or maybe he thought he could catch you by surprise."

"It would be more impressive if I hadn't been wearing armor," Davidson conceded as he followed her into the shower. "Do you want me to scrub you down?"

Kat felt her face heat. Modesty was impossible to maintain at Piker's Peak, where the cadets were bunked together without regard for age or sex. And Davidson had seen her naked countless times before, back when she'd been a mere midshipwoman. It was a tempting offer—her body remembered his touch far too well—but she knew she couldn't allow it, not now. They were now senior officers, not junior crew.

"No, thank you," she said as she washed the sweat off her body. "I'm sorry, but . . ."

Davidson didn't show any signs of obvious regret when she turned to look at him. If anything, she noted, he was more muscular than before, but he'd picked up a handful of nasty scars on his chest. Marines kept their scars, she recalled him telling her, even when modern medical science could leave their skin as smooth and untouched as a baby's bottom. It was how they kept score.

"I don't remember those scars," she said. "How'd you get them?"

"Some bastard planted an IED far too close to the Rover," Davidson explained. "I got slammed in the chest by the wreckage and sent howling to the ground. If I'd been wearing my armor . . ."

Kat nodded. Marine armor was almost impossible to penetrate without heavy weapons, but it was also hellishly intimidating, not the sort of thing that should be used when the Marines were trying to win hearts and minds. Davidson's other enhancements were under the skin, impossible to detect without a deep scan. Some of them, she knew, were so highly classified that no one outside the Royal Marines was supposed to know about their mere existence let alone what they actually *did.*

She felt his gaze passing over her body. "You're still perfect," he said. "You didn't pick up a single scar?"

"They faded quickly," Kat said. Her body didn't allow scars to last for more than a few weeks. She might spend a long time healing, but anything that didn't kill her outright wouldn't inflict permanent damage. Or so she had been told. "I don't have the ego required to show off my cuts and bruises."

Davidson smirked. "Paper cuts and coffee stains?"

Kat gave him a one-fingered gesture. "Vacuum scars and plasma burns," she said, remembering a major systems failure on *Thunderous.* She'd spent a week in Sickbay afterwards, having the damage repaired. "I don't think I could hack it as a groundpounder."

"You have the bloody-minded determination to press on until you get killed," Davidson said snidely. "Everything else would come, in time."

Kat shook her head, then stepped out of the shower into the drying room. She picked up a towel and dried herself swiftly, then reached for the small pile of clothes she'd left on the bench. Part of her was very tempted, she knew, just to turn and take Davidson into her arms. They both knew there would be no strings attached. But she knew better than to allow it, not now. She was the ship's commander. It was quite possible she would have to order him to his death.

She shivered at the thought as she pulled on her panties and bra, then donned her trousers and jacket as Davidson joined her. He dressed himself with formidable speed—he'd always had that habit, she recalled—then sat down on the bench. Kat checked her appearance in the mirror, decided she passed muster, and then sat down facing him.

"I meant to ask," she said, "how are your Marines coping with shipboard life?"

"They're surviving," Davidson said. He smiled suddenly. "And they're glad of the chance to practice boarding starships, despite the complaints from the freighter commanders."

Kat had to smile. The convoy master had been hearing from his subordinate captains and he'd passed their complaints on to Kat. She wasn't surprised—no civilian starship crews enjoyed seeing Marines prowling through their ships—but it wasn't something she intended to stop. Given where the ships were going afterwards, she wanted to make sure they were searched thoroughly before they were allowed to leave.

"Anyone would think they had something to hide," she mused.

"Oh, they do," Davidson said. He shrugged at her expression. "There's always a market for smuggled goods, Kat. Something as simple as the latest AV recording or bootleg flick will bring in thousands of crowns if sold to the right distributor. And then pornography from Tyre or Paradise will fetch a high price on one of the dourer worlds in the Commonwealth."

"True," Kat agreed. "Though I don't see what people enjoy about modern music."

The thought made her smile. Candy had patronized—in all senses of the word—a dozen up-and-coming musicians, often lobbying her father to use his influence to keep others from pirating their music. But it was a losing battle. There might be musical stars who were famous on a particular planet, yet they rarely saw any royalties from anywhere outside the system. It was just too easy for a starship crewman to copy their recordings, upload them to the datanet on a different planet, and then start distributing them. Their father had eventually banned Candy from speaking to him outside family gatherings, if only because she just wouldn't shut up about her latest pop star boyfriend.

"Everyone has different tastes," Davidson said. He paused. "It's a little more dangerous for those freighter crews, though."

Kat nodded, sourly. Years ago, a freighter crew had been arrested and jailed by enforcers for daring to bring pornography into the Theocracy. There had been no evidence that the crew had intended to distribute the porn, but it hadn't mattered. The Commonwealth was forced to make a number of increasingly sharp diplomatic protests before the crew was finally released. They hadn't had a good time while prisoners.

"I hope you warned them," she said.

"Oh, we did," Davidson said. "Porn isn't illegal within the Commonwealth. But the Theocracy . . ."

Kat understood. They'd all heard from the refugees. Anything the Theocracy didn't like was destroyed, starting with religious sites and eventually including schools for girls and mixed-sex gatherings. The Theocracy had picked up the worst, she sometimes thought, of its predecessors as well as the best. If they genuinely believed God would only grant them victory if they worked for it . . . they might well be very dangerous opponents.

She stood. "I have paperwork to do," she said dryly. "I wish we had more time to just chat."

Davidson gave her a sly look. "Shore leave on Cadiz?"

"Only if you let me borrow a suit of armor," Kat said. She rather doubted the *entire* planet was dangerous, but she knew better than to take chances. "Don't let anyone's complaints slow you down."

William read the latest series of complaints from the convoy master with a rather jaundiced eye. The convoy master didn't seem to have any sense of proportion; first, he complained about the marines poking their way through his ships, then demanded compensation for the fuss and upset. Given that most of his crews actually had very little to do until they reached Cadiz, William rather suspected the convoy master was trying to hide something. Or perhaps he just resented having marines tramping through his ships.

Sighing, he looked up at the bridge display, half hoping that something would happen to spare him the monotony of endless paperwork. But there was nothing on the display, apart from the nine freighters and the live feed from the drones in front of them. Operating them at such a remove was tricky—yet another source of complaints from the convoy master—but he had to admit the idea had worked out well. If there was someone lurking ahead of them, the drones would spot them before they realized they'd discovered the convoy.

He put the complaints to one side, promising himself that he would write out a proper response later, then turned his attention to the personnel reports. Department heads *always* waited until they were in hyperspace to do the reports, which wasn't entirely a bad sign. If there had been a crewman who was a real problem, he or she would have been reported before they left the spacedock. The absence of such a report was heartening. But it was clear, as he skimmed through the reports with a practiced eye, that there was at least *one* problem that might need his intervention.

"Idiots," he muttered, under his breath. It *always* happened, no matter what he said or did—or what anyone else said or did, for that matter. *There's always one idiot—and someone ready to take advantage of an idiot.*

It was surprising how certain indicative patterns could appear in the data. The Navy automatically held half of its wages in reserve, in the Naval Bank, but the other half was always transferred to the starship's database. A crewman's bank balance could be accessed anywhere in the Commonwealth—or onboard ship—and used for anything from souvenirs to small luxuries. Or gambling. The data in front of him suggested there was a gambling ring on the ship. And it was starting to get out of hand.

"Bloody fucking idiots," he swore.

Roach looked up from his console, where he'd been running tactical exercises. "Sir?"

"Belay that," William growled, annoyed at his own loss of control. "Go back to work."

"Aye, sir," Roach said.

William glared at the lieutenant commander's back, then worked his way through the data. He was no accountant, but there was no logical reason for repeated transfers of money from one account to another, apart from gambling. Gambling was not—technically—against regulations, where almost anything else would get the participants dishonorably discharged from the Navy. It hadn't been *that* long ago when a senior chief had been convicted of running a prostitution ring on a superdreadnought. He'd been put in front of a court martial board, dishonorably discharged, and finally shipped to Nightmare. His associates had served prison terms of their own.

He sighed as he finished putting the picture together. Gambling. It had to be gambling. And he was right. It was definitely getting out of control.

Shaking his head, he typed a message on his console, ordering the senior chief to have a few words with the gamblers. There were always one or two assholes at the center of the ring, he knew from bitter experience, one or two crewmen cunning enough to lure inexperienced young men and women into bad habits. Perhaps this ring would be smart enough not to take it too far, something that would require his intervention, or into criminal realms. The captain would have to become involved as well, and there would be a full investigation. And the Navy Police would start rooting through the ship's internal affairs to find out just what had happened and why.

His review of the remaining files passed without incident, much to his relief. The older hands, who had won that title by being assigned to *Lightning* as soon as she was commissioned into the king's service, had been helping the newcomers grow accustomed to the ship. Meanwhile, the newly qualified officers were doing well, apart from one who might have become ensnared by the gamblers. He made a note to speak to her if the disturbing financial transfers continued, and perhaps offer a few words of fatherly advice. If there was one thing he knew from his pre-Navy life, it was that the game was always rigged.

"I've completed the exercise, sir," Roach reported, breaking into his thoughts. "It seems to work fine, Commander, but we really need more cruisers to form a full squadron."

"And a command vessel," William noted as he strode over to Roach's station. The *Uncanny*-class hadn't been intended to serve as command vessels. Their designers had configured them more for independent operations, pointing out that they were heavily armed *and* fast enough to run away from anything bigger than themselves. Given that they'd said the same about battle cruisers, William wasn't too impressed. "We'd need another ship to coordinate the datanet."

"We might be able to reprogram the tactical computers to handle a datanet," Roach said. "It would be risky, because we don't have as many laser communicators as a dedicated command vessel or a superdreadnought, but it could be done."

William considered it for a long moment. "We'd also mark ourselves out as a target," he warned, finally. "Every ship in the enemy fleet would fire on us."

"Probably," Roach agreed. He tapped his console. "But we could make the same modifications on every other starship in the squadron. We'd *all* look like command vessels."

"I'm sure that would endear you to their crews," William said. No one liked being a target, even if they were inside a superdreadnought's formidable shields. "But it would also make it easier to keep the datanet up and running, wouldn't it?"

"I think so," Roach said. "Right now, losing a command vessel means losing the datanet, even for superdreadnoughts. It takes time to relink the ships together, which gives the enemy time to fire on suddenly-isolated vessels. But if we had multiple datalinks up and running, we could just switch command and control to a different starship."

"Work out a plan," William ordered. "Forward it to me once you're done; we'll go through it and see how well it holds up in the simulator."

And then we will have to test it for real, he thought, tartly. There was no other way, short of combat, to know how well a theory would work in practice. *If Admiral Morrison lets us do any exercises at all.*

"Sir," Lieutenant Robertson said, "we're picking up a distortion zone alarmingly close to us."

William walked over to her console and looked down at the display. No one had a real model for predicting energy shifts within hyperspace, which meant that starships might have to change course at unpredictable intervals. Flying through the distortion zone wouldn't be as bad as flying through a storm, but it would disrupt sensors and communications. It was the perfect place for an ambush.

"Pass the word to the freighters," he ordered. The captain had given him blanket authority to change course if he deemed it necessary. "Order them to prepare to change course to"—he studied Lieutenant Robertson's console carefully—"the following coordinates."

He walked back to the command chair as the small convoy started to alter course. The distortion zone was growing stronger, he noted, sweeping towards the clustered vessels like an ever-expanding storm.

Scientists sometimes wondered if the starships in hyperspace actually *attracted* storms and distortion zones. They sometimes did seem to blow up out of nowhere and overwhelm passing ships.

"There's going to be some disruption," Lieutenant Robertson reported. "I . . ."

There was a *ping* from Roach's console. "Commander!" he snapped, interrupting the navigator. He would only interrupt if he thought it was urgent. "I think we have company."

William took a look at the sensor display, then nodded. There was *something* out there, hidden in the distortion zone. It was impossible to be sure, but they had to assume the worst.

He keyed the console. "Red alert!" he said. "I say again, red alert! Captain to the bridge!"

CHAPTER EIGHT

"Report," Kat snapped.

Her XO was already rising from the command chair. "One starship on intercept vector," he said. "She's coming out of the distortion zone."

She must have been lurking in ambush, Kat thought. It wouldn't have been too difficult for someone on Tyre to ping a signal ahead of them, inviting a pirate ship to take up position and wait for the convoy to arrive. *Not bad timing on their part.*

"Bring the ship to battle stations, but do not raise shields," she ordered. Shields didn't work well in hyperspace and their mere presence would almost certainly tell the enemy that they weren't approaching a helpless freighter.

"Aye, aye, Captain," Roach said.

"How close can they come without getting a hard visual of our hull?"

"They probably won't have a good look at our hull until they're much closer, Captain," Roach replied, "but it's impossible to be precise."

Kat nodded, reluctantly. Hyperspace did weird things to sensors, even visual scanners and crude telescopes. It was possible the enemy ship would reach point-blank range before realizing that something was badly wrong—and equally possible they would get a visual from thousands of kilometers away and shy off before Kat could open fire. All she could do was hope for the former.

She ran through the tactical situation in her mind as her crew raced to battle stations. The enemy ship was coming up behind the convoy, which suggested its crew believed *Lightning* was at the prow of the formation. No pirate would dare tangle with a heavy cruiser if there was any way to avoid it. If they'd been right, the ambushers would definitely have a chance to pull a freighter away from the convoy before her escort noticed something was wrong.

"All stations report combat ready," her XO said. "Weapons systems are online, ready to fire; point defense datanet online, ready to go active on your command."

Kat smiled. They'd run exercises nearly every day since they'd left Tyre. They damn well should be at battle stations by now. She thought, briefly, of Davidson and his marines, taking up position to aid with damage control if necessary, then pushed the thought to the back of her mind. There were more important issues to handle.

"Pass the word to the convoy master," she said. She wished, suddenly, she knew the man better. But she'd resisted meeting with him after the endless barrage of complaints. "Inform him that we have company and that the convoy is to remain in formation. They are *not* to scatter."

The XO nodded without argument. Kat hadn't expected one. A single pirate ship could be handled easily—Roach could blow their unwelcome companion out of space now, if she hadn't wanted to take the pirate ship intact—but scattering would expose the convoy to any other pirate ships in the area. She looked down at the live feed from the sensors, trying to determine if there were any other vessels nearby, then scowled in irritation. It was impossible to be sure.

But at least there isn't anyone close enough to be noticed, she thought, relieved. *We won't have to worry about multiple enemies.*

Kat settled back in her command chair and watched as the pirate ship slowly closed in on the rear of the convoy. The ship's crew seemed to be playing it carefully; unless she was much mistaken, she was sure they could have caught up with her by now. But they had plenty of time to close in on their target, all the while bracing themselves to run or crash back to real space if *Lightning* put in an appearance. Kat allowed herself a cold smile. She wanted the pirate ship intact, she wanted prisoners to interrogate . . . but she wouldn't shed any tears if the vessel was accidentally blown apart or destroyed by a hyperspace storm. Pirate crews had gone far outside any standards of morality. They deserved nothing less than death.

An alarm buzzed. "They just swept us," Roach said. "I think our ECM fooled them."

"Prepare to fire," Kat ordered, sharply. If the pirates had realized what *Lightning* actually was, they'd have started to run. She'd only have a few minutes to kill them before hyperspace hid them from her sensors once again. "Lock weapons on target, but do not go active. I say again, do *not* go active."

"Aye, aye, Captain," Roach said. He would have kept a firm lock on the pirate ship as soon as they'd detected her, but the order had to be repeated. "Weapons locked; I say again, weapons locked."

Kat felt her heart thumping within her chest as the pirate ship seemed to hesitate, then glided closer. The pirates had been fooled! ECM was always tricky, even in real space. The slightest mistake could render one of the most expensive systems in the Navy worse than useless. But it had definitely worked. The pirates still thought they were crawling towards a harmless freighter.

She thought, fast. Civilian sensors were rarely military-grade. What would be a reasonable time for the freighter they were pretending to be to detect the pirates? The pirates knew that anyone who detected them would alert their escort, which meant . . . the pirates would probably issue their demands as soon as they believed they'd been detected. Ideally, they'd want to do it before their target could scream for help.

"Go active when they reach *here*," she ordered, tapping a point on the display. By then, a basic civilian-grade kit should have located the pirate ship. "Sweep them, but make it look sloppy."

Roach turned to grin. "Aye, aye, Captain."

Kat looked up and saw the XO's face. He looked as pleased with the situation as Kat felt—more so, in fact. Kat recalled his file and understood. Tyre had never been attacked by pirates—even during the worst days of the Breakdown, the system had been heavily defended against rogue starships—but Hebrides had been attacked several times. It hadn't been until the Royal Tyre Navy had established a permanent presence in the system that attacks had died away, leaving a legacy of bloody slaughter and slavery. No one from the XO's homeworld would show any mercy to pirates.

Nor will I, Kat thought.

But she knew she had permission to offer the pirates their lives in exchange for information. Life on Nightmare would be far from fun—the last report had suggested the exiles had set up small communities and were raiding each other—but it wasn't death.

We need the intelligence only they can provide, she reminded herself as she looked back at the holographic display. The red icon representing the pirate ship was drawing closer, while a wave of distortion was coming into view ahead of the convoy. *Letting them keep their lives is a small price for actionable intelligence.*

Kat gritted her teeth as the distortion washed closer. If she'd been in command of the pirate ship, she would open communications once the distortion was close enough to make it difficult to signal *Lightning*. They'd get their threats in first, followed by promises few spacers would believe. But if the crew refused to cooperate, the pirates could simply launch a missile barrage and blow their ships into atoms, even though it would gain the attackers nothing. There was hope, their victims might think, even if the pirates took them as slaves.

She shuddered at the thought. She'd seen pirate slaves—men and women liberated after HMS *Thomas* had captured a pirate base. They'd been broken beyond repair. The lucky ones had skills the pirates could use, so they'd been press-ganged into joining pirate crews, but the unlucky ones had been raped, then put to work as manual laborers. Human slavery and trafficking was alive and well on the edge of explored space, despite the best efforts of the more civilized powers. Even the Theocracy cooperated when it came to hunting down pirates.

"Captain," Lieutenant Ross said, "I'm picking up a tight-beam radio signal."

"Put it through," Kat ordered.

". . . under the guns of a warship," a harsh male voice said. There was so much static that it was hard, even with computer enhancement, to be entirely sure they were hearing the entire message. "You are ordered to cut your drives and prepare to be boarded. Do not attempt to alert any other ship in your convoy. If you cooperate, your lives will be spared."

Kat's lips twitched. Few spacers would believe promises from pirates. If *she'd* been a merchant skipper, she might just have tried to ram the pirate ship. It wouldn't have had a hope in hell of working in real space, but it would definitely have had a chance in hyperspace. And even if it failed, the pirates would have been forced to blow their own prize rather than take it intact. It might cost them dearly, in the long run. Pirate economics demanded a constant supply of prizes just to feed their market.

"Tell them that we will cooperate," she said, "as long as our lives are spared."

Her smile grew wider. "And try to sound scared when you say it," she added. "Let them think we're feeling vulnerable."

She could imagine the reaction on the pirate ship as someone young, female, and apparently helpless begged for mercy. They'd probably find it funny, she knew, as well as a lure pulling them closer. If their crew hadn't been psychotic before they'd boarded their ship, they probably would be by now. Some of the men they'd tried to rescue, the ones who had been forced to work onboard the pirate ships, had been just as bad as their enslavers by the time they'd been found. Others had zoned out completely.

"They're ordering us to fall back from the convoy slowly," Lieutenant Ross reported. "And not to signal anyone else."

"Unsurprising," Kat commented. She looked at the helmsman. "Comply with their directive. And remember we're posing as a freighter."

"Aye, aye, Captain," Weiberg said. "Reducing speed . . . now."

"Establish a tight-beam link with the convoy master," Kat ordered. "Inform him of our situation and order him to keep his ships in formation. I don't want anyone to come looking for us."

"Aye, Captain," Ross said.

"And order him not to reply," Kat added quickly. "We don't want the pirates to hear it."

"They might pick up our signal," the XO warned softly. No one else could hear him. "This is hyperspace."

Kat nodded. Hyperspace did weird things to radio signals, no matter how carefully they were transmitted. It was quite possible that a tight beam signal would be scattered, allowing the enemy to pick up on it despite being on the other side of the transmitter. If that happened . . . the pirate ship would probably open fire, intent on punishing the freighter that had dared defy orders. Kat would have no choice but to kill the attackers as quickly as possible.

Seconds ticked away. It rapidly became clear that the pirates hadn't picked up the signal.

"Picking up another signal," Ross said. She sounded rather surprised. "They're ordering us to hold position and be ready to greet them. All weapons are to be stowed in lockers; any onboard security systems are to be disabled."

The XO snorted. "Who do they think we are?"

Kat had to smile. It was common for passenger liners and select shipping freighters to have onboard security systems, but rare for standard freighters to have anything beyond a safe and security locks on the computers. The pirates might have assumed the worst, though; it *was* a logical precaution. And the order to stow all weapons suggested they didn't intend to take additional risks.

Or perhaps it will give them an excuse to break their agreement, she thought, grimly. *But they don't really need the excuse.*

"They're entering approach vector now," Roach reported. "I don't think they're interested in maintaining plausible deniability any longer."

"Good," Kat said. Her lips curved into a tight smile. The game was about to come to an end. "Neither am I."

Pirate crews had never impressed her with their intelligence, but it was unlikely they would get much closer without taking a hard look at her hull. Roach's passive sensors were already filling in details, suggesting that the pirate ship was an old frigate, probably one dating all the way back to the Breakaway Wars. A number of such ships had gone missing after the wars had come to an end, although no one was quite sure how many. The UN had kept extensive records—every little thing had to be detailed, according to the bureaucrats who actually ran the government—but the records had been destroyed on Earth. Speculation over just how many ships remained in existence had been a common topic of conversation at Piker's Peak.

"I have hard locks on their drive section," Roach reported. He sounded pleased with himself. The locks had been established without needing to run an active sensor sweep. "I can pop a hammerhead missile into their ass, no problem."

"Excellent," Kat said. In normal space, she would have used energy weapons, but they were dangerously unpredictable in hyperspace. There was a reason most people preferred to avoid fighting battles outside real space. "Prepare to fire on my command."

She braced herself. One of the *other* reasons why fighting in hyperspace was so dangerous was that explosions tended to attract energy storms. They could score a damaging hit on their target, allowing them to board the hulk, yet an energy storm could blow up around them and destroy the crippled vessel before it could be claimed. Even a hammerhead missile, a warhead designed to inflict limited damage, ran the risk of drawing a storm to them. But there was no real choice. The only other option was blowing the pirate ship into dust.

There was a *ping* from Roach's console. "They swept us, Captain," he warned. Red lights flared on the console. "They know what we are."

"Fire," Kat snapped.

Lightning shivered as she launched her missile, aimed right at the enemy drive section. If Kat and her crew were lucky, the pirates would have no time to either return fire or take evasive action. But they hadn't been alert at all. They didn't even have their point defense on automatic, ready to blast unexpected threats out of space. The missile slammed into their rear section and detonated.

"Open a channel," Kat ordered. She waited for the nod from Ross before speaking. "Pirate ship, this is Captain Falcone of the Royal Tyre Navy. If you give up now, without further ado, your lives will be spared. You have one minute to surrender before I blow your ship into atoms."

There was a long pause, long enough that Kat wondered if the pirate ship had lost all power along with her drive section. A military starship shouldn't have had that problem—there would be batteries, at the very least—but it was quite possible the pirates hadn't kept up with their maintenance. Military discipline wasn't part of their lives. Besides, she knew, the ship was over a hundred years old. They might well have done a poor job of refitting her with the latest sensors and weapons systems.

She thought rapidly. If the pirates couldn't communicate, she would have to send the marines into the hulk, knowing the pirates could be waiting for a boarding party before blowing their own ship, taking the marines out as well as their crew. Or, if they'd lost life support completely, it was equally possible that most of the crew were trapped in sealed compartments—or dead.

But we could pull evidence from their hull, if we looked, she thought.

"Picking up a weak signal," Ross reported. "They're begging to surrender."

Kat keyed her console. "This is your one chance," she said. "Cooperate with the marines and your lives will be spared. Any resistance will result in the destruction of your vessel."

She switched channels. "Colonel, you have permission to launch," she told Davidson. The marines had been waiting in their shuttles, ready to launch as soon as the pirate ship was crippled. "Good luck."

The display updated rapidly as shuttles arced away from *Lightning*, heading towards the crippled ship. Kat tensed as the Marines entered weapons range, knowing that a single energy weapon could pick off a shuttle before any of the troops even knew they were under attack. Davidson was in command, of course. Even if it had been permissible for him to remain behind, he wouldn't have done so. The thought hurt more than she'd expected. It was one of the things she'd loved about him.

"Contact the convoy master," she ordered, trying to distract herself. "The convoy is to hold position until we have searched the pirate ship, then we will resume our journey to Cadiz."

"Aye, Captain," Ross said.

Kat's console bleeped. "This is Davidson," a voice said. His tone was calm and steady, betraying no excitement or concern. "We have boarded the pirate ship. No resistance. I say again, no resistance."

"Very good," Kat said. She looked at the XO. "We need to put an investigative team on the vessel."

"I'll see to it," the XO said. "With your permission, I'll take an engineering and tactical crew with me. They'll be able to pull information from what remains of the enemy's computers."

"And determine if she can be safely towed to Cadiz," Kat agreed. Taking the ship as a prize wouldn't win the crew much in the way of money, but it would be *something*. Besides, a full team of analysts from Cadiz might discover something her crew didn't have the expertise to find. "If not, place scuttling charges and abandon the hulk. I doubt she can move under her own power now."

"Aye, Captain," the XO said.

Kat nodded, then smiled round the bridge. "Our first real combat test," she said, "and you all did very well."

She paused. "Stand down from battle stations," she added. "But continue to monitor local space. Our friend out there may have friends of her own."

CHAPTER NINE

"You'll want to keep your face mask on," the marine rifleman said as William climbed through the airlock and into the pirate ship. The rifleman's name tag read HOBBES. "The ship stinks like a brick shithouse on a very hot day."

"Thank you for that mental image," William said dryly. Marines tended to be blunt and crude, something he normally appreciated. But not today. "Where are the prisoners?"

"They're being held in the mess," Hobbes said. "If you'll come with me, sir . . ."

William followed him through the dark corridor, wondering just how the pirates had managed to keep their ship operational for so long. This particular section was some considerable distance from the drive compartment, yet half of the lighting elements seemed to have been blown out while the onboard datanet had been completely lost. Clearly, the UN's fetish for multiple redundancy—something shared with engineers the galaxy over—hadn't endured past the ship falling into pirate hands.

The corridors looked filthy, coated with dust and grime, as if the pirates had never bothered to clean their living space. He glanced into one cabin—the door had been jarred open—and saw a messy space with datachips and bedding scattered everywhere. One bulkhead had chains hanging down towards the ground, ending in manacles. He shuddered, realizing that someone had been kept prisoner in the room. Whoever it was, he hoped they'd been rescued rather than killed. It hadn't been *that* long since his homeworld had been raided almost every year by pirates.

They walked into the mess. William stopped dead. A handful of armored marines were guarding thirty prisoners, all men. The prisoners were lying on the deck, their hands cuffed behind their backs, their clothes largely torn from them. Some were whimpering to themselves, their world suddenly turned upside down. William looked down at them for a long, chilling moment, then looked at Hobbes. None of the prisoners looked very impressive.

"Which one of these pieces of shit is in command?"

"The captain is dead," Davidson said, entering from the other hatch. His face was set in a permanent frown. "So are most of the senior officers."

"Dead?" William repeated. "How?"

"Suicide implants," Davidson said. He motioned for William to follow him. "That's odd, for pirates."

William mulled it over as they walked up the corridor and onto the bridge. Pirates rarely used personalized suicide implants. They were normally only used by secret agents and military personnel. All they did was kill their user if the command was sent or if the user was on the verge of spilling specific secrets to interrogators. William knew better than to trust the implants completely. They were perfectly capable of mistaking an accident that left someone badly hurt for torture, and killing their bearer.

The bridge was a shambles. Several consoles had exploded—he'd never seen that happen outside a bad entertainment flick—and a handful of bodies lay on the deck. Two of them had clearly been sitting at the consoles, judging from the wounds, but the remaining five all looked surprisingly peaceful. But it was clear they were dead. The corpsman kneeling beside one of the bodies looked up, then saluted.

"Commander," he said gravely. "Their brains were turned to ash, along with their implants."

"Understood," William said. There was no point in looking for alternate causes of death. "I assume the implants are beyond recovery?"

"Almost certainly," the corpsman said. "I'll have the analysts plough through the dust, but I'd be astonished if they found anything beyond traces of their presence. The damage was total."

William looked down at the pirate commander. He was a tall man, so extensively muscled that William would have bet good money it was the result of cosmetic treatment, wearing an outfit that showed off his frame to good advantage. His belt, lying beside him, had carried two pistols, a monofilament knife, and a neural whip, the latter probably used on his crewmen when they misbehaved. Pirate commanders had nothing but force to keep their men in line.

And most of them are probably challenged by their subordinates, he thought. Assassination was a common way of moving up the ladder on a pirate ship. There was certainly no such thing as promotion for merit. *He would have had to keep his men under tight control, but not too tight.*

William looked round the bridge. "Why did their implants trigger? Why not simply blow the ship itself?"

"Good question," Davidson agreed. "We *did* smash their datanet to hell and gone, so they might have tried to trigger the self-destruct and failed. Or there wasn't a self-destruct in the first place. I can't imagine pirates being very willing to sail under one."

William nodded, turning back to the marine. "How many did we take alive?"

"Thirty-one confirmed pirates, we believe," Davidson said as they left the bridge and headed down another corridor. Judging by the stains on the bulkheads, the pirates had been in the habit of urinating on the deck. "Fifteen slaves, all but two female, which we are holding in this compartment. They just can't be trusted."

"I know," William said, as they stepped into the compartment. "Stockholm syndrome."

Inside, a number of women lay on the deck, their hands bound behind their backs. It wasn't fair or right to treat them as prisoners—they were victims of the pirates, rather than willing assistants—but he knew there was no choice. After so long as nothing more than slaves, the prisoners might have developed a kind of loyalty to their captors, just to keep their minds from cracking completely.

The two male captives had been pushed against the far wall, away from the women; the marines eyed them warily. It was quite possible, despite their obvious mistreatment, that they were pirates posing as captives in the hopes of escape.

Or that they were forced to partake in forbidden pleasures, William knew. It was the standard treatment pirates gave to prisoners who were too valuable to the ship to hold for ransom, or simply put out an airlock. *Once they got their hands dirty, they knew they could never go home again.*

"Have them all moved to *Lightning*," he ordered bluntly. They'd probably have to be put in stasis, after the doctors took a look at them. Once the ship reached Cadiz, they could be transferred to a specialized medical facility. "Do we have anyone who might know anything among the prisoners?"

"Not as far as we know," Davidson stated. "They all claim to be ordinary crewmen."

"Have them interrogated, then transferred to stasis cells," William said. "If they happen to know anything useful, we can follow up on it at Cadiz."

The next hour went slowly as the investigation team carefully searched the pirate ship, finding very little apart from hundreds of pornographic datachips and plenty of evidence that the ship had been involved in dozens of attacks. Most of the main computer had been destroyed—*that* part of the self-destruct system had worked perfectly—and what remained was scrambled beyond immediate use. William watched as the damaged cores were removed from their compartment, knowing that the techs on Cadiz would have their work cut out for them. It was highly unlikely they'd be able to produce anything more than gibberish or standard operating files.

"None of the crew kept a journal," Hobbes told William as he returned to the airlock. The marine brandished a little black book. "Or, at least, none we could use. This book details sexual conquests, rather than anything else."

William wasn't surprised. The military banned its personnel from keeping personal logs, knowing that enemy intelligence agents would try to access them in hopes of finding actionable intelligence. It was clear the pirates probably felt the same way too. If one of their crew had kept a journal, it might wind up being used against them. A note of a pirate base's location alone would be disastrous.

"Add it to the evidence locker," he said. He had no wish to read a sexual journal belonging to a pirate. "Can this ship be taken under tow?"

"The chief engineer believes it can be towed by one of the freighters," Hobbes said. "But its hull is badly damaged. There won't be much prize money."

"There will be a baseline rate, if nothing else," William pointed out. Taking a pirate ship out of commission alone was worthwhile. If any actionable intelligence was pulled out of the hulk, even on Cadiz, the crew would be in line for another bonus. "Besides, we can always melt the hull down for scrap."

He smiled as the marines pulled their prisoners to their feet, none too gently, and pushed them towards the airlock. Some of the pirates looked panicky as they were shoved through the hatch, as if they expected to discover the airlock opened into empty space, while others just looked resigned. They'd had enough time, he decided, to come to terms with the fact that their reign of terror was over.

"Doctor," he said, as Doctor Katy Braham entered the compartment. "What do you have to report?"

Doctor Braham—she had always insisted on being called Katy—looked grim. She'd been in the navy almost as long as William himself and she'd seen more than her fair share of horror, but she had always seemed optimistic. Not this time, William suspected. Pirate ships were always houses of true horror.

"All but one of the women will require extensive rejuvenation treatments as well as counseling," she said bluntly. She never bothered to sugarcoat bad news. "The good news is that the sheer scale of their wounds implies they were definitely captives; the bad news is that they will probably have to be permanently supervised by female personnel until we reach Cadiz. Their . . . conduct will leave much to be desired."

"They attempted to come on to the marines," Hobbes put in.

"*Thank you,* young man," Doctor Braham snapped. She glared at Hobbes, then switched her attention back to William. "They've had servitude beaten into them, Commander. It's the only way they know to guarantee their safety. I don't think they will ever return to what they were before they were captured."

William winced. "Do we know who they were?"

"We're running their DNA through the records now," the doctor said. "But I would be surprised if we found a match. Their genetic patterns don't suggest any high-tech world."

They could have come from Hebrides, William thought. The pirates hadn't wanted much from his homeworld, apart from food, drink, and women. And the planetary government had no choice but to send them whatever they wanted. Some of the girls had volunteered. Others . . . had been drafted. *Can we take them home?*

Doctor Braham cleared her throat loudly. "The two male captives have been beaten, quite badly," she continued. "They were worked over by professionals. The damage was not extensive or permanent, but it would have been very painful. I think we can safely assume they're not willing pirates."

"Keep an eye on them anyway," William ordered. Stockholm syndrome could strike any kind of captive, no matter how badly they were treated. And if the pirates had forced their captives to get their hands dirty . . . he shook his head. "And see if they memorized anything they can tell us."

"I'll have my staff supervise the transfer to *Lightning*," the doctor said, as though she expected objections. "I think we will probably need to put most of the former prisoners in stasis. There're too many of them for my staff to handle."

"See to it," William said. He sighed. Yet another problem. "But they will need to answer questions eventually."

He took one final walk through the vessel, noting the sheer lack of maintenance that had contributed to her quick defeat, then returned to the shuttles as the crew prepared to leave the pirate ship for the last time. The female prisoners, according to Davidson, had experienced real problems with boarding the shuttles until two of the female marines had removed their own armor. Even so, the prisoners had shied away from them. The doctors had eventually resorted to sedating all of the pirates' former captives, with the intention of leaving them out of it until the ship reached Cadiz.

"The interrogations will begin in thirty minutes," Davidson informed him. Interrogating the former pirates was a marine chore. "Do you wish to witness?"

The honest answer was no, but William knew he should be there. "I'll catch a cup of coffee and a shower, then join you," he said instead. He was ruefully aware he stunk after spending several hours on the pirate ship. "Hold the interrogation until I arrive."

He walked back to his cabin, showered, took a long drink of coffee, and then returned to Marine Country. The prisoners had been separated, ensuring they couldn't come up with a shared story to tell the marines, although William would have been surprised if they'd managed to cooperate in any case. Pirates weren't used to cooperating with one another, no matter the prize. He forced himself to look impassive as he walked into the interrogation chamber and peered through the one-way glass.

The pirate *definitely* didn't look impressive, he decided, as the marines cuffed him to the chair and then attached a pair of monitors to his forehead. He was a young man, barely out of his teens; William suspected, despite himself, that he knew the boy's story. Like so many others, he would have viewed a career in space as more glamorous than a life behind the rear end of a mule on the ground. And he would have rapidly found himself so desperate for work that he would have taken the first job that came along. It was sheer bad luck it had been on a pirate ship.

Young and impressionable, William thought. *And desperate.*

It was never a good combination.

"The corpsman did a quick medical check," Davidson said as he entered the compartment. "There are no medical issues, nor any interfering implants. It's unlikely he knows anything of substance."

"We'll see," William said. It was impossible to say in advance what would serve as a clue to lead the navy to the pirate base. The pirate might have seen something that would fit in with another piece of information from a second pirate. "I . . ."

He broke off as Hobbes began the interrogation.

"These devices," Hobbes said, "allow us to monitor your brainwaves as you respond to our questions. Should you try to lie to us we will know about it. If you try to lie to us repeatedly, we will put you in a lab and access your memories directly. This process tends to result in the victim becoming brain-dead. Do you understand me?"

The prisoner nodded, rapidly.

"Good," Hobbes said. He stepped backwards and smiled. "Where were you born?"

"Roslyn," the pirate said.

William watched with growing impatience as Hobbes slowly built up a baseline on the pirate's brainwaves. It was the closest humanity had come to a perfect lie detector, he knew, but it wasn't entirely perfect, even without the problem of separating between *subjective* truth and *objective* truth. And it could be fooled by a set of implants, if the pirate had been deemed important enough to have them. Instead, it was starting to look as though he knew nothing beyond his duties. The pirates certainly didn't bother to tell him where they were going or where they were based.

The odd piece of data, however, concerned two men who had joined the pirate crew as senior officers, then died with the other officers. Surprisingly, they hadn't joined the pirates in their games, even when they'd had new victims for their pleasures. Instead, they'd just alternated between the bridge and their cabin while the captain fawned on them. The pirates had suspected the newcomers were actually paying their wages, such as they were. But their commander had always discouraged questioning.

"They didn't mind if we destroyed our targets," the pirate explained, frantically. He seemed almost desperate to help the interrogator now. It was the only way he could hope to keep his life. "We got paid anyway."

William and Davidson exchanged glances. Pirate economics were haphazard at the best of times, but there were some understandable principles. A destroyed ship, her cargo smashed to atoms, was worthless. The pirates wouldn't be able to take her cargo to one of the poorer worlds, a place where no one would ask questions, and sell their takings. They wouldn't even be able to have fun with the crew. And they would have to replenish the weapons they'd fired. The bastards would *lose* money on the raid.

"That's odd," Davidson said. He seemed to want to say something, but held his tongue. "We need to bring this to the captain's attention."

"Yes," William agreed. He'd noticed that Captain Falcone and Davidson spent a great deal of time together. It wasn't uncommon—the captain could hardly confide in anyone else—but she seemed to take it to excess. "And we will, once we've interrogated the remaining prisoners."

He sighed as he looked back at the prisoner, who was currently outlining some of the raids he'd seen. It was the same story, he knew; once seduced, the pirate had nowhere else to go. But William was damned if he would feel sorry for the idiot. He could have walked away, even gone back to his homeworld. Instead, he'd made the choice to stay with the pirates and join in their atrocities wholeheartedly.

"I hope the bastard chokes on Nightmare," William said bitterly. "Or that he gets killed on the surface."

"He might well discover he's a very small fish among sharks," Davidson agreed. His tone was expressionless. "The very worst of the Commonwealth can be found there."

William nodded. It wasn't death, he knew. Or at least it wasn't immediate death, meted out by his own hands. But it was close enough.

CHAPTER TEN

"They were happy to destroy the ships?"

"Yes, Captain," Davidson said. "They still got paid."

Kat frowned. She'd been sitting in her office, writing the first report on the encounter for the Admiralty, when the XO and Davidson had requested an audience. But their report was unbelievable. What sort of pirate actually took *losses* on his raids?

But one of the lessons she'd had to endure from her tutors bubbled up in her mind. "The government can subsidize a service from taxpayers' money, even though the service is operated at a loss," he'd said. "Sometimes this serves a practical purpose. The service is necessary . . ."

She looked at her XO. "Someone is subsidizing the pirate operations," she said. "The two strangers on the ships might well have been working for the Theocracy."

It made sense, she told herself. There was no logic to pirates destroying ships, but if they were actually being paid anyway, no matter the outcome, they'd be happy to smash as many freighters as they could find into atoms. The report would have to be rewritten.

"If that's the case," the XO said slowly, "why didn't they just launch a missile at us as soon as they had a lock on our location?"

"Greed," Davidson speculated. "They'd have had a chance to sell our hull and cargo as well as collect their paycheck from their backers."

"Or have their fun with the crew," Kat added tartly. The medical report had made for horrifying reading. "But this is a worrying development."

"Yes, Captain," Davidson said. "It's also problematic because we have no proof the Theocracy is behind it. There are other multisystem powers in the galaxy."

"None as threatening as the Theocracy," Kat countered, but she knew he was right. "What did the autopsy show?"

"Nothing we can use to identify them," Davidson admitted. "The dead men could have come from anywhere. There are no specific genetic traits linked to the Theocracy. The men did have basic enhancements, but they couldn't be narrowed down to a single world."

"They could have gotten them from anywhere," Kat said. It would have been more surprising to encounter baseline humans in space. Even newly contacted worlds made the effort to get medical enhancements for its population. "So we have no real proof?"

"And no way to hunt down the pirate base," the XO said. "It could be anywhere."

He sighed. "None of the surviving pirates know anything important," he added. "Their hands are caked in blood, their souls stained by their crimes, yet they know nothing we can use to track their bases down and destroy them. All we can do is drop them off on Cadiz for transfer to Nightmare."

"Put them in stasis," Kat ordered. It was two weeks to Cadiz and she was damned if she was feeding the prisoners. They could be dropped off at the planet, where they would be held until the next leg of their journey. "Is there any point in continuing to sweep the pirate ship?"

"I don't believe so," the XO said. "The ship's computers are smashed, her datanet is shattered, and her navigational systems completely wiped. Cadiz might be able to pull something from the wreckage, but we don't have a specialized forensic team."

"Then have her taken in tow by one of the freighters," Kat said. "Offer to double their pay if they do it without complaining."

The XO smiled. "Aye, aye, Captain."

"We should get a bonus out of this, if nothing else," Kat added. *She* didn't need the prize money, but her crew would be delighted. "Please inform the crew that we will get underway in"—she checked her wristcom—"thirty minutes. Hopefully, nothing will happen until we reach Cadiz."

It was a dismissal and William recognized it as such. He stood, saluted, and marched out of the hatch. Kat watched him go and then looked at Davidson. Her former lover was smiling, slightly.

"I think he's grown a little more accepting of you," he said bluntly. "You did well today, you know."

"I had a good crew," Kat said automatically. She smiled at him. "Thank you."

Davidson stood. "I'll get the prisoners into stasis," he said. He sighed. "One of them *did* show up on the records."

Kat lifted an eyebrow. There was enough storage capacity in a single computer core to list every man, woman, and child in the entire galaxy, but records were far from complete, even in the Commonwealth. She'd expected the pirate crew to come from the edge of settled space, where there were no records and plenty of worlds happy to take stolen goods, no questions asked. It was unlikely that any files from those worlds would be added to her ship's database.

"Ronan Yedica," Davidson said. "Child of a nagging mother and largely absentee father. Ran away from home four years ago; never found, until today. God alone knows how he ended up on a pirate ship."

"Let him write a letter home, if he wishes," Kat said. She understood the impulse to run away from home, but hers had been much more constructive. Surely this runaway could have applied to Piker's Peak . . . or one of the more basic training academies. There were plenty of openings for merchant spacers. "But we can't make an exception for him."

"No," Davidson agreed. "We can't."

He paused. "Have you told the XO about your father's concerns?"

Kat shook her head. It would have only heightened his sense that Kat had pulled strings to be assigned to *Lightning* as her commanding officer.

"Probably a good idea," Davidson said. "But I think he's a keen observer. You will need him at Cadiz, if what your father suspects is true."

"I know," Kat said, reluctantly.

Davidson gave her a smile that reminded her of their time together. "You may be the captain," he said, "but you're not alone. You certainly don't have to do everything yourself."

"The buck stops with me," Kat countered. The commandant of Piker's Peak had that burned into every desk in the building. It had taken years for the cadets to understand its true meaning. "I can't let him risk his own career for me."

"I think he's loyal," Davidson said. "And you probably upset his universe by handling the pirates so well."

He saluted, then turned and strode out of the cabin. Kat looked back at her terminal, then started to rewrite her report. Once it was completed, she wrote out a second message for her father. It was possible her report would be lost somewhere within the bureaucratic channels, but a more direct message wouldn't go missing. At least it would serve as evidence that *something* was badly wrong along the border.

She sighed, then stood. She wanted to be on the bridge when the convoy resumed course and then start carrying out additional drills. The next pirate ship they encountered might just launch a missile at them rather than try to take her ship intact. Or they might open fire on the prow of the convoy instead . . .

We need more escorts, she thought sourly. More light units would need to be detached from the battle squadrons for escort duties, weakening the fleets patrolling the border. *And that might be precisely what they want us to do.*

♦ ♦ ♦

"I'm afraid they all had to go into stasis," Doctor Braham said of the pirate's former prisoners when William entered Sickbay. "I just don't have the facilities to even begin healing them all."

William nodded, unsurprised. "You did manage to remove the cuffs first? Or take statements?"

"Yes to the first, no to the second," the doctor snapped. She eyed him unpleasantly. "I think you don't understand just how badly they were treated. They really need to spend several weeks in a regeneration chamber, not answer questions from you or any other men."

"I understand," William said quickly. Annoying the ship's doctor was never a good idea. "Do we know who they are?"

"I didn't find a match when I ran their DNA against the records," Katy said. She pointed to a chair on the far side of the compartment, motioning for him to sit down. "But two of them were probably from pastoral worlds. There aren't many within six months of here."

William sat, reluctantly. "You're sure?"

"They were baseline humans—and I mean *baseline*," Katy assured him. She dragged a chair over and sat down facing him. "Someone like you has genetic enhancements and improvements, even if they're not spliced into your bloodline. They, on the other hand, have no enhancements at all. My best guess is that their homeworld was a dumping ground for a religious sect the UN decided didn't deserve to stay on Earth."

She folded her hands on her lap. Only someone who knew her well would have picked up that sign of tension.

"The poor girls were on the verge of death," she added. "I've never seen a group quite so riddled with disease. I'm surprised they even managed to survive the shock of being rescued."

"Some didn't," William said. Other bodies had been found when the marines searched the pirate ship. "What sort of idiot doesn't go for the boosted immune systems, at the very least?"

Katy frowned. "Genetic engineering hasn't always been as precise as starship engineering," she said, after a long moment. "The early engineers often pushed ahead in hopes of developing a provable science before they were shut down by their governments. Some of their experiments produced . . . horrors. Others actually laid genetic time bombs in their test subjects that wouldn't explode until their grandchildren were born."

She shrugged. "Back then, there were strong reasons to oppose widespread genetic engineering," she added. "There were quite a few sects dedicated to maintaining the purity of humanity's bloodline. One of them could have founded the women's homeworld."

William shook his head. Hebrides had never asked to be a low-tech world, but the Breakdown had ensured the settlers were thrown back on their own resources long before they were ready. They'd managed to hold on to some technology, yet it hadn't been enough to protect them against pirates and raiders. Or, for that matter, to avoid having most of the population working in the fields just to feed the colony. Why would anyone *want* to trap themselves on such a world?

But humans were strange creatures. Perhaps some of them were strange enough to want to spend the rest of their lives on a farm.

"Thank you, Doctor," he said. The former slaves wouldn't be needed to testify against their captors, at least. "Please let me know when they are ready for transfer to Cadiz."

"I'd be happier if they were sent to another world," Katy said. "Cadiz is hardly the most peaceable of locations."

"That's where we're going," William said.

Katy nodded. "You're overdue for your physical, by the way," she added. "I need you back in here within a week."

"I think you just enjoy poking and prodding at me," William teased. "I'm sure regulations give me at least another two months before it becomes mandatory."

"Only if you count from the day we left spacedock for the final time," Katy informed him, reaching for a glove. She snapped it, meaningfully. "If I have to go hunting for you, Commander, it will be a *very* uncomfortable medical inspection."

William snorted. "I'll come back in two days," he said. By then, any problems with the crew after the battle should be apparent. He didn't expect any, but the thought of prize money had been known to make crewmen do stupid things. "You'll have the table ready?"

"Of course," Katy said. She paused. "Was there anything else you wanted to talk about?"

"I . . ."

William hesitated. Just as the captain could talk to the senior marine, the XO could talk to the ship's doctor. They shared responsibility for the health and well-being of the crew and were expected to meet at least once a week, if only to compare notes. But he wasn't sure he wanted to talk about his personal doubts with her.

"No, thank you," he said, finally. He stood. "I'll see you in two days."

He strode out of Sickbay and started to walk to the bridge, then changed his mind and walked to the observation blister instead. The hatch opened at his approach, revealing the eerie lights of hyperspace. At least it wasn't occupied, he noted as he stepped inside, the hatch hissing closed behind him. Crewmen and women had been known to use the observation blister for a little bit of privacy from time to time.

It seemed as if there was nothing between him and the hyperspace storms alarmingly close to the starship's hull. Colors no human had been able to name flickered and flared in the darkness, clouds of glowing mist that looked almost *real*, if one stared at them for too long. He stepped up to the transparent blister and sighed, remembering just why he preferred living in space to a planetary surface. It was a dangerous life, as the battle they'd fought proved, but it was boundless. One day, perhaps he would buy a ship of his own and head out beyond the rim of explored space. Who knew what might be lurking out there?

He sat down on the bench, mentally reviewing the battle. The captain had done well . . . hell, she'd done *very* well. A pirate ship was rarely a formidable opponent for a full-sized warship, but it could easily have turned nasty. He'd known commanders who would have blown their target away at maximum range or risked allowing the pirate ship closer . . . Captain Falcone had done neither. She'd handled the battle just right.

And what does that say, he asked himself, *about her competence?*

The thought was galling, but it had to be faced. He'd assumed the captain had been promoted through her father pulling strings, rather than merit. No, he knew there had been a great deal of string pulling involved. She simply didn't have the experience to be assigned to command a heavy cruiser, at least not without succeeding her commander after his death. And her conduct since assuming command proved her limited experience. Even being an XO on a battle cruiser wasn't enough to simply jump straight into a command chair.

She'd made mistakes. They had all been minor, but she'd made them. And he'd worried about what she'd do when faced with a real challenge.

But she'd come through it admirably. She'd crippled the pirate ship, captured a number of pirates, and collected physical evidence that suggested someone was bankrolling the operation rather than taking a commission on their loot. There were other, more experienced commanders who might not have handled it so well.

And *that* meant that he'd underestimated her.

It wasn't something he could talk to anyone about, not even to the ship's doctor. Naval officers had no right to privacy. The ship's doctor had a duty to break her oath of confidentiality if she believed one of the crewmen was a serious danger to himself or his fellows. And he wasn't sure what Doctor Braham would do if he confessed his doubts to her. Grumbling about the captain, no matter how she'd been given the job, would be a severe breach of military etiquette.

Not that, in the end, it had mattered.

He'd been wrong about her. She was inexperienced, she needed to learn fast, but she wasn't grossly incompetent. Nor had she hidden behind her rank or her father's title. She had acted as befitted a good commanding officer and he had to admit that, even though it was only in the privacy of his own head. And he should take it into account. The contingency plans he'd been devising to take command if necessary, an act that could be construed as mutiny if the Admiralty happened to want a scapegoat, shouldn't be taken any further. He owed her the same trust and confidence he owed every other commanding officer, at least until the man had proved himself beyond redemption.

She wouldn't be the first officer to need to learn fast upon assuming command, he thought. He'd started his career as a crewman, after all, watching the senior chiefs gently manipulate young officers into becoming paragons of virtue. The Army did it all the time. It was only the Marines who insisted on having everyone spend a few years as an infantryman first before assigning them to other roles. *And I need to stop being so suspicious of her.*

He turned his head as the hatch opened behind him, revealing a young woman wearing a midshipwoman's uniform. Midshipwoman Cecelia Parkinson, he reminded himself. She was young enough to be his granddaughter, with short red hair and a freckled face. He couldn't help noting that she looked rather pale and worn, unsurprisingly. But was it the stress of going into combat or something worse?

"I'm sorry, sir," she said, flushing. She stumbled backwards so rapidly he thought she was about to trip over her own uniform. "I thought the compartment was free."

"I forgot to lock it," William said. Had *he* ever been that young? The captain was barely ten years older than Cecelia, with far more poise and self-control. "It isn't a court-martial offense to walk through an unlocked hatch."

The poor girl's face grew even redder and she muttered something incoherent.

"Don't worry," William said, rising to his feet. "I was just leaving."

She opened her mouth to object, but he stepped past her and through the hatch before she could say a word. It was probably her first real chance to take a break and look out at hyperspace and he wasn't about to deprive her of it. No true officer would act in such a fashion. And besides, if he remembered what he'd seen in the files correctly, she probably needed some time to think.

Making a mental note to have a word with the senior chief, he strode down the corridor and back to the bridge.

CHAPTER ELEVEN

"Captain," the XO said. "We are ten minutes away from Cadiz."

Kat nodded, then sat. The two weeks since the pirate attack had passed almost without incident, apart from a brief sensor contact that might have been another pirate vessel—or just another random glitch thrown up by hyperspace. All they could say for certain was that the contact hadn't attempted to close the range and attack.

"The convoy master will be pleased," she said. He hadn't been too happy when he'd discovered his starship had been tapped to tow the pirate hulk. "Take us back into real space as soon as we reach optimal coordinates."

She studied the display as *Lightning* and her convoy plunged towards Cadiz. Unusually, there were several semi-permanent energy storms near the planet, limiting the number of hyper-routes starships could use to reach the planet. There were guardships within hyperspace, monitoring constantly for incoming fleets, although she knew there would be far too many false alarms. She'd half expected the approaches to be mined when she'd read the files, but 7th Fleet's CO had apparently decided there was too great a risk of accidentally destroying a civilian ship. If there hadn't been a war looming, Kat would have thought he was right.

"We are entering optimal coordinates now," Weiberg reported, breaking into her thoughts. "Vortex generator online; ready to return to real space."

"Take us out," Kat ordered. It would be a relief to see stars again, even if it marked the start of her mission. "Now."

Space twisted in front of them, then parted, as though an angry god had torn a hole in the very fabric of reality. Kat gazed at stars shining their light into hyperspace before the first freighters slid through the tear and back into real space. Her ship brought up the rear, closing the tear behind them. An odd feeling ran through the ship, a sensation no one had ever been able to fully describe; then it faded away.

They were back where they belonged.

"We have entered the Cadiz System," Weiberg said, formally.

Kat looked at her XO. "Please make a note in the log," she said. They'd moved from one command region to another. "And then transmit our IFF code to Cadiz."

"Aye, Captain," the XO said. Lieutenant Ross echoed him a moment later.

Kat looked at the display as the passive sensors started to suck in and process data from all over the Cadiz System. It didn't take an expert eye to realize that the system looked *odd*, as if it hadn't quite followed normal development patterns. There were installations orbiting the gas giants and mining stations in the asteroids, but there were relatively few stations near Cadiz itself. The brief guide to the system she'd read during the flight had stated that several corporations had actually invested in terraforming packages for Cadiz V, a Mars-type world on the very edge of the habitable zone. It was a recipe for later trouble.

She sighed. Normally, a Commonwealth world would have a unified government able to handle off-planet development—and a solid claim on their star system. Cadiz, on the other hand, had no unified government;

the only power that patrolled the outer edges of their star system was the Royal Navy. Corporate investment in the system had been made without the permission of any local government, thus ensuring that Cadiz's inhabitants received no true benefits from their resources. It was just another problem fuelling the growing insurgency on the planet's surface.

But we didn't have a choice, she told herself.

And her thoughts mocked her. *The strong have always told themselves they have no choice but to steal from the rich.*

She rubbed her eyes. Cadiz sat directly between the Commonwealth and the Theocracy, a world that either side could use as a jumping-off point for an attack into the other's space. It could not be allowed to remain apart from the Commonwealth, some had argued, because the Theocracy had shown no hesitation in invading worlds incapable of defending themselves. And yet the locals hadn't *wanted* to join the Commonwealth. They might not have been as successful as Tyre, but they had made a solid investment and intended to work towards the future on their own. But the Commonwealth, reluctantly, hadn't respected their wishes.

They called it an annexation, Kat knew, and claimed it was for their own good. But the locals weren't happy. And, because it was impossible to form a stable government, Cadiz was losing control over its own resources. Indeed, if Cadiz V became a settled world in its own right, it would just sow the seeds for more tension. Cadiz might become nothing more than an economic backwater while Cadiz V controlled the system.

The display bleeped as it picked up the starships orbiting Cadiz. Kat sucked in her breath as she saw the icons for three superdreadnought squadrons, followed by numerous smaller icons representing cruisers, destroyers, and gunboats. It looked, at first, like an unstoppable force, a gathering of the most powerful warships in the galaxy. And yet, as more and more detail appeared on the display, it became evident that something was wrong—7th Fleet should be moving around rather than holding the same position.

She cringed inwardly as she thought through the implications. There was almost no control over civilian starships moving in and out of the system. *Any* of them could be a spy ship, reporting to the Theocracy; they'd know *precisely* where to find their targets. Standard procedure was to have the fleet in constant motion, or at least change position every few days, but Admiral Morrison seemed to believe it wasn't necessary.

"Captain," Lieutenant Ross said, "we have picked up a formal response to our IFF codes."

Kat glanced at her display. It had been nearly twenty minutes since they'd sent the codes. It shouldn't have taken more than ten minutes to receive a reply.

"Sloppy," her XO muttered. His face was grim. "They should have detected our arrival and challenged us at once."

"True," Kat muttered back. They'd come out of hyperspace five light minutes from Cadiz, but the twist in space-time should have been detectable from right across the system, instantly. Cadiz should have sent a challenge the moment they'd arrived, the signal crossing the IFF codes *Lightning* had sent back. "They definitely should have challenged us."

She cleared her throat. "Did they send us specific orders?"

"No, Captain," Ross said. "They just acknowledged our arrival."

Kat wondered, for a brief moment, if the system had already fallen. The thought sent a chill down her spine. Were they flying right into an ambush? But it seemed unlikely. The superdreadnoughts orbiting Cadiz were Royal Navy designs, while there was no sign that a battle had been fought in the system. No matter the readiness level of 7th Fleet, she found it impossible to believe the system had fallen without a battle. *Someone* would have tried to fight.

"Keep us on course," she ordered. "And request orbital slots for the convoy."

"Aye, Captain," Ross said.

More disturbing signs started to appear as *Lightning* flew towards the planet. The fleet in orbit should have had at least some of its starships at battle readiness at all times. Instead, their drives and sensors were stepped down to the point it would take nearly an hour to bring them back up to full power. Every ship was also supposed to keep its shield generators on standby, but she had a feeling they hadn't even bothered to take *that* basic precaution. She shook her head in growing disbelief. Superdreadnoughts were tough, built to take a staggering amount of punishment, but an antimatter warhead impacting against an unprotected hull would be disastrous. She realized 7th Fleet was staggeringly vulnerable.

"They should be running gunboat patrols too," the XO said, through their implants. It was rude to use implants to talk in front of other people, but it helped keep their conversation private. "Someone could be sneaking up on the ships under cloak right now and they wouldn't even have a clue they were there."

Kat couldn't disagree. Cloaking systems were only perfect if the starship under cloak stayed very still, pretending to be a hole in space. A starship under power emitted faint radiations that weren't completely concealed by the cloak, though the vessel would still be hard to track. Gunboat patrols should have made it impossible for someone to sneak up on the fleet, yet the only gunboats she could see on the display were performing routine maneuvers. They certainly weren't patrolling space as aggressively as she would have liked.

She turned her attention to Cadiz itself. There was a smaller orbital presence than she would have expected from a world at its development level, but there were dozens of freighters in orbit, along with several commercial stations. And, she realized slowly, 7th Fleet didn't seem to be doing anything to inspect the freighters coming in and out of Cadiz. They could be moving heavy weapons down to the surface, yet no one was even searching the ships before they entered orbit! And, by Commonwealth law, any freighter that was allowed to enter orbit was immune from further searches without clear proof of wrongdoing.

There's no single authority here, she thought grimly. *And because of that, it's hard to monitor everything that happens within the star system.*

The only remotely encouraging sign was the level of security round the orbital StarCom, although she would have preferred considerably more. A handful of automated weapons platforms guarded the structure, while a bubble of clear space was enforced by gunboats and Marine shuttles. But then losing the StarCom would be disastrous, even if the system didn't come under immediate attack. How would the corporate representatives on Cadiz communicate with their superiors without it?

She smiled humorlessly. *Perhaps I should arrange for something to happen to it*, she thought. *Losing the StarCom would unite all the corporations against Admiral Morrison.*

It was nearly thirty minutes before another signal arrived from Cadiz. "Captain, we have been assigned orbital slots," Ross reported. "There's also a private message for you."

"Pass it over," Kat ordered. Who would send her a private message? But she knew the answer before the message popped up in her in-box. Admiral Morrison, according to her father, was a contemptible social climber. Making the acquaintance of Duke Falcone's daughter could only benefit him in the long run. "And inform System Command that we will take up our orbital slots as quickly as possible."

She frowned as she saw the slots appear on the display. The freighters would be entering low orbit, while *Lightning* herself would be permitted to remain in high orbit, which would allow them some maneuvering room if the shit hit the fan. It didn't look very safe at all, but there was no point in picking a fight with Admiral Morrison—or the system's controllers, such as they were—so quickly. Instead, she rose to her feet and nodded to the XO.

"Mr. XO, you have the bridge," she said. "Inform me when we enter orbit."

"Aye, Captain," the XO said.

Kat saw her forebodings reflected in his eyes as she walked past him and into her Ready Room. Inside, she waited until the hatch had hissed closed behind her, then sat down at her desk, and accessed the private message. It was keyed to her specific command implants, which was oddly amusing. Admiral Morrison might not have been interested in her if she'd still been a commander and XO of a starship, responsible to her captain. It would have suggested she wasn't interested in pulling strings on her own behalf.

The thought made her feel coldly furious at her father. She hadn't even *looked* at the message, but she was sure Admiral Morrison wanted to make use of her. She'd run into other senior officers with the same ambition, yet this was different. *This* commanding officer, thanks to her father, had evidence that she *was* interested in pulling strings on her own behalf . . .

Gritting her teeth, she pressed her palm against the terminal, then frowned as the holographic image appeared in front of her. Thankfully, the message had been recorded and sent before they were close enough to Cadiz for a real-time conference. Admiral Morrison was strikingly handsome, with muscles on his muscles, his uniform tailored to show his looks and build off to best advantage. But his appearance was too handsome, too striking, to be real. It suggested deep insecurities that even a minor visit to a cosmetic bodyshop had been unable to cure. Even the genetic engineering that had shaped Kat's appearance had given her something more *natural.*

But it's easy to see why he impresses some civilians, she thought as she keyed the switch to start the playback. *He looks the very model of a modern space admiral.*

"Captain Falcone," Admiral Lord Buckland Morrison said. His voice was perfect too, almost as practiced as one of the political leaders speaking in the houses of Parliament. But there was something about it that suggested it was far from natural. "Please allow me to welcome you to Cadiz."

Kat nodded, impatiently. It wasn't common for starship commanders to be sent messages of welcome by the station commander. They were meant to be good little subordinates and present themselves to the admiral's office as soon as they entered orbit. Sending Kat a message, she knew, was not a good sign.

"I look forward to meeting you in person," the admiral continued. "You are welcome to visit my office once your ship has entered orbit. I would also like to invite you to a party at my estate the following week. You would be more than welcome."

"A party," Kat repeated, incredulously. Who the hell did the admiral think she was? Candy Falcone? "He wants me to go to a *party*?"

"Your crew are, of course, welcome to begin their shore leave roster while the convoy prepares itself for its next destination," the admiral concluded. He smiled at her. It would have been attractive if she hadn't been so sure it was fake. "And I look forward to meeting you in person."

Insecure, Kat thought as the message came to an end. She couldn't help being reminded of her first boyfriend, although they'd both been teenagers at the time. *He told me the same things twice, as if he were afraid I'd miss what he was saying or go somewhere else. And so did the admiral.*

Her father would have wanted her to get to know the admiral, she knew, although it was because *he* wanted evidence he could use to stick a knife in Morrison's back. Kat herself . . . would have preferred to spend as little time with the admiral as possible. But a direct invitation from her superior officer would be hard to avoid, even with her family connections. Someone without them would have had to humor the admiral, at least as long as they valued their career.

She winced. Suddenly, the condition of the orbiting superdreadnoughts made a great deal of sense.

You're jumping to conclusions, she thought, coldly. *You don't know if the superdreadnought commanders have been spending too much time on the planet's surface.*

But it did seem alarmingly plausible.

"Record," she ordered, after she was sure she could trust her voice to remain even. "Admiral Morrison, I will land on the planet's surface once my ship has entered orbit. I look forward to meeting you in person.

However, I have duties to my ship and I may not be able to attend your party. Thank you for your time."

It was borderline rude, she knew; she'd known officers and aristocrats who would have exploded under much less provocation. But she had a feeling Admiral Morrison would let it slide. She sent the message with a tap of the console, then called the XO into her Ready Room. When he arrived, she replayed the message for him, smiling to herself at his reaction.

"I will not be attending his . . . *party*," she said, making the word a curse. "But I can't avoid visiting him in person."

The XO didn't disagree. "It's protocol," he said. He hesitated, noticeably. "You should take a Marine detachment with you."

Kat made a face. The official press releases claimed that violence on the surface was declining, but the instructions for traveling from the spaceport to Gibraltar—the planet's capital city—suggested otherwise. She would be traveling in an armored convoy, guarded by several platoons of soldiers. It didn't suggest the planet was even remotely safe.

"That would probably violate some unwritten rule," she said. She took a long breath. "Do we have a list of frontrunners for shore leave?"

"Yes, Captain," the XO said. He pulled his datapad off his belt, then held it out to her. "I've put myself on the list, of course."

They shared a smile. It was an old joke. An XO who couldn't manipulate the system to his own advantage was in the wrong job.

"Once I return to the ship, I'd like you to go with the first party," Kat said. "I need your impressions of the planet's surface too."

She paused. "Besides, you need some leave," she added. "I know you haven't had any for the last nine months."

"I've had worse," the XO said. He hesitated. "Captain, I don't believe we should risk allowing more than fifty crewmen down to the surface at any one time. If the system comes under attack . . ."

He allowed his voice to trail off, but it didn't matter. Kat had already thought of it for herself.

"See to it," she ordered. There was one major spaceport on the planet and a handful of minor ones. Getting her crew back to the ship if the system came under attack would be a nightmare. "And make sure we have enough manpower on hand to fight if necessary."

The XO saluted, then withdrew, leaving Kat alone with her thoughts.

CHAPTER TWELVE

"They're diverting us to a different approach route," Midshipman Thomas Morse said. "I'm not sure why."

Kat nodded as the shuttle fell through Cadiz's atmosphere, heading towards the giant spaceport thirty kilometers from Gibraltar. The locals might not have access to many heavy weapons, but the reports suggested that they *had* obtained some antiaircraft missiles they had fired at a handful of vehicles, including shuttles. Shooting down a helicopter would be annoying, but hardly fatal; shooting down a shuttle carrying a starship commander would be a political nightmare. Even Admiral Morrison's backers would find it impossible to cover up the disaster.

She leaned forward as the spaceport came into view, a giant sprawling complex stretching out for miles. That alone was alarming, she knew; the average spaceport was nowhere near so large, even when handling military deployments. The briefing pack had noted that most of the shore leave facilities were within the wire, allowing starship crewmen to stretch their legs and relax without ever actually seeing the planet itself. Dozens of large hangars and military barracks dotted the landscape, while countless helicopters, attack craft, and shuttles sat on the ground, ready to launch at a moment's notice. It looked very far from peaceful.

The shuttle came to a halt over the spaceport, then dropped down to the landing pad. Kat had a brief impression of hundreds of soldiers jogging over the base, all carrying weapons slung over their shoulders, then the shuttle hit the ground. The shock surprised her, although she knew it shouldn't have. A hovering shuttle was terrifyingly vulnerable to more weapons than the expensive antiaircraft missiles that might have been smuggled into the district.

"The shuttle will be remaining here," Morse said, consulting the live feed from the spaceport's control tower. "Do you wish me to remain with it?"

Kat considered it briefly. She rather doubted she would be back anytime soon, even if the meeting with Admiral Morrison lasted less than an hour. The journey to and from the capital city alone would take quite some time. On the other hand, Morse was a young and inexperienced officer. Allowing him to wander the spaceport on his own might turn into a disaster. But it was his first time on the planet's surface . . .

"You may explore the complex," Kat said, after a moment. "I'll call you when I'm on my way back to the shuttle. Keep your wristcom with you at all times."

She paused. "And *don't* drink anything even remotely alcoholic," she added. "This isn't shore leave."

"Aye, Captain," Morse said.

Kat smiled to herself, then scrambled out of the shuttle and onto the tarmac. The heat struck her at once, a wave of warm air that sent sweat crawling down her back. She looked round and saw a handful of soldiers wearing gray urban combat dress heading towards her, led by a corporal. He saluted as he approached, his eyes flickering over her and then meeting her eyes. Professional, Kat noted mentally. *That* was a relief.

"Captain Falcone," the officer said. "I'm Corporal Whisper. I've been assigned to escort you to government house."

"Thank you, Corporal," Kat said.

She allowed him and his men to lead her through the complex towards the vehicle park, where they helped her into a large armored vehicle that seemed a cross between a truck and a tank. The windows were transparent battle steel, she noted, allowing her to see out, but proof against anything short of a nuclear blast. It didn't bode well for the security situation either, she decided, as the vehicle jerked into life. A handful of smaller vehicles, some of them carrying mounted machine guns, followed them as they headed towards the gates. That *definitely* didn't bode well for local security.

Corporal Whisper seemed to have appointed himself her local guide and pointed out a number of landmarks as they drove through the complex. The swimming pool, the library, the giant strip of shops, bars, and brothels intended to separate spacers from their money . . . and the prison, where irreconcilable insurgents were held, pending their exile to Nightmare. Kat made a mental note to ensure the pirates were handed over for transport, then pushed the thought aside as she saw a long line of locals being searched by military police.

There was almost no privacy, she realized. The locals had to endure countless humiliations just to enter the complex.

"They used to smuggle in bombs," Corporal Whisper explained when she asked about the searches. "Eventually, we insisted that anyone who refused to actually *live* within the complex had to be searched thoroughly whenever they went in or out of the gates. We found quite a few nasty surprises over the years."

Kat shuddered. She'd never liked being searched during security exercises—and the locals had to endure it almost every day. It was just another humiliation piled on top of losing control of their homeworld to outsiders . . . No matter the justification, she couldn't help thinking the Commonwealth would come to regret annexing Cadiz. But what other choice had there been?

They passed through the gates and out into the countryside. The road was surprisingly wide, she noted, wide enough to make it difficult for someone to plant IEDs along the roadside without making them instantly noticeable. Defoliants had been used to clear the bushes away from the road, ensuring that it was hard to set up ambushes too. There would be no new growth for years, Kat knew. Just something else for the locals to hold against the occupation force. And the stripped roadway wouldn't stop a sniper from taking a shot at the convoy as it raced towards the city.

Still, Cadiz was beautiful, she thought with a trace of wistfulness. She had never been able to climb mountains or even hike before joining the Navy, even when she wasn't surrounded by bodyguards and interfering tutors. Davidson had taken her mountain climbing once or twice, before their relationship had come to an end. The mountains she could see in the distance looked challenging, just the type of experience he loved. But she doubted they were safe for anyone, unless they were surrounded by armed Marines.

She sucked in her breath as they entered Gibraltar, after being waved through the gates by armed soldiers. Inside, hundreds of cars and motorbikes—some so primitive they were actually fueled by gas rather than power cells—buzzed round, while the locals who were on foot glowered at the passing convoy. Kat frowned when she saw them, realizing just what—or rather who—was missing. There were almost no women. The only women on the streets were little girls or old mothers and grandmothers.

"Odd," she said, out loud. "Where are the girls?"

"They're normally kept indoors," Corporal Whisper explained. "It's quite a conservative culture here, Captain. A young woman's reputation is the key to finding her a good match. If there are suggestions she . . . compromised herself with a young man, she won't have a hope of getting married into a reputable family. She might even be kicked out of the house."

Kat shook her head in disbelief. "And the young men?"

"No one cares about their experience," Corporal Whisper said. "They spend more time at the brothels than working or even taking potshots at us."

He smirked. "We have a medical clinic responsible for handling sexually transmitted diseases," he added. "And do you know how many times it's been attacked?"

"No," Kat said.

"It hasn't," Corporal Whisper informed her. "None of the insurgents have ever gone anywhere near it."

Kat started as a bullet pinged off the canopy, followed by a rocket that slammed into the vehicle and shook it, but inflicted no real damage. Their escorts opened fire, sweeping the nearby buildings with bullets, then relaxed as the incoming fire slacked off and died. There was no way to tell if they'd killed the snipers or merely forced them to take cover, but it hardly mattered. They weren't sticking around for a fight.

She looked at the buildings and shivered. Half of them were pockmarked with bullet holes and other signs of damage, while the other half looked as though no one had bothered to do any maintenance for years. But she could hardly blame the locals, she realized as they swept past the buildings and across a firebreak. There was no point in repairing buildings that might be shot up again at any moment. She turned to look at Government House as it came into view and sighed again. It looked like a giant fortress, surrounded by solid walls and patrolled by soldiers on the battlements.

They passed through the gates, revealing a number of short-range guns behind the walls. If someone lobbed mortar shells into the complex, she reasoned, the gunners could track the shells back to their point of origin and return fire. And, if they reacted quickly enough, they might even kill the enemy mortar team before they could escape. But the cost in civilian life had to be quite high.

The vehicle came to a halt. Corporal Whisper opened the hatch, revealing a grim-faced woman in a tight-fitting uniform that had to have been specially tailored to show off her body to best advantage. Kat felt a flicker of sympathy. It was clear, just from her stance, that the woman didn't want to wear the uniform, but it had been forced on her.

And it was easy to guess just *who* had decided such a revealing uniform was a good idea.

"Captain Falcone," the woman said. "I'm Commander Jeannette Macintyre, the admiral's aide. Welcome to Cadiz."

Kat studied her for a long moment. Commander Macintyre was beautiful, with long red hair and a perfect face, but her stance was all wrong. Someone had insisted she have her body upgraded, Kat decided, although it was impossible to say who. The look on Macintyre's face also suggested she wasn't inclined to share any confidences with Kat. She probably assumed the worst of her.

"Thank you," Kat said, holding out a hand. "It's been an interesting tour."

Macintyre smiled as she grasped Kat's hand and shook it, firmly. In the distance, Kat heard the sound of explosions.

"It isn't a safe place for anyone," Macintyre said finally. "The admiral is waiting to see you."

Kat followed her through a network of corridors and then a collection of offices that seemed to be crammed with bureaucrats and officers trying to maintain the occupation. She couldn't help noticing that most of them happened to be young and female—and almost none of them looked local. But *that* wasn't a surprise, she told herself. If none of the locals could be trusted, they couldn't be allowed to work in government. And yet, that would ensure Cadiz would have almost no one versed in running a government when the Commonwealth finally withdrew. They'd fall into chaos almost at once.

Perhaps that's not a bad thing, she thought, *at least for the workers. They would be taken for collaborators.*

She pushed that thought aside as Macintyre led her into the admiral's office. Kat had to keep her face under strict control as she glanced round—there was a staggering amount of gilt embedded in the walls, surrounding a number of artwork from Cadiz—and then looked at the admiral, who was standing in front of a holographic display. In person, he was even more striking, but it wasn't *real.* He'd definitely not had his looks spliced into his genes before birth. Like Macintyre, there was something subtly wrong about how he moved.

"Captain Falcone," he said. He held out a hand. "Welcome to Cadiz."

"Thank you, sir," Kat said. She grasped his hand, allowing him to shake hers. His handshake was perfect, too perfect. It was just like the curtseys would-be aristocratic women were expected to drop every time they encountered someone from a high-ranking family. "It's good to be here."

Admiral Morrison studied her for a long moment, his gaze seemingly welcoming . . . but Kat detected an element of cold calculation behind his smile. She forced herself to hold still under his scrutiny, then allowed herself a moment of relief as he finally let go of her hand and motioned her towards a chair. Kat sat down and crossed her legs, then frowned inwardly as the admiral sat on the sofa, facing her. His poise was again perfect, too perfect. It was just like the rest of him.

"I understand that you have had an eventful trip," Admiral Morrison said. "A captured pirate ship, no less!"

Kat's eyes narrowed. *She* hadn't sent any report to the admiral, not yet. By tradition, the first report was always supposed to be made in person. But the convoy master might have filed a report of his own . . . or someone might have noticed they were towing a pirate ship with them. There were too many possibilities . . .

"Yes, sir," she said. "We took the ship intact, capturing some of its crew and liberating some of its slaves, all of whom are currently held in stasis. I would like to transfer them to the planet's surface as quickly as possible."

The admiral made a dismissive wave with his hand. "You can make arrangements with my aide for the prisoners to be added to the holding pens," he said. "The former captives can remain in stasis until they can be shipped to Tyre."

Kat frowned. "They can't receive treatment here?"

"There are better facilities on Tyre," the admiral said.

Kat felt her frown deepen. There might well be better facilities on Tyre, but not by much, and certainly not better enough to justify keeping the former captives in stasis until they were transferred to yet another planet. But it was the admiral's call. If the situation on the ground was as bad as it seemed, the hospitals on the planet's surface might be overflowing with casualties. Besides, sending them back to Tyre would make it harder for anyone to cover up the pirate attack.

"Yes, sir," she said, finally. "We also found some disturbing evidence on the pirate ship."

She briefly outlined what they'd discovered—and the conclusions they'd drawn, afterwards. The admiral seemed attentive enough, but she'd enough career experience to tell he wasn't really interested. She *couldn't* tell if he was playing dumb or if he genuinely didn't care, but either way it was worrying. It was also in line with everything else she'd seen since entering the system.

"Admiral," she concluded, "someone is backing the pirates. There is simply no other explanation."

"They're *pirates*," Admiral Morrison said with a sneer. "They're hardly an organized fighting force."

"They don't have to be," Kat said. "All they have to do is attack and destroy our shipping."

She thought, briefly, of her father's warnings. If freighters continued to be lost to "causes unknown," insurance rates would start to rise steeply. This would lead to increased shipping costs, which would drive many of the smaller firms out of business and force the larger firms to tighten their belts. It was quite likely, she knew, that the bigger corporations were downplaying the situation purely to avoid an economic downturn. But they couldn't keep the pretense up indefinitely.

"The pirates are taking losses too," Kat added. "They couldn't operate their starships without a backer, certainly not if they're blowing up prizes rather than selling them."

"There's no proof," the admiral said. "I do not believe that accusations of *anything* would improve relationships between ourselves and the Theocracy."

"We have plenty of evidence that *something* is very wrong," Kat insisted. "Who *else* benefits?"

Admiral Morrison offered a look of nonchalance. "I hope you will attend my party," he said. "There will be dignitaries from all over the system in attendance."

The sudden change in subject left Kat feeling breathless. "Admiral . . ."

"I believe most of my superdreadnought commanders will attend," Morrison continued, as if she hadn't spoken. "The CEO of Cadiz Incorporated will *also* be attending. He was particularly interested in meeting you."

"Oh," Kat said.

"Indeed," the admiral agreed. "I think he has a proposal he wishes to put before you."

"I have no say in the affairs of Falcone," Kat said flatly. It was true. Her eldest brother would inherit most of the family stock, leaving her with just her trust fund and a bundle of nonvoting stock. "The discussion would not be productive."

She took a breath, knowing she was about to put her career on the line. "Admiral," she added, "how can you ignore the growing threat to our shipping lines?"

For a moment, she saw a trace of anger behind the admiral's eyes, and then it was gone.

"The decision to annex Cadiz was, in my view, a mistake," the admiral said, finally. His voice was so flat she just *knew* he was using implants to keep it under control. That too was rude, at least in private conversation. "We did something very provocative, something that could have provoked a war, something that could have torn our government apart, purely for our own selfless interests. It would be smart for us to refrain from any other provocative actions in the future."

He cleared his throat, loudly. "Your ship will escort the convoy to the border in five days, once several pieces of cargo have been loaded onto the freighters," he continued. His tone made it clear he considered the assignment a punishment. "After that, we will discuss your future . . . operations."

Kat fought down the urge to grind her teeth in frustration. How could the admiral be so blind? But the hell of it was that he had a point. The decision to annex Cadiz had come alarmingly close to tearing the Commonwealth apart, no matter the justification behind it.

"Thank you, sir," she said, rising to her feet. "I will return to my ship."

"My aide will show you out," the admiral said. He stood and then held out a hand. "And I do trust I will see you at one of my parties, Captain. I believe you have a great deal to offer."

"Yes, sir," Kat said. She shook the admiral's hand reluctantly. "But my starship always comes first."

CHAPTER THIRTEEN

Night was falling over Cadiz Spaceport as the shuttle dropped down to the landing pad and landed neatly, the pilot shutting down the drives moments later. William climbed to his feet, opened the hatch, and stepped through onto the tarmac. The air was cooler than the captain had reported, but there was a strange smell that bothered him more than he cared to admit. It reminded him of his homeworld.

Behind him, the forty-nine officers and crew who had been assigned to the shore leave roster strode out of the shuttle. He turned round to face them, sighing inwardly. There was something about the prospect of shore leave that turned even the most disciplined spacers into a rowdy mob. He cleared his throat loudly and they quieted, knowing he could still bar them from leave, even now.

"You should all have reviewed the safety briefing before boarding the shuttle," he said, knowing some of them probably wouldn't have taken the time to even skim the file. "Do *not* attempt to leave the spaceport or enter any secure zone. Should you do either . . . you'll probably spend an uncomfortable night in the cells before I come and get you."

He paused as the sound of helicopters clattered overhead before fading away in the distance, then continued.

"Do *not* spend more than you have on your credit card, do *not* come stumbling back to the shuttle drunk, and do *not* do anything you don't want to appear on your service record," he added. He turned and pointed towards the shore leave section. "Dismissed."

The crew cheered, then ran past him and through the gates. William snorted, knowing he'd been just as enthusiastic once upon a time, and then strode after them with casual measured steps. The thought of shore leave was hypnotic, he had to admit, but it wasn't really what he wanted, not now. Forty-eight hours was hardly enough to relax properly. Once upon a time, he'd booked himself into a hotel and just spent four days in bed.

He smiled as he passed through the gates and peered down the long road. It *looked* like any other strip of entertainment intended to keep spacers happy on shore leave: a line of bars, strip clubs, gambling arcades, and brothels. His smile grew wider at some of the memories, then he sobered as he caught sight of two armored marines patrolling the street. No matter how hard they tried to disguise it, the spaceport was a prime target for the insurgency. It wouldn't be hard for a spy to slip through the gates and cause trouble.

A line of spacers, the gold badges on their collars marking them as superdreadnought crew, came pouring out of one of the bars, heading towards the brothels. They'd clearly not spent much time on shore leave, William decided, recalling his own adventures. It was generally better to go to the brothel first rather than the bars or gambling joints. The only spacer he recalled spending much time gambling while on shore leave had been an asexual teetotaler, someone who wasn't interested in anything else. Everyone else knew the games tended to be rigged, no matter what the house promised.

He sighed, feeling too responsible to just go to a brothel and carouse, then turned and walked towards the bar at the top of the road. The title, emblazoned on the door in glowing letters, read **OFFICER DOWN**. It wasn't particularly funny, he decided, as he pushed the door open, but it was unlikely any of the junior ranks would dare enter. The establishment was meant for officers and officers alone.

No doubt there's a higher class of prostitute here, he thought as he closed the door behind himself and glanced round. The interior looked like a high-class cafe on Tyre, one of the places that sold cakes and cream teas along with expensive liquor and fancy drinks. *And I'm too poor to spend any time here.*

"William," a female voice called. "It is you, isn't it?"

William stared. He *knew* that voice.

"William," Commander Fran Higgins said. "Long time no see."

"You too," William said. He walked over and sat down facing her. "I didn't know you would be here."

"I'd have called you if I'd known," Fran agreed. She smiled as the waiter arrived, carrying a small notebook in one hand rather than a data terminal. "My friend here would like a Cream Plum, thank you."

The waiter bowed and retreated. William blinked in surprise, then looked at Fran. She looked almost as he remembered, with short brown hair and a face that was solid rather than pretty, but she looked tired. In a way, she looked older than William himself—and he knew she was ten years younger.

"It's good to see you again, Fran," he said. "But why are you drinking here?"

Commander Higgins gave him a sharp look. "Why are *you* drinking here?"

"Touché," William said. "I'm here because I don't want to have fun in front of the crew."

Fran snorted, rudely. "Snap."

The waiter returned, carrying a small glass, which he placed in front of William. The XO eyed it doubtfully—it seemed too fragile for him to pick up—then reached for it and took a sip. The taste was surprisingly strong, but there seemed to have relatively little alcohol. But that probably shouldn't have been a surprise. Officers were not meant to get drunk in public.

He settled back and looked at Fran, taking in the signs of someone who had been worked to breaking point. Her hands twitched constantly, her eyes kept flashing from side to side and she looked . . . *worn*. He couldn't help wondering if he should book a hotel room and implore her to actually sleep for a few short hours, perhaps with the help of a sedative. But he knew she'd kick him somewhere painful if he even dared *hint* she should take a break.

"I only just arrived," he said, once the waiter was out of earshot. They'd have more hope of keeping their conversation private in one of the louder bars further down the strip. "How long have you been here?"

"Years," Fran said. She eyed her drink, but made no move to take a sip. "Or at least it feels that way. I think it's been round eleven months."

William felt a shiver of alarm. "You *think*?"

"I try to forget it," Fran said. "*Defiant* is not a happy ship."

"I see," William said, after a moment. "But you're her XO, aren't you?"

"Of course," Fran said. She tapped her uniform meaningfully, drawing his attention to the silver badge on her shoulder. "Only one XO and that's me."

She sighed. "And a whole fucking pile of shit on my shoulders," she added. "You want my advice? Run. Run far."

"I don't think that's an option," William said. He took a breath. "Fran . . . what's happening here?"

Fran sipped her drink. She was already marginally drunk, William realized, or she wouldn't have let *anything* slip. The Fran Higgins he remembered had been a paragon of efficiency and emotional control. If *she* was turning to liquor . . . it wasn't a good sign. *Defiant*—a superdreadnought—was definitely not a happy ship.

"We were a good squadron when we were assigned to Cadiz," Fran said mournfully. "The commodore might have been a political appointee, but he was a good man; the captain had years in the service, plenty of time to know what to do himself and what to leave to me. I thought a deployment to Cadiz would allow us plenty of time to train and exercise for the war. But I was wrong."

She shook her head. "It's all fucked up, William," she added. "Like I said, take your ship and run."

"I can't do that," William said. "What's wrong?"

Fran laughed, bitterly. "Where do I even start?"

She shrugged. "No training exercises," she said. "Half the crew on shore leave at any one time. Shore Patrolmen getting into trouble because they don't have the sense to stay out of shit. The captain spending most of his time on the planet's surface; the commodore kissing up to the admiral rather than sticking up for his crews. I can't run regular maintenance cycles and the ship is practically unserviceable. We're fucked if we have to get into a fight without at least a week to prepare for action."

William blanched. "It's that bad?"

"It's worse," Fran said. She took a long swallow, finishing her glass, then waved to the waiter. "Another!"

"Water would be better," William said, quickly.

"You're not the boss of me any longer," Fran thundered. "You didn't try to screw me. The captain is certainly trying to screw me."

Her voice slurred for a long moment, then recovered. "If someone inspects the ship, I'm screwed," she said with heavy satisfaction. "I will take the blame."

She wouldn't take the blame alone, William knew, at least if regulations were honored and the IG carried out the inspection. The buck stopped with the vessel's commanding officer. But if the captain and the admiral carried out the inspection, it *might* be possible to blame Fran . . . assuming no one took a close look at the reports. And, with Fran a nobody, politically speaking, it might just be shoved under the rug.

"Shit," he said.

"Yeah," Fran agreed. "Shit."

She met his eyes. "You have no idea just how many problems we've had," she said darkly. "One of the Shore Patrolmen walked out an airlock, another was beaten halfway to death by someone—we still don't know who. Exercises would help the crew pull back together, but I'm not even allowed to run them. Apparently, they cost too much money."

William winced. Naval bases had a specific budget each year. If there was a shortfall, canceling training exercises seemed an excellent way to save funds. But it was a false saving. Troops and starship crews who had no time to exercise tended to lose competency alarmingly fast. If they had to go into battle, they'd be screwed.

He placed his hand on top of the drink when the waiter placed it on the table. "Is 7th Fleet combat capable?"

Fran surprised him by laughing, hysterically. "I doubt there's a single ship in the fleet that can move under her own power," she said. "The superdreadnoughts certainly can't without some hasty repair work."

William hoped—desperately—she was exaggerating. If she was correct, 7th Fleet was effectively a sitting duck. Cadiz had some planet-side defenses, but hardly enough to make a real difference if the Theocracy came knocking. Besides, the locals would definitely rise up against the occupation force—and move from the frying pan into the fire. The Commonwealth meant well, even though it had blundered badly. Theocratic rule would be far worse.

He took a long look at her, feeling pity intermingled with rage. The Fran Higgins he'd known had been a capable officer, not a drunken wreck. She deserved better. Hell, the crews on the fleet's starships deserved better too. They were wasting away because their commanders were more interested in partying than actually carrying out their duties.

If any of her subordinates saw her like this, he knew they'd lose all respect for her.

"Tell me something," he said. "Have you not filed a complaint?"

"Nine of us did," Fran said. "We never heard anything back from the IG."

William swore under his breath. Admiral Morrison might well be able to prevent a formal complaint from ever leaving the system, assuming he had a crony or two in charge of the StarCom. But he couldn't move against the complainers without ensuring they had their chance to face a court-martial board. Instead, he seemed to have just left matters as they were. It wasn't a smart way to behave.

He signaled the waiter. "I understand you have rooms upstairs," he said. He placed his credit chip on the table. "I want one of those rooms and a sober-up injection, now."

"Yes, sir," the waiter said. He took the chip with practiced ease, then stepped back. "If you will come with me . . ."

William helped a protesting Fran to her feet, then half carried her through the door and up a flight of stairs. One of the doors on the next floor was open, revealing a naked man and a girl kneeling in front of him, sucking his penis. William was silently grateful he didn't recognize him, even though he had to be a fairly senior officer. He knew, intellectually, that his superiors had sexual drives too, but he didn't want to think about it. Thankfully, Captain Falcone didn't seem to be interested in patronizing bars or brothels.

The room was larger than he'd expected, certainly larger than any room in a more average brothel. He positioned Fran on the bed, took the injector from the waiter, and pressed it against her neck. She glared daggers at him as the injection shot into her system, then stumbled to her feet and into the toilet. Moments later, he heard the sound of vomiting as the alcohol left her bloodstream, along with everything she'd eaten over the past few hours. He waited as patiently as he could until she walked back into the bedroom, looking murderous.

"You're a bastard," she said as she sat down on the bed and removed her jacket. Her uniform was badly stained. "You could at least have let me go back to the shuttle before I took the injection . . ."

"Friends don't let friends fly shuttles while drunk," William pointed out. "Besides, I dread to imagine what would happen to your service record if you were found drunk and disorderly."

"Under the circumstances," Fran said, "that wouldn't be a problem."

She placed her head in her hands, embarrassed. "I'm sorry, William," she said, refusing to look up. "You shouldn't have seen me like that."

"I'm glad you still have some dignity left," William said gently. "Besides, I can't chew you out any longer."

"I suppose not," Fran said. She paused. "How much did I tell you?"

"Enough to worry me," William said. How much had she drunk? Short-term memory loss wasn't normally a problem. "Is your captain really leaving everything in your hands?"

Fran looked down at the grubby floor. "Yes," she said, finally. "But I don't even begin to have the tools to fix this mess."

William, for the first time in far too long, found himself completely at a loss. He'd prepared himself on the assumption he would be doing most of the work on *Lightning*, an assumption that had rapidly proven false. But Fran . . . Fran definitely seemed to be doing most of the work, without the crew or authority that would make it possible. He honestly had no idea how to proceed. There were ways to handle a misbehaving crewman, even to manipulate a tyrannical commanding officer, but this . . . ?

The IG needs to come here, he thought numbly. Like most officers, he hated the Inspectorate General, viewing them as a bunch of useless bureaucrats or desk jockeys who didn't have the slightest idea of how things really worked, but they were needed now. *This isn't one ship, this is the entire goddamned fleet.*

He looked at her. She shouldn't go back to her ship, not in such a state.

"Tell me," he said. "How long until you're due back on *Defiant*?"

"Two days," Fran said. "But I should go back earlier."

William let out a sigh of relief. "You can stay here and sleep," he said, firmly. "I want you going back to the ship in tip-top condition."

"For what?" Fran asked, bitterly. "I can't make it all better."

"You can try," William said. "And besides, you owe it to yourself."

He thought briefly about telling her about the pirate attack and the worrying pattern behind it, but then decided it could wait.

"I'll get you a sedative," he said, instead. "You can sleep here until you wake up naturally."

Fran objected loudly. William understood—he hated the idea of being sedated too, even with someone he trusted in the room—but there was no choice. In her state, Fran was unlikely to sleep very well without chemical aid. He keyed the console, requesting a sedative, then cast his eye down the list of other options. Some of them were truly alarming; others were merely amusing. What sort of commanding officer would want a pair of leather handcuffs?

Maybe one who has dreams of whipping crewmen, he thought. It was understandable. There were quite a few crewmen he'd met who might have benefited from a whipping. *Or maybe one who's just a sadist.*

He picked up the sedative when it arrived, then held it up in front of her. "Lie down," he ordered, firmly. "You're about to go to sleep."

Fran sighed. "I feel like a failure," she said. Her tone was so bitter that William almost insisted she see a counselor, but he thought better of it. Few officers would gladly visit someone who could have them removed from duty with a word. "I've failed the crew . . ."

"You'll have a chance to make it better," William promised. The captain wanted his impressions of the situation on the ground. She'd get more than she ever expected, particularly once he started looking up other friends attached to 7th Fleet. "And you can't fight for your crews without a good night's sleep."

He pressed the tab against her arm, then sat back and watched as she fell into slumber. Her face relaxed until she was almost the younger officer he remembered, before she'd been assigned to Admiral Morrison's command. He felt a spark of bitter hatred, even though he'd never met the man. What could have gone so badly wrong that it would cripple a woman he'd once known to be a good officer?

And not just her, he told himself. *Whatever rot started here has spread through the entire fleet. If the Theocracy comes knocking . . .*

He shuddered. If half of what Fran had said was true, the thought was far from comforting.

CHAPTER FOURTEEN

Kat waited until her steward had served her XO and Davidson steaming mugs of coffee, taking another cup for herself as well, then leaned forward, placing her hands on her desk.

"The situation looks bad," she said. "Just how bad is it?"

"Disastrous," the two men said, together.

They exchanged surprised looks, then Davidson motioned for the XO to continue.

"I spoke to several other officers I know," William said. "All of them agreed that 7th Fleet is in no condition for a fight. The average superdreadnought is at forty percent efficiency, which may be an optimistic assessment. It's a little better for some of the smaller ships, as they still have useful work to do, but not *that* much better. The list of problems seems endless."

Kat nodded, slowly. A cruiser could expect to serve as anything from an independent scouting platform to a convoy escort or colony guardship. No sane CO would risk allowing his ship to decline too far, knowing he might have to switch tasks at any moment. But superdreadnoughts spent far too much of their time near fleet bases, close to shore leave facilities for officers and crew alike. It took a strong-minded commander to keep his crew at peak efficiency when the temptations of the nearby planet were so strong.

The XO sighed. "Overall," he added, "it seems likely that a mere squadron of superdreadnoughts could best 7th Fleet if they attacked tomorrow."

He ran his hand through his graying hair. "Some of the officers I spoke with have been attempting to do something about the problem, but they haven't been able to get any response from the Admiralty. And Admiral Morrison keeps pooh-poohing their concerns. A handful of officers who pushed it too far, apparently, were relieved for cause and assigned to asteroid bases in the sector. None of them were sent home for court martial."

"Because a court martial would have required open discussion of just what was happening on Cadiz," Kat said, thoughtfully. "Instead . . . their careers were destroyed."

She cursed under her breath. Her trust fund ensured she didn't have to work a day in her life if she wanted to resign herself to an eternity of lazy luxury. But no one outside the aristocracy had that option, even a senior naval officer. The officers would have noted what happened to others who questioned too loudly and shut up, despite the growing risk of attack. They wouldn't want to see their careers blighted too.

"Yes, Captain," the XO confirmed. "Admiral Morrison seems to have been remarkably successful in keeping matters under wraps."

Kat looked at Davidson. "And what did you hear?"

Davidson looked . . . irked. "I called a handful of Marine officers on the surface," he said darkly. "Most of them agreed the situation is dire, both in space and on the ground. The insurgency is still holding strong, the occupation forces are having to fight hard to hold their ground, and senior officers are losing control. There have even been rumors that the insurgents have been dehumanized to the point where atrocities have been covered up. I wish I could say it surprises me."

Kat lifted her eyebrows expressively.

"Occupation duties are always tricky," Davidson said. "A soldier on patrol can lose sight of common decency when confronted by a civilian population that either does nothing or actively supports the insurgents. The urge to just hit out and smash the grinning bastards into paste becomes overwhelming. It doesn't help that there simply aren't enough forces on the ground to keep the entire planet under control. Our troops have been substituting superior firepower for boots on the ground."

The XO frowned. "So an area is only under control as long as we have troops on top of it?"

"Yes," Davidson agreed. "Once the troops move away, the insurgents move back and take control again. Anyone who collaborated with our forces gets brutally murdered. By now, the only people willing to work with the occupation forces are locals without connections or people who believe we can protect their families."

He winced, noticeably. "But even they are bearing the brunt of suspicion," he added. "I heard a dozen horror stories from a couple of marines. If we didn't have overwhelming firepower in orbit, Captain, I think we would have lost Cadiz by now."

"But we have handled insurgencies on other Commonwealth worlds," Kat said thoughtfully. "Why can't we handle *this* one?"

"Every other world had a large majority in favor of joining the Commonwealth," Davidson reminded her. "All we really had to do was train and bolster the local security forces, then assist them in asserting control over the hinterlands. Hell, most of the insurgencies faded away when the benefits of Commonwealth membership became apparent. Here . . . the locals largely hate our guts, with reason. The insurgency shows no sign of going away."

"And we can't build up a local force allied to us," the XO said. "But surely some of them see the advantages . . ."

"Not enough of them," Davidson said, cutting him off. "The whole situation is FUBAR, Captain. We can't fix the occupation and we can't abandon the star system."

"Perhaps we should simply abandon the planet itself," the XO said. "It isn't as if we *need* to have installations on Cadiz."

Kat took a moment to breathe. Interstellar law was an odd thing, all the more so now the aftereffects of the Breakdown were slowly fading away. Technically, whoever owned Cadiz owned the entire system, which meant the investments made in the system would be at risk if Cadiz was abandoned and allowed to go its own merry way. There were a dozen large corporations in the Commonwealth that would refuse to accept losing control of their investments. But with Cadiz V being terraformed, there might soon be a second settled world in the system. It was a horrible, ghastly mess.

But we would have overwhelming firepower, she thought slowly. *What would it matter what Cadiz thought if they couldn't reach orbit?*

"It would look very bad," she said, finally. "It wouldn't play well at home and it wouldn't play well with the other interstellar powers—or even the other independent worlds along the Rim. The Theocracy will probably make use of the whole story to convince people we can't be trusted."

"They'd have to be out of their minds," the XO commented. "Haven't they been *listening* to what the refugees told us?"

"It's easy to manipulate the news," Kat said, remembering one of the few lessons she'd had directly from her father. The Falcone Consortium owned a large chunk of the mainstream media. No editor would dare run a story that impinged on the corporation's interests. "And the Theocracy is very good at it."

She remembered the reports and shivered. There were no independent media outlets on Theocratic worlds, no one pushing anything but the official version of events. The locals welcomed the Theocracy; they either converted happily or lived in peace under their own religions and everything was simply wonderful. Kat knew the refugees told a different story, but they simply didn't have the reach and exposure Theocratic propaganda had. And, the farther away a planet was from the expanding border, the more likely its population would believe the Theocracy's version of affairs.

We should be telling them the truth, she thought. But the truth sounded less attractive than a barrage of lies. *Or we should forward the refugees on to them.*

"The overall situation is dire," Kat said, finally. She took a sip of her coffee. "Mr. XO, there are some things we need to discuss with you."

The thought made her feel a twinge of pain. She'd had the sense the XO had come to respect her, at least to some degree, after they'd tackled the pirate ship. Maybe she was still too young for her role, but at least she'd handled the situation competently. And yet . . . now she had to discuss her father's request for information with him. It was easy to imagine him considering her willingness to cooperate with her father a form of disloyalty to the navy.

She shook her head. What choice did she have?

"I wasn't just assigned to command this starship," she said, hesitatingly. "I . . . was also asked to carry out an independent review of 7th Fleet—and Cadiz's security."

The XO's face went blank. Kat sighed, mentally bidding farewell to their new rapport, then pressed onwards. Davidson showed no reaction.

"I have a backchannel through the StarCom," she continued. "The message I send won't be intercepted or read by prying eyes. I intend to write a full report on what we've observed over the last two days."

"Admiral Morrison will be furious if he finds out you've gone behind his back," the XO said mildly. "This isn't sending a private report to the IG, is it?"

He hadn't asked who would receive Kat's message, she noted. Was it that obvious?

Of course it is, she told herself angrily. *Who else would request a report from right outside the normal channels from YOU?*

"No, it isn't," Kat said. She loved her career, but she could give it up if necessary. Besides, she could always formally protest an assignment to an asteroid station and demand a court martial. She had a feeling Admiral Morrison would bend over backwards to avoid putting her in front of a Captains' Board. "But I don't see any other option."

"You would be making yourself a pawn in a political struggle," the XO said in the same mild tone. It was impossible to tell if he approved or disapproved of her actions. "Whatever happened, Captain, your career would never be your own again."

"It never has been," Kat said, unable to keep the bitterness from *her* tone. She looked at him, wishing she could read his face. "The entire report will be under my name."

The XO shook his head. "I just saw an officer I trained, an officer I respected, trying to drink herself to death," he said softly. "She just couldn't cope any longer with the strain placed on her by her superiors. It has to be stopped."

He paused. "Feel free to put my name on the report as well," he offered. "It might help if your readers think it isn't just your work."

Kat gave him a relieved smile, even though she knew he had far more at stake than she did. Her XO was a powerless nobody, someone who hadn't even been born a Commonwealth citizen. His career could be blighted or destroyed completely with a word or two from Admiral Morrison. Kat could fund him, perhaps even find him a place within the Falcone Consortium, but it wouldn't be the same. Yet he was offering to place his career at risk for her.

"Mine too," Davidson said, breaking his silence. He hesitated, minutely. It would have been unnoticeable if Kat hadn't known him so well. "Captain, I confess I have no idea why General Eastside has not reported the situation to Tyre. But I do have to make a report myself."

Kat wasn't surprised. The Marine Corps, always on the tip of the spear, encouraged its junior officers to send reports and feedback back to Tyre. There were times when it allowed officers to do an end-run around a sometimes stodgy military bureaucracy. But someone should have *already* reported the problems, not settled for rumors and innuendo. Why hadn't the senior marine on the spot reported the problem himself?

"Add it to mine," Kat advised. "I don't want anyone to read the report until it reaches Tyre."

The XO smiled. "Afraid of what the admiral will say?"

"I'd prefer not to pick a fight with him right now," Kat said. Part of her would relish the confrontation, but it would be disastrous. The issue at hand could be easily buried if enough people were convinced she was a snotty little brat who initiated a feud because she wasn't happy with her orders. "And I would prefer to have the IG send out a team without any more fuss than strictly necessary."

"Their presence might alert the Theocracy that their window for attack is closing," the XO agreed. He looked down at the table, thoughtfully. "The Admiralty might want to assign three new squadrons of superdreadnoughts to Cadiz, then remove Admiral Morrison and call back 7th Fleet for refit."

Kat leaned forward, alarmed. "It's that bad?"

"I think several of the superdreadnoughts will need months of hard labor before they'll be anything like combat capable," the XO said. He paused. "You know you can download fleet statistics from the datanet?"

"Yes," Kat said. She'd *been* an XO. Maybe not as long as *he'd* been an XO, but she knew a few tricks. It had been an eye-opening experience in many ways. "Most of the captains spend their days on the surface."

"There's supposed to be a note in the database every time a component is requisitioned from naval stockpiles and sent to a starship," the XO said. "Right now, only a hundred or so requisitions have been made over the last four months."

"That's absurd," Kat said. *Lightning* alone had made over five *hundred* requisitions since she'd taken command. "A superdreadnought should have"—she tried to work it out in her head—"at least a thousand a month."

The XO gave her a cold smile. "Or they're not doing any maintenance," he said. "Naval components are tough, but standing orders are to replace them long before they reach their expiration date. If they're not being replaced regularly . . ."

Davidson cleared his throat. "This is starting to look like more than incompetence," he said, grimly. "This is starting to look like outright treason."

The XO blinked. "Are you suggesting Admiral Morrison is in the pay of the Theocracy?"

"Someone should have reported this up the chain of command," Davidson said. He tapped off points on his fingers as he spoke. "There's a duty—a legal duty—for Marine officers to report superiors who are grossly incompetent. Naval officers . . . well, someone might well have tried to blow a whistle by now."

"Fran did," the XO said, quietly. "So did others."

"And those reports haven't reached the Admiralty," Davidson said. "I certainly wasn't told more than rumors when I received my orders—and there should have been a full briefing from Marine Intelligence. This smacks of outright treason."

Kat considered it, slowly. It was possible, she had to admit, but it didn't seem likely. The admiral could have surrendered the planet to the Theocracy by now, if he'd been working for them directly. A few careful orders prior to attack and 7th Fleet would be utterly incapable of defending itself. Why would the Theocracy play a waiting game when the chances of their agent being exposed would only grow stronger with each passing day? *Someone* would eventually get a message to the Admiralty . . .

"Admiral Morrison is the blue-eyed boy of a number of politicians," she said finally, remembering her father's files. "They put him in position in the hopes of preventing any further . . . adventurism."

"This is madness," Davidson said. "His political backers can't save him from a shit storm of that magnitude."

"I don't think they give a damn about his career," Kat said. "All they care about is ensuring we don't blunder into a war."

"As opposed to having one rammed down our throats when the Theocracy comes over the border," Davidson said dryly. "Are they out of their minds?"

But Kat understood. Reality was a flexible concept if one happened to be as wealthy and powerful as the highest families on Tyre. Wealth insulated them from the cold equations of everyday life. Indeed, no matter how much money they spent, it was unlikely they could ever bankrupt themselves. But some problems couldn't be bought off by money.

She had a feeling, when the investigation finally took place, that they wouldn't discover a vast overarching conspiracy. Instead, they'd discover a thousand tiny decisions that made sense, individually, but added up to disaster. She could understand Admiral Morrison wanting to avoid provocation; she could understand the shipping companies wanting to avoid a rise in insurance rates; she could understand officers not wanting to blight their careers; she could understand bureaucratic supply officers not wanting to give up their supplies . . .

Or was it a conspiracy after all? It seemed absurdly paranoid. A conspiracy on that scale would be either unworkable or unstoppable. She knew how hard it was to keep even a small organization a secret. And yet even paranoids had enemies.

"I will write the report," she said. "We're scheduled to leave in four days, escorting the convoy to the border. I'll transmit it just before we leave."

Davidson frowned. "I can't say I'm happy with doing this in such an . . . underhand manner," he confessed. "Is it *right*?"

Kat hesitated. Davidson had always been honorable. It was one of the things she'd loved about him. He preferred to do things in a direct manner, if possible, rather than sneak round behind his superior's back.

"I don't see that we have any choice," the XO said. "If we file a report through channels, it will go missing somewhere along the way."

"I agree," Kat said simply. "We can't take the chance."

"Then I will write a formal report for Marine HQ," Davidson said. "Can you send it with your message?"

"Yes," Kat said. Her father might try to use what she'd sent for political advantage. If the report went to Marine HQ too, it would be harder for him to suppress it. "And I'll also suggest reinforcements be sent before anything else happens."

She dismissed them both, then sat back in her chair, feeling very old. Part of her *hated* the idea of sneaking around a senior officer—and that, she knew, was precisely what she was doing, no matter how she tried to disguise it. Admiral Morrison wore the same uniform and she was conspiring against him. Yet she knew there was no choice. The condition of 7th Fleet grew worse every day.

Slowly, she reached for her private terminal and started to write.

CHAPTER FIFTEEN

"Transit completed, Captain," Weiberg reported.

"Good," the captain said. "Set course for the rendezvous point."

"Aye, Captain," Weiberg said. "Estimated flight time: two days."

William nodded to himself, knowing the die had been firmly cast. He and the captain had spent the last four days writing a careful summary of their observations, attaching a number of off-the-record comments from his contacts on the fleet, then uploading it into the StarCom message buffer. The codes the captain had been given, he'd been told, should ensure that the message would be transmitted at once, then wiped from the buffer. It should be impossible for any unfriendly eyes to read the report without the correct codes.

And if we're wrong about that, he thought morbidly, *our careers will be in the shit hole.*

He pushed the thought aside as he watched the display update. Ten freighters—another had joined them at Cadiz—were slowly making their way through hyperspace, shadowed by the giant heavy cruiser. William rather doubted the ships would be attacked, particularly if the Theocracy *was* backing the pirates, but he knew better than to take that for granted. After all, it would look even more suspicious if Theocracy-bound freighters were the only ones spared pirate attacks.

A dull quiver ran through the ship and he smiled. They were on their way. There had been some good-natured grumbling from the lower decks about the shortage of shore leave—he'd ended up giving some of the crew only a few short hours on the planet's surface—but it felt good to be heading away from Cadiz. He didn't want the lethargy affecting the fleet to infest *Lightning*—and it wouldn't, not while he was XO. Even if Admiral Morrison insisted on keeping them at Cadiz, he would ensure an endless series of training exercises to keep the crew sharp.

He looked at the captain's blond head and felt an odd flicker of affection. It had been brave of her to tell him the truth, knowing he might start disliking her again—or take it to the admiral. Her career would probably have survived, but no one would ever have trusted her again. What CO would trust an officer who had spied on another officer? She might start spying on him next.

But her father was right, he had to admit. There was something *deeply* wrong at Cadiz Naval Base. He'd gone through the records and watched, in alarm, as standards had slowly dropped ever since Admiral Morrison had been appointed CO. Maybe it *was* deliberate after all, he wondered, although there was no way to tell. And, if so, was it for political reasons or outright treason? The sooner the IG carried out a full audit, the better.

"Mr. XO," the captain said, formally. She turned to face him. "You may conduct your inspection of the *Wandering Soul*."

"Aye, Captain," William said.

He saluted, then turned and walked through the hatch towards Marine Country, where Davidson, a platoon of Marines, and a handful of inspectors were already waiting for him, the Marines carrying weapons and looking thoroughly intimidating. William wasn't expecting trouble onboard the *Wandering Soul*, but it was well to be prepared.

He hadn't bothered to tell the freighter's CO there would be an inspection. It would only have upset him ahead of time.

They scrambled into the shuttle, then launched from *Lightning* and flew towards the *Wandering Soul.* Like most freighters, William noted, she was ugly as hell, little more than a boxy superstructure with a drive section attached to the rear. There were no weapons, according to the manifest, although *that* meant nothing. He wouldn't have been surprised to find a handful of weapons fittings *mounted* on the starship's hull.

He keyed the communicator. "*Wandering Soul,* this is Commander McElney," he said. "I intend to board and inspect your vessel for contraband goods. Please open an airlock for my shuttle."

There was a long pause. "Commander, I must formally protest," a belligerent voice snapped. "My ship was inspected at Cadiz and we have not made landfall elsewhere . . ."

"We have authority to inspect any freighter traveling in convoy at any moment," William said, cutting him off. He already knew the ship had been inspected—or at least that the records *claimed* the ship had been inspected. "If you do not comply, your ship will be boarded and seized—and you and your crew will be held in custody."

"An airlock has been cleared for you," the voice said quickly. Too quickly. "But I must warn you that I will file a formal protest."

"Take us in," William ordered, ignoring the protest. They *were* within their legal rights—and besides, if they found anything illegal he knew the protest would fade away. "I want to search the ship as quickly as possible."

They docked, then swarmed onto the ship, weapons at the ready. No one offered resistance; William was mildly surprised, at least at first, to discover there were no women in the crew. But it made a certain kind of sense if they were dealing with the Theocracy. Captain Norton, a burly man who looked too big for his uniform, protested loudly, then reluctantly passed William his papers. William inspected them while the Marines checked the ship and then allowed the inspectors to go to work.

"You don't seem to be carrying very much," he observed, lifting his eyes from the manifest. "Why do you think you can sell civilian-grade sensor suites?"

Captain Norton smirked at him. "We already have a deal with an agent," he said. "They'll take as many suites as we can deliver for thirty percent over the market rate."

"Odd," William noted. He could understand the Theocracy wanting military-grade sensors, but civilian grade? They could obtain the plans just about anywhere in the Commonwealth and then produce the systems for themselves. "Do you know what they want with them?"

"Of course not," Captain Norton sneered. "I don't ask too many questions, Commander. I merely deliver what I'm told to deliver."

William frowned. It made no sense . . . which probably meant he was missing something. The Theocracy wouldn't throw away money on something they could produce for themselves. He checked the rest of the manifest and noted that it included other starship components, including a handful of drive motivators. Some of them were designs that had first been produced before the Breakaway Wars. Were the Theocrats trying to wage subtle economic warfare by buying up starship components? Or did they have some devious plan to use them against the Commonwealth?

"So it would seem," he said, finally. "And are you carrying anything you'd hate to have us discover?"

"Commander," Norton snapped, "we are a *clean* ship!"

"Remarkable," William commented. He shrugged, expressively. "Just remember we won't be able to help you if you run into trouble with the Theocracy's authorities."

"They do tend to be anal," Norton agreed. "But they pay well, so we put up with their crap."

My brother and you would probably get along, William thought darkly.

He keyed his wristcom, making no attempt to hide his action. "Chief?"

"We've opened a couple of crates," the chief said. "So far, everything checks out."

"I told you we were inspected on Cadiz," Norton put in.

"Yes, but I wouldn't trust the inspectors on Cadiz to find a spacer in a brothel," William retorted. The inspection had either been alarmingly light or someone had merely flagged the ship as inspected, probably after being paid a large bribe. It was yet another problem caused by the lack of a unified authority for Cadiz. "And you are aware of the dangers of taking the wrong thing into Theocratic space?"

"I am a businessman," Norton said stiffly. "I don't care about politics."

"Politics cares about you," William said. He tapped his wristcom. It was tempting to spend the next few hours tearing the ship apart, but it would have triggered a more serious complaint from the independent merchant's guild. "Open a couple more crates at random, Chief, then search the cabins."

"Looking for women?" Norton asked. His voice was mocking. "I'm afraid we had to leave them behind on Cadiz."

"Probably for the best," William agreed.

He looked at Norton for a long moment. Perhaps the man could offer some useful intelligence, if nothing else. "What happens when you reach their world?"

"Well, we just off-load," Norton said. "They search the ship, then take crates out through the airlock and tranship them to another freighter. It must cost a bomb, Commander, but they seem to swallow the cost. Then we just wait until they arrange an escort to chivvy us back to the border."

William frowned. "Do they let you land on a planet's surface?"

"Never," Norton said. "They don't offer any shore leave facilities. The closest they come to entertainment is allowing a missionary to board our ships to preach to us. We generally listen politely until he goes."

"I see," William said. His wristcom buzzed. "One moment."

He lifted the device to his lips. "Go ahead."

"We've found nothing illegal in the second set of crates or the cabins," the chief said. "Do you want us to search the rest of the ship?"

"No," William said, after a moment. They were probably just wasting their time. "Return to the shuttle, Chief. I'll join you there in a moment."

"I told you so," Norton said, with some pride. "We are a *clean* ship."

"I know," William countered. "It's very suspicious."

He winked at the man, then turned and walked to the shuttle. Midshipwoman Cecelia Parkinson was standing just outside the hatch, looking nervous. It would be her turn to lead the next search, commanding men who had more years in the Navy than she'd had in her life. And William would have to remain behind in the shuttle and hope she didn't screw up too badly . . .

"Nothing to report, sir," she said. Judging by her voice, she expected to be blamed for not finding something contraband. She hadn't found her confidence yet. "The ship appeared to be clean."

"That's a good thing," William assured her. He'd rather hoped she would shape up before now. "I'd hate to be caught by the Theocracy if I *did* have something contraband on my ship."

He led the way through the hatch and into the shuttle, then motioned for the pilot to disengage from the freighter and take them to the next ship. As soon as they were in motion, he looked down at the copy of the manifest and frowned. As far as he could tell, the Theocracy was spending money—well over the going rate too—on items that were practically worthless. It didn't make *sense*.

Midshipwoman Parkinson coughed when he said that aloud. "Sir," she said, "it *might* make sense."

She cringed when he looked at her sharply. "I . . ."

"Theories are always interesting," William assured her. Honestly, what did they *teach* young officers at Piker's Peak? "What do you think it means?"

"They're buying something they should be able to make for themselves," Parkinson said, "but they're *not* making them for themselves or they wouldn't need to buy them. What are they doing with all that productive capacity if they're not using it?"

William felt his blood run cold. Out of the mouths of babes . . .

"They're not producing civilian-grade components for their freighters because they're busy producing military-grade components for their warships," the senior chief said. "It makes sense, sir."

It did, William noted. It made far too much sense.

"I'll bring it to the captain's attention," he promised. Midshipwoman Parkinson would get a note in her file commending her for the deduction. He'd see to it even if the captain didn't. "But how much production capacity do they *have*?"

He mulled it over as they moved from freighter to freighter, inspecting them all one by one. There were no surprises, apart from a large porn stash one of the freighter crewmen had kept for himself despite the warnings. William warned his CO to have it confiscated and thrown into space, then ordered the inspection team to return to *Lightning*. He had an important report to make.

"You did good today," he told Parkinson once the shuttle had returned to *Lightning*. "Take a break, then write your report. Be sure to mention your deduction as well as everything else."

"And that your approach was textbook perfect," Davidson added. The marine gave the young officer what was probably intended as a reassuring smile. "But you probably need to consider the unpredictable as well."

◆ ◆ ◆

"They're purchasing civilian-grade starship components from us," Kat mused as she read the report. Her Ready Room felt unusually cold. "The midshipwoman would appear to be correct, wouldn't she?"

"Someone must have noticed," Davidson said. "If there was a steady pattern of components being drained into Theocratic space . . ."

"They wouldn't," the XO said gruffly. "We're not looking at classified pieces of kit here, Major. There isn't anything on the list that can't be obtained for a few hundred crowns just about anywhere in the Commonwealth. I'd bet good money that most of the components on that ship were third- or fourth-hand by the time they were purchased by the Theocracy's agents. As long as the money was upfront, no one would ask too many questions."

"But the Theocracy shouldn't need the components," Kat mused. It was a puzzle, all right, one that made little sense. "Or is their industrial base weaker than we supposed?"

"I've studied command economies," Davidson said. "It's quite possible they're very good at producing warship tech, but less good at meeting their economic needs. They might have thrust everything they had into building their navy, then discovered they needed a civilian economy too."

Kat nodded, slowly. It made sense.

"But we know almost nothing about the Theocracy's internal structure," she mused. All they really heard from the Theocracy was propaganda, and she was fairly sure that it was mostly lies. "Could they be far weaker than we thought?"

"Bluff and bluster?" Davidson asked. He sounded as though he liked the idea. "*The Wizard of Oz* in space? Pay no attention to the absence of starships behind the border? Maybe they don't have anything larger than a light cruiser and they've been bluffing everyone they've met?"

"We know they took some worlds that should have been able to mount a defense against one or two ships," the XO said sharply before anyone could get too excited. "I don't think they would be so keen to press up against our space if they were truly too weak to put up a fight."

He shrugged. "Besides, their world was a careful investment, as carefully planned as Tyre herself," he added. "They didn't owe the UN crippling amounts of money. I don't think we dare assume they didn't manage to put together a first-rate industrial base of their own. It's in their damned doctrine."

"They do seem to believe that one has to deserve to win to actually win," Davidson agreed sourly. "It will make them dangerous, certainly far more dangerous than their predecessors."

"So we have something else to report once we get back to Cadiz," Kat said. She sighed. It was quite possible her father would have sent a reply, but it was equally possible that someone had noted the message and traced it back to her, even if they couldn't read it. "Did you find anything else even remotely suspicious?"

"No," the XO said. "Cargo and crew manifests checked out. We ran the crews against the database and identified most of them. A handful weren't registered with the various trade guilds, but that means nothing. Membership in the guilds isn't compulsory."

And is keenly discouraged in places, Kat thought. Tyre had strict laws governing how unions could form and what they could do. Her grandparents had helped write them.

"They could be enemy agents," Davidson suggested. "The shipping firms would be a good place to hide an intelligent asset or two."

"And then have them report back while under guise of being searched," the XO said. "It could work."

"Yes, it could," Kat mused. "But we don't have grounds to hold any of them, do we?"

"None," the XO said. "Some of the ships were skirting the edge when it comes to shipping regulations, but they're out on the border. No one will give a damn if we report them."

"It's their lives at stake," Kat agreed. Besides, if they pushed the limits too far, no one would insure the ships against accidents, let alone pirate attacks. "And out of our jurisdiction."

She straightened up. "Write a full report," she said, "and we'll attach it to the next message we send back to Tyre. And then get some sleep. We'll need to be alert when we reach the rendezvous point."

"Aye, Captain," the XO said. "Will you get some sleep too?"

"I'll do my best," Kat said. The thought of sleep was tempting, but she had far too much paperwork to grind through. She'd downloaded everything she could from Cadiz before they'd departed the system, trying to put together a picture of just how 7th Fleet had decayed into a useless mass. "It's still a day to the RV point."

"Plenty of time to sleep," Davidson rumbled. He rose. "I'll prep the teams to inspect the next set of ships, Captain."

Kat almost asked him to stay, but held her tongue just in time. Instead, she nodded.

"See to it," she ordered. The freighters from the Theocracy would have to be inspected carefully, *very* carefully. Who knew what they might be carrying? "And get some sleep too."

"I'll sleep when I'm dead," Davidson said. He headed for the hatch, which hissed open in front of him. "Goodnight, Captain."

The hatch hissed closed behind him.

"I'll write the reports," the XO said. He looked as though he was on the verge of saying something himself, then thought better of it. "Please make sure you get some sleep."

"I will," Kat promised. She watched him leave the room, then sighed. "But I don't know if I'll have time to sleep."

CHAPTER SIXTEEN

The dull red star had no name, only a catalogue number. It had been visited once, according to the files, by a UN survey team that hadn't spent any longer than necessary in the system, then simply left alone until an RV point had been required for transhipment between the Commonwealth and the Theocracy. The otherwise useless star system had seemed a perfect place for ships from both sides to meet with nothing at stake.

Kat studied the system display, feeling more than a little boredom. There was *nothing* in the system, not even a comet or a handful of asteroids. And the Theocratic ships were late. She settled back in her command chair, reaching for her private terminal, then paused as an alarm sounded. Moments later, a blue-green icon flashed up on the display.

"One vortex detected, Captain," Roach said. "I'm picking up seven freighters and one starship of unknown design. Mass readings suggest a light cruiser."

Kat leaned forward, interested, as the Theocratic ships spilled out of the vortex. The freighters looked practically identical to other designs used all over the galaxy, but the light cruiser looked as though it only carried energy weapons instead of a mixture of energy weapons and missile tubes. She could see some advantages in the design, yet she knew the enemy ship would be vulnerable to a missile-armed attacker engaging from outside her own range.

She might have been designed to serve as a point defense cruiser, Kat mused, thoughtfully. *It would make a certain kind of sense.*

"We're being scanned," Roach warned. The display washed red as the enemy sensors caught sight of *Lightning* and her convoy. "They have a solid lock on our hull."

"Yellow alert," Kat ordered. The Theocratic ships would have to come a great deal closer if they wanted to catch her by surprise. "Send them our IFF codes."

There was a long pause. "They're requesting an open channel," Ross reported as the enemy ships came closer. "Captain?"

"Open channel," Kat ordered. She cleared her throat. "This is Captain Falcone of HMS *Lightning*."

Twenty seconds passed before the reply arrived. A grim-faced man appeared in front of her, wearing a green uniform covered in gold braid and unfamiliar writing. He wore a green skullcap on his head, his beard trimmed into a neat goatee. A beard meant something among the Theocracy, Kat recalled, although she couldn't remember what. Was it devotion or something else?

"I am Captain Zaid of the *Faithful Companion*," he grated. He sounded coldly furious, although there was no way to tell why he was annoyed. "Transmit your manifests now."

Kat kept her face impassive with an effort. "Transmit the manifests," she ordered, then turned her attention back to the Theocratic officer. "Transmit your own manifests."

There was a long pause as both sides analyzed the manifests against what they'd been promised. "Everything appears to be in order," Captain Zaid said, reluctantly. "We will transfer our freighters to your command."

"Picking up data packets from the freighters," Ross injected. "Everything seems to be in order."

"We will transfer ours to you," Kat said, feeling a moment of sympathy for the merchantmen. They would be going into Theocratic space, where they would be at the mercy of the Theocrats and their clerics. "And thank you for your time."

Captain Zaid's face twitched, then his image vanished from the display. Kat watched, feeling an odd tingle of unease as the Theocratic starship opened a vortex, then ordered the Commonwealth freighters through the tear in space-time. As soon as the last of the freighters were through, the warship followed, departing without even a final message. It was oddly rude, Kat noted, as if Captain Zaid hadn't wanted to talk to her any more than strictly necessary.

"He probably had someone looking over his shoulder," the XO muttered, so quietly that only Kat could hear. "They wouldn't risk allowing him to be *friendly*."

Kat nodded, sourly. "Open a vortex into hyperspace," she ordered. "Order the freighters to proceed into hyperspace, then take us in after them."

She looked up at the XO. "You'll have to search their ships, one by one," she said. "Good luck."

"Thank you, Captain," the XO said. "I'll let you know what I find."

The first two freighters were normal, William was surprised to discover, insofar as anything was normal on a Theocratic starship. There was a captain and crew, but there was also a cleric whose job seemed to be keeping an eye on the crewmen for impure thoughts. He insisted on staying with the crew at all times, refusing to allow them to be interviewed in private by the Marines—and the crew themselves seemed reluctant to be interviewed without him. They'd need his testimony, William suspected, to prove they hadn't said anything they shouldn't to the infidels.

But it was the third freighter that set alarm bells ringing at the back of his head. It was simply too good. He was used to freighter ships pushing the margins, not freighter ships where everything was shipshape and Bristol fashion. The crew looked far too good to be merchantmen, while the captain didn't even seem outraged at having outsiders tramping through his ship. And *that* was far from normal.

"Search this ship *thoroughly*," he ordered, finally. "And check every last item against the manifest."

Captain Junayd looked . . . placid. His cleric looked absolutely furious, but the captain looked completely unconcerned. The alarm bells grew louder. William had *never* met a freighter commander who hadn't resented having Marines boarding his ship and poking through his hold. And yet this commander didn't seem to care. Spitefully, William ordered the vessel's cabins searched too. But that didn't provoke any reaction either.

"As you can see, we have nothing to hide," Junayd said an hour later. He seemed far too amused at William's discomposure. "The ship is clean."

"So it would seem," William agreed. "But we are far from finished."

He looked down as the engineering crew inspected the freighter's control systems and—finally—found something out of place. The vessel's drives and shields were civilian grade, no more capable than anything from the Commonwealth, but her sensors were top-of-the-line military gear. Her passive sensors were on a par with *Lightning*'s, the engineers reported, while her active sensors might actually be better. Now that they had a clue, the engineers pushed harder and reported that there was a whole secondary computer network concealed within the hull.

The ship looked like a harmless merchantman, William concluded, but she was a spy.

At his command, five armored marines came onto the bridge. "I'm afraid we will be taking you and your ship into custody," William said. "I would ask you not to do anything stupid."

Captain Junayd, for the first time, showed a hint of something other than amusement. "We have been cleared to deliver our cargo to Cadiz," he said, his voice darkening. "To hold us is a breach of the trade agreement between the Theocracy and the Commonwealth. It will have the most unpleasant repercussions for your career."

"I'll take that chance," William said. He checked the crew manifest, quickly. There were seventy men on the ship, thirty more than any halfway competent crew needed to operate the vessel. What were *they* doing on the ship? "You and your crew can be held in reasonable comfort onboard my vessel or you can be held in stasis."

The cleric swore vilely in a language William didn't recognize. There were few samples of the language the Theocracy used, mainly because their personnel always used English when talking to outsiders, but it didn't sound pleasant. Captain Junayd gave him a sharp look, somehow shutting the cleric up instantly. *That* was interesting. None of the other freighter commanders had shown anything like that degree of control over their watchdogs.

"We will file a formal protest, of course," Junayd said. "But as long as you're bringing my vessel to Cadiz anyway, we will be happy to accept quarters of reasonable comfort."

"Of course," William agreed. He looked round the bridge for a long moment, then back at the Theocratic officer. He was *sure* he was looking at a naval officer, not a civilian merchantman. "I suggest you order your crew to behave themselves. They are under our jurisdiction now."

"I took the ship's sensor system apart, piece by piece," Lynn reported four hours later. He sounded tired but grimly amused. "She doesn't have a lick of justification for such an elaborate sensor suite, Captain."

Kat nodded, slowly. Taking a Theocratic ship, even a freighter, into custody would raise eyebrows right across the Commonwealth. There would be questions asked, both by Admiral Morrison and in Parliament. The evidence had to be gathered completely by the book, she knew, or someone would move to dismiss it as tainted. Luckily everything seemed to be in place.

"If she entered the Cadiz System," she mused, "she would be able to determine much about 7th Fleet purely from her passive sensors."

"Yes, Captain," Lynn agreed. "The suite is really quite elaborate. They'd be able to intercept radio traffic and monitor the situation on the ground, as well as record the fleet's emissions. And the only way to find it was to carry out a full search and examination of the ship."

"Which you did," Kat said, nodding to the XO. "What tipped you off?"

"The crew was just too good," the XO said. "Most freighter crews are . . . well, not sloppy, but lax. They cut corners, don't update records, wear their uniforms poorly if they wear them at all, all bad habits we try to keep out of the military. This crew was far too good to be true."

"Better than you might think," Davidson put in. His voice was very cold. "You noticed there were more crewmen than strictly necessary?"

The XO nodded, impatiently.

"I watched some of them through sensors as they filed into the holding cell," Davidson said grimly. "I'd bet good money they're special forces, *not* regular crewmen. There's something about their cocky attitude that is familiar."

"Theocracy marines?" Lynn asked. "Are they better than you?"

"Of course not," Davidson huffed. He looked at Kat, his eyes worried. "Those guys are definitely trained soldiers, Captain. Give them weapons and armor and they'd be able to cause one hell of a mess on Cadiz."

"Or onboard ship," the XO said. "We do have them under close guard?"

"Yes," Davidson said. "But they have to be watched carefully at all times."

Kat rubbed her forehead. "And the other freighters?"

"We've searched two additional freighters," the XO said. "They seemed normal, as far as we could tell, but we have four more to go."

"It's unlikely there will be more than one spy ship," Davidson commented. "They wouldn't want to heighten the chances of detection."

The XO leaned forward. "And what do we do with our new prisoners?"

Kat had given the matter some thought. "We have to take them to Cadiz, along with their ship," she said. Regulations admitted of no ambiguity in such matters. "Admiral Morrison will have to decide their fate. In any case . . ."

She took a breath. "We have legal authority to hold them for questioning," she added. "And we have precedent on our side. The Theocracy has held some of our crews for quite intensive questioning in the past."

"They're not going to like that," Davidson rumbled.

"Tough," Kat said. "If they want to hold our crews, we can hold theirs."

"Yes, Captain," the XO said.

"But it could cause a diplomatic incident," Davidson cautioned. "We could have made a fuss over them holding our crews, but we didn't."

Kat muttered a curse under her breath. The bigger shipping lines had been interested—very interested—in opening links to the Theocracy. They'd had visions of a colossal new market opening up in front of them, which had pushed them to ignore any reports of crews being mistreated or threatened with prosecution under Theocratic law. She sighed, inwardly. Her father, at least, should have known better. Trading was always unstable when one party felt free to ignore civilized convention at its leisure.

Evict the crews if you like, she thought. *But holding them for crimes that aren't crimes where they come from opens a dangerous set of precedents.*

She pushed the thought to one side and forced herself to smile. "Search the rest of the freighters, then report back to me when you're done," she ordered. "I'll be writing my own report."

"Aye, Captain," the XO said.

Kat watched him go, then keyed her console, accessing the live feed from the makeshift cells. She'd spent enough time with Davidson to recognize soldiers as well and she had to admit he had a point. The Theocracy crewmen didn't *look* like crewmen. They had the finely honed confidence of men who knew they were the best of the best, just like Davidson and the other marines she'd met. And there were definitely too many of them to man the freighter.

She checked the manifest again. The crew manifest had only been submitted upon request, a slip that would probably have gone unnoticed under other circumstances. Who would have thought anything of a sloppy civilian crew? But if the Theocracy had been lucky, the soldiers could have been landed on Cadiz without anything counting them in and then counting them out again. Even now, they could walk off ship and make their way to the local guild house, then vanish after their mothership had left the system. It wasn't as if anyone would be surprised to see a Theocracy freighter shedding crewmen.

Spies, she thought darkly. But she knew it had been a risky trick for the Theocracy to try to pull. *They took a blatant risk in sending a spy ship into our space.*

The thought didn't bring her any comfort. There was no way to know how many *other* ships might have been slipped through as part of the regular convoys. Or, for that matter, if there were spy ships that *weren't* part of the convoys. Perhaps the captain and her crew had been *meant* to find this one, just to convince them that they had caught all of the spies. But they might be wrong.

And if they're sending spy ships now, they must be preparing their attack, she concluded. It might be too late to save 7th Fleet. *Checking their figures before they launch a final assault.*

She shuddered. How long would it take her father to arrange for the IG to make a visit to Cadiz? Weeks, perhaps months. Admiral Morrison had some damn good political cover. It might well be too late. And if that was the case . . .

She shuddered again. Cadiz wasn't vital, but 7th Fleet was largely irreplaceable in less than a year. And the war might be lost along with it.

◆ ◆ ◆

"That filthy unbelieving infidel," the cleric thundered. "How dare he lay his hands on . . . ?"

"Enough," Admiral Junayd said. There were times when he felt that clerics had their brains—or at least their common sense—removed before they were permitted to grow the unkempt beards that marked them as keepers of religious orthodoxy. "You never know who might be listening."

The cleric shut up, at once. Junayd allowed himself a tight smile and then lay back on the bunk. As prison cells went, it was remarkably comfortable. The infidels hadn't even broken out truth drugs or torture instruments, both of which would have been used by the Inquisition back home. It wouldn't have helped—his crew all had suicide implants to prevent them from talking—but it did suggest the infidels weren't taking the threat very seriously. In their place, Junayd would have destroyed his own ship to make sure there was no chance of any intelligence getting back home and sworn blind it had been a terrible accident.

He thought rapidly. Flying into enemy space himself had been a risk, he knew, but it had been necessary. It was difficult, if not impossible, to trust reports from spies, no matter how well the agents had covered their tracks. There was just too much temptation for the spies to send the reports they thought their superiors wanted to hear. But who would have thought the Commonwealth had finally decided to start giving freighters more than a cursory inspection before clearing them to dock at Cadiz? Really, it was quite surprising they'd worked up the nerve.

The cleric mumbled prayers to himself, clearly unsure what was about to happen. Junayd kept his thoughts to himself. It was unlikely the Commonwealth would detain them for long, unless they somehow figured out just who he was. And if they had . . . he thought briefly of the suicide implants, then sighed. He didn't want to die, but he didn't fear death. God was waiting for him in His Heaven.

He knew what would happen to a spy ship captured within Theocratic space. The crew would be interrogated, the technicians trying to beat the suicide implants, while the ship itself would be carefully dismantled. Did the Commonwealth have the nerve to kill him and his crew? It was possible, but the trade links the Theocracy had dangled in front of their greedy corporations would mediate against it. They wouldn't want to give up the chance to make money, even if it meant accepting humiliation after humiliation. Really! It was unbelievable just how much the Commonwealth's government was prepared to swallow in exchange for trade links and a few other concessions.

But he knew how they thought. Money talked; common sense walked. Everything had a price, even religious fervor. It was insulting to think that someone—anyone—believed the Theocracy would surrender its principles for *money*. But as long as the infidels believed they could manage the Theocracy, the Theocracy would have all the time in the universe to prepare. Even if Junayd didn't return home, he knew, the attack would still go ahead.

And the Commonwealth's rich worlds and industrial base would be theirs for the taking.

CHAPTER SEVENTEEN

Duke Lucas Falcone disliked the houses of Parliament. As a veteran of the political wars that shaped Tyre's government, he knew better than most that 90 percent of activity in Parliament was meaningless. Most political decisions were made after careful backroom discussions, well away from the media, and then presented to Parliament as a done deal. If the discussions were handled properly, there was little meaningful pushback from His Majesty's Loyal Opposition. They benefited from the end result as much as the government.

He silently cursed the planet's founders under his breath as he took his seat and started to review his briefing notes. They had wanted to ensure that Tyre's political system grew and changed as the planet itself changed, knowing that taxation without representation was sure to lead to an eventual revolt and civil war. But with the House of Lords and the king controlling much of the planet's wealth—and thus power—the House of Commons had become more of a talking shop than its creators had envisaged. Anyone driven enough to become successful could simply take out a patent of nobility and advance to the House of Lords.

The chamber filled slowly as lords, MPs, and reporters slid into the room and found their seats. Lucas's implants matched names to faces, although he didn't need the data to identify the true movers and shakers of the Commonwealth. Others, elected on platforms that failed to match any of the political parties currently in existence, were strangers to him. They simply didn't command enough of the vote, let alone political power, to be important. The hell of it, he knew, was that some of them knew it. Their showmanship did nothing more than waste time and amuse the reporters.

"This session will come to order," the speaker said, the sound field automatically projecting his voice to every corner of the room. "The doors will now close."

A dull thud echoed through the chamber as the doors closed with majestic grandeur. Lucas kept his face impassive with an effort. The designers of the chamber—and many of the chamber's traditions—had wanted to create a sense of dignity, of timeless power and majesty, but he had a feeling they'd failed. There was no sense of forward thinking, merely staunch conservatism. The only advantage to the whole system, he'd decided long ago, was that anyone trying to be fashionably late would be barred from the chamber, unable to enter or cast a vote. A handful of MPs had lost their jobs over failing to vote, recalled and sacked by their constituents. It never failed to amuse him.

The party whips moved through the chamber, noting attendance as the dignitaries settled down. There was no need for the whips, Lucas knew, but their act was tradition too, warning any MP considering independent action that his or her party was watching. It wasn't unknown for MPs to cross the chamber from government to opposition, yet there was always a high price tag. Only the most principled—or confident—MP would risk the recall election that would automatically be called if he or she switched party allegiance. Still, for some, the gamble paid off.

"We are called to debate the issue of Cadiz Naval Base," the speaker said. There was no sense of surprise in the chamber. Anyone who was anyone had sources within the government, sources that would have informed them of the debate's subject, even though it hadn't been officially announced. "The Honorable Eustace Perivale is called to speak."

Lucas allowed himself a tight smile as faces turned in his direction. Perivale was *his* creature, an MP who had sold his soul and his vote to the Falcone Consortium in exchange for money and political backing. There would be no doubt among the movers and shakers who had organized the debate, even though nothing—again—had been said officially. It was just another part of the political game.

"Mr. Speaker, Members of Parliament, My Lords and Ladies," Perivale said. He didn't look impressive—like most MPs who aimed for an air of dignity he didn't have the wealth or self-confidence to pull off—but he had a fine speaking voice. "Cadiz Naval Base is one of the most vital facilities in the Commonwealth. It is required to support naval operations, provide convoy escorts, and defend the border. But I have received evidence that the base has been allowed to fall into disrepair."

The speaker keyed his switch. "I invoke parliamentary rights," he said. "The house will now go into closed session."

Politics, Lucas thought, as the reporters were shooed from the room. There would be rumors that something was badly wrong on Cadiz now, but no specific details. It would force the government to do something without provoking panic or encouraging the Theocracy to jump now. Or so he hoped.

Perivale waited until the chamber fell silent again, then continued. "The evidence suggests that the base is no longer capable of maintaining operations," he said. "The 7th Fleet is not in a better state. Furthermore, there are strong suggestions that evidence of incompetence, even wrongdoing, has been actively suppressed."

There was a low buzz of chatter from the benches and, more importantly, dozens of private encrypted signals sent from MP to MP. Lucas watched, keeping his face impassive, as the loyalists spoke urgently to the prime minister, who didn't look pleased. He might be the leader of the strongest political party—and a loyal servant of the king—but he didn't have the power to change anything unless the rest of the Commons backed him. And *that* was unlikely.

Lucas wanted to sigh, but kept the expression to himself. The true problem with politics at such a high level was that everything was interrelated. Admiral Morrison's posting to Cadiz had been part of an elaborate quid pro quo, giving several parties that had nothing else in common incentive to maintain the status quo. And he wasn't entirely sure who among the aristocracy was pushing it. Someone who wasn't interested in Cadiz—*that* was a given—or thought there was no prospect of war breaking out. But there were quite a few aristocrats with the combination of power and political beliefs to make the conspiracy work.

The prime minister rose to his feet. "My Honorable Friend wishes you to believe the situation on Cadiz is out of control," he said. "But anyone should know that the task of integrating Cadiz into the Commonwealth, a task undertaken at the behest of a majority of the house, will be a long and difficult one. Immediate success was never likely, nor was it expected."

Lucas didn't quite resist the urge to roll his eyes like his daughter. The prime minister's retort answered nothing. Bland generalities rather than specific details. He *must* be rattled, he noted, with a hint of amusement. Or someone higher up the food chain had been working on him. Just who, he asked himself again, had put Admiral Morrison's name forward for command of Cadiz?

"With respect, Prime Minister," Perivale said, "that answer is far from sufficient. We are not talking about the need to provide security on the planet's surface, but the condition of the naval base and fleet charged with defending our borders. The fleet is simply incapable of carrying out its duties."

This time, the buzz of chatter was louder. Lucas watched, quietly monitoring the signal bursts, trying to determine who would jump what way. The decision to annex Cadiz had almost torn the Commonwealth apart, he knew; there were MPs who had no intention of allowing any further annexations . . . or anything that might be deemed provocative. In their world, the Theocracy was an innocent victim of the Commonwealth's paranoia. And besides, why would anyone want to fight a full-scale war? There were enough resources in space for everyone.

But that assumes the Theocracy follows the same logic as ourselves, Lucas thought, grimly. *And everything we've seen suggests they don't.*

He shivered. The Believers had been exiled from Earth. They had been weak; their enemies had been strong. Lucas could understand why they would seek to take control of as much space as possible, quite apart from their duty to spread their religion. They wouldn't want to be weak again.

And then there was the constant stream of refugees . . . and missionaries. It boded ill for the future.

On the floor, tempers were running high. The prime minister was trying valiantly to defend the situation, while the Leader of the Opposition was being goaded into pushing for an independent parliamentary investigation of the situation. *That* would be a mistake, Lucas knew; independent parliamentary investigations tended to become political very quickly. But it would provide political cover if someone wanted to remove Admiral Morrison, then swear blind they'd never heard of him.

However it would also be used to undermine the occupation of Cadiz itself. There was a small but substantial group that wanted to abandon Cadiz, along with the investments the Commonwealth had made in the system. A parliamentary investigation would give them ammunition to aim at the government, perhaps even seduce other MPs and lords to their side. And then the base might simply be abandoned . . .

He sighed. *Politics.*

"Please be seated," the speaker said. The noise-cancelling field silenced the rest of the MPs, who glowered at the speaker before resuming their seats. "I believe it would be better for us to take a break. We will reconvene in two hours."

Lucas nodded, then stood and followed the rest of the lords as they made their way to the restroom. There would be a chance for a drink, something to eat, and some political scheming . . . or maybe not. He stopped as a new message blinked up in his implants, inviting him to the Royal Palace. His majesty had clearly been monitoring the whole debate. Lucas hesitated, thinking hard, and then sent back a brief acknowledgement. It was time he spoke to the king.

The Royal Palace looked almost undefended, Lucas noted, as he strode through the garden path leading from the houses of Parliament to the glowing structure. It was built of white marble, just like the rest of the city, reflecting the sunlight into his eyes. And yet he happened to know that successive monarchs had worked armaments and shields into the building until it was almost as tough as a planetary defense center.

He sighed inwardly as he passed through the security screen and walked into the palace, where the king's aide—a middle-aged woman with a hatchet face—met him and led the way up the stairs. Tyre had originally been built by corporate families, families who had councils to elect the person who would succeed the previous CEO . . . and put limits on his power, if necessary. Combined with an open invitation to anyone successful to join the nobility, it helped ensure that the people in charge had a firm grip on reality. But the Royal Family passed inheritance—and the bulk of their power—down a strict line of succession. One of his nightmares was an incompetent monarch rising to power.

The king is not incompetent, he told himself as he was shown into the private audience chamber. *He is merely young*.

"Your Grace," King Hadrian said. "Thank you for coming."

"It was my pleasure," Lucas said as he took a seat. There was little formality in the private chambers, thankfully. "It has been far too long since we spoke."

The king smiled, although it didn't touch his eyes. Lucas sighed inwardly again. The king was barely two years older than Kat, yet he had inherited far more wealth and power than anyone else in the Commonwealth. He was young, with short dark hair and darker eyes, and a drive to match his father that needed to be tempered. But then his father had built the Commonwealth and started the buildup against the Theocracy. It would be hard for anyone to live up to such a man.

He wouldn't have succeeded me, Lucas thought coldly. *The family wouldn't have accepted someone with so little experience.*

"Perivale made an impressive speech," the king said. "How much of it did you write for him?"

"Enough of it," Lucas said. He didn't bother to deny his involvement. The king and his advisors would have known before Perivale opened his mouth. "The situation on Cadiz is growing dire."

Lucas took a breath. "Admiral Morrison needs to be removed now," he added. "Whatever he's good for, Your Majesty, it isn't command of a fleet base on the brink of war."

"Politics," the king said. There was a bitter tone in his voice. "Accepting Admiral Morrison as the fleet base's CO was the price we paid for getting the last naval budget through Parliament."

"Politics be damned," Lucas said evenly.

"They're very keen to prevent another Cadiz," the king pointed out. "They don't see the real danger."

Lucas wasn't too surprised. The hell of it was that there were good arguments against annexing worlds that didn't *want* to be annexed. If nothing else, occupying them was a steady drain on the Commonwealth's resources. Admiral Morrison could be relied upon to do nothing, if that was what they wanted. He certainly wouldn't invade Theocratic space on his own authority. But what would he do if the Theocracy attacked?

"Then we need to sideline Morrison," Lucas said. There were plenty of ways to remove someone from effective power while leaving them with an impressive job title. He'd used them himself on members of the family who didn't deserve to wield power. "Separate his command responsibilities. Put someone else in command of 7th Fleet, but leave Morrison in an oversight role."

"They'd resist any change in the status quo," the king said. "We couldn't undermine Morrison's position without risking a political confrontation."

"Some confrontations have to be fought," Lucas said. "And *your* position can't be undermined so easily."

"Their position can," the king said. "They will fight tooth and nail to keep Morrison in command."

"Then find something you can offer them in exchange for cutting Morrison loose," Lucas snapped. "He has to *go*!"

But he knew it wouldn't be easy. Political patronage was a fact of life. Any aristocrat worthy of the name had a whole string of clients who accepted his money and political support in exchange for service. Admiral Morrison had reached high office through being a client of someone much more powerful, but his very position gave him influence over his patron. If nothing else, cutting Morrison loose would damage his patron's reputation for defending his clients, making it harder to attract new ones in the future.

Not for the first time, he cursed the system under his breath. Push Morrison too hard and the whole system might come tumbling down. And the Theocracy would be glad to take advantage of the political chaos. If Kat was correct and they were backing the raiders, they had to be almost ready to jump. They wouldn't risk alerting the Commonwealth until it was too late to matter.

They could be crossing the border now, he thought. *Cadiz might already be under attack.*

"We need to take steps," he said instead. "Something to ensure we can replace Morrison quickly, if war breaks out."

The king nodded. "I intend to dispatch Admiral Christian and 6th Fleet to backstop 7th Fleet," he said. "The fleet movement will be kept classified, but they'll be in position to reinforce Cadiz if necessary. I'll add sealed orders for Christian too. If the war begins, he is to relieve Morrison without further ado."

Lucas eyed him, feeling an odd flicker of suspicion. Had the king, who *was* Commander-in-Chief of the Navy, planned for redeployment all along? Or had he made it up on the spot?

"It may be impossible to save Cadiz," the king added. "In that case, we will fall back and hold the line elsewhere."

"You've been giving this some thought," Lucas observed. The king had wanted a naval career, but the shortage of heirs had ensured he would never be allowed to serve. "Have you been talking to the Admiralty?"

"Yes," the king said flatly. He leaned forward. "I will need your assistance to get this through the Defense Committee," he added. "We dare not take it to Parliament."

"Very well," Lucas said. The king was right . . . but Lucas was unable to shed the feeling that he'd been manipulated. "But we do need to limit Morrison's ability to do harm."

"Tricky," the king observed. "Do you have any ideas?"

"We could always recall him for consultations," Lucas said reluctantly. "There are some matters that can't be discussed over StarCom."

"True," the king agreed, "but his patrons would smell a rat."

Lucas shook his head in disbelief. Had anyone, the king's father included, realized that by annexing Cadiz they would cause the entire political system to gridlock? There was just too much opposition to *any* form of adventurism to allow Admiral Morrison to be removed. Lucas could understand their point, particularly after Cadiz had been such a dismal failure. But what would happen if it was the *Theocracy* who started the war?

"I'll speak to some of them," he said. "Perhaps we can find something to trade in exchange for kicking Morrison upstairs—and into somewhere harmless."

"Good luck," the king said. "And give your daughter my best wishes."

Lucas wasn't surprised the king knew who'd contacted him. No one would send such a damaging—and uncompromising—report back home unless they were assured of political cover. Kat was almost certainly the only person at Cadiz who would, even though it might cost her a career she'd worked hard to build. Anyone who checked the fleet lists would find her name and look no further.

"Yes, Your Majesty," he said. He'd once hoped that Kat would be one of the king's playmates, but it hadn't worked out. The prince, like most boys before adolescence, had been more interested in spending time with his male friends. "I'll give her your good wishes."

CHAPTER EIGHTEEN

"You *released* the spy ship?"

Kat stared at Admiral Morrison in absolute disbelief, the two sitting in his office. She had thought herself prepared for anything, from a lecture on telling tales to her father to a demand she turn in her command codes, badge, and uniform. She'd spent the return flight telling herself that she could survive if she had to fall back on her trust fund. Perhaps she could buy herself a starship and set out as an independent trader. But she had never considered the admiral simply letting the spies *go*.

She caught her breath. "Admiral," she said, "we caught them red-handed!"

"A modern sensor suite doesn't make them spies," Admiral Morrison said with unaccustomed firmness. "They were hardly crammed full of weapons."

Kat's eyes narrowed. "*Intelligence* is a weapon, Admiral," she said. "Why did you release them?"

"The trade guilds were furious," Admiral Morrison said. "I had complaints coming in to my office almost as soon as you arrived. I skimmed the evidence, decided you had overreacted, and ordered the ship released."

"You released them because the traders complained," Kat said. She had to fight to keep her voice under control. "Admiral, that was *not* a trading ship."

"You should know better than I just how many . . . non-standard trading ships there are along the border," the admiral said. "There are quite a few with military-grade gear."

"But a sensor suite that is better than anything generally available?" Kat demanded. "And far more crew than they need to run the ship?"

She shivered. Having enemy commandos onboard her vessel, even unarmed and under heavy guard, had been a nightmare. It had been a relief to reach Cadiz and transfer them to the planet's security forces. She should have known it wouldn't last.

"Trade with the Theocracy brings a considerable amount of money to this planet," Morrison said. "The Occupation Government was most upset. They actually wanted me to formally censure you for your . . . overreaction."

He gave her a smile that was probably meant to be reassuring. It came off as condescending.

"I understand how hard it can be to avoid letting go of one's first impressions," he continued smoothly. "My first glance at the records didn't leave me with a good taste in my mouth either. But, upon mature reflection, I decided there was simply not enough evidence to hold them against their will. There would be . . . diplomatic repercussions."

"The Theocracy is unlikely to want to draw attention to their spy ship," Kat snapped. She rather suspected the crew would simply have been abandoned to their fate. "And the trade guilds don't make *that* much money . . ."

"They have quite a few links to corporations back home," the admiral said. He gave her a wintery smile. "Your father might not be pleased to get a report that his daughter had damaged his investment."

Kat thought rapidly. Did the admiral know she'd sent a report to Tyre? It didn't sound like it—and the security codes should have prevented the message from being intercepted. Or had he set out to lure her into a false sense of security? There was no way to tell.

"My father is not part of this discussion," she said finally. "I have my duties as a naval officer . . ."

"You have a duty to obey orders," the admiral countered. "In this case, the evidence has been reviewed and found to be lacking. We cannot justify holding on to the freighter. I will not put a note in your file about the incident, Captain, but I would advise you to be careful in the future."

Kat looked past him, out the window. In the distance, a plume of smoke was rising into the air while a pair of helicopters flew overhead. The insurgency was alive and well, even in Gibraltar itself. Just how much worse would it become, she asked herself, if the commandos she'd captured added their skills to the mix? And were they the first ones to make it to the surface?

I should have wiped their computers, even destroyed the cores, she thought. Davidson *had* suggested it, which would have rendered the ship completely useless without a major refurbishment, but she'd wanted to preserve the evidence. There would be no chance to do it in the future either, not now that the charges had been formally dropped. The spy ship could collect her intelligence at leisure and then make her way back to the Theocracy. Somehow, Kat doubted she would be allowed to escort the next convoy.

"Yes, Admiral," she said, finally.

"Now, onto more pleasant matters," Morrison said. "I am hosting another party in four days, Captain, and I would like you to attend."

Kat fought down the urge to grind her teeth. She *hated* parties; she'd always hated them, particularly after she'd realized that her birthday parties were a chance for her parents to network rather than dote on their daughter. And who could attend parties when war was looming in the distance? The mere presence of the spy ship suggested the Theocracy was merely making sure of its figures before launching the attack.

"This will be a good opportunity for you to meet your fellow commanding officers," the admiral continued, unaware of her inner turmoil. "And there are quite a few others who would like to meet with you as well."

I'm still not in a position to influence my father, Kat thought. But she knew saying it out loud would be pointless.

She forced herself to think logically. The admiral was right about one thing, at least. It *would* be a chance to meet the other commanding officers and take their measure. None of the reports sounded promising, but maybe things could be better in person. She could talk to them, even try to warn them about the oncoming storm. Perhaps they would listen . . .

Or perhaps they will see me as someone promoted ahead of her competence, she thought bitterly. *And they won't listen to me.*

"I'll attend," she said, finally.

"Splendid," the admiral said. "I'll have my society aide get in touch with your steward about dresses and suchlike. It's completely informal, Captain. We wouldn't want anyone allowing their rank to get in the way of pleasure, would we?"

Kat had to draw on her implants to keep her face still. Candy had spent hours trying to play dress up with Kat, even after they had both reached their majority. She *hated* playing dress up as well. If there was one advantage to naval dress uniforms, which were universally hated too, it was that no one could try to outshine everyone else. It wasn't something anyone could say of society balls. If two different women happened to wear the same dress, it could start a feud that would last for years.

"Yes, Admiral," she grated. She would have to give her steward some very precise instructions. Some of the dresses society butterflies had been known to wear in public barely covered anything. She was damned if she'd be talking to her fellow commanders while looking like a whore. "I look forward to it."

There was a flash of light in the distance, followed by a fireball rising up into the sky. Kat shook her head, feeling a moment of pity for everyone on the surface caught between the insurgents and the Commonwealth military. If half of the reports Davidson had forwarded to her were accurate, the Commonwealth was definitely losing control over its long-serving soldiers. The number of "incidents" was on the rise.

And those are only the ones we know about, she thought. *How many more haven't been recorded, let alone investigated and punished?*

The admiral was speaking. Kat winced, inwardly. She'd distracted herself.

"I'm sorry, Admiral," she said. "I was staring at the blast."

"You get used to them," the admiral said. "I was suggesting you spend some time in the facilities here. They're designed for senior officers."

Kat wanted to go back to *Lightning*, but she knew she should have a look round the government complex. Who knew when she'd have another chance?

"It would be my pleasure," she said finally. "Your aide can escort me."

The admiral nodded, then summoned Commander Jeannette Macintyre and issued orders, ending with a wink. Kat sensed trouble long before Commander Macintyre escorted her out of the admiral's office and down a long flight of stairs to a restaurant that wouldn't have been too out of place on Tyre itself. Kat couldn't help being reminded of the Hotel Magnificent; the waiters looked snooty, the customers looked rich . . . and half the tables were empty.

"I've already eaten," Kat said when Macintyre started to steer her towards a table. "I'd just like to see the rest of the complex."

It was larger than she'd realized, Kat discovered, as Macintyre gave her a short tour. And it was also surprisingly luxurious. There were two swimming pools—one for enlisted, the other for senior officers and bureaucrats—both of which seemed to be incredibly busy. Behind them, there were three bars, again separated by social class, and a large gym. It was better equipped than the compartment on *Thunderous*—or *Lightning*.

"Most of the workers here can't leave the complex," Macintyre explained. "There's no shore leave, not even a brief trip to the spaceport. They have to find their entertainment here."

Kat shook her head in disbelief. She knew a little about funding, thanks to her father, and she had a sneaking suspicion that the bureaucrats had spent more than they should have had available to decorate their living quarters. The Commonwealth had poured a vast amount of money into Cadiz, but where had half the money gone? She knew, all too well, that the bureaucrats had to spend their entire budget or it would be cut. If they hadn't been able to spend it on Cadiz, had they spent it on themselves?

Another flash of light in the air caught her attention. "That's a mortar shell," Macintyre explained, utterly unperturbed. "We shoot them down before they can strike the complex, vaporizing the bastards. Everyone loves seeing them explode."

Kat heard the sound of guns, firing from the other side of the complex. "And those?"

"Firing back at the bastards," Macintyre said. "We try to kill as many mortar crews as possible."

"I see," Kat said.

Macintyre leaned forward. "Would you like some companionship?"

Kat felt herself flush. She'd never really explored the brothels near Piker's Peak, even though they catered to both male and female customers. It shouldn't really have surprised her that there was a brothel attached to Government House. The admiral would probably have ordered one if it hadn't been there already. But they had never really been her style.

"I think I would like to go back to my ship," she said instead. "There's nothing for me here."

Commander Macintyre offered no objection, somewhat to Kat's surprise. Instead, the aide just called the security commander and arranged for a convoy to escort Kat back to the spaceport. Kat wasn't surprised—but more than a little alarmed—to discover that shuttles weren't allowed to land in the complex or even overfly the city. It was clear that the situation on the ground was actively degrading, far worse than any of the reports suggested. She couldn't help imagining what would happen if the Commonwealth ever lost control of the high orbitals. It would be a nightmare.

"The admiral is a busy man," Macintyre said, apologetically. "He will have more time for you in the future."

Kat kept her opinion of that to herself. The less time the admiral had for her, the better. She silently composed a second report to her father as they waited for the escort, then climbed into the small tank and took her seat. This time, there was no transparent window allowing her to see out into the city. All she could do was sit and wait for the vehicle to reach the spaceport, hearing from time to time bullets pinging off the armor. It was clear the insurgents weren't afraid to challenge the occupation force directly.

They're wearing us down, she thought, morbidly. The occupation force had powered armor and access to the best medical treatment in the galaxy, but there was still a steady stream of casualties heading back home. If it grew worse, she suspected, there would be more urgent questions asked in Parliament, perhaps even widespread protests against the war. It hadn't happened before, but Cadiz was a special case. There wasn't even a glimmer of light at the end of the tunnel.

Kat let out a sigh of relief when they reached the spaceport and the hatch opened, allowing her to scramble out onto the tarmac. She wasn't claustrophobic—it was impossible to serve in the Navy if one was scared of tight places—but she had disliked being in the vehicle intensely. It probably wouldn't have been any better if she'd been able to see outside, knowing bullets and homemade rockets would be hurled in her direction. She walked towards the shuttle, then climbed through the hatch and ordered the pilot to take her back into space. It would be a relief to be away from the planet's surface.

And if it can do this to me, she thought grimly, *what does it do to someone who spends months here?*

She called the XO and Davidson as soon as the shuttle docked, inviting them both to her Ready Room. As soon as they arrived, she explained—briefly—what the admiral had done to the spy ship. Both of them reacted with horror, but there was nothing they could do. The spy ship had been released and there might not be a chance to search it again, after she left Cadiz.

"The admiral isn't interested in preparing for war," Kat said. She'd checked the message buffer. Her father hadn't replied. "And it might take too long for any new orders to arrive from Tyre."

The XO leaned forward. "Your father can't do anything?"

"My father isn't all-powerful," Kat pointed out. "Someone is backing Admiral Morrison and that someone will have to be . . . dissuaded. It's never easy when so many different political personalities are involved."

She ran her hand through her blond hair. "We need to make some contingency plans of our own," she added. "And we need to bring in others from the rest of the fleet."

The XO's eyes narrowed. "I received a message only an hour ago, inviting me to the Dead Donkey," he said. "That's a bar in the spaceport, Captain. It has quite a bad reputation."

Kat had to smile. "For Cadiz?"

"Yes," the XO said. "But it's also one of the places the Shore Patrol doesn't dare go."

"Sounds like someone wants to chat," Davidson said. "Do you want me to come with you?"

The XO shook his head. "The message was unsigned," he said. "If it's someone Fran might have pointed in my direction, Major, they won't want to see a Marine. They might assume the worst."

Kat cleared her throat. "How many officers do you know—and trust—on the fleet?"

The XO hesitated. "I've recognized round thirty names," he said. "There might well be others. Pretty much all of them are mustangs with their heads screwed on properly."

Kat took a breath. What she was about to propose was not—technically—against naval regulations. On the other hand, the admiral might well be able to class it as conspiracy to commit mutiny or barratry, both of which carried the death sentence. Kat's father would be able to save her, if at a cost, but anyone else who took part was doing so at the risk of their life. And their reputation would be shot to hell.

"I'll make an assessment of the other commanding officers at the admiral's party," she said, "but we have to assume the worst. We need to convince your friends to help prepare 7th Fleet for battle as quickly—and covertly—as possible."

The XO frowned. "That will be difficult," he said. "Even the most data-constipated bureaucrat would be unable to avoid noticing the sudden upswing in requisitions."

Kat cursed under her breath. He was right.

"It has to be done," she said, finally. She looked at Davidson. "Can you warn the marines on the ground that the system might come under attack?"

"I can try," Davidson said. "But if the fleet isn't ready to defend the planet, the marines on the surface will be screwed."

"I know," Kat said. Any other planet would have countless loyalists ready to resist the Theocracy. But Cadiz was different. They'd learn their mistake soon enough, if the refugees were telling the truth, yet it would be too late to save the forces on the ground. "Do what you can."

The XO gave her a long look. "What guarantees can I offer my colleagues?"

"I don't know," Kat admitted. It was possible her father would be able to arrange for her to get wide authority, perhaps quasi-sealed orders she could use to justify her actions. But they would have to be procured from the Admiralty and there would be resistance, not least because she was such a junior captain. "They may be risking their lives as well as their careers."

The XO didn't object. In some ways, that worried her more than she cared to admit.

"I'll meet with this contact," the XO said, "and then get in touch with my old friends. No one will think anything of us meeting in a bar for a drink and a yarn about old times."

"Thank you," Kat said. She wished she had more contacts, but the XO had been in the Navy longer than she'd been alive. Most of the officers she knew were on Tyre. "If it does go to shit, I'll do what I can."

"I know you will," the XO said. He sounded as though the last of his reservations had faded away. "Thank you, Captain."

CHAPTER NINETEEN

Finding the Dead Donkey was not an easy task in the evening darkness, William discovered. The bar didn't have any lights advertising its presence, apart from a single slit in the door that hinted there was something inside. It had no windows and no sign, save for a drawing of a donkey lying on the ground, surrounded by flies. But it did have had one thing going for it, he decided as he walked through the door; it was the perfect place to meet someone without the Shore Patrol interrupting the meeting.

He gritted his teeth as he looked round, searching for the rendezvous point. The Dead Donkey was a large bar, decorated with pictures of animals in the wild, but the tables were separated by privacy walls, while several expensive—and only semi-legal—ECM generators were operating, making it extremely difficult for anyone to overhear anything. Even the air was tainted with foul-smelling smoke. Gritting his teeth, fighting the instincts that warned him the air was badly contaminated, he walked into the section and sat down. There was no sign of his contact.

He looked up as the bartender appeared, one hand clutching a battered-looking terminal. "A drink, sir?"

"Water, please," William said. He wanted something stronger, but he had a feeling he'd need all of his wits about him. "And a small packet of peanuts."

The bartender nodded and withdrew. William sighed and studied the pornographic images someone had drawn on the privacy wall. They were very imaginative, if somewhat impractical. Besides, no one would come to the Dead Donkey hoping to pick up a woman for the night. There were brothels for that back towards the more civilized parts of the spaceport.

"Billy," a voice said. "You look as young as ever."

William stared. ". . . Scott?"

His brother slipped into the compartment and sat down facing him, resting his hands on the table. "You were expecting someone else?"

"Yes," William said, flatly.

He studied his brother carefully. Scott was older by ten years, but he looked younger. His hair was still brown, rather than graying; he wore a merchant spacer's uniform and wore it well. But there was no starship ID on his collar, suggesting he was trying to conceal his vessel from prying eyes. That, William knew, was no surprise.

"I caught sight of your captain this morning," Scott said as he pulled a privacy generator out of his pocket and placed it on the table. "She's very pretty—and quite young." His eyes gleamed with amusement as he activated the generator. "Do you ever feel you made the wrong choice?"

"No," William said. His brother had always been able to get under his skin. "I don't."

"You should have your own ship by now," Scott said. "You've had thirty years in the Navy, seven of them as an XO. But she has powerful connections and I guess those trumped your experience."

He smiled, then twisted the expression into a leer. "But she's young," he said, again. "Do you ever pull her over your knee and spank her when she makes a mistake?"

William tapped the table sharply. "Is there a reason you asked me to come here?"

"Yes," Scott said. "But aren't you remotely pleased to see me?"

"You're a disgrace," William said. "I haven't seen you for nearly thirty-five years."

"You've probably heard of me," Scott said. He leaned back, placing his hands behind his head and leaning on the partition. "Not under my real name, of course."

William sighed. Scott had loved a girl on their homeworld, a girl he had hoped to marry when he grew old enough to start a croft of his own. But she'd been sacrificed to the pirates to appease their wrath only a year before the Commonwealth had arrived. Scott had obtained a starship and departed Hebrides, refusing to listen to either their parents or William himself. And he'd become a smuggler. There were times William wondered if his brother hadn't crossed the line into piracy too.

"Probably not," he agreed. "What are you doing here?"

"There aren't many barriers to free trade here," Scott said absently. "You never know what one might be able to pick up in this system."

William glared at him. "Are you shipping weapons to the insurgents?"

"I never disclose secrets belonging to my clients," Scott said. He smirked as he saw William clenching his fists. "But I have other places to serve right now."

"Oh," William said. "And those are?"

His brother smiled, then held up a hand as the bartender returned, carrying a tray of glasses and a packet of peanuts. William's eyes narrowed as he realized his water was nowhere in sight.

"I took the liberty of ordering some Highland Ale for us both," Scott said. "You do remember drinking ourselves stone cold drunk one day?"

"Yeah," William said. He wasn't blind to the underlying message either. Highland Ale was cheap on their homeworld, but expensive elsewhere. Scott was displaying his wealth without ever quite bragging openly. "Dad was not pleased."

Scott tapped the privacy generator again as soon as the bartender withdrew, switching the frequencies. This time, William gave the generator a closer look. It wasn't civilian, he saw, despite a careful paint job. It was military grade. His brother followed his gaze and smiled, coldly.

"It's astonishing just how much falls off the back of a shuttlecraft," he said mildly. "If you know who to ask, of course."

"Of course," William echoed. "Why did you ask me to come here?"

Scott took a sip of his beer. "Can I ask you to keep some parts of the story to yourself?"

"Maybe," William said.

Scott studied him and then nodded. "I've been smuggling for nearly forty years," he said bluntly. "You've probably heard of my alias, which I won't share with you right now because it would cause you a conflict of interest. Suffice it to say that I have a small fleet of smuggler ships and don't give a damn about borders."

William put two and two together. "You've been smuggling goods into the Theocracy," he said suddenly. "*That's* why you're here."

"Yes," Scott said simply. He leaned forward, resting his elbows on the table. "It's astonishing how much those wankers are prepared to pay for smuggled goods. Anyone would think they didn't believe in their religion."

His face twisted with remembered pain. William winced in sympathy. Scott had been a regular churchgoer, just like the rest of the family, until he'd lost his girl. It might have been better if the priest hadn't tried to convince him that one girl was a small price to pay for their safety. Scott had to be dragged off the badly beaten priest and he'd never gone back to the church since then, despite pleas from their mother and thrashings from their father.

"They want porn," Scott said. "And luxury goods."

"Stuff regular traders aren't allowed to send them," William commented. "How do you get away with it?"

"Large bribes," Scott said. He shrugged. "Honestly. The Theocracy isn't that different from . . . well, Cadiz. As long as you know who to pay off, and keep them sweet, no one touches you. The Inquisitors even have a sideline in very rough porn."

William frowned. "Do I want to know?"

"Probably not," Scott said. "You were always more straight-laced than me."

"Oh," William said. Their homeworld had been very conservative. It had been a shock to discover that nude photographs, video clips, and VR simulations were freely available in the Commonwealth. And then the porn just became more and more hardcore. He was used to it now, but it sometimes still shocked him, even though he knew everyone involved were actors. "Is there a point to this?"

"I've been hiring out more ships to work within the Theocracy," Scott said. "I don't mean just smuggling work, either. I mean hauling just about everything you can imagine from star to star."

"You'd think they have their own freighters for that," William said slowly. A very nasty idea was starting to build up in his head. "What happened to them?"

"A very good question," Scott agreed. "Time was we couldn't penetrate more than a few star systems into the Theocracy. The officials got more and more expensive to bribe. Hell, some systems were off-limits no matter what we offered. But now . . . now, we're actually hauling freight for them regularly. It's all rather odd."

William shivered. Civilians might think of the Navy as being nothing more than warships, but the fleet train—the freighters that transported missiles, spare parts, and other essentials—was just as important. A large part of Cadiz's importance lay in the stockpile of supplies that had been built up in the system ever since it had been annexed. But if someone had wanted to launch an invasion of hostile space, they would need freighters to keep their warships supplied with everything they might need to function.

"They're reserving their freighters for some other reason," William said slowly.

"That's right, Billy," his brother said. "And I don't think it bodes well for your mistress."

He smirked, then pressed on. "Not the only odd thing too," he continued. "I've seen agents moving through the underground, looking to hire mercenaries and pirate ships. But I think you've already seen some evidence of this."

"You have a pipeline into the admiral's office," William said.

"The occupation government leaks like that bucket you dropped down the gorge," Scott said. "I didn't have to spend more than a few hundred crowns to get a look at the report your captain filed. Most of your conclusions were correct. Someone is paying pirates handsomely to destroy ships rather than try to take them as prizes."

"If you have proof of this," William said, "it's your duty to share it with us."

"I don't have a duty," Scott said. "Am *I* a Commonwealth citizen?"

William winced again. His brother had never been quite the same since his girl had been taken by the pirates. Once, he would have been as selfless as anyone else raised by a poor but proud family. Now, he looked out for himself, first and foremost. He'd certainly never done anything to help the rest of his family, although that might have been a favor of sorts. Their parents wouldn't have accepted anything from such a tainted source.

"If war comes . . ."

"There will be room for us," Scott said, cutting him off. "We can make deals with whichever side comes out on top."

"If you believed that," William said, swallowing his anger, "you would never have come to me at all."

Scott smiled openly. "True, I suppose," he said.

William pressed his advantage. "The Theocracy is prepared to tolerate you—now," he said. "That will change, I think, if they win the war. They certainly won't want to see their civilians corrupted by outside influences. I think you'll be invited to a meeting that will be nothing more than cover for a mass slaughter."

"Perhaps," Scott said.

Scott took a breath. "Let me be blunt, then," he added. "Myself and my associates are unwilling to take a side formally. We have . . . contacts who will be outraged at the thought of us working with you. Some of them are more scared of the Commonwealth than the Theocracy. Others just want to stay out of the firing line.

"But we're prepared to provide intelligence, for a price."

William wasn't surprised. "What price?"

"I suppose that depends on what you're prepared to offer," Scott said. He leaned forward, smiling coldly. "What *are* you prepared to offer?"

"And what," William asked, "are *you* prepared to offer?"

"It depends on what *you* are prepared to offer," Scott said. "I . . ."

William slapped the table. "Stop playing games," he snapped. "If there's something you want, say so."

"Money," Scott said. "And certain . . . events . . . being officially forgotten."

William thought fast. The captain had a discretionary fund she could use to make deals if necessary—and she had her trust fund too, he reminded himself. It was quite possible they could simply purchase whatever Scott had to offer . . . and he was fairly sure his brother wouldn't try to cheat them. If he did, there would be no grounds for a long-term relationship.

"Money we might be able to offer," he said.

Scott met his eyes. "*Might*?"

"You didn't tell me who I'd be meeting," William snapped. "I certainly didn't make any preparations to pay you any actual cash!"

He reached into his pocket and pulled out his credit chip. "I can offer you a few hundred crowns, if you like."

"Point," Scott agreed.

He leaned backwards, then took a long swig of his beer. "I have a considerable amount of navigational data," he said. "You are aware, no doubt, that most of the hyper-routes into Theocratic space are mined or patrolled. But a handful of the more . . . hair-raising routes are largely unguarded. You might find the information useful."

"I'd prefer to know more about pirate bases and contacts," William said.

"I bet you would," Scott said. "But I'm afraid"—he tapped his forehead meaningfully—"that isn't on the table."

Scott paused. "I will say that demand for our services has actually been growing stronger," he added. "You may discover that you have less time than you think."

William sighed. "Are you saying you'll close a deal with them if we refuse or that we might not have long until the war breaks out?"

"Maybe both," Scott said. "It'll cost you at least a hundred crowns for a definite answer."

Scott reached into his pocket and produced a datachip. "I brought something as a gesture of good faith," he said. "My crews have a habit of recording everything picked up by their passive sensors, including local news broadcasts. This . . . is everything they recorded from a visit to Heaven's Star. You used to know it as Abadan."

William checked his implants. Abadan had been settled just before the Breakdown and remained largely untouched by the Breakaway Wars and other galactic affairs, at least until the expanding Theocracy had rolled over it. There was nothing else listed in the files, not even a mention of refugees. But if the world had been a stage-one colony before the Breakaway Wars, it was unlikely they'd had any homebuilt space industry of their own before it was too late. The only advantage they'd had was that their debts to the UN had died with the UN itself.

"You won't find it very reassuring," Scott said. "We can provide more, for a price."

"Of course," William said.

His brother leaned forward. "Can I ask you a question?"

William hesitated, then nodded.

"I could give you a command," Scott said. His voice was very soft, as if he feared being overheard. "I have a handful of former warships in my fleet. Someone like you, with the skills of the common spacer and bearing of an officer, would be very helpful. Why don't you join me?"

He pressed forward before William could say a word. "You would rise on your own merits," he added. "You wouldn't have to take orders from a girl who was born with a silver spoon in her mouth. You would be free."

"Tell me," William said, "how you giving me a command is any different from the captain's father giving *her* a command?"

"You've proved you can handle command," Scott said. "And none of my people would dispute it."

He reached out and touched William's hand. "Come with me," he said. "This star system is a disaster waiting to happen. Don't stay and die for a Commonwealth that doesn't appreciate your service."

William stared down at the table, his thoughts awhirl. He *was* tempted, he had to admit, even though he would never have said it to his brother's face. Command *was* his dream, yet it seemed increasingly unlikely that he would ever have a starship of his own. Even if he succeeded to command *Lightning*, the Admiralty would probably find another commander to replace him. And an independent shipping captain had far more autonomy than a naval commander.

"It's immoral," he muttered.

"I do have legit businesses," Scott said. "You wouldn't have to dirty your hands if you didn't want to."

The hell of it, William suspected, was that his brother was being sincere. Their relationship had died the day Scott had turned his back and walked away, yet before then he had always looked out for his younger brother. And the offer was tempting. If the captain had been half the brat he'd feared, he would have seriously considered turning his back on the Royal Navy. But Kat Falcone was a better person than he'd dared hope for.

"I have my duty," he said, firmly. "And my pride."

"Pride doesn't put food on the table," Scott snarled.

William's lips twitched. "I'm not that desperate," he said finally. "Thank you for your offer, Scott, but no."

Scott stood. "I'll pick up the tab," he said. He dropped a second datachip on the table, then picked up the privacy generator. "There's a contact code for my current location on the chip. Should you try to trace it . . . well, I'm afraid it won't work. And you won't see me again. Send me a message, tell me who you'll be bringing, and we will see."

"Understood," William said. "How long will you be in the system?"

"I'm not sure," Scott admitted. "If the system comes under attack . . . well, I'm gone."

He nodded to William and then walked away.

William looked at the bottle of beer and then took a long swig himself. It tasted worse than he remembered, but was oddly familiar nonetheless. Part of him was tempted to order more, to drink himself as senseless as they'd done years ago, but he knew his duty. Leaving the rest of the beer on the table, he stood and walked through the bar's doors. Outside, there was no sign of Scott. All he could see was a flashing light advertising a nearby brothel. He was tempted to knock on the door, to find a girl for the night, but he pushed the thought aside.

I have to get back to the ship, he thought. *And then work out what I'm going to tell the captain.*

CHAPTER TWENTY

"Don't worry about having a smuggler in the family," Kat said the following morning. "I have politicians in mine."

The XO looked relieved. Technically, he should have declared any potentially . . . *embarrassing* family connections when he'd joined the Navy. His brother might not have been quite as notorious as he'd hinted at the time, but it would still look very bad on his service record. And, if his brother was one of the smugglers wanted by the law, it was unlikely his career would survive.

"Thank you, Captain," the XO said.

Kat looked down at her hands. "I'll send the information to Tyre," she said, flatly. "And add it to every other factoid we've collected. But I don't know if anyone will pay attention."

The XO sighed. "Did your father not send anything back to you?"

"Nothing useful," Kat admitted. "All he sent was a brief acknowledgement and a note that the matter would be discussed."

She sighed. "And I have to waste time going to the admiral's party rather than patrolling the border or doing something useful."

"Yes, Captain," the XO agreed. "Think of it as a chance to gain some useful intelligence."

"Think of it as a chance to practice removing lips from my ass," Kat countered, crossly. Morrison's guest list had been announced on the planetary datanet, as if anyone cared who the admiral chose to invite to his parties. Most of the guests were either naval officers or civilian administrators looking for posts in the private sector after they finished their terms of office on Cadiz. "I should take a blowtorch and a monofilament knife for swift removal."

The XO smirked. "And can you do anything for them?"

"I doubt it," Kat said. "I was never groomed to take an important place within the corporation."

She rose to her feet and started to pace the compartment. "How long do we have?"

"I wish I knew," the XO said. He stayed in his seat, watching her. "I'll be speaking to my friends tomorrow night."

"Have fun," Kat said. She wished she could go, but she knew the XO's friends would talk much more freely without her around. "And tell them they will have my full support, if necessary."

"I wish it were that easy," the XO said. "What about your family's people within the system?"

"Few of them are in any place to assist us," Kat said, slowly. "But I do plan to talk to them when I have a moment."

The XO stood. "I'll inform you of the outcome," he said. "The only other problem right now is shore leave rota. There have been complaints."

"I know," Kat said. She'd heard from Davidson that there had been grumbles. "But we're not allowing the crew levels to drop below seventy percent, not now. I want to be ready to fight if the shit hits the fan."

The XO nodded. "Aye, aye, Captain."

"Dismissed," Kat said.

She waited for him to leave, then sat back down at her desk and called up the file the admiral's office had sent her. It was clear, alarmingly so, that Morrison had imported personal staff from Tyre and then put them on the occupation force's budget. One staff member had sent Kat details of the frock the admiral expected her to wear at the party. Instead of a dress uniform he wanted her to wear a little black cocktail dress. She'd look good in it, Kat had to admit, but she wouldn't look *anything* like a commanding officer. It would be hard to restore discipline if any of her crew saw her in the getup.

Bastard, she thought, angrily. *What the hell is his game*?

It was depressingly easy to hire a bar for the night, William discovered. The captain had given him a credit chip with a sizable balance, which had allowed him to reserve the entire bar, buy a considerable amount of alcohol, and give the staff the night off. It had required a deposit of an extra thousand crowns to secure their absence, but it was worth it. There would be no eavesdroppers when he and his friends met to discuss the situation. God alone knew what rumors would start if anyone overheard.

We'd probably all get charged with plotting a mutiny, he thought as he watched Davidson and Corporal Kevin Loomis scan the entire bar for bugs. They'd already found and disabled a couple of monitors, but he was feeling paranoid. *Or perhaps with using common sense in the vicinity of a senior officer*.

"It's clean," Davidson confirmed finally. "The security fields should ensure no one can overhear you."

William nodded. "Go back to the shuttle," he ordered as he checked the bar. The supplier hadn't bothered to do more than drop the crates of booze behind the bar. It didn't bother him. "I'll call you if I need you."

"No shore leave for us," Davidson agreed. The Marines had to stagger their shore leave, just like everyone else. "Good luck, Commander."

"Thank you," William said.

It was nearly twenty minutes before the door opened for the first time, revealing Commander Fran Higgins. William smiled at her, then tossed her a bottle of beer and waved her to one of the chairs. She gave him a puzzled glance, but said nothing as the door opened again to allow two more officers to enter the bar. William passed them both drinks and smiled, waving away their questions. There would be time to talk once everyone had arrived.

"William," Commander Trent said, "is there a reason for this gathering?"

"Patience," William said. Trent was a friend, rather than a former subordinate. It put them on more equal terms. "I'll get to the meat of the matter when everyone has arrived."

He couldn't help noticing that several of the officers, perhaps suspecting the truth, had brought privacy generators of their own. His implants monitored the intermingling fields, decided they were suitable, then ignored them. He kept passing out bottles of beer, waiting for the final few officers to arrive. As soon as they entered the bar, he closed and locked the door before walking round the table and sitting down.

"I suppose you're wondering why I called you here," he said. There were some chuckles at a joke that had been old before humanity had reached for the stars. "Before we start, I should tell you we can speak freely. The bar is clean and there are at least twelve privacy generators operating within the room."

"Doesn't *look* very clean," Commander Jove said. He waved a hand towards a dark stain on the wall. "I dread to imagine what *that* is."

"Me too," William said. As Jove had probably hoped, the jokey comment broke the ice. "I should also warn you that this discussion will be very sensitive. You were all invited because I trust you to have your heads screwed on properly—and to have enough sense to keep the subject of our discussion a secret. As far as anyone else is concerned, we're meeting for a chat and a session of swapping lies about our heroic exploits."

He paused, trying to gauge their mood. Some of them, including Fran Higgins, seemed to understand what they were actually being told, others looked mildly bemused. And to think he hadn't even reached the crux of the issue yet. It was quite possible that he'd misjudged one of them and they would be betrayed as soon as the meeting came to an end. The only upside of such a disaster was that it would be impossible for the admiral's patrons to hide or cover up.

"The Theocracy is preparing to invade this system," he said flatly.

There were no objections, much to his relief. Some of them would have already seen the writing on the wall, either through reports of pirate attacks or the simple decline of 7th Fleet into a mass of combat-ineffective units. None of them were stupid, after all; mustangs commonly had a very hard time of it until they proved themselves to officers who had been through Piker's Peak, rather than rising from the ranks. And *none* of them trusted the Theocracy.

He ran through the gathered evidence as quickly as possible, then pressed on. "I do not believe that anyone from Tyre will handle the situation in time to dissuade the Theocracy from attacking," he warned. "We *know* there's an enemy spy ship in the system *right now*. They will *know* just how weak we are—and how much damage they can do if they hit us within the next few weeks. And if that happens . . . are we in any state to beat them off?"

"No," Fran Higgins said.

No one disagreed. William felt chills running down his spine. They'd all been can-do people when he'd met them, mustangs who had risen because they believed nothing could truly stop them. To see them so broken, so fatalistic, was disturbing. And yet, what could they do?

"I don't know what Admiral Morrison is playing at," William said. "His patrons appointed him because they knew he wouldn't rock the boat. But it's equally possible he's a traitor, someone in the pay of the Theocracy. Or he may simply be as incompetent and greedy as the evidence suggests. What I do know is that we need to make contingency plans to do something if—when—the Theocracy attacks."

Commander Trent leaned forward. "It seems to me, William, that you're talking about mutiny."

William sighed, inwardly. "No," he said. "I'm talking about doing our damn duty."

He took a breath. "It won't be easy to repair the damage without higher authorities realizing what we're doing," he added flatly. "A sudden upswing in demands for spare parts alone would be noticeable. But we have to do what we can to prepare for a sudden attack on the system."

"Without anyone noticing," Fran Higgins said. "You do realize that discipline is in the shitter?"

"Time to get it *out* of the shitter," William said. A crew could endure much, but not a slow decline in standards, followed by a demand to revert immediately to the old ways. It was one of the reasons military training was so damn hard. "You can work with senior chiefs and petty officers to ensure that the really bad cases are dumped on the planet or assigned to punishment duties."

He paused. "Between us, we have over five hundred years worth of experience," he said. "We ought to be able to think of something."

"Break up gambling rings by swapping crews round," Trent suggested. "God knows we should be able to move crewmen round without getting our commanders to sign off on it."

William nodded. First officers had considerable power to handle crew transfers, duties that would merely waste their commander's time. Any gambling—or worse—rings could be broken up and scattered over a dozen ships if there was any reason to believe those involved could be redeemed. And the real hard cases could simply be assigned permanently to the planet. That would probably sit very well with them until the Theocracy attacked.

The thought caused William a flicker of guilt. He hadn't attended to the gambling ring on *Lightning* yet. He'd hoped the problem would sort itself out, but he simply hadn't had time to check. Making a mental note to see to it as soon as he returned to the ship, he sat back in his chair and listened as his friends discussed potential ideas. Training schedules could be fixed, given some time and effort; hell, with a little fiddling, they could be used to make the commanding officers look good. If presented properly, most commanders would simply sign off on it without considering the deeper implications.

"The King's Cup is being held in nine months," Jove pointed out. "We could try to put together a team."

William had to smile. The King's Cup was awarded to the starship with the finest gunnery crews in the fleet. It was an important award, which was at least partly why the commanding officers would want it for themselves. If they were convinced they had a chance to win, they'd resist the admiral if he started trying to prevent the crew from engaging in gunnery exercises. It wasn't as if they would be preparing for war.

"I have a question," Commander Stroke said. "What happens if we are attacked *before* we have a chance to prepare the fleet for doing more than spitting helplessly in their general direction?"

"We run," William said simply.

None of his friends looked happy at *that* prospect, but they all understood the situation. The 7th Fleet represented a vast investment, one that couldn't be replaced in a hurry. The ships could be repaired, their crews could be retrained . . . but only if they got out of the trap before the Theocracy destroyed them. Keeping the ships intact was their first priority.

Stroke scowled at him. "And what if we receive orders to fight to the death—or surrender?"

William took a breath. Nothing he'd seen on Cadiz had convinced him that Admiral Morrison would command the fleet effectively, even if he was able to take command without problems. The admiral rarely showed his face on his flagship, preferring to command the system from Government House. An all-out attack on the system might start and finish before Morrison even managed to make it back to orbit, assuming the attack wasn't coordinated with insurgents on the ground. It was what *William* would have done.

And the Theocrats sent commandos to the system, he thought slowly. *Were they meant to sneak into the secure zones and cause havoc?*

"We retreat," he said. "Preserving the fleet is more important than trying to defend Cadiz."

"A few months of occupation by the Theocracy would teach them a lesson or two," Fran Higgins muttered darkly. "Let them see what a *real* invasion force can do to helpless civilians."

"They're not *that* helpless," Trent pointed out mildly.

"We operate under strict ROE," Fran countered. "Our forces aren't trying to reshape their society, merely trying to convince them to accept a role in the Commonwealth. The Theocracy, if the refugees are to be believed, will crush any resistance with maximum force, then start encouraging mass conversions to their faith. Cadiz will simply become another Theocratic world. And good riddance."

Stroke cleared his throat, loudly. "You're talking about disobeying orders in the face of the enemy," he said sharply. "That will get us all shot."

"Better we get shot than lose every ship in the fleet," Trent snapped.

William opened his mouth, but Stroke overrode him. "Or can your . . . *captain* guarantee we keep our lives?"

It took William several seconds to calm his temper. "There are no guarantees of anything, beyond this," he said icily. "The Theocracy is planning an invasion; 7th Fleet is in no condition to defend this system against overwhelming force. We are making contingency plans to take action in the event of an attack before we are ready to meet it."

He braced himself. "We swore to defend the Commonwealth when we signed up," he added slowly. "I don't intend to allow Admiral Morrison to weaken the defenses to the point the Theocracy can just walk in and take over. And nor should any of you.

"If we are discovered, or betrayed"—he shot a sharp look at Stroke—"it is quite possible we will be charged with planning a mutiny," he warned. "There will be no guarantees that the captain's influence, such as it is, will save us from anything. But I don't believe any of us were *ever* offered any guarantees when we signed on the dotted line and gave our lives to the Navy."

His gaze moved from face to face. "If you don't want to take the risk of being involved," he concluded, "you can back out now. As long as you keep your mouths shut, there shouldn't be any danger, at least from your superior officers. The danger from the Theocracy will not go away."

There was a long pause. "Count me in," Fran Higgins said finally. "But it will not be easy to get the supplies we need."

"We could always bribe the bureaucrats," Stroke offered. "Or simply play silly buggers with the supply manifests."

There was a thought, William knew. The senior bureaucrats wouldn't know anything was wrong if the junior bureaucrats helped their friends camouflage their actions. He might have to make some promises—the *captain* might have to make some promises—but it should be doable. If nothing else, a promise of guaranteed employment in the Falcone Consortium should unlock a few hearts and minds.

The discussion raged backwards and forward for nearly two hours before William called it to a halt and produced a handful of datachips from his pocket. "These are cutting-edge encryption codes," he said. It had been alarmingly easy to obtain them, a factoid he would not be including in any report to Tyre. "We can use them to send messages through the planetary datanet, if necessary."

He paused. "I think we should meet again three days from now," he added. "That will give us time to see what needs to be done, then start planning to do it."

Stroke sighed. "And what if the bastards attack tomorrow?"

William glowered at him. "We die," he said. "Any more questions?"

There were none. He smiled to himself, handed out a final round of beers, then dismissed his colleagues with a warning to stagger their return to outer space. A couple would probably seek solace in the arms of a prostitute before returning to their shuttles. It was hard to care about their choice, he knew, even though he didn't have time to find companionship himself. There was no way to avoid one simple fact.

The die was well and truly cast.

CHAPTER TWENTY-ONE

The admiral's mansion was magnificent, Kat had to admit as the aircar descended towards the building. It resembled the Royal Palace on Tyre, but where the palace was built from white marble the admiral's mansion was built of red brick. Brilliant lights illuminated the garden, allowing guests to make their way through the foliage even as night fell over Cadiz. Kat couldn't help being reminded of her family estate on Tyre, though there were fewer guests there. Her family historically had so little privacy that it valued what it did have.

She braced herself as the aircar touched down, then stood and adjusted her dress as the hatch hissed open. Candy would have *loved* the black dress, Kat knew, but she disliked showing off her body in this way. It wasn't something she'd earned, not even something she'd paid for herself; her looks had been shaped by her father's genetic engineers long before she'd been more than a glint in his eyes. The dress made her look younger than she was, young enough to pass for a teenager. If she'd shown up on the bridge wearing it . . .

The thought made her smile as she stepped out of the aircar and looked towards the giant mansion. It was clear the admiral had decided to have some fun at the expense of his guests. The men all wore fancy uniforms, some dating all the way back to pre-space Earth, while the women all wore variants of the same cocktail dress Kat wore. Some of them had even cut the dresses shorter to expose as much of their legs as they could without showing underwear. Kat smirked at the thought of them bending over to pick something up, then smiled inwardly as a maid hurried towards her. What was it about powerful men, she asked herself, that they insisted on dressing their female servants in revealing outfits?

Power, she thought. Her father didn't indulge his power in such a manner, but his father had been born to wield power. He had never been insecure, not like the admiral and the newly rich. *They* flaunted their power out of fear it would fade away if it wasn't displayed to the world. And yet they wouldn't have obtained their Patents of Nobility if they hadn't had the wealth and power to back them up.

"Captain," the maid said. She was clearly a local, her voice accented yet understandable. "The admiral requests the pleasure of your company in the reception room."

Kat sighed, inwardly. She would have preferred to wander the gardens. It had been clear, from a single glance, that absolutely nothing useful would be accomplished by attending the party. But the maid would be blamed for failing to convince Kat to attend upon the admiral . . .

"It will be my pleasure," she lied smoothly.

The maid led her through the gardens, up a long flight of stairs, and into the building itself. Kat's first impressions didn't fade as she looked round while they walked through a long corridor and down another flight of stairs. The building was crammed with artwork, each piece probably worth at least ten thousand crowns, gathered together merely to show off the sheer wealth of their owner. There was no elegance, Kat noted, nor any attempt to do more with them than just show off. The admiral was definitely one of the newly rich.

She sighed again as the maid paused, nodding to a footman standing halfway down the stairs. The man stepped forward, then announced

Kat in a loud, booming voice that echoed through the entire room. Men and women turned to look at her, their collective gaze under strict control. Kat kept her own face under control as she descended the final stairs and walked towards the admiral. Their emotionless faces suggested they were wondering just what she could do for them.

"Lady Falcone," Admiral Morrison said. He was wearing a uniform with so much gold braid that it threatened to blind anyone who looked at it. "Thank you for coming."

"It was my pleasure," Kat lied. She couldn't place the admiral's uniform, but she had a feeling that whoever had designed it had hated officers. It would make an excellent target for a sniper watching from a distance. "How could I refuse your kind invitation?"

Morrison either missed or chose to ignore the hints of sarcasm in her tone. Instead, he took her hand—his gaze flickered over her chest, then looked back at her eyes—and led her through the room, introducing her to dozens of people. Kat filed their names and titles away in her implants for further investigation, then chatted politely about nothing with each of them before the admiral led her to the next one. None of them seemed to have anything interesting to say.

"It's a disgrace that the brothels are allowed to remain open," one elderly guest snapped, her hand catching Kat's shoulder as though she was a young child. "The morals of our officers and men will suffer."

Kat resisted—barely—the temptation to slap her. She'd met far too many elderly women like her, women who saw themselves as anointed monitors of society. To them, life wasn't complete unless they held the moral high ground and used it ruthlessly to lecture and belittle their juniors for not living up to their moral standards. But then, they were rarely actually powerful, if only because few would vote them into power. Their preaching and whining was all they had.

"They should be shut down," the woman continued. She hadn't let go of Kat's arm. "And the sheer quantity of alcohol swigged by serving men and women is dreadful . . ."

"It is also all that makes serving here bearable," Kat said, feeling her patience snap. Her training had its limits, particularly when she knew shore leave facilities were a vital necessity for the health and morale of her crew. "And besides, do you think they wouldn't be able to find companions and alcohol if the spaceport bars were closed?"

The woman stared at Kat as though she had started speaking in tongues. "I . . ."

"Do you have the slightest idea," Kat asked, "why the bars and brothels exist?"

Admiral Morrison interrupted before the woman could think of a response. "Katherine Falcone," he said, "there's someone I would like you to meet."

"Of course," Kat said smoothly. The woman was gaping at her in shock. It would be dangerous to her reputation in society to badmouth a Falcone. "I would be honored to talk with someone intelligent."

Admiral Morrison led her across the room and through a large door, which led into a dance hall. A band was sitting on the dais, murdering a tune that Kat vaguely recognized as having been fashionable ten years ago. Guests didn't seem to be following any set dance, she decided; couples were merely moving round the hall, hand in hand. It wasn't the sort of dancing Kat enjoyed, though she had to admit it had its moments, but only when she was dancing with someone she actually liked.

"Katherine Falcone," the admiral said, "I'd like you to meet my son, Adam Morrison."

Kat took one look and just *knew* they weren't going to get on. Everything she knew about the admiral told her that he would do anything to maintain his position and the favor of his patrons because his position could be undermined quite easily. Adam Morrison lacked even *that* level of self-awareness. His face was strikingly handsome, so handsome it was almost bland. The suit he wore, rather than a fake uniform, was cut tightly enough to show off his muscles to best advantage. But it was clear, from the way he moved, that he had no training at all.

"Charmed," Kat lied once again.

She had to fight to keep her face under control, particularly when Adam's eyes dropped towards her chest. She knew what was happening. The admiral's son was unmarried—and the admiral had ambitions. Even a short marriage between Adam Morrison and Kat could secure the admiral's place in High Society. She sighed, inwardly. It was hardly the first time someone had tried to introduce her to his children. But it said a great deal about High Society that Adam wasn't the worst she'd encountered.

"Charmed," Adam echoed. He held out one hand. "Shall we dance?"

Kat took his hand and allowed him to lead her onto the dance floor. He wasn't a bad dancer, she discovered to her surprise, but his hands kept creeping downwards as he whirled her round the room. The admiral was nowhere to be seen after the first dance, depriving Kat of any easy excuse to escape. Instead, she found herself pulled into a second dance.

"I understand you're in command of a destroyer," Adam said, putting his lips close to her ears. "Do you enjoy being in command?"

"A cruiser," Kat corrected icily. "And command is enjoyable."

"I bet it is," Adam said. He leered at her, his hands crawling downwards again. "And do you ever want to just relax?"

Kat stepped backwards, forcing him to jerk his hands back up. "I walk fifty miles a day to relax," she said, "and then spar with marines."

"I spar with marines too," Adam said. "Do you know I hold a reserve commission in the planetary militia?"

"No," Kat said. She was *sure* Adam didn't spar with anyone, just from the way he moved. A graduate of Piker's Peak unarmed combat course could have taken him. "What do you do in the militia?"

"I command the reserve defense unit," Adam informed her. "We aced our last evaluation."

"You must have a wonderful sergeant," Kat said, unable to keep the sarcasm out of her voice. "What does he do for you?"

"He takes the burden of command off my shoulders," Adam said.

He keeps you from getting everyone killed in training exercises, Kat translated mentally. It wasn't uncommon for young noblemen to hold reserve commissions, but it was clear that Adam didn't even meet the bare requirements. Even her older brothers were expected to spend at least three days a month with their units. *Poor bastard.*

"Come on outside," Adam urged. He pulled her towards a large pair of doors that led out into the gardens. "You'll love it."

He would have been right, Kat decided, if he hadn't been with her. Whoever had designed and shaped the gardens had done so as a labor of love. Instead of the sheer tackiness of the building's interior, there were flowers, bushes, and trees planted according to a pattern that pleased the eye, also serving as a home for all kinds of wildlife.

"It can be a hard life out here," Adam observed as he led her down to a large pond. "I rarely speak to anyone my equal."

Kat had to bite down a laugh. On Cadiz, Admiral Morrison and his family were at the very pinnacle of High Society. They could distribute patronage freely while everyone looked up to them as something to emulate. But on Tyre they'd be nothing more than junior aristocrats at best. Adam was deluding himself if he thought he could go back to the core of the Commonwealth and still be top dog. There were people back home who wouldn't hesitate to poke his bubble if he tried to maintain the illusion.

That might be why the admiral introduced us, she thought. *A marriage would improve their status immeasurably.*

It would also not be approved, she knew. She *was* the youngest child, without the obligations of her elders, but she only had her trust fund in her own name. If her father decided not to approve the match, she wouldn't be granted any voting stock or anything else she could use to influence politics. Admiral Morrison's dreams of marrying his son into the highest tier of the aristocracy would crash and burn . . .

. . . and Kat knew she wouldn't accept Adam in any case.

"How lucky for you," Kat said. She looked up. The moon was slowly rising in the sky, casting an eerie light over the scene. "I think we should go inside now."

"There's no one in there but boring people," Adam said. His voice became a whine. "Wouldn't it be better to stay outside?"

"I don't think so," Kat said. She couldn't quibble with his assessment of the party guests, but she did need to speak to some of her fellow commanding officers. Perhaps one or two of them could be talked into helping prepare 7th Fleet for combat. "You should be showing your face to the guests."

"They don't care about either of us," Adam said. He reached for her hand and caught hold of it, pulling her towards him. "Wouldn't it be much more fun to . . ."

His lips met hers. Kat froze for a second in genuine astonishment—no aristocratic buck she'd ever met had crossed the line so blatantly—and then she pulled her hand free and shoved his chest, hard. He lost his footing and tumbled backwards, falling over the edge of the pond and hitting the water with a giant splash. Kat smirked, then carefully pulled her dress back into place. She couldn't help wondering, despite the seriousness of the situation, just what Adam would tell his father.

"You are an idiot," she said as Adam surfaced. It was clear that the pond was deeper than she'd thought. His fancy uniform was dripping wet, completely ruined. The nasty part of Kat's mind hoped it had cost hundreds of crowns. "Did you really think I would give myself to you out here?"

Adam stared at her in shock. Kat glared back, recognizing the symptoms. Adam, like far too many aristocrats, had been raised in an environment where no one could say no. From some of the things Kat's elder brothers had muttered when they thought she couldn't hear, their father had been *much* less permissive than some of the other fathers on Tyre. But then, they *were* being groomed to take his place.

"Stay there until I'm gone," Kat ordered. She was tempted to ask him just what his father had said, but she didn't want to talk to him any more than necessary. "And I suggest you *think* about what could have happened."

She turned and walked back to the building, straightening her dress further as she walked. Behind her, she heard splashing, but nothing else. She listened anyway, half expecting to hear him come charging after her. Thankfully, he had more sense than to believe he could just give chase and catch her before it was too late. It was *already* too late.

Shaking her head in disbelief, she slipped through a side entrance and made her way into the nearest refresher. It was empty, surprisingly; normally, the bathrooms were packed with women chatting about men. She paused and then looked at herself in the mirror, feeling her heartbeat finally starting to race. Her training had kept it under control until she was safe.

I've had worse, she told herself firmly. Vacuum training at Piker's Peak had been nightmarish. She'd shaken for hours afterwards, the first time. And then there had been unarmed combat training . . . it had been her first real experience with physical violence and it had shocked her. There were female marines, she knew, but she couldn't have been one of them. She just didn't have the endurance.

She washed her face and then forced herself to think coldly and rationally. She *could* file a complaint, she knew, but it wasn't enough to have Adam convicted of anything, let alone take down his father with him. It would look like a date gone wrong, rather than attempted rape; hell, she wasn't even sure if he *had* wanted to rape her. She'd met enough aristocrats who had refused to press any further when it was clear their attentions were unwanted. The whole situation would not only look very bad, but it would distract attention from the very real problems facing 7th Fleet.

Bastard, she thought. She checked her implants and noted the time. If she spent another hour chatting to the other captains, she could leave afterwards without upsetting the Grand Masters and Mistresses of Etiquette. Cursing, she looked down at her dress. It would be hard enough to convince them to take her seriously without wearing a dress that made her look like a damned teenager . . .

The admiral must have wanted me to look attractive for his son, she thought. Oddly, the thought made her smile. *I wonder if he still likes me.*

The building shook. Moments later, she heard the sound of shooting.

Insurgents, she thought, horrified. She'd checked the map. The building was over a hundred miles from the closest settlement. But the sound of shooting—and screams—echoing through the building suggested the insurgents had managed to get an attack force into place anyway. Another explosion rung out, sending pieces of plaster dropping from the ceiling and down to the floor. Kat shook herself out of her shock and activated her implants, trying to send a distress signal. Moments later, a warning message popped up in front of her eyes.

DATANET DOWN, it read. The local data nodes had been corrupted—or simply destroyed. She remembered the maid, a local girl with access to the building, and shivered as a second message popped up. **UNABLE TO ACCESS PLANETARY NET.**

Kat swallowed a curse, unsure what to do. Outside, the sound of shouting and screaming was growing louder. The insurgents had clearly broken into the building. Her training had never covered combat on the ground, at least not in anything other than theoretical detail. They'd always been told to leave ground combat to the Marines.

Get out, she told herself. Someone *had* to have noticed that Morrison's mansion had come under attack. But this was Cadiz. No one had impressed her with their competence since she'd first set foot on the planet. *Get to the aircars and contact the Marines. Or . . .*

She froze. The door was opening.

CHAPTER TWENTY-TWO

"Hands in the air," the insurgent snapped.

Kat obeyed, studying the insurgent carefully. He wore a black mask that concealed his features, but she was sure he was male—and young. It was clear he had received some training, just from the way he held his weapon, but it wasn't complete. She wasn't too surprised. The insurgent masterminds had to know anyone assigned to attacking the admiral's mansion was unlikely to return. They wouldn't waste their best men on such an operation.

"I'm just a maid," she said, trying to stammer convincingly. Her name and face had been flashed across the planet's society pages, but the little black dress made her look completely different. "I . . ."

She straightened, trying to push her breasts forward. The insurgent's eyes dipped, just slightly. It was possible, she told herself, as he advanced on her, that he wasn't as well disciplined as he should be. Did he *know* it was a suicide mission?

Kat braced herself as he came into reach, then looked up pleadingly into his eyes. He looked amused rather than suspicious. Kat shoved the gun to one side and slammed her fist into his throat. He choked, then stumbled to the floor. She let out a sigh of relief as he let go of the rifle without pulling the trigger and alerting his companions that something had gone wrong.

Taking the rifle, she checked it quickly. It was an unfamiliar design, but the principles were almost identical to weapons she'd used at Piker's Peak. She held it in one hand, then searched the insurgent with the other. He was also carrying a small pistol and several clips of ammunition. Kat picked them up and cursed. Her dress didn't have any pockets for storing bullets. She tore off his mask and used it as a makeshift carry.

She stepped over to the door, listened carefully, then stuck her head outside. There was no one in the corridor as far as she could tell, but she could hear the sound of loud protests in the distance. She wondered, absently, just where the admiral had gone before deciding it didn't matter. If the insurgents had any sense, they'd make damn sure they didn't kill him. His replacement could hardly be any less competent. Gritting her teeth, she advanced out of the room, trying desperately to remember the way back to the aircars. Perhaps it would be better to slip out of the door and move round in the gardens . . .

An insurgent was guarding the door. Kat cursed under her breath as she yanked her head back, then tried to think of something else she could do. Of *course* the insurgents would be guarding all the exits and entrances . . . she turned and headed towards the stairs. If the admiral was even remotely competent, there would be a spare communications suite in his bedroom, automatically linked into the fleet command network. It was a gamble, but she couldn't think of anything better. She knew she couldn't singlehandedly beat however many insurgents there were.

She froze as she reached the stairs, then ducked into the shadows as she heard people—several people—moving towards her. Three of them were insurgents, she realized as they came into view, but the others were maids and manservants. They weren't prisoners either, she noted, unsurprised. Clearly, the insurgents had been plotting the operation for quite some time. Local labor was cheaper than importing servants from

Tyre—and besides, the locals couldn't demand better treatment under Commonwealth Law. As long as they seemed trustworthy, she knew, they would be hired.

The thought made her shiver as the insurgents walked past and vanished into the distance. How many local men and women were working at the spaceport? Or in the government complexes scattered all over the planet? Hell, the prostitutes alone probably heard enough pillow talk to keep the insurgents informed of everything that happened on the planet before it hit the media. The only thing preventing a general uprising, she knew, was 7th Fleet and the orbital defenses.

But the Theocracy's attack would deal with them.

She felt a stab of pity for the brain-dead men and women who had attended the admiral's party, then made her way up the stairs as soon as the insurgents were out of sight. The building was eerily quiet—she couldn't help wondering just what the insurgents intended to do with their prisoners—but she pushed the thought aside as she reached the top of the stairs and turned right, down the corridor. A noise caught her ear and she froze, then looked into one of the larger rooms. A number of men and women lay on the ground, their hands bound behind their backs. It took her a moment to realize that they had to be the servants who had remained loyal—or at least hadn't been part of the insurgency from the start. She briefly considered freeing them, then dismissed the idea. There was no way to know if they could be trusted.

No loyal retainers here, she thought morbidly. Her bloodline had entire *families* serving as retainers, almost part of the Falcone family itself. Most of their children tended to start their lives as playmates for the aristocratic kids, then become servants as they grew older. But it simply wasn't possible to build such an edifice on Cadiz. *No one can be trusted completely.*

Kat took one last glimpse at them, then strode onwards. Her implants kept blinking up warning messages—the house nodes were flickering on and off, suggesting that their software was trying to overcome a viral attack—but she'd already downloaded and saved a copy of the mansion's floor plans. The admiral's bedroom was at the end of the corridor, through a large wooden door. She stopped dead as she heard someone speaking ahead of her, then peeked through the door. Two insurgents were ransacking the room, hunting for something the admiral might have concealed in his bedroom. They turned and stared at her, then reached for their weapons. Kat shot the first one instinctively, then swung her weapon to target the second insurgent. He threw himself at her too late. She shot him, then jumped to one side.

His body hit the floor, already dead.

She fought down the urge to throw up as she checked the body. She knew she'd taken life before, but it had always been at a distance. She'd never seen any of the men and women who had died under her fire. Now . . . she swallowed hard, then looked round the chamber. The admiral hadn't stinted on his personal quarters. Everything was designed for comfort, particularly the bed. It was large enough for five or six people to sleep comfortably. She kept staring round until she located a solid wooden cupboard and then pulled it open. For once, Morrison had followed regulations. He'd installed a full communications system in his quarters.

Kat let out a sigh of relief, then reached for the controls, inputting her access codes. There was no point in calling the local government, not now. God alone knew what else might be going on. She needed to call her ship.

"This is the captain," she said as soon as the channel was open. "We have a situation."

♦ ♦ ♦

Captain Patrick James Davidson knew, without false modesty, that he wouldn't rise any higher than command of a company of Marines. Fortunately, he didn't *want* to rise any higher. He would be happy with his company of Marines and a chance to test himself against the best and brightest the enemy had to offer. In a way, he'd even mourned when the Theocratic commandos hadn't tried to break out of the hull before they'd been handed over to local authorities on Cadiz. He'd been *sure* they would have tested his men to the utmost.

He pushed the thought aside as the shuttle raced through the atmosphere towards the admiral's mansion. The report had been precise and to the point; the captain was stranded inside the mansion, while the building was occupied by an unknown number of insurgents with unknown objectives. Judging from the situation, Davidson rather suspected their objective was to blow the mansion and escape, leaving the occupation government with a black eye and a great deal of embarrassment. But the attackers couldn't be allowed to get away with it.

"Prepare to jump," he ordered. He'd brought two platoons with him, both wearing light combat armor. The remainder of the company would remain in reserve until they were called forward. Thankfully, the local authorities hadn't tried to interfere with his mission planning. They'd been caught flat-footed by the attack. "Now!"

He was first out of the shuttle, plummeting down towards the building. It was impossible to tell if the insurgents knew they were coming or not; they didn't seem to have any active sensors operating near the mansion, but they might well have agents somewhere within the planetary air traffic control. No ground fire rose up to meet the marines as they fell, their antigravity units arresting the group's descent bare seconds before they would have hit the rooftop. Davidson tore open the hatch with his armored hands, then jumped down into the building. There was no sign of any enemy forces.

WARNING, his suit buzzed. COMBAT JAMMING ENABLED.

Patrick nodded, then dismissed the alert as he led the way forward. Being deprived of microscopic spies was irritating, but hardly a surprise. His suit picked up the sounds of someone shooting in the distance, perhaps Kat. He put on a boost of speed, hastily comparing his current location to the mansion's floor plans. The captain had said she was hiding in the admiral's bedroom. As he rounded the corner, he saw she was under attack.

He threw himself forward, landing among the terrorists before they knew he was there. At such close range, there was no way he could miss, certainly not with his inbuilt stunner. He knocked them all out rapidly and then muttered orders to the rest of his platoon. The terrorists might have the remainder of the guests under guard, but stun grenades would knock out everyone—hostages and insurgents alike. It might be the only way to prevent them from blowing up the building, taking everyone inside with it.

"Captain," he called, "the corridor is clear."

It had been odd seeing Captain Falcone again after their relationship. They'd parted on good terms—he was too realistic to think they had a chance of staying together forever—but part of him had been tempted to try to restart their relationship when they'd found themselves assigned to the same ship once again. But he'd known it wasn't a good idea . . . Now, he found himself staring at her as she inched out of the room, weapon in hand. Her dress was torn, one of her legs was badly bruised . . . and he thought she'd never looked more beautiful.

"Captain, are you all right?" The voder would ensure that no one heard the tremor in his voice.

"Yes, thank you," Kat said. Her eyes were shining despite the situation. And the dress. "Status report?"

Davidson checked his HUD. "We're advancing on the hostages now," he said. "We don't have time to waste."

The captain nodded. "And the admiral?"

"Unknown," Patrick said. "With your permission . . ."

"Good luck," the captain said. "Try to take some of the insurgents alive, if possible."

"Yes, Captain," Patrick said. "We will try."

♦ ♦ ♦

Kat sat back in the corridor, feeling her body shaking with a combination of relief and fear—and frustration that she couldn't do anything but wait. Davidson didn't need her getting in the way, nor could he spare anyone to stay with her. She kept the rifle on her lap and waited, listening carefully to the sound of stunners and grenades echoing through the vast building. It was nearly forty minutes before the jamming cut out and her implants started to work normally again, reporting the sudden arrival of a small army of soldiers from the spaceport.

"Captain," Davidson said, "we have shuttles inbound from the ship. Do you want to return to *Lightning*?"

"I want to know what happened to the admiral," Kat said. "And his son. What happened to his son?"

She watched as the stunned guests were carried out of the building for transport back to the spaceport, where they would recover in the hospital. Behind them, soldiers moved among the insurgents, flexi-cuffing and then searching them before marking them down for transport to the nearest holding cell.

"That was surprisingly easy," Davidson observed. "They didn't even have the building rigged to explode by the time we attacked them."

Kat gave him a sharp look. The insurgents had clearly spent months laying the groundwork for the assault, an assault that had only managed to kill a handful of officers and bureaucrats before it failed spectacularly. They'd had a stroke of bad luck—the attackers had probably assumed she would be captured with the rest of the commanding officers—but it was still odd. The more she thought about it, the more she realized something was badly wrong.

"Maybe they were trying to embarrass the admiral," she said slowly. The insurgency *had* to know that someone more competent would be sent to replace Morrison if he died. "Or just to embarrass the occupation government itself."

"Could be," Davidson agreed. "Men and women can be replaced, Captain. A reputation cannot be repaired so quickly."

Kat nodded. No doubt Admiral Morrison would have incentive to minimize the scale of his failure.

"This wasn't the commandoes," Davidson added. "They're still in the spaceport."

Kat ground her teeth, then looked up sharply as the admiral appeared and made his way over to face her. "Admiral," she said coolly, "where the hell were you?"

"The hero of the hour," Morrison said. He completely ignored her question. "I believe the press wants to meet you."

"I have to see the doctor," Kat said quickly. She leaned forward. "Admiral, where *were* you?"

"The panic room," the admiral said. He looked embarrassed. "My staff shoved me inside as soon as the attack began."

Kat's eyes narrowed. "And you couldn't call for help from there?"

"I tried," the admiral said. "But no one replied."

Davidson touched Kat's arm lightly. "Someone did manage to get the word out," he said, quietly. "You weren't the first to call for help."

Kat stared at the admiral for a long moment, fighting to control her temper. Morrison had wasted her time with a useless party, pushed her into the arms of his leech of a son, and then had the gall to cower in the panic room while his guests were menaced, threatened, and killed by armed insurgents. Only sheer luck had saved him from a disaster that would have ended his career, along with the occupation itself.

Could her father save her from execution if she shot the admiral? She was tempted to find out.

"I believe a starship has to be assigned to patrol the border," she said. The previous cruiser was due back in a day or two. "I would like *Lightning* to be assigned to that role."

The admiral opened his mouth but then apparently thought better of whatever he'd intended to say. Instead, he merely nodded.

"I will have routing orders cut for you," he said. "And you have my thanks, Captain. You will be honored for this."

Kat wanted to roll her eyes in disgust. Somehow, she resisted the temptation.

"I would be honored to discuss it when I return to Cadiz," she said. She had no doubt the admiral would try to award her the highest honor he could bestow just to avoid calling attention to his failures. "But for the moment I need to return to my ship and see the doctor."

Her voice hardened. "But thank you, Admiral, for a party I will never forget."

She allowed herself to lean on Davidson's armored arm as they walked towards the shuttle and straightened up as soon as they were out of sight. Her body ached, but it was tiredness rather than bruises or broken bones. She reached the shuttle's hatch and then paused. A line of men and women with bound hands were making their way into a large transporter.

"The former servants," Davidson explained grimly. "They will be interrogated to see what they knew about the whole affair."

"And if they're not insurgents by the time they go into the detention camps," Kat muttered, "they will be when they're released."

She stepped through the hatch, cursing the admiral under her breath. He'd be looking for a scapegoat, someone to take the blame for the whole affair. Chances were some innocent bureaucrat would be made to take the fall, either through accusations of incompetence or threats of criminal investigation. But the true cause of the problem would be left in command, utterly unmolested. The admiral had set the tone for his entire command.

The shuttle's drives powered up, then propelled the vehicle up through the atmosphere and out into space. Kat let out a sigh of relief as they passed through the edge of the atmosphere, silently promising herself never to set foot on Cadiz again. It was a promise, she knew, she might well be unable to keep.

"Put us alongside the emergency air lock," Davidson ordered. "I want to go directly to Sickbay."

"Aye, aye, sir," Midshipwoman Parkinson said.

Kat opened her mouth to object, but Davidson shook his head. She saw his stubborn expression and gave in. He thought she needed Sickbay and he would damn well *take* her to Sickbay.

"Pass me a uniform jacket and ship suit," she ordered crossly. It was increasingly hard to maintain her dignity in the black dress. "I'm damned if I'm wearing this on the ship."

Davidson, thankfully, didn't argue.

CHAPTER TWENTY-THREE

"Some cuts and bruises," Doctor Braham said briskly. "But no real damage."

"Thank you," Kat said. "Can I be dismissed now?"

"There *is* still the matter of your medical checkup," Doctor Braham said. "By regulation, all senior officers are to undergo a full medical scan every three months. You haven't been scanned once."

"I was scanned on my previous posting," Kat pointed out, although she knew she had already lost the argument. She should have found time while *Lightning* was in transit to have her scan. "There wasn't anything wrong with me."

"I'll be the judge of that," the doctor said. "Lie back on the bed and take a deep breath."

Kat sighed, but held her peace as the doctor ran a series of scanners over her body. Her implants kept flashing up alerts, each one noting that her body's secrets were being exposed and dissected. It wasn't a real problem, Kat knew, but it was still annoying. And as the doctor was the only person who could relieve the captain of command, it was rare for a captain to willingly turn herself in for a medical scan.

"Your genetic engineer was a master," the doctor commented as she ran through the final set of scans. "Or was he one of those who believed he could create the superman?"

"I think my father didn't allow any experimentation," Kat said. There were a hundred research institutions seeking newer ways to enhance the human mind as well as the body, but none of them had succeeded in improving the basic level of intelligence. Direct computer interfaces helped more than genetic rewriting. "At least he didn't allow it on any of us."

"Probably wise of him," Doctor Braham noted. She stepped backwards, then sent a silent command to the scanners, which withdrew. "You're as fit and healthy as could reasonably be expected, under the circumstances. I'll see you in another three months."

"Yes, Doctor," Kat said as she sat up and reached for her uniform jacket. "How are you coping with the crew?"

"No serious problems, apart from a couple of cases of excessive intoxication after shore leave," the doctor informed her. "No matter the sheer number of bars on the surface, there's always someone who goes to an unlicensed place and drinks something strong enough to pickle their brain cells. But I think the crew could do with shore leave somewhere safer."

Kat nodded. Piker's Peak had stressed the importance of an active shore leave—and they hadn't just meant Intercourse and Intoxication. The XO should be organizing activities for the crew, everything from skydiving to power boating or simply enjoying the sun on a sandy beach. But there were no such facilities on Cadiz. Even if they had located a beach far from a local settlement, Kat wouldn't have trusted it. The insurgents might have seen it as an opportunity to winnow down her crew.

She pulled her jacket over her chest, then stood. "We're due to rotate back to the core in a few months," she said, with the private thought that the war might well have started by then. "There will be time for more active shore leave later."

"It could explain some of the situation here," the doctor offered. "Crews without the prospect of a meaningful shore leave . . ."

Kat snorted. She'd never been an ordinary spacer, but she *had* appreciated the chance to get off the ship for a few days, even as a midshipwoman. A few days at the spaceport would have satisfied her, although it wouldn't have satisfied Davidson or any of the more active crewmen. But there were no real facilities on Cadiz outside the spaceport itself and there was nothing she could do about it. A complaint to the admiral would probably get her nowhere.

She nodded to the doctor, then walked out of the small compartment. Davidson was outside, pacing the deck like an expectant father. Kat had to suppress a smile at the mental image. She nodded to him as he came to attention. If she knew him—and she did—he was probably planning to escort her back to her cabin. The thought both pleased and annoyed her. Part of her wanted the company, but part of her resented anyone thinking she needed help.

"I'm fine," she said as she turned to lead the way through the hatch. "And your men?"

"They're fine," Davidson said. His blue eyes watched her with undisguised concern. "But we trained for this sort of shit."

Kat said nothing as they walked through the corridors and finally reached her cabin. She hesitated, then opened the hatch and beckoned him into the barren room. Davidson looked surprised at the lack of decor, but Kat had never felt the urge to collect artwork or show off her wealth to her officers. The only decoration she had allowed herself was a painting of HMS *Thunderous* an officer had done, years ago. Kat had liked it enough to keep for herself.

She felt her body sag as soon as the hatch hissed closed. Davidson caught her and helped her over to the sofa, then sat next to her as she started to shake. Kat looked down at her hand, watching in dismay as it betrayed her, then up at him. His eyes were worried, yet unsurprised.

He'd expected her to go into shock, she realized. She wanted to scream at him for not warning her, although what could he have said?

"It's all right," he said. One of his arms enveloped her and Kat relaxed into his embrace. "It's a natural reaction."

"Oh," Kat muttered. It was hard to think straight. Now that the whole incident was over and she was safe, her imagination was providing hundreds of ideas about what could have gone wrong. She could have been taken as a hostage. There were stories about kidnapped officials who had been held for months before they were released—or killed, their bodies found by patrolling soldiers. "What's happening to me?"

"You weren't trained as an infantryman," Davidson pointed out. He didn't sound accusatory, for which Kat was grateful. "Now that the crisis has passed, your body is reacting."

"Damn it," Kat muttered. She *hated* showing weakness. Even as a young officer, she'd done everything in her power to avoid showing even the slightest hint of fear. It could have destroyed her career. "I'm sorry."

"It isn't your fault," Davidson assured her. His hand was stroking her back, lightly. "Just relax and let it pass."

Kat glowered at him, but did her best to follow his advice. He was right, of course; she'd never had any real ground combat training. The Royal Navy had discussed boarding and counterboarding actions, but no one had seriously expected the enemy to try to board a starship in the midst of combat. They'd be more likely to force the ship to surrender and *then* send in the Marines. Or whatever the Theocracy used in place of Marines. No one had thought Kat and her fellow cadets would ever go into battle on the ground.

"I didn't have the shakes after I fired a starship's weapons in anger," she muttered resentfully. "Why do I have them now?"

"Ground combat feels different," Davidson said. He let go of her and stood, then walked over to the coffeemaker positioned against the bulkhead. "Tea?"

"Something warm," Kat said. She wanted him back holding her and to hell with discipline or her reputation. "Anything."

Davidson poured her a mug of tea, then walked back and held it under her nose until she managed to force her hand to take it and hold it to her lips. It tasted remarkably good, even though she knew naval tea and coffee came from the lowest bidder. But then, she was alive and her enemies weren't . . . She giggled despite the situation, almost slopping hot tea on her legs. At least she'd managed to get rid of the damned dress. She would have hated to wear *that* while the doctor was poking and prodding at her.

"That's a normal reaction," Davidson said. He shrugged, then sat down next to her. "Did I ever tell you about the balls-up at boot camp?"

Kat shook her head, feeling her hair caressing her face.

"We were meant to crawl under a hail of incoming fire," Davidson said. "The drill instructors had rigged up a set of machine guns to fire over our heads. It was absolutely terrifying, but we told ourselves that it was perfectly safe. Somehow, despite the deafening racket, we managed to crawl through the trench until we were midway to our destination. We were just starting to get used to it when the machine guns went out of control and bullets started hitting the ground right next to us."

"Shit," Kat said.

"That's precisely what I did," Davidson admitted. He smiled at her expression. "We all froze, then crawled for the end of the trench as fast as we could, despite the mud and . . . other stuff in our path. And we all had the shakes afterwards."

He paused. "We learned later that the whole thing was just another test and there was no real danger, but it was mortally convincing," he added. "I never had the shakes again after that day."

"I'm not surprised," Kat said. She took another sip of her tea and then wrapped her arm round him. "But I don't think I'll be applying for boot camp anytime soon."

"You probably wouldn't have made it," Davidson told her bluntly. "Boot camp is nothing like as genteel as Piker's Peak."

He was probably right, Kat knew. Even apart from ground combat training, Piker's Peak was focused on turning out officers and gentlemen rather than groundpounders who could run fifty miles and then attack the enemy without a pause. Kat's training had touched on a great many issues; Davidson's had focused on killing the enemy and breaking things. There were times when she envied the handful of aristocrats who *had* gone into boot camp. None of *them* were ever accused of having used connections to put themselves ahead of the rest.

No mercy, she recalled. It was the motto of the Marine Boot Camp. There were no allowances for weakness or family name. Those who graduated were the best of the best; those who were discharged for medical reasons were honored for having tried, even if they hadn't made it. And those who quit bore no shame.

She finished her tea, then stared down at her empty cup. Too much had happened in one day for her to think properly. She knew she should consider the admiral's actions, and the actions of his son, and perhaps even report them to her father. But the raid on the mansion had pushed such petty concerns out of her mind.

"I'm buggered if I'm leaving the ship again," she said flatly. "It isn't safe down there."

"Good idea," Davidson said with suspicious enthusiasm. "You'll be the number one target of the insurgents right now."

Kat eyed him. "Oh?"

"I reviewed the planetary datanet while the doctor was examining you," he said. "The admiral's PR department has already credited you with escaping the terrorists and defeating them, practically singlehandedly. Apparently, you're some kind of super starship captain, a mistress of martial arts as well as a tactical genius . . ."

Kat put her head in her hands. "I'm never going to live this down, am I?"

"Of course not," Davidson said. "At last report, the admiral was planning to grant you the Combat Infantryman's Badge."

"Fuck," Kat said. "I'll be a laughingstock."

She felt her fists clench round her mug and hastily put it down on the deck. The coveted award was given to soldiers who had seen combat and, more rarely, spacers who had found themselves fighting on the ground. It brought a considerable amount of prestige, but little else. But, as far as she knew, it had never been awarded to someone who had escaped a bunch of insurgents long enough to radio for help, then hide until help arrived.

"You won't have to worry about it," Davidson said. "I don't think General Eastside will allow the award to go through."

"Saved," Kat said. She sighed, then stood. "I really should sleep, shouldn't I?"

"I've already spoken to the XO," Davidson said. "Your schedule has been altered. You won't have to stand watch until tomorrow evening."

Kat hesitated. Under normal circumstances, the watch rota wasn't vitally important when the starship was orbiting a heavily defended planet. It was generally seen as a good time to give junior officers a chance to practice without too much opportunity to screw up. But on Cadiz . . . she'd insisted that senior officers remain on watch at all times. The Theocracy could attack at any moment.

But she knew she needed the rest.

"Thank you," she said, finally. She looked down at him, feeling an odd mix of sensations in her breast. "Will you . . . will you stay the night?"

Davidson hesitated, briefly. It would have been unnoticeable if she hadn't known him so well.

"Are you sure?" he asked, finally. "You could regret this . . ."

"Yes," Kat said. She wanted to feel *alive*. "Come with me."

After a moment, Davidson rose to his feet and followed her into her bedroom.

◆ ◆ ◆

"You do realize someone will have noticed?" Davidson said the following morning. "I didn't bed down with the bootlegs."

"I think it's none of their business," Kat said. It had been a long time since she'd kissed anyone, let alone slept with them. The admiral's son certainly didn't count. "Besides, we're in orbit, not on deployment."

"That isn't what I meant and you know it," Davidson said. "There could be . . . *problems*."

"Then we will handle them," Kat said. She reached for her terminal and skimmed through the handful of messages. "The admiral has sent us our deployment orders."

She read them, quickly. *Lightning* was to patrol the border, investigate any hints that starships might be crossing the border without permission, render aid to any ship attacked by pirates, etc., etc. Patrol duty was boring, she knew, but it was necessary. Admiral Morrison had even thoughtfully outlined the precise route they were to follow, close to the border but not close enough to cause problems. Or so he clearly hoped.

Every ship follows the same course, she thought after a check of the records. *They're not even trying to vary their flight plan.*

"Good," Davidson said. "When do we leave?"

"Tonight," Kat said. She tapped a key, forwarding the orders to the XO, then swore as she read the next message. "The spy ship left orbit yesterday."

Davidson looked up, meeting her eyes. "Coincidence?"

"Perhaps not," Kat said. "They might well have been there to watch what happened when the admiral's mansion was attacked."

"Or it was just a coincidence," Davidson said. "I'd hate to be the officer who tried to coordinate an operation across interstellar distances."

Kat shrugged. It didn't matter. What *did* matter was that the Theocracy probably had up-to-date sensor readings on 7th Fleet's condition—and the XO's old friends had barely started trying to get the fleet combat capable once again. Kat's most optimistic estimate was that the fleet needed at least a month of uninterrupted repair work . . . and she knew it wasn't going to get it. The Theocracy would lower the hammer within weeks.

"It does make me wonder," Davidson said. "Did the Theocracy authorize the operation?"

Kat considered it carefully. By any reasonable standard, decapitating the enemy command network was a reasonable goal in war. But if they'd killed Admiral Morrison and his command staff, she reasoned, they could hardly have hoped for his replacement to be so incompetent. It was unlikely the admiral's patrons could put someone equally useless in his place. But did the Theocracy *know* Admiral Morrison was so incompetent? Or did they consider him a typical commanding officer?

"They might have hoped the occupation would collapse in the aftermath," she mused. Word would have reached Tyre by now. Questions would be asked in Parliament. "That would give them Cadiz without a fight."

"Maybe," Davidson agreed. "Or they might have been horrified at losing their chance of taking out 7th Fleet."

"There's no way to know," Kat said morbidly. She glanced at the next message, then froze. It was from her father. "One moment."

The message wasn't informative. Her father had been unable to determine just who was backing Admiral Morrison. It took Kat several moments to understand the full enormity of what she'd been told. Duke Falcone commanded a patronage network that touched all levels of the Royal Navy, from the junior crewmen to very senior officers. If he couldn't determine who was backing Admiral Morrison, it had to be someone *very* high in the aristocracy.

Or perhaps it's just someone good at covering his tracks, she thought. *But who?*

Her father's note concluded with authorization to call on the Falcone-owned faculties in the system if necessary and order them to assist her. She felt a chill run down her spine as she studied the wording. It was more corporate authority than she'd ever been offered—or expected to wield. Kat hesitated, then forwarded both the authorization and the contact details to the XO. The bureaucrats probably wouldn't notice if the Falcone-owned facilities started requesting spare parts as long as they were paid. The spare parts could then be forwarded to the starships that needed them without sounding any alarms.

"I hate this," she said. Frustration bubbled up in her mind, seeking an outlet. "We're sneaking round our own officers, trying to get ready for war."

"There's no choice," Davidson said. He looked down at the table. "At least *some* of us will be ready when the shit hits the fan."

Kat nodded reluctantly. "I'd better get the ship ready for departure," she said. She felt much better after sex and a good night's sleep. "And remind the crew I exist."

"I'm sure none will dare disobey the martial arts artist," Davidson said.

"Thanks," Kat said sourly. "I'll be expected to try out for the martial arts team next."

CHAPTER TWENTY-FOUR

"I have the bridge," the captain said.

"I stand relieved," William said as he rose from the command chair. Two days of patrolling the border had turned up nothing, apart from some additional navigational data that would be forwarded to the weathermen when they returned to Cadiz. "With your permission, Captain, I have disciplinary matters to attend to."

The captain nodded. William took one last look at the display, then walked off the bridge and headed down towards his office. The designers had clearly not seen the value in placing it right next to the bridge, but he had to admit it was sometimes useful to have his private space right on the edge of Officer Country. He knew crewmen who would hesitate to walk onto the command deck, no matter the cause.

Shaking his head, he stepped through the hatch and tapped instructions into the terminal, alerting the senior chief. He'd put the matter off for far too long, hoping and praying that it would resolve itself before he had to actually take action. But it hadn't. If anything, he noted as he looked at the figures, it was growing worse. Something would have to be done before a handful of promising careers were ruined. He sat down behind his desk and waited. Ten minutes later, the hatch beeped. Someone was waiting outside.

"Enter," he ordered.

William looked up as Crewman Third Class Jonny Steadman entered the compartment. He was a fearsome brute, as muscled as a marine, without the discipline that separated the Marines from the common spacers. His bald head and bare arms were covered in tattoos that pushed the limits of what regulations allowed—but then, Steadman knew he was unlikely to see promotion. If he hadn't been good at his job—and he was, according to the senior chief—he would have been discharged long ago.

Steadman saluted. "You wanted to see me, sir?"

"I did," William confirmed. He'd known enough men like Steadman in his career to know that the slightest hint of weakness would be fatal. "Sit."

He studied Steadman for a long moment, contemplating his options. The man seemed to be trying to decide which of his offenses had led to the summons, but it was impossible to tell if he knew which one had caught the XO's attention. Most disciplinary issues below decks were handled by the senior chief, with the XO only becoming involved if matters were serious. Which one, Steadman had to be wondering, was *serious*?

"You've been running a gambling ring," William said finally. "Haven't you?"

Steadman's eyes narrowed for a brief second. "Gambling isn't against regulations, sir."

Bingo, William thought. Steadman wouldn't be trying to mount a defense if he hadn't realized why he was in the shit. And he might already have worked out just what had gone wrong—and why.

"Of course gambling isn't against regulations," William said. "Of course gambling is common on a starship. I am shocked, *shocked*, to hear that there might be gambling going on below decks."

Steadman smiled at the quote. It vanished a second later as William glared at him.

"Gambling is tolerated as long as it falls within acceptable limits," he said. "And you've been breaking the limits, haven't you?"

He allowed his voice to become contemplative. "A young officer, fresh out of Piker's Peak, untried in the ways of the universe . . . wouldn't you say she was easy meat? A young officer, trying her hardest to be liked by the rough crewmen under her command, partaking in gambling with her subordinates. And a young officer, too naive to realize that the game is rigged—that the game is *always* rigged—losing her salary to her subordinates . . ."

Steadman's face suddenly went very cold.

"Oh, don't be an idiot," William said sharply, before Steadman got any ideas about retaliation. "I monitor bank accounts on this ship, you ninny. She didn't come crying to me. But once I noticed the pattern . . ."

He allowed his voice to trail off meaningfully. Steadman rose to the bait.

"We didn't *ask* her to play, sir," he said. "And we didn't encourage her to keep playing."

William lifted his eyebrows. "Are you trying to tell me you didn't want such a poor player to keep playing?"

He pressed his hands against the table and went on before Steadman could say a word. "It's already getting out of hand, isn't it? She can't give you more money . . . how long will it be, I wonder, before you start using her debt against her? Will you ask her to help you with your less-than-savory activities? Or merely to cover your ass when you get into trouble? Or will you simply try to get her into bed? I'm sure *that* would give you bragging rights below decks."

Steadman looked as if he wanted to say something, but common sense was keeping his mouth firmly shut. William was almost disappointed. He had no proof of anything that could be used to throw the book at Steadman, beyond his own suspicions and the details from the bank accounts. And Steadman was right. Gambling wasn't against regulations. But William knew, all too well, just how easily it could lead to *real* trouble.

This is why more officers should be mustangs, he thought. *They'd have some experience at handling problem cases before they became officers.*

He glared at Steadman. "I will not order you to return her money," he said. "You won it legitimately. What I *will* order you to do is to refrain from inviting her to play any more games. Do you understand me?"

"Yes, sir," Steadman said.

"In addition," William added, "you are not to gamble—ever—for anything more than petty cash. If you want a high stakes game, you can go to the casinos on Cadiz and play there."

William sighed. Money wasn't the only stake in shipboard games. Everything from duty rosters to games and pornographic datachips could be included, if the gamblers were willing. But they tended to cause far too many problems. He'd seen crewmen try to hold down double or triple shifts because they'd gambled and lost. It could not be tolerated.

"I will have my eye on you," he warned. "Step out of line just once more and it will be the Captain's Mast."

Steadman flinched. Even if he wasn't—technically—guilty of breaching regulations, a Captain's Mast could destroy his career. The captain had wide authority to determine what constituted a crime and issue punishment as she saw fit. Steadman *might* be able to convince higher authorities to overturn Captain Falcone's decision, but it would be a major black mark on his record. And he would almost certainly never take up another posting on a starship.

William rose to his feet. "Report to the senior chief," he ordered flatly. "I dare say he has some work for you."

"Sir," Steadman said. He didn't look happy. There was never a shortage of unpleasant or uncomfortable jobs on a starship, which tended to be reserved for punishment duties or for very junior crewmen. "I . . ."

"Out," William ordered.

He watched Steadman go and then sat back at his desk. Steadman wasn't a problem. Men and women like him wouldn't go anywhere, not unless they cleaned up their act. If he stepped out of line again, it would be the end of his career. And he'd made a career of knowing just how far he could push regulations before they broke. But his second visitor would be much more of a problem. Her career, which had been promising, might have just run into a brick wall.

The hatch beeped again. "Enter."

Midshipwoman Cecelia Parkinson entered, looking as though she had been ordered to face the headmaster—or a firing squad. If headmasters on Tyre were anything like headmasters on Hebrides, she might have preferred the firing squad. The midshipwoman closed the hatch and walked towards the desk, nervousness written all over her face. She stopped precisely the right distance from his desk and saluted.

"Be seated," William ordered.

He took a long moment to study her. She really *was* young, he knew, young and naive. The captain had been older when *she'd* graduated from Piker's Peak but Kat Falcone hadn't shown the same level of promise as Midshipwoman Parkinson. And yet, if there hadn't been a looming war, it was unlikely she would have been allowed to graduate so early. Rumor had it that quite a few newer officers needed more polishing and encouragement from the senior chiefs than before.

And Steadman probably saw her coming, William thought, morbidly. Parkinson lacked the self-confidence to stand up to men like Steadman. *And once he had his hooks in her . . .*

He shook his head. She should have approached the XO or one of the lieutenants for help. No doubt Steadman had pointed out that her career would be at risk if her superiors knew she'd been gambling. Or maybe she'd been horrified at the thought of being a sneak. The captain had had similar doubts over landing Admiral Morrison in the shit.

"Midshipwoman, do you know why you're here?"

Parkinson shook her head, unconvincingly. She knew, all right, or at least she had a very good idea. William wasn't surprised. Given her behavior over the last few weeks, she had clearly thought too much about just how badly she'd damaged her own career. He should have tackled the matter earlier, or asked one of the lieutenants to give her some friendly advice. But he'd failed her.

"Gambling," William said flatly. "How much do you owe Crewman Steadman?"

Parkinson hesitated. "Five hundred crowns," she said, finally. "I . . ."

William sighed. Half her income would be inaccessible as long as she was onboard ship, a precaution against this very situation. But Steadman wouldn't have pushed her to withdraw it when she was on Cadiz, not when having her in his debt would be far more useful in the long run. Parkinson was beautiful. Who knew *what* the crewman had had in mind?

Maybe I should just beat him up, William thought. *Or ask the marines to encounter him in a dark alleyway one day.*

"Five hundred crowns," he repeated. It was a sizable part of her wages, particularly with half of her money being held in reserve. "You're in debt to an ordinary crewman to the tune of five hundred crowns?"

"Yes, sir," Parkinson said. Her hands twisted on her lap. "I . . ."

"You were lured into the game," William said. It was time for some fatherly advice. Technically, it wasn't his job to mentor young officers—that was normally handled by the senior chiefs—but he had a feeling Parkinson would listen to him more than the NCOs. "I believe there was a course at Piker's Peak on maintaining the proper distance between yourself and crewmen?"

"Yes, but . . ."

William cut her off. "But what?"

Parkinson swallowed. "Sir," she said, "I was a fool."

"Good," William said. "That is a *far* more useful attitude."

He met her eyes. "You went into Piker's Peak because you have the makings of a fine officer," he said. He'd checked her record. As far as he could tell, she didn't have any aristocratic or naval connections. "But, you must understand, the universe is *full* of people who will take advantage of you if you show them the slightest hint of weakness. Gambling with your subordinates was a dangerous mistake."

"Yes, sir," she said.

"It could easily have been a great deal worse," he added. "You have been entrusted with rank, which brings power and responsibilities. He could have exploited you for his own personal benefit, either by forcing you to work for him or simply by offering to write off part of your debt in exchange for going to bed with him. Do you understand just how close you came to disaster?"

Parkinson flinched. "I wouldn't have . . ."

"It is amazing," William cut her off, "just how far someone will go with the proper manipulation. He would have started small. Perhaps he would have asked you to alter the duty roster in his favor, a tiny act that wouldn't have caused any real harm. And then he would have slowly worked his way up until you were completely in his pocket. You would have been his slave, all the time telling yourself that you wouldn't go any further. I've seen it happen, *midshipwoman*. It can get so far out of hand that the IG has to be called in to sort out the mess."

He met her eyes. "You're lucky," he said. "If he'd been a little more careful about covering his tracks, no one would have noticed until it was far too late. Your career would have been destroyed. As it is, you *will* have to pay the price for your carelessness.

"There are people who depend on you," William added, trying to sound firm but not overly harsh. "You will be leading those people into battle one day. The universe is *not* a safe place for careless young officers."

"I know, sir," she said. Tears were glistening at the corners of her eyes. "I'm sorry, sir."

William reached for a handkerchief and handed her a tissue, suddenly feeling very old. They came from very different worlds, literally.

He'd served in the ranks before becoming a mustang; she'd never served on a starship until she'd completed her course at Piker's Peak. She had self-confidence issues he'd never experienced. He wondered, absently, if the captain ever had such issues. But she would have been raised to give orders to her subordinates.

"You have to make a choice," he said, once she'd wiped her eyes. "You can have NJP—non-judicial punishment—from me or you can face the captain."

He waited. When he'd been a junior crewman, he would have hated the thought of facing the captain, even though the senior chiefs had been very good at inventing unpleasant punishments for misbehaving crewmen. NJP punishments simply weren't added to a crewman's permanent record. He would have to make a note in Parkinson's file that she'd had an NJP, as she was an officer, but by long tradition the matter would be assumed closed as long as there were no repetitions. Besides, it also cut down on paperwork.

"I'll take the NJP," Parkinson said finally.

William nodded, respecting her choice. "There's no point in docking your wages," he said. He *could* have docked her reserved wages, but it would have been petty and cruel. "I *will* strip your seniority through a retrospective beaching. It will be pointless on this ship, yet the promotions board will take it into account when they consider promotions."

He saw the wince she couldn't quite hide and nodded. Seniority in a given rank was important, even though Parkinson had only four months as a midshipwoman. It might make the difference between early promotion and remaining a midshipwoman for several months longer after she completed her first cruise. Unless she did something heroic, of course, that jumped her ahead on the list. It was always possible.

"In addition, you will spend some of your off-duty hours training with the Marines," he added. Parkinson had done poorly in her unarmed combat course and hadn't, according to the records, practiced with her firearm since boarding *Lightning*. "They will teach you how to fight and defend yourself, which will boost your confidence. And believe me, you need your confidence."

"Sir," Parkinson said, "I can't fight . . ."

"You're in the wrong career if that is literally true," William said. He'd known people who had been too quick to fight and people who had been held back by their inner demons, but he'd never met anyone who was literally incapable of fighting. "The Marines will make sure you develop the confidence to kick some ass, the next time you need it. And you will."

"Yes, sir," Parkinson said reluctantly.

"There is a war coming," William said. "We cannot allow young officers to avoid their duties."

He hesitated, then reached for his rank pips and removed them from his collar. "You should have come to me or one of the other officers at once," he added. "I understand why you didn't, but you should have. You would have been lectured and reprimanded, of course, yet you would have been helped. We are here to advise you if necessary."

"Yes, sir," Parkinson said.

"Report to Major Davidson this afternoon, after your shift," William said. He smiled at her frightened expression. "The Marines look fearsome, but they *will* help you overcome your doubts and make you more confident. And you *need* confidence."

"Yes, sir," Parkinson said.

William nodded. He'd repeated it enough, he hoped, for it to sink in. If she didn't grow a spine, with or without the Marines, she would be in deep trouble when she was expected to fight.

He rose. "Dismissed, Midshipwoman," he ordered. "I will call you back in a week or two from now. By then, I expect you to have a plan worked out for your future development."

Midshipwoman Parkinson hesitated, as if she wanted to say something, but then turned and walked out of the hatch. William watched her go, then picked up his rank pips and slowly returned them to his collar. Had she picked up the underlying message? He'd given her advice she had to hear, but not advice he could give as the XO. He sat down and wrote a brief note into the log and then reached for the endless list of issues that needed to be considered. If nothing else, border patrol duty was good for testing the ship, without actual combat. Or interference from bureaucrats on Cadiz.

He continued to think of Parkinson and what she was going through, feeling a flicker of sympathy. On Hebrides, confidence would have been hammered into her head before she reached puberty. But Tyre was kinder to its children.

Poor girl, he thought. *All alone in the night.*

CHAPTER TWENTY-FIVE

"Captain," Ross said, "I'm picking up a distress signal."

Kat swung her chair to turn and face the communications officer. "Is it real?"

"I think so," Ross said, after a long moment. "There's none of the oddities hyperspace throws up when a message has been bounced hundreds of light years."

"Show me its location," Kat ordered. The display altered, showing a location on the near side of the border that was far too close to a hyperspace storm for comfort. "And is it genuine?"

"Unknown," Ross said.

Kat hesitated. By law, and interstellar agreements, ships were meant to respond to distress calls, no matter who sent them. There was also an agreement against sending *fake* distress calls, an agreement she knew the Theocracy had never signed. It was quite possible that the call was a ruse, intended to lure her ship into a trap. But it was her duty to respond to the call unless she *knew* it was a fake. And she knew no such thing.

"Alter course," she ordered. "Yellow alert. I say again, Yellow alert."

She settled back in her chair as the drumbeat sounded, calling her crew to action stations. If it was a trap, so close to the border, they might find themselves in a fight at any second. An ambush in hyperspace would be risky, but the Theocracy might deem it a worthwhile risk if they wanted her ship destroyed. Taking her intact would be a little harder.

"Launch probes," she added. Hyperspace would dim their signals, but there might be some advance notice if they were flying towards a trap. "And monitor them closely."

She glanced up as the XO came onto the bridge and checked the situation. He took his seat next to her. He looked tired. It struck her, suddenly, that he'd been sleeping when she'd sounded the alert. She threw him an apologetic look, then looked back at the display. The signal source was getting closer, but it was still obscured by bursts of energy. Hyperspace roiled and boiled, as though it were a living thing.

And if it's a trap, Kat thought, *what better way to hide it from our sensors?*

"I'm picking up weapons fire," Roach snapped. "There isn't one ship there, Captain. I'm picking up at least two."

Kat sucked in her breath as the two contacts suddenly came into view. One of them was a freighter, clearly modified to carry at least some weapons and heavy defense shields. The other was a destroyer of unknown design, but definitely modern. She checked the records and found no match. They had to be looking at another indigenous Theocratic design. And it was clearly on the verge of blowing the freighter apart.

"The freighter is hailing us, Captain," Ross reported. "They're begging for assistance."

Kat looked at the XO, who looked back evenly. They were in Commonwealth space, but they didn't have the slightest idea of what was actually going on. For all they knew, the freighter was crewed by terrorists or pirates and the Theocrats were doing the right thing by hunting them down. It was equally possible the crew were refugees, fleeing the Theocracy's iron grip on their worlds. There was no way to know without boarding the ship.

And she had orders to protect the border.

"Contact the Theocratic ship," she ordered. "Warn them off."

There was a long pause. "They're opening a channel," Ross reported.

"Put it through," Kat ordered.

The image was so badly distorted by hyperspace that it was hard to make out any details about the speaker. His face seemed dark, but she couldn't tell if he had a beard or if it was merely his uniform. The audio channel was clear enough, however. She could hear the speaker without problems.

"The freighter has been stolen," the voice said. The speaker didn't even bother to identify himself. "You are ordered to allow us to recover our ship without interference."

"Ordered?" the XO repeated. "Unless he has some secret weapon mounted in that hull, Captain, we outgun him by an order of magnitude."

"Red alert," Kat ordered. Alarms howled through the ship as she touched his console, linking her into the audio channel. "This is Captain Falcone. Your vessel has engaged in hostile acts within Commonwealth space. You are ordered to stand down. The freighter will be boarded, then towed to the nearest Commonwealth naval base. You may request its return there."

"They just swept us," Roach snapped. "They're locking weapons onto our hull!"

Kat blinked. "Are they mad?"

"They may not want to report failure," the XO said softly. "What will their superiors say if they back down now?"

It seemed absurd, Kat considered. *Her* superiors wouldn't expect her to pick a fight with a starship several times her size, not over a mere freighter. *That* suggested there was something important about the freighter, something that needed to be recovered at all costs, no matter the risk. Unless it was a trap, of course. The freighter had really been quite lucky, suspiciously lucky, that *Lightning* had picked up her distress call.

"Lock weapons onto their hull," Kat ordered. They'd clearly been trying to take the freighter intact, but they might change their minds now *Lightning* had arrived. "And prepare to cover the freighter if necessary."

There was a long pause. "Your attempts to shield the freighter are an act of war," the enemy commander said finally. "Stand down and allow my forces to board the freighter or you will be fired upon."

Kat thought fast. Her orders were somewhat contradictory, thanks to Admiral Morrison and his bureaucrats. She was supposed to patrol the border and defend Commonwealth interests, but she wasn't allowed to fire first under any circumstances. It might start a war. Yet she knew the war was likely to start anyway . . .

If we had a few weeks to prepare, she thought. *But we won't get those weeks . . .*

She keyed her console, opening the channel. "This is Commonwealth space," she said, firmly. "I will not allow acts of aggression within our territory. You will have your chance to issue a demand for the freighter to be returned to you and any prisoners to be extradited. I . . ."

"Incoming fire," Roach snapped. Red icons blazed to life on the display. "Multiple missiles incoming; I say again, multiple missiles incoming!"

"Launch decoys," Kat snapped. In hyperspace, point defense would be dangerously unreliable. "Return fire!"

Lightning shuddered as she unleashed a broadside, aimed right at the Theocratic vessel. Kat braced herself as the wave of incoming missiles altered course, some suckered away from her vessel by the decoys, others picked off neatly by the point defense. But two survived long enough to slam into her shields.

"Energy disturbances registered," Lieutenant Robertson reported. "Hyperspace has started to become dangerously unstable."

Kat winced. "Pull us away from the disturbances," she ordered. On the display, the enemy ship had taken seven hits and was spinning out of control. "Raise the Theocratic ship. Order them to . . ."

She broke off as the enemy craft exploded, ripped apart by the disturbances in hyperspace, her crew wiped out before they could hope to get to the lifepods. Kat felt a moment of true horror at what she'd done, then pulled herself back to reality. If their actions provoked a full-scale hyperspace storm, escape would become extremely difficult. Fortunately, hyperspace seemed calmer than she had any right to expect.

"Target destroyed," Roach said. "I'm not picking up more than a few fragments of wreckage."

"Understood," Kat said.

She shuddered. The war might have just begun . . . assuming, of course, the Theocracy figured out what had become of their vessel. It was quite possible they'd assume the destroyer was lost in hyperspace, particularly if the freighter they'd been chasing was desperate enough to ram them amidships.

"Contact the freighter," she ordered. "Inform them they are to hold position, stand down all weapons and shields, and prepare to be boarded."

The XO looked at her. "With permission, Captain, I should accompany the Marines," he said. "One of us may have to make decisions in a hurry."

Kat hesitated. It was possible, although unlikely, that the Theocracy had been in the right. If so, their crew had fought and died for nothing. But it was far more likely they were dealing with political refugees or defectors. Either case would require some quick decisions.

"Do so," she ordered. "But be careful. This could all have been arranged to trick us into lowering our guard."

"They threw away a destroyer to do so," the XO pointed out. "It doesn't seem likely."

"We shall see," Kat said. "Watch yourself."

She watched the XO leave the bridge, then turned to watch the display. The freighter seemed innocent, too innocent. Kat felt suspicions flickering through her mind as the marine shuttles launched, heading right towards the freighter. What *was* it carrying that was so important that an enemy commander had been prepared to risk almost certain death just to prevent the ship from falling into Commonwealth hands? Or was it meant to convince the Commonwealth that they'd captured something vital?

All she could do was wait.

♦ ♦ ♦

Up close, it was alarmingly obvious that the freighter had been in a battle. Scorch marks covered its hull, revealing moments where the shields had failed and allowed directed energy weapons to caress the ship. Someone had bolted weapons and sensors—even shield generators—from several different eras to the hull, trying to give her some extra—and unexpected—punch. William was alarmingly impressed with whomever had done the work, even though it was far too sloppy to be tolerated on a Royal Navy starship. They'd somehow managed to get the different systems to work together.

He pushed his admiration aside as the shuttle dropped towards the nearest airlock. According to the plans, they should be within a few meters of the bridge—much of the freighter was nothing more than cargo holds—but it was impossible to be sure. The freighter was old enough to have been refitted to be anything from a passenger liner to a garbage scow. A dull clunk echoed through the shuttle as she mated with the airlock, and then a hiss sounded as the hatch opened and air pressure matched.

"Stay here," Davidson said to the XO. The armored marines would take the lead. "Watch our backs."

William scowled as the marines stepped through the airlock, ready for anything. Cold logic suggested it wasn't a trap, but he had to admit the captain's paranoia was grounded in reality, particularly after hearing some of the tales from the refugees. The Theocracy hadn't hesitated to call down strikes on their own positions just to kill insurgents and freedom fighters. If they thought it was important enough, they could have easily sacrificed a destroyer just to make sure the freighter was taken into custody.

But if they intended the ship to serve as a Trojan Horse, he thought, *it wouldn't work. We'd never allow it anywhere near the fleet base without checking it thoroughly first, would we?*

"Commander," Davidson said, "you might want to take a look at this."

William stepped through the hatch. Inside, the vessel was as dull and gray as any other freighter from the early expansion era, but it wasn't the bulkheads that caught his attention. The men standing at one end of the chamber, their backs pressed against the gray metal, were cyborgs. Their bodies had been extensively modified in a manner he could only deem *crude.* Half of them had had their arms replaced by weapons, the other half had electric eyes or implants growing out of their heads. And they looked . . . oddly unconcerned.

"They're under orders to do nothing," a soft voice said. "They will obey."

William turned to see a slim man wearing a white robe. There was something effeminate about his movements—and his face, come to think of it. If he hadn't had an Adam's apple, William would have wondered if he was a girl, pretending to be a man.

"Obey?" Davidson repeated. "What have you done to them?"

"They volunteered to be bodyguards," the man said. "The doctors programmed them to be obedient."

William felt sick. It was easy to use implants for thought control, to direct someone along an approved route of thinking—or simply to puppet their body like something in a simulation. But it was banned, so completely that anyone who dared suggest using it risked being summarily sacked, while standard implants had built-in safeguards to prevent anyone from hacking them and turning the user into a slave. It wasn't something he would have used on anyone, even a volunteer.

He gathered himself. "How many people are there on this ship?"

The young man hesitated. "Will you swear not to return us to the Believers?"

William felt his eyes narrow. The Theocracy called its people the Believers, but hardly anyone else did. He'd thought he was dealing with refugees from a border world, yet the presence of the cyborgs argued otherwise. Something was deeply wrong. He drew on his experience and studied the young men, then pasted a reassuring expression on his face.

"If you're seeking political asylum," he said, "the case will be heard at the nearest naval base. However, I can assure you that you will not be returned unless you are guilty of crimes under interstellar law. The ship may have to be returned; you can stay. But we need you to cooperate now."

The young man took a breath. "There are seventeen crew, nineteen bodyguards, and twelve passengers on this ship," he said. "The passengers are important."

William gave Davidson a sharp look, then looked back at the young man. "There isn't any more time for games," he said. "I need you to answer the questions. *Who* are the passengers and why are they here?"

The young man straightened upright. "They are the Princess Drusilla and her maidservants," he said. "And they request that you protect them from their enemies."

Davidson could only gape. "Pardon?"

"Search the ship thoroughly," William ordered. He'd expected a defector ever since he'd seen the bodyguards, but he hadn't anticipated a *princess*. Everything they knew about how the Theocracy treated women suggested they were neither seen nor heard. How could one of their *princesses* have stolen a ship and escaped? "The captain will have to meet with the princess, in person."

"She cannot meet any unrelated male," the young man said quickly. "She . . ."

"Will have to get used to our customs if she wishes to stay," William said. If the princess couldn't meet an unrelated man, what about the man facing him? Or her cyborg bodyguards? But the cyborgs could probably be programmed to ignore her. "Now, if you don't mind, we will search your ship."

♦ ♦ ♦

Kat had grown up in a society where men and women were largely equal. A baseline woman might be physically weaker than a man, but an enhanced woman could be stronger than an unenhanced man, and technology had liberated them from the drudgery of life in the past. She had to admit she was curious about a woman from a very different society, particularly one who had managed to escape her family's grasp. Kat could sympathize. But, at the same time, it was a major diplomatic headache.

She felt a trickle of dislike as soon as Princess Drusilla was shown into her Ready Room by two female marines. The princess was slender with dark skin, darker eyes, and an air of helplessness only betrayed by the sharpness in her eyes. She was no fool, Kat knew, despite her air of fragile vulnerability. This was a woman skilled in manipulating others to get her way.

Just like Candy, she thought, but Candy could have abandoned her manipulations at any point and lived her own life. She had a feeling Princess Drusilla would never have been able to live on her own. Nothing they'd heard from the refugees had suggested women had good lives in the Theocracy. It seemed to be more common for them to become nothing more than baby factories. Given the Theocracy's expansion rate, Kat could well believe it.

"I did not believe them when they told us a woman commanded this starship," Princess Drusilla said. Even her voice was enchanting. Kat couldn't help being affected, although she was well aware of the manipulation. By now, it was probably habit for the princess to manipulate those round her. "And you're so *young*."

"Thank you," Kat said, tartly. She swallowed her reaction as best as she could. "I just killed a destroyer to help you escape, Your Highness. Your mere presence is going to cause considerable problems for my government. I don't have time for games."

The princess lowered her eyes. Kat wondered, absurdly, if she really thought a gesture of submission would help her case—or if she was thinking of Kat as a man in a woman's body. The thought made her smile. Swapping sexes permanently wasn't common, but anyone who felt they'd been born the wrong sex could have a proper sex change. She shrugged, dismissing the thought. Under the circumstances, it hardly mattered.

"I need answers," Kat said. She kept her voice under tight control. "Why did you come here?"

"To escape," the princess said. Her voice became urgent. "And to warn you. They're already preparing to attack your worlds."

Kat studied Princess Drusilla carefully. She certainly *sounded* as though she was telling the truth, but . . . but it was hard to be sure. Growing up while considered to be an inferior being would have taught her how to lie and mask her reactions far more effectively than anything Kat had endured.

"I think you'd better start from the beginning," she said. "And don't leave anything out."

The princess bowed her head, then began.

CHAPTER TWENTY-SIX

"My father is the Speaker," the princess said. Even on a display screen, she was stunning. "I was his oldest daughter."

William frowned, studying her. The princess hadn't been crude, but she *had* been alarmingly seductive. He *wanted* to make her happy, he *wanted* to protect her . . . and, even though he *knew* it was an act, he still found it hard to resist. Making a mental note to ensure she only dealt with female crew, he watched as the recording played out.

"He wants to launch an attack against the Commonwealth while he's still in office," Princess Drusilla continued. "I believe he thinks such a proof of God's favor will ensure his son can take up the role of Speaker after him. The attack fleets are already being positioned to take the offensive against your worlds."

"And why," the captain's recorded image said, "did you come to us?"

William glanced at the captain. The way she sat suggested she was tense—and that she disliked the princess on sight. William wasn't sure why, but he knew that women tended to pick up on subtle points men missed. Or maybe she just felt dowdy when compared to the princess.

"My father promised me as a reward to the admiral who conquered the Commonwealth," Princess Drusilla said. "I protested. He told me I would be . . . rewritten to suit the admiral's tastes in women. It would kill me, destroy my personality. I planned an escape with the help of my bodyguards and made it off world. But then they gave chase."

The princess leaned forward, her every motion screaming *earnestness.* "I have copies of some of their plans," she said. "You have to believe me. I won't go back. I can't."

William could well believe it. If the Theocracy took a dim view of backsliding among new converts, he dreaded to think what they would do to the daughter of their leader if she betrayed them. And she *had* betrayed them, unless it was an elaborate trick. But his years of service in the Royal Navy told him it was too elaborate to be a trick. They'd have to be damn near omnipotent to pull it off successfully.

The captain tapped the table. "Doctor?"

Doctor Braham leaned forward. "I have examined the princess and her handmaidens," she said. "The princess is not baseline human—there's some genetic engineering and reshaping in her DNA—but she isn't outfitted with any implants, not even a basic neural link, apart from a simple tracking implant. I think it is comparable to a prisoner tracking implant from Tyre, although it doesn't have a stunner included. Fortunately for Princess Drusilla, the implant was apparently disabled. I have since removed it."

"Good thinking," the captain said.

"Her handmaidens don't have any implants either, but they have definitely undergone some conditioning," Doctor Braham said. "They're very . . . obedient. Princess Drusilla is apparently their mistress, but they will obey any orders as long as they don't conflict with any from the princess. However, they may well have other orders in their minds that might be activated at any moment. We lack the deep-scan facilities to make sure of it."

William shivered. Conditioning—a form of brainwashing—could be used on almost anyone, unless they had implants to prevent it. The technology was the stuff of nightmares, he knew all too well; a loyal officer could be turned into a spy with only a few hours of enemy conditioning. Or worse. Someone could be turned into a slave if they encountered someone with bad intentions and no scruples. There were always lingering rumors about rings that specialized in conditioned slaves . . .

"The conditioning wasn't perfect," Davidson said. "Not if they weren't able to alert the security forces that the princess was planning an escape."

"Or they might not have known what was in the princess's mind," Doctor Braham said. "I think they're also very ignorant, at least outside their specialized fields. One of them is clearly a doctor, charged with tending the princess, but she knew almost nothing about life on a starship."

She paused. "I can't offer any guarantees," she added. "I simply don't have the equipment to be sure they don't have additional commands buried within their minds. All we can do is keep them in stasis until we return to Cadiz."

William nodded. The crew of the Theocratic freighter had, much to their relief, already been moved into stasis and placed in storage. He had a feeling that none of them would want to go home, no matter how terrifying they found the idea of living among infidels. The Speaker would probably have them tortured to death for daring to assist in his daughter's escape. And the bodyguards, after a brief set of scans, had joined them in stasis.

"She claims she would have been brainwashed," Davidson said. "Is that plausible?"

"The technology to create Stepford Wives—or Husbands—exists," Doctor Braham said flatly. "It isn't actually *that* difficult to remove a person's ability to decide which orders to follow, or have their minds automatically interpret any instruction as an irresistible order. There have even been worlds where such techniques were used regularly, particularly on companions and servants of the local rulers. Would it be used in this case?"

She sighed. "Princess Drusilla has no implants, nothing that would protect her mind," she added. "It's certainly *possible* that someone *could* use the technology on her."

"We already know what the Theocracy thinks of women," the captain growled. "It might well seem an ideal solution for them."

William wondered, absently, if any of Tyre's aristocracy had ever used such technology on their wives or children. It was certainly possible . . . and someone with the wealth and power of the captain's father could have covered it up afterwards. But if it got out, it would utterly destroy the perpetrator's family. They'd be lucky if they weren't lynched in the streets by outraged citizens. *No one* took the idea of having his or her mind altered lightly.

And if the princess tells her story back home, he thought, *the public will be outraged.*

"We have a problem," the captain said, tapping the table. "Is this a genuine defection or is this an elaborate trick?"

She keyed a switch, activating the holographic display. One star glowed red. "If the princess is telling the truth," she added, "the Theocracy's attack fleet is gathering here, preparing to surge across the border and invade. But she doesn't know when the attack is actually planned to start, which leaves us with a dilemma. Can we believe her?"

William looked at Doctor Braham. "Can you confirm her identity?"

"No," Doctor Braham said, shortly. "We don't have any DNA records from her family for comparison. However, I monitored her brainwaves while she was speaking to me and she certainly *believes* she's telling the truth."

Davidson stroked his chin thoughtfully. "This does seem to be too elaborate to be a trick, Captain," he said. "They'd have to be able to track us through hyperspace just to be sure we were in position to save Princess Drusilla from her pursuers. And hyperspace could easily have swallowed their distress call before we ever heard it. If they wanted us to intercept the destroyer and blow it to pieces, Captain, they really got quite lucky."

He paused. "It would have made more sense to have them enter Cadiz before threatening to destroy the ship," he added. "There were just too many things that could go wrong."

The captain frowned. "So you believe it isn't a trick?"

"I don't think so," Davidson said. "This could be the break we've been waiting for."

"Captain," Roach said, "it's nearly three weeks from here to their homeworld. How did they manage to avoid interception for so long? And how did they even get the ship in the first place?"

"Sheer audacity, if you believe them," Davidson said. "I debriefed the princess's assistant extensively. He managed to get all the paperwork filed, allowing him to slip the princess and her escorts up to the freighter in spacesuits so no one knew who was travelling, then used the bodyguards to take over the ship and set off into hyperspace."

William considered it. The story sounded plausible; starships had been hijacked by passengers before, particularly largely unarmed freighters. If the crew had been promised their lives, they might cooperate long enough to get the ship into hyperspace and headed towards the Commonwealth. Quite a few things could easily go wrong, but given what was at stake . . . he felt a sudden flash of admiration for Princess Drusilla. She'd clearly managed to turn her status as a second-class citizen into an advantage.

"Boarding the ship wouldn't have been easy, not if they wanted the princess alive," Davidson added. "A skilled crew might just have managed to remain away from the destroyer for three weeks."

"Something to check," the captain said. She paused. "Opinions?"

Roach spoke quickly. "Captain, I don't buy this," he said. "We're talking about a handful of uneducated women, from a world where women are expected to be little more than baby factories, and their bodyguards capturing a starship and traveling for three weeks without being intercepted by an immensely more competent and capable crew. And she's someone so important we *have* to treat her with kid gloves. There are just too many unanswered questions for me to believe she's what she claims to be."

"But they don't benefit," Davidson mused. "If we believe her and go on the alert, they're not going to be able to launch their attack against unprepared defenses. How do they gain the upper hand from letting us have a woman we think is their leader's daughter?"

"Perhaps they want to make us look like aggressors," Roach speculated. "Or perhaps they want to lure us into a trap."

Davidson snorted. "Make us look bad in front of *whom*?"

He had a point, William knew. There *were* other interstellar powers, but none of them seemed inclined to worry overmuch about the Theocracy—or the Commonwealth, for that matter. They believed the Theocracy would either wind up hemmed in by the Commonwealth or simply collapse under its own weight. There were few low-tech worlds left for the Theocracy to conquer with a single destroyer, then occupy with a few thousand armored soldiers. Then its people would start asking if the constant state of emergency, with all production going to the military, was worth it. There would be no good answer the Theocrats could give.

But they could keep their people in ignorance for quite some time, he thought. *Unless a bigger power decided to intervene.*

The captain tapped the table again, harder this time. "Major?"

"The story seems plausible," Davidson said. "And we are well aware of the possibility that it is a trick. However, I honestly don't see how they benefit. Right now, they couldn't ask for a better chance to clobber 7th Fleet. Why put us on the alert when it gets them nothing but the certainty of stubborn resistance?"

The captain's face flickered, just for a second. She didn't like what she'd been told, but why? William knew she was well aware of the danger from the Theocracy. She'd even risked her own career to send messages back to Tyre. It made no sense.

"It could be meant to cause political trouble," Roach suggested. "Wouldn't there be questions asked in Parliament if we went on alert?"

"There's a difference between putting the defenses on alert and storming across the border, looking to kick ass and take names," Davidson snapped. "They'd know the difference."

William smiled. "Would the politicians?"

The captain cleared her throat, loudly. "They certainly don't seem to benefit," she agreed reluctantly. "But it could still be a trick."

She shook her head. "We have to report it to Tyre anyway," she said. "We'll put a crew on the freighter, then head back to Cadiz at best possible speed. Once there, we will brief the admiral on our discovery. The attack could begin at any moment."

William frowned. "But why haven't they jumped already?"

Davidson leaned forward. "They could be waiting for His Majesty's birthday," he said. "We'd have most of our personnel down on the surface, getting rat-assed drunk, with only skeleton crews on the ships. It's pretty much tradition by now. And if they caught us then, we'd have our trousers round our knees and our . . ."

"Thank you," the captain said quickly. "But His Majesty's birthday is three months away. Think what we could do with three months."

"Get 7th Fleet ready for a fight," William agreed. He wondered, suddenly, what would have happened if the insurgents had managed to kill the admiral and most of his commanding officers. The efficiency of the fleet would probably have doubled. "And even get some reinforcements out here."

"They may understand Admiral Morrison very well," Davidson grumbled. "I don't think they'd expect him to change the habits of a lifetime."

Captain Falcone looked torn. William understood. Speaking disrespectfully of a superior officer was a court-martial offense. But it was hard for anyone to argue that Admiral Morrison *deserved* respect.

Whatever he'd done to earn his place on Cadiz, to buy patronage from powerful people, it hadn't been based on a lifetime of dedicated service, skill, and efficiency.

She rose to her feet. "I will be writing the report to Tyre," she said. "Mr. XO, please see to putting the crew on the freighter, then getting us underway. I want to be back at Cadiz as soon as possible."

"Aye, Captain," William said.

"We do have an issue with the handmaidens," Doctor Braham said before the captain could take her leave. "Should we put them in stasis too?"

"Please do," the captain said, after a moment. "Mr. XO, Major, I want you to assign two officers to debrief Princess Drusilla as extensively as possible. *Female* officers."

"Aye, Captain," William said. "We'll find out what she knows."

The captain nodded, then turned and walked out of the compartment. William looked from face to face, silently dismissing them, then reached for his terminal and started to assign a crew to the freighter. There would be no prize money for *this* ship, he was fairly sure, but it would give some of his crew a chance to stretch their legs and spend time away from *Lightning*. After a moment, he added a pair of engineering techs to the roster. If there were any unpleasant surprises on the freighter, they'd find them before the ship got anywhere *near* Cadiz.

"I'm going to assign one of my marines to the princess," Davidson said slowly. "Do you have a suitable officer to assign to her?"

William considered it, carefully. Midshipwoman Parkinson was probably young enough to seem unthreatening, at least to a woman who hadn't grown up surrounded by powerful and self-confident young women. It was quite possible Princess Drusilla would be scared by one of the female marines. But Parkinson didn't have the confidence to stand up for herself . . . it was possible Princess Drusilla would overwhelm her.

But she'll have a marine to supervise, he thought. *She'll do.*

"I think so," he said, finally. "We also need to sort out a list of questions for her, see if we can pick holes in her story."

Davidson nodded. "Kid gloves," he said. "But at least we can monitor her brainwaves. If she lies to us, we'll know about it."

"Let's hope so," William said. One possibility that *hadn't* been raised at the meeting was that the princess might believe she was telling the truth but had actually been lied to by her father. "I dare say we'll find out soon."

♦ ♦ ♦

Kat sat in her Ready Room, feeling oddly conflicted.

She had no doubt the Theocracy was planning an offensive—and a great deal earlier than His Majesty's birthday. The date was simply *too* obvious. Besides, by then, someone might have replaced Admiral Morrison with a more efficient officer. But, at the same time she disliked Princess Drusilla. The reaction was so strong it surprised her. She'd encountered society butterflies and madams who hadn't irritated her anywhere near as badly whenever they'd opened their mouths. It primed her to disbelieve anything the princess said, on principle.

An officer cannot afford to let her personal feelings interfere with her job, she told herself sternly. But her own thoughts mocked her. *Do you dislike the princess because she could be you, if things were different, or because Patrick finds her attractive?*

Angrily, she pushed the thought aside, then started composing the next message to her father. Given half a chance, Admiral Morrison would probably sit on the whole affair—or try to hand the princess back to the Theocracy just to avoid a diplomatic incident. He couldn't be allowed to hide anything. And yet . . .

She finished writing about the bare bones of the incident, then added notes about her own reactions and that of her officers. The story would play well on Tyre, she knew. Perhaps *too* well.

She muttered curses under her breath as she called up the recordings and reviewed them again. Princess Drusilla was good, very good. Manipulation was second nature to her—and, in truth, it was hard to blame the girl. What other tools did she have to exercise some control over her life? And if she was telling the truth about her father's plans for her . . . Kat couldn't blame her for running. God knew there were aristocrats on Tyre who'd fled just to escape their families and *they* had never been threatened with brainwashing. Even the most manipulative aristocrat on Tyre wouldn't consider rewriting his children's minds just to suit himself.

"We'll see," she concluded. "But where do we go from here?"

CHAPTER TWENTY-SEVEN

"I have received orders from Tyre," Admiral Morrison said. He looked angry, although Kat couldn't tell if he was annoyed at his orders or angry that he had to leave his comfortable lodgings and meet Kat at the spaceport. "These orders, in my view, are provocative."

Kat sucked in a breath. The admiral had wanted to put a lid on the whole affair, as she'd feared, but it had been too late to prevent her from sending a message to Tyre. This time, he seemed to be aware she'd sent the message, even though he hadn't called her to rip her head off. The thought brought her no pleasure. Given what had happened at the party, it was quite likely the admiral was reconsidering his plans for her.

"They are our orders, sir," she said, trying to sound respectful. It wasn't easy. "The Admiralty needs hard data."

The admiral looked thunderous, but she thought she saw a hint of fear on his face. It was hard to blame him. The Admiralty's orders, sent back a day after *Lightning* had returned to Cadiz, admitted of no ambiguity. Kat was to take her cruiser, slip over the border, and investigate the reported staging base directly. If she found an enemy fleet there, she was to hightail it back to Cadiz and inform the Admiralty that the war was about to begin. And *that* would bring the admiral's failings to the attention of his superiors.

"So it would seem," he said, finally. "But there are too many risks involved in this operation."

"Orders are orders, sir," Kat said. She couldn't help feeling nervous at the prospect too, even though she was grateful that someone was finally doing *something*. "And we have to *know*."

She smiled. Admiral Morrison had wanted to keep the princess at Cadiz, but the Admiralty had ordered Kat to dispatch her to Tyre as quickly as possible. Thankfully, a light cruiser had been on the verge of heading home and it had been a simple matter to arrange a transfer. The handmaidens would go with her, while the remaining bodyguards and starship crewmen would be held at Cadiz until a decision was made, one way or the other. Kat would have preferred to send them to Tyre too, but no one was quite sure what they wanted to do with themselves.

"So we do," the admiral said gratingly. "You'll depart tomorrow, Captain. And I wish you the very best of luck."

He turned and strode out of the conference room, leaving Kat alone. She sighed to herself, then looked over at the navigational display. The star Princess Drusilla had highlighted *would* make a good staging base, she knew, if only because it was as worthless and unremarkable as the star they'd used as an RV point for the convoy. It was highly unlikely that *anyone* would consider visiting the area unless they had something to hide. Civilian shippers probably wouldn't go anywhere near the place.

But it was *getting* there that would be the problem.

"The admiral wasn't pleased," she said when she reached her shuttle. Her XO was waiting for her, his face pale. "But our orders have been confirmed."

"Good," William said. Neither of them had been happy at being called down together, even though the XO had to be debriefed while Kat spoke to the admiral. "Did he give you any updated navigational information?"

Kat shook her head. The Theocracy's border was dangerous to starships, with energy storms moving randomly though space. There *were* a handful of known hyper-routes, but the Theocracy would have plenty of time to mount patrols, lay minefields, and take other precautions to discourage anyone from visiting. Taking *Lightning* through a carefully surveyed route would be *asking* for detection.

"I expected as much," the XO observed. "But I did have a thought."

Kat looked at him, putting two and two together. "Your brother?"

"He might have something to help us," the XO said. He looked at his terminal. "But I don't even know if he's still here."

"Send a message," Kat said. "If he's here, we can ask him if he has anything useful for us."

"Aye, Captain," the XO said. He keyed the message into his terminal, but then hesitated. "Do you want to accompany me?"

"I'll be needed to authorize the credit chip," Kat said. She had a feeling the XO didn't want her along, but she wanted to meet his brother, particularly if she was paying him out of her trust fund. It was unlikely she'd ever be able to claim it back from the government. "And besides, meeting him can hardly be more dangerous than the admiral's party."

The XO snorted as a reply popped up in his terminal. "I'd recommend changing into civilian clothes, Captain," he said after reading the message. "You don't want to attract attention."

The street of bars, brothels, and gambling arcades looked different in daylight, Kat decided, as they strode down the road an hour later. Bright sunlight obscured some of the charm, revealing hints that some partygoers had partied too hard and were now suffering hangovers and other aftereffects. A gang of locals wearing bright uniforms was trying to sweep the road, while a handful of crewmen shouted unhelpful advice from the side. Kat eyed the locals suspiciously, wondering if they could be trusted. If the admiral's servants had turned on him . . .

"This bar caters to smugglers and other forms of lowlife," the XO muttered as he escorted her into a tiny building. "It's very secure."

Kat nodded, thoughtfully. Her implants were blinking up warnings, stating that the building was *drenched* in privacy fields. One or two of them might be countered by modern surveillance technology, but several fields working in unison would be enough to defeat even the most sophisticated system. Using so many in one place, she suspected, was technically against the law, although she doubted the case would ever go to court. The general public disliked the idea of being spied on by anyone.

"It would have to be," she muttered back. Even in the semidarkness, it was clear that *no one* came to the Dead Donkey for the ambience. Kat saw a cockroach scuttling across the floor, suggesting the owner didn't care about health and safety regulations . . . if, of course, there were any on Cadiz. Such matters were the task of the local government and Cadiz had none. "Why else would anyone come here?"

"Billy," a voice caroled. "Over here!"

Kat turned and saw a man who looked like a younger version of her XO. Only the eyes, hard and cold, suggested he was actually the older brother. His gaze flickered over her once, then locked on to her eyes, a motion that warned her it would be dangerous to underestimate Scott McElney. The shirt she'd found was a size too tight, but he hadn't even *looked* at her breasts, just her eyes. *He* wasn't going to underestimate her.

"You must be Katherine Falcone," Scott said. He held out a hand. "It is a pleasure to meet an aristocrat who actually gets her hands dirty from time to time."

"Thank you," Kat said. She shook his hand and then allowed him to motion her towards a bench in a private compartment. "How many aristocrats have you met?"

Scott tapped his nose, but said nothing.

The XO leaned forward. "This isn't a friendly chat," he said. His voice was tense, as if he hadn't wanted to have company when he spoke to his brother. "The last time we met, you mentioned navigational data. Do you have such data on hand?"

"I have quite a bit of data on hand," Scott said. "What, precisely, are you looking for?"

"Unguarded routes into the Theocracy," Kat said. "A way to slip into their space without being detected."

"I have several," Scott said. "Some safer than others, but more likely to attract attention."

He paused. "But what are you prepared to pay?"

Kat exchanged a glance with her XO, then reached into her pocket and produced a blank credit chip. She held it up so he could read the balance—zero—then pressed the coin into the palm of her hand, using her implants to authorize the transfer. The credit balance jumped up to one thousand crowns. And it would be largely untraceable, she was sure. The crowns would still exist, but they would no longer be connected to her.

"One thousand crowns, up front," she said. She sensed her XO's shock, but pressed on anyway. There was no time to bargain. "And I will pay another thousand crowns upon our successful return."

"You could be caught—or reveal the existence of the passageway," Scott said smoothly. "I dare say it won't remain a secret after you report it back to Tyre."

Kat suspected he was right. But she also knew he was trying to see how much she was prepared to pay. "I will put the other thousand crowns in an escrow account," she said shortly. "If we don't make it back, the board of inquiry will determine the cause of our deaths. The account will then be unlocked if the problem isn't with your directions."

And if it is, she added silently, *there will be a number of hard questions for you.*

"It sounds like a decent offer," Scott said. "But what happens if the Theocracy starts guarding the passageway?"

"They haven't started guarding it yet, even though you've probably used it yourself," the XO grated. His voice was very cold. "They could start guarding it tomorrow or from the moment the war breaks out."

"True," Scott agreed. "But I do have commitments . . ."

Kat studied him for a long moment, then sighed. "I will put two thousand crowns in the escrow account," she said. "It will be released to you upon our safe return, no further questions asked. And we shall do our best to remain undetected."

"Very well," Scott said. "One thousand now; two thousand afterwards."

"And you will add a guarantee of secrecy," the XO added. "You're not allowed to trade anything you might have picked up today to anyone else."

Kat swore inwardly. She'd grown up among the aristocracy . . . and she'd never considered the possibility of betrayal. But it was far too possible. The smugglers lived in the void between the two interstellar powers, trying to play each of them off against the other. Scott might be loyal enough to his brother not to consider betraying him to the Theocracy, but there was no way they could take it for granted.

"Very well," Scott said. "You will have exclusivity."

He reached into his pocket, produced a datachip, and pressed it against his palm. There was a long pause as he worked silently, then removed the chip and passed it to Kat. She took it and scanned it with her own implants, discovering that there were five navigational files on the chip and nothing else. After a moment, she passed him the credit chip and pocketed his datachip. The smuggler smiled and rose to his feet.

"One moment," the XO said. "What else have you heard about recent events?"

"Not much," Scott said. "For once, the admiral's office is very quiet. It's quite suspicious."

"Good," Kat said. "Let us hope it stays that way."

William couldn't help brooding as they made their way back to the shuttle, then flew into orbit and returned to *Lightning*. His brother was a disgrace, both to the family and his entire homeworld. There was no avoiding the fact he'd made his fortune smuggling everything from guns to farming equipment—and probably slaves. William had no illusions about life on primitive farming worlds. There was no shortage of worlds that would be grateful if smugglers shipped in young boys and girls, children who could be taught how to farm. Or equipment they simply couldn't afford for themselves.

He wondered, briefly, what the captain had thought of Scott, but she hadn't said a word to him. Instead, she seemed almost meditative, perhaps contemplating the task ahead of their ship. Even if the navigational data was as good as Scott clearly believed, it would be difficult to sneak across the border without being detected. But they had no choice. Orders were orders—and besides, if they discovered an attack fleet preparing to launch, it would wake up the Commonwealth to the oncoming storm.

"I need you to review this data," the captain said as they entered the navigational compartment. Lieutenant Nicola Robertson was sitting inside, studying the latest update from the weathermen. "If this is a safe course to use, we need to depart this afternoon."

Lieutenant Robertson took the chip and slipped it into a reader. "Not a standard piece of navigational data," she noted. "Can I ask where it came from?"

"No," William growled.

The captain shot him a look, but said nothing.

"Interesting," Lieutenant Robertson said. "This course would take us right through the Seven Sisters."

William swore. "The bastard!"

The captain leaned forward. "But is it usable?"

Lieutenant Robertson hesitated. "If the data is accurate, there is a passage through the region," she said. "But it wouldn't be a very *safe* passage. I'd honestly not recommend sending an entire fleet through in a body. And a handful of mines could be used to close the passage permanently."

William studied the display, thinking. The Seven Sisters—seven stars that orbited each other—projected an odd gravitational pattern into hyperspace. Smart navigators deemed the entire area impassable and refused to go anywhere near it, but smugglers would probably consider it an ideal place to meet and transfer stolen cargos in private. They could be almost assured of avoiding detection, even by border patrol ships. The sheer level of hyperspace distortion made any form of patrolling almost impossible.

"It might be doable," he said, reluctantly. "But it will be very risky, Captain. A single mistake and we might be forced back into normal space or vaporized by a hyperspace flare."

The captain nodded. "But they're not guarding that approach route," she said, slowly. "If we could get through the passageway, we'd be almost assured of a safe voyage to our destination."

"But they might well be keeping an eye on approach routes to the star itself," William mused. "We could be detected then . . ."

"That would prove they had something to hide," Captain Falcone said. She smiled. It lit up her entire face. "There's no point in guarding, let alone mining, the approach routes to a useless red dwarf star. The only reason for having guardships in place would be to protect a secret, such as a waiting attack fleet."

She took a breath. "Inform the crew that we will depart in"—she checked her wristcom—"two hours from now. Once we are in hyperspace, we will set course for the Seven Sisters and try to thread the needle."

"Aye, Captain," William said.

She had nerve; he had to admit. There were experienced commanding officers who had been decorated for heroism who would have thought twice about trying to fly through the Seven Sisters, no matter the stakes. And her family's position wouldn't protect her from hyperspace storms if one lanced out and enveloped their ship. The number of starships that had survived a direct encounter with a hyperspace storm could be counted on the fingers of one hand.

"And then contact your friends," she added. "Send them a message, update them on the general situation, and . . . suggest they speed up their preparations."

"Aye, Captain," William said softly.

The captain nodded. "How long do we have?"

It was the question, William knew. How much did the Theocracy know about what Princess Drusilla had known before making her escape? And did they know she'd been rescued by the Royal Navy? In their place, William would have assumed the worst when their destroyer failed to return, but how long were they prepared to hold out hope before drawing the correct conclusion? The Theocrats had to know that starships could rarely be held to a precise schedule. No one could predict when a hyperspace storm might blow up and push them dozens of light years off course.

He thought, grimly, of the reports from the debriefing. Princess Drusilla hadn't been expected to know anything beyond how to look pretty. All she'd learned had come from sympathetic tutors and a handful of servants, many of whom had been stunningly ignorant themselves of anything more than the basics. The princess could neither read nor write, either in the Theocracy's written language or Galactic Standard English. He honestly didn't know *any* high-tech world that *didn't* insist its civilians learn Galactic Standard as a second language.

But would the Theocracy expect her to know about their plans?

It was hard, very hard, to think like the Theocrats. William had grown up on a world where women were to be protected, but anyone who treated them as property would have rapidly come to regret it. Hebrides *bred* strong women. Who would want a shrinking violet when the rough environment demanded someone who could do almost anything a man could do? Even now, even with genetic enhancement, his homeworld had never developed a tradition of engineering women for beauty. They preferred strength and stamina.

But the Theocrats had considered Princess Drusilla a child. No, worse than a child; they'd considered her *property*. It was alarmingly possible that they honestly hadn't realized she could think for herself, which might have explained why the princess and her servants had managed to steal a freighter. The security officers had been conditioned not to treat women as serious threats.

There might be an advantage for us in that, he thought as he saluted and turned to the hatch. *Maybe they won't take a female captain seriously either.*

Putting the thought to one side, he headed for the bridge. Running through the Seven Sisters would be dangerous. It was time to prepare the crew for the coming ordeal.

CHAPTER TWENTY-EIGHT

"We are approaching the Seven Sisters," Lieutenant Samuel Weiberg reported. "I estimate we will enter the passageway within twenty minutes."

"Distortion levels are increasing rapidly," Lieutenant Robertson added. "Sensors are at thirty percent efficiency and failing fast."

Kat kept her face impassive with an effort. As a young girl, she'd tried to take up canoeing, only to discover her family forbade her to test herself against any of the really exciting rapids. Now, she felt something of the same attraction, mixed with a sick feeling in her gut. Her ship—and her crew—could be blown to atoms in a second, before they ever knew they were in trouble. And no one would ever find a trace of their remains.

They'll never see us coming, she thought. If the navigational data was accurate, they could emerge from the passageway in a haze of distortion, then leave on almost any route they chose. It would require a stroke of very bad luck for any guardship to see them coming. *But we might not make it at all.*

"Keep us steady," she ordered. She wondered, suddenly, if she should have updated her will. Her nonvoting stocks and shares would be reabsorbed into the family, but her trust fund would be distributed among her former crew—if they survived—and their families. "Take us into the fire."

She linked into the ship's sensors through her implants and recoiled. Giant flashes of lightning cracked through space, each one powerful enough to swat her ship as easily as a human would stamp on an ant. Great rolling waves of energy blazed round the gravitational shadow cast by Sister III, while flickers of energy pulsed between Sister IV and Sister V. It was a maelstrom far more powerful than anything produced by mankind, Kat knew. No one, despite some proposals, had ever managed to tap hyperspace as a source of energy. All attempts had been universally disastrous.

Look at us, the storms seemed to say. *You puny humans. So smug and secure. You're nothing compared to us.*

Alerts flashed up in her implants as she disconnected herself from the sensors. Her heartbeat was racing so fast she found sweat trickling down her back. Kat forced herself to take a deep breath, then composed herself with an effort. There was a reason officers and crew were discouraged from peeking through the starship's hull when they were so close to a hyperspace storm. Mentally kicking herself for her mistake, Kat gripped hold of her command chair and braced herself for the first hint of trouble. The hull started to shake gently seconds later.

"Picking up waves of gravity turbulence," Weiberg reported.

The XO leaned forward. "Can you see the passageway?"

"Yes," Robertson said. "But it's very thin, sir."

Kat took a breath. "Take us in," she ordered. "Best possible speed."

There was no point in trying to sneak through, she knew. The passage might be safe, at least when compared to the remainder of local hyperspace, but their mere presence would excite hyperspace and trigger more storms. All they could do was race through it as fast as possible and hope they outran any surges of energy chasing them. She studied the display, carefully edited by the computers to be as unthreatening as possible, then braced herself. The shaking grew worse a moment later.

"Storms are picking up," Robertson reported. "But they're not closing in on us."

The shaking abated, just long enough for Kat to relax, then it rapidly grew worse. On the display, waves of energy seemed to be spiraling towards them, almost as if the passageway were intelligent and rejecting their very presence. But *Lightning* passed through into the passageway without further incident, finding safe space at the very heart of the storm. It wouldn't last, Kat knew, but she relaxed for a long moment anyway. All she could do was watch and wait.

She tracked their progress on the display. They'd be passing closer to Sister VII than she would have preferred, but it seemed as though the navigational data was largely accurate and the passage was safe. But, behind them, storms were gathering. Kat wondered, in a moment of gallows humor, if the Theocracy intended to use the passageway to send their fleet into Commonwealth space. They'd lose at least half of their ships if they tried.

Another dull quiver ran through the ship, then a long series of tremors that had Kat bracing herself, praying under her breath in a manner she hadn't used since her first exposure to vacuum, back at Piker's Peak. The lights seemed to dim for a second, then came back to life, just before something *hit* the prow of the ship hard enough to shake the entire vessel. Kat felt stunned, then confused, then finally realized they'd rammed right into a gravity wave. A physical impact would have blown the entire ship to bits.

Ramming always works, she thought, remembering lessons at Piker's Peak. *But it's hard to ram when both ships are under power.*

"Incoming gravity waves," Robertson snapped.

Kat snapped out of her trance. "Brace for impact," she snapped. "All hands brace for impact . . ."

The hull rang like a bell; then they were suddenly back in clear space. Behind them, the passageway was thoroughly blocked as storms flashed and flared through the space they'd been, only seconds ago. Kat let out a sigh of relief as the shaking rapidly faded away, even though there were still distortions nearby. But it would be almost impossible for anyone to track them through the haze.

"Alter course," she ordered. "Take us around the distortion, then pick a random course and head into Theocratic space."

She took a breath. Her uniform was so soaked in sweat that she wanted to change, but she knew there was no time. They might still be unlucky before they put some distance between themselves and the Seven Sisters, and then headed for their target star. She keyed her console, opening the link to engineering.

It was several minutes before the engineer replied.

"No major damage, Captain," he reported. "A number of circuit breakers blew, but nothing worse. I have damage control teams replacing them now."

Kat nodded. Energy surges were among the most dreaded effects of hyperspace storms, all the more so as they sometimes materialized in starship systems without any prior warning and wreaked considerable damage. They'd been lucky, she told herself. Another passage through the Seven Sisters might well be the end of them. She silently thanked whoever had been crazy—or desperate—enough to plot out the course, then turned her attention back to the display. They were pulling away from the Seven Sisters now.

"Tactical," she said, "are we in clear space?"

"As far as I can tell," Roach reported. He didn't sound happy. "Our sensor range has been cut down quite badly here."

Kat didn't blame him for worrying. If their sensors were unreliable, a Theocratic superdreadnought could be right on top of them and they'd never know about it. The only upside to the whole affair was that the superdreadnought probably wouldn't see them either, unless the Theocracy had produced a major breakthrough in hyperspace sensors. She considered it, then dismissed the thought. If the Theocracy could track starships in hyperspace with perfect precision, the war was within shouting distance of being lost before it had even begun.

"Alter course," she ordered. "Take us towards our target star, best possible speed."

"Aye, Captain," Weiberg said. "Estimated ETA: nineteen hours."

"Good," Kat said. Despite the situation, there was nothing to gain by pushing the drives until they overloaded. She'd only risk stranding her crew in enemy space. "Keep a close eye on the sensors. Assume that every contact is genuine and alter course to avoid detection."

"Our course will become quite erratic," the XO warned. "And we may be considerably delayed."

Kat nodded. There was no accurate data on shipping lines within the Theocracy, but hyperspace had been known to throw up false contacts on a regular basis. It was quite possible they *would* be delayed, yet there was no alternative. The last thing she wanted was to have an enemy fleet on her tail because they'd ignored a possible contact until it was too late.

She rose to her feet, silently cursing the uniform designers. They'd gone for style—on the theory that every girl loved a spacer—and ignored some of the practicalities. Her shirt simply wasn't absorbing sweat. She wanted a shower, a change, and a nap before they reached the enemy star system. There would be time, at least, to get them.

"Mr. XO, you have the bridge," she said. She leaned close so no one else could hear. "Make sure you get some rest too."

"Aye, Captain," the XO said.

Kat walked out of the bridge and headed for her cabin, then changed her mind and went on a walking tour around the ship. Most of her crew, she was gratified to see, looked to have survived their close brush with a hyperspace storm without ill effects, although some looked paler than normal and a handful had made their way to Sickbay for a sedative. Kat was silently relieved the princess and her handmaidens had been off-loaded—they would have been terrified by the storm—then made mental notes to try to ensure her crew got a proper shore leave period as quickly as possible. But she knew it wasn't likely to happen. If the princess had been telling the truth, the war might start alarmingly soon.

She finally made her way back to her cabin, then hesitated as she stepped through the hatch and heard it close behind her. It would be easy to call Davidson to her cabin, to invite him to sleep with her . . . and she *knew* she needed something to work the tension out of her body. It wasn't like the aftermath of the insurgent attack, when she'd been shaking so badly she wanted someone to hold her, to hell with regulations. She could call him . . .

Angrily, she pushed her feelings aside, undressed, and walked right into the washroom. It felt absurdly luxurious, given *Lightning*'s size compared to a superdreadnought or even a battle cruiser, but for once she was grateful. She showered, dried herself, and then stumbled into bed. It felt as though she hadn't slept at all when the alarm rang, but when she checked her wristcom it was clear she'd slept for nearly eighteen hours. The whole experience had drained her in a way she hadn't expected.

But you should have expected it, she told herself as she checked the ship's status. They'd only had to change course twice to avoid a potential contact, something that both pleased and worried her. What if they'd missed something?

She had to admit the Theocracy kept a careful watch on its side of the border, preventing civilian craft from passing without a license and a convoy escort. They wouldn't want to encourage free trade between star systems when that could undermine their position. Or, for that matter, allow refugees to escape.

She dressed, then walked back to the bridge. The ship's logs showed that the XO had taken a break, much to her relief, but he'd still managed to be back on the bridge before her. She took her command chair, nodded to him, and concentrated on reviewing the reports from various departments. Thankfully, the storms definitely hadn't left any lingering problems in their wake.

"Captain," Weiberg said, "we are forty minutes away from our destination."

Kat looked down at her display, thinking hard. The star Princess Drusilla had identified was a red dwarf, largely useless for anything other than secret meetings and hidden colonies—assuming, of course, that it had any planets, asteroids, or comets at all. It was unlikely the Theocracy would go to the expense of mounting dedicated sensor platforms to watch for intruders popping out of hyperspace, not if they had nothing permanent in the system to defend. But a fleet of starships would certainly have their own long-range sensors . . .

"Take us out at the planned location," she said, finally. They'd have to crawl into the system, just to pick up anything useful, but it would make it harder for any watching passive sensors to detect their arrival. "And then cloak us immediately."

She forced herself to relax as the minutes became seconds and then ticked down to zero. Hyperspace roared and seethed, then opened up to allow *Lightning* to slip back into real space, the gateway closing a second later. Kat tensed, despite herself, as the cloaking device hastily shielded their arrival. It was quite possible that, if there happened to be a guardship on duty nearby, their arrival would have been detected, no matter what precautions they took. No one had managed to find a way to cloak a starship's arrival from hyperspace . . .

"Passive sensors are clear," Roach reported. "If there's anything active within engagement range, I can't see it."

Which proves nothing, Kat thought. Guardships rarely announced their presence. One of them could be lurking in space, drives and shield deactivated, watching through passive sensors for any uninvited guests. *Or they could be hiding under cloak, watching and waiting for us.*

She shivered, very slightly, as the ship-mounted passive sensors sucked in data from the nearby system. It seemed almost as barren as the last red dwarf she'd visited, although this time there was a small asteroid field and a handful of comets orbiting the dying star. Someone might have established a hidden colony here, she thought, in the days before the Breakaway Wars, but there was no way to know. Either they were hiding from the Theocrats or the Theocrats had occupied their colony years ago. Or they'd thought themselves far enough from the UN not to need to hide and had headed for a G2 star instead. There were three nearby.

"Captain," Roach said, "request permission to deploy the passive sensor arrays."

Kat hesitated. Admiral Morrison had hemmed and hawed about allowing her to take them—and if she hadn't had her overriding orders from Tyre, she had a feeling he would have refused to allow her to even *think* about removing the systems from Cadiz. They were not only staggeringly expensive, but highly classified. Using them in an enemy-held star system ran the risk of having to destroy the arrays rather than bring them back onboard her ship.

"Deploy them," she ordered. She wanted to know as much as she could about the enemy star system before she crept closer. "But be ready to recover them at all times."

Long minutes passed as the systems were deployed, then activated. They were far more capable than starship sensors, she'd been told, although there were limits. Like all passive sensors, they were dependent on their target emitting something that could be tracked. And, unlike *Lightning's* sensors, they could be blinded if something too powerful appeared far too close to them.

"I'm picking up limited drive emissions," Roach said. "They're clustered round the asteroids, Captain. It could be a staging base."

"They'd have to be powerful if we can pick them up from this distance," the XO commented. "Superdreadnoughts, perhaps."

Kat nodded. "Can you draw more data from the passive arrays?"

"I don't think so," Roach said. He paused, his hands flying over his console. "There are a handful of other drive sources in the system, but most of them are concentrated round the asteroids."

Kat studied the display, then nodded. "Recall the passive arrays," she ordered. "We'll have to go deeper into the system."

We should have brought two ships, she thought, although she knew two ships might not have made it through the passageway. *One to sneak close, one to watch from a distance—and run if the shit hits the fan.*

"Launch probes on ballistic trajectories," she added. "Then launch a relay platform to link their laser communicators to us."

"Aye, Captain," Roach said.

Kat forced herself to watch as the probes moved into the system, feeling the tension rise as the hours ticked by. The drive sources slowly took on shape and form in the display as *Lightning* followed, her passive sensors watching carefully for anything that might betray the size or capabilities of the enemy starships.

Kat swore under her breath as three of them suddenly snapped into view, marked clearly as superdreadnoughts. The UN had never built superdreadnoughts, let alone sold them to the Theocracy. Any doubts she'd had about the Theocracy having its own starship construction program had vanished.

"They look larger than ours," the XO commented. He didn't sound impressed. "But their drive systems are actually sloppy compared to our ships. And their datanets don't seem to be as capable."

He paused. "But they might have stood them down here," he added. "They won't be expecting this system to come under attack, even if we launched a preemptive strike."

Kat knew he had a point, but she hoped the enemy datanet was flawed. Superdreadnoughts carried more missile tubes than a whole squadron of heavy cruisers, giving them a formidable long-range punch, while their energy weapons could rip *Lightning* apart at close range. The thought of facing just one of them was worrying. An entire squadron would be frighteningly powerful. And the sensors seemed to indicate that there were at least three entire squadrons of superdreadnoughts holding position near the asteroids. Anything that evened the odds would be more than welcome.

"I think they have escort ships too," Roach said. New contacts flashed up on the display as *Lightning* moved closer. "A handful of cruisers, several destroyers . . . and there are definitely some gunboats—I think they're carrying out limited exercises."

"Odd," the XO said. "You'd think they'd be interested in exercising as much as possible if they were expecting to go to war. And have more escort ships attached to the fleet."

Kat couldn't disagree. "Perhaps they're standing down in preparation for the attack," she said. But then exercises tended to be more regular than genuine military operations. It was quite possible the enemy CO was giving his crews a rest. "Or . . ."

An alarm sounded. "Captain," Roach snapped, "they just swept one of the drones!"

CHAPTER TWENTY-NINE

"We should be launching the offensive by now," the cleric said. "Do you not have authority to launch the attack at the best possible moment?"

Admiral Junayd sighed. The cleric had not coped well with his brief imprisonment on the Commonwealth cruiser, even if the authorities on Cadiz had been *very* apologetic when they'd released the freighter and her crew. Junayd had merely been relieved that he'd been able to leave the system without being interrogated by the Commonwealth, but the cleric had spent most of the return journey performing rituals to cleanse himself after setting foot on an infidel world. At least it had kept the man out of Junayd's beard for a few glorious days.

"We do not have the fleet train assembled yet," Junayd said firmly. It was infuriating. He'd gathered his attack fleet to start the invasion, yet the attack would fail if he wasn't guaranteed resupplies. Commonwealth weapons, assuming any were captured, were not designed to be fired from his ships. "Once the freighters are here, we will take the offensive."

"But the infidels caught us," the cleric insisted. "They could be preparing their defenses right now."

He was right, Junayd knew, which didn't make him any less irritating. The Commonwealth *had* caught the spy ship, after all. But they hadn't had any *proof* . . . at least, not enough to satisfy their legalistic-minded admiral. And yet . . . he recalled the private message from the Speaker with a tinge of horror. Who knew *what* would happen if Princess Drusilla actually made it to Commonwealth space?

Shaking his head, he turned back to the display. His spacers and troops hadn't been allowed to grow rusty, even though they'd spent the better part of three months orbiting a worthless star. He'd worked them like dogs, forcing them to undergo exercise after exercise, training simulation after training simulation. The crews had responded splendidly, particularly when he'd started offering rewards for best performances. They knew far more about their enemy than the Commonwealth knew about them.

There were still too many unanswered questions, though, no matter how many simulations they ran. Would Commonwealth superdreadnoughts be better than Theocratic superdreadnoughts? Would the Commonwealth's greater industrial might prove decisive if the early campaigns were unsuccessful? Would the Commonwealth's far wider breadth of research and development give them another advantage? Would the Commonwealth's merchant marines rally behind the flag or flee like frightened children? There were just too many questions nothing but war would be able to answer.

He had no doubt the Theocracy—or at least the Believers who mattered—would be solidly behind the war. Expansion had brought great rewards, after all, along with millions of new converts. But how well would the system endure in a long war? In hindsight, he suspected, they should have built more freighters as well as warships, but anyone who suggested it would have been hauled off to face the Inquisition. The True Faith would never allow itself to be defenseless, not again. They would never allow someone else to determine their fate.

The cleric cleared his throat. "Admiral," he said, "God will not grant us victory if we refuse to take advantage of the opportunities He offers us."

"I know," Junayd said. "But God also expects us not to become too reliant on Him."

It was the age-old problem, he recalled, that had spurred the growth of the True Faith. The older faiths—Judaism, Christianity, and Islam—had all been too reliant on God's help and support, rather than doing anything to actually *earn* that support. Their followers had fallen into disbelief and idolatry, resting on laurels that dated back hundreds of years, while their enemies had steadily undermined their positions and prepared them for the kill. In the end, the core of those faiths had died on Earth. But the True Faith had survived and prospered.

Of course we did, Junayd thought. *We took nothing for granted.*

An alarm sounded.

"Report," he snapped.

"Admiral," one of his staffers said, "the outer edge of the spiderweb was just brushed."

Junayd swore. He'd thought the spiderweb was a boondoggle, a waste of time and resources that had only been put into production because the designer happened to have powerful family connections. But it seemed it had paid off after all . . . unless, of course, it had been brushed by a tiny asteroid—something so small it had escaped the scans the attack fleet had done of the system when they'd arrived.

"Sensor focus," he ordered. They could use the contact for yet another drill, even if it was nothing more dangerous than another piece of space debris. "Lock on and track the contact, then bring up active sensors. I want space *dissected*."

"It's a probe," the staffer said. On the display, the contact suddenly came into sharp focus. A probe, Commonwealth design. Moments later, its onboard systems decided there was no hope of escape and triggered the self-destruct. "Target destroyed."

"Bring the fleet to battle stations," Junayd ordered. Probes were hardly FTL-capable. If one had brushed the edge of his fleet, so far from enemy territory, there had to be a mothership out there somewhere, watching them.

His fleet had been located by the enemy.

"Launch gunboats in a search pattern," he ordered, "then continue to sweep space with active sensors."

He thought it through, rapidly. The enemy commander would keep his distance from the fleet, if only to stay out of weapons range, but he couldn't be *that* far away. Maintaining control of the probe would become harder as the light-speed delay between mothership and probe grew longer and longer. It was just possible the gunboats could catch the enemy ship before she made her escape. And even if they didn't . . .

"They know we're here," the cleric said.

"Yes," Junayd agreed. The cleric was actually *right*! Given how little the bastard knew of military strategy, it was a small miracle in and of itself. "And there's no other reason to be here, apart from staging an invasion of Commonwealth space."

"Then we have to take the offensive now," the cleric said. "Before they manage to warn the Commonwealth."

Junayd nodded. On the display, a red icon representing the enemy ship had just popped into view. The gunboats were already altering course, sweeping towards their new target, but it didn't take more than a glance to tell him they wouldn't intercept their target unless the enemy commander decided to wait around for them. It wasn't likely to happen.

"Inform the fleet that we will be departing in an hour," he ordered. "And then power up the StarCom. We need to alert our operatives that the war is about to begin."

He took a breath. Years of careful planning and preparation were about to face their first true test, as was the Theocracy itself. Every previous conquest had been largely unable to defend itself, not against a pair of destroyers taking the high orbitals. But the Commonwealth was heavily defended, a multistar political system with its own ideology that might well undermine the Theocracy's control over its population, given time. Even if expansion hadn't been one of the tenets of the revised True Faith, Junayd suspected, there would have been war. The galaxy simply wasn't big enough for both of them.

It wasn't going to be easy, he knew. There would be a delay in offensive operations, a delay that could prove costly. But there was no alternative. If they let the moment pass, the enemy might have an opportunity to prepare to meet the oncoming storm. And that could prove disastrous.

We have to win quickly, he told himself. *Or we may not win at all.*

He pushed the thought aside. Defeat was unthinkable.

♦ ♦ ♦

"They caught the probe," Roach said. "Their fleet is coming to battle stations now."

Kat nodded. Dozens of starships were bringing up their active sensors, revealing their positions to *her* sensors. The enemy fleet was bigger than they'd thought, although it *was* still strikingly light in escort ships. Perhaps they'd crammed more point defense into their superdreadnoughts then she'd realized, she wondered, or perhaps they'd simply concentrated on superdreadnoughts to the exclusion of all else.

The display washed red, just for a second. "They caught us," Roach added. The display turned red again. This time, the color refused to fade. "I think they have a solid lock on our position."

"Crap," the XO commented. "Do they have something new?"

Roach looked down at his console. "I think they ramped up standard sensors," he said after a moment's thought. "I don't think they've got anything *new*, sir."

But you could be wrong, Kat thought. *They're not stupid. They might have developed something we missed.*

She pushed the thought aside as red icons separated themselves from the enemy fleet and raced towards *Lightning's* position. Gunboats. She cursed under her breath, remembering tactical analysis reports that had suggested the Theocracy had no gunboats. Clearly, someone had dropped the ball somewhere. Kat wasn't particularly surprised. Even if the Theocracy's scientists hadn't come up with the idea for themselves, they'd have no trouble stealing it from the Commonwealth or one of the other independent powers.

"Gunboats will enter engagement range in five minutes," Roach warned.

Kat thought fast. They'd already learned more than she'd expected to learn—and more than she'd wanted to learn—about the enemy fleet. There could be no doubt of its objective, not now. The only logical reason to mass a fleet round a useless star, where it couldn't hope to defend an inhabited planet, was to prepare to mount an invasion of enemy space. Even exercises could be carried out in a populated star system.

"Helm, take us out of here," she ordered. An engagement with enemy gunboats might prove disastrous depending on what weapons they carried. Shipkiller missiles would rip *Lightning* apart if they were launched from very close range. "And then set course for the border, maximum speed."

"Aye, Captain," Weiberg said.

"I'm picking up drive emissions from the enemy superdreadnoughts," Roach said. "They're powering up their drives."

Kat exchanged a glance with her XO. They hadn't just found proof of the imminent offensive, they'd *triggered* it. She *had* tried to warn the XO's friends and allies on 7th Fleet, but would they be ready to fight when the Theocracy arrived? Somehow, Kat couldn't help feeling as though disaster was about to unfold. It was vaguely possible the offensive wasn't about to begin . . . she shook her head, angrily. That was wishful thinking and she knew it.

They've lost the element of surprise, she thought. *But if they act fast they can still give us a pounding before we're ready to meet them.*

"Vortex opening," Weiberg said. Behind them, the enemy gunboats broke off as it became clear they wouldn't be able to catch *Lightning*. "We are gone."

"Take us to the border," Kat ordered as the eerie lights of hyperspace enfolded her starship. "Don't worry about stealth. Just get us to Cadiz as fast as you can."

She thought rapidly. Thankfully, they did have some advantages. The enemy might give chase, but it was unlikely they could get a ship into hyperspace fast enough to actually *track* her ship before she put enough distance between them to be effectively invisible. But then, they'd have no real doubt of her destination. Cadiz was still the closest Commonwealth world with a StarCom. Once she reached Cadiz, she could scream a warning that would outrace any Theocratic attack fleets. But the first invasion fleet would be hard on her heels.

Assuming they're not pushing their drives to the limit, she thought, *how long would it take them to reach Cadiz?*

She played with tactical simulations on the display but the solutions changed, depending on the variables she entered. If the Theocracy pushed its drives to the limit, there was a good chance they'd reach Cadiz within seventeen hours, just after *Lightning's* own arrival. But if they decided not to risk burning out their drives within enemy territory, they'd take around twenty hours to reach Cadiz, giving the defenders several hours to prepare for the attack. It wouldn't be enough.

"We might run into a guardship," the XO warned. "Or a minefield."

"We have to take the risk," Kat answered. "We don't have time to try to sneak back through the Seven Sisters."

She gritted her teeth. One day, she told herself, someone would invent an FTL communicator small enough to be mounted on a heavy cruiser, one that would save future ships from having to flee with the forces of hell snapping at their heels. It was possible, in theory, to mount one on a superdreadnought, but as StarCom units were staggeringly expensive and power intensive, it was unlikely anyone would try. The Commonwealth had preferred to establish a single StarCom in orbit round each of its populated worlds. God alone knew what the Theocracy had done with *their* StarComs.

But the XO was right. They might well run into a minefield if they weren't careful, although part of her suspected the Theocracy might have disabled its own mines in preparation for the invasion. Mines weren't known for being good at telling the difference between friendly and unfriendly targets, particularly in hyperspace. IFF signals were dangerously unreliable in hyperspace, after all. It was one of the reasons the Commonwealth had never bothered to mine even rarely used hyper-routes.

That might cost us now, she thought, grimly. *The Theocracy will have free reign to move through hyperspace to our worlds.*

"Prepare messages for your allies," she ordered, grimly. "Tell them that time is about to run out."

She reached for her terminal and started to compose a message to the Admiralty. If it had the right priority tags, it would be bumped right to the top of the queue for processing and transmitting, as soon as they reached Cadiz. The admiral would be informed, of course, but he wouldn't be able to stop the message. She attached the raw sensor recordings to a follow-on message, then pulled up the records and started to study them, hoping to draw something from the raw data. But she knew it would take a team of analysts to parse the data successfully. The only hopeful sign was a suggestion that enemy datanets were nowhere near as capable as the Commonwealth's systems—and she knew better than to take *that* for granted. It was equally possible the enemy systems had merely been stepped down.

"Captain," Roach said, "we may have an enemy contact."

Kat looked at the display. A yellow icon had appeared . . . not quite blocking their path to Cadiz, but alarmingly close. There was no way to tell if it was a warship, a smuggler, or simply a glitch in the sensors.

But surely even the most paranoid guardship wouldn't be expecting a heavy cruiser hightailing it out of Theocratic space.

"Keep us on course," she ordered. "If they come within engagement range, prepare to open fire without further warning."

"Aye, Captain," Roach said.

Kat forced herself to relax. She'd done all she could. All they could do now was keep running to Cadiz—and pray to God they got there in time.

She accessed her implants, then linked directly to Davidson. "I want you to carry a message to the CO on the ground," she subvocalized. "He needs to be informed that his garrison may come under heavy attack."

"Understood," Davidson said. There was a pause. "Do you want to disembark my company?"

"I don't know," Kat said, honestly. If Cadiz was about to come under attack, the defenders would need all the help they could get. But unless the situation was better than she thought, she would be sending Davidson and his men to certain death. "Do you believe it's necessary?"

"They'll need support, Captain," Davidson said. He sounded solidly confident, although he rarely sounded excited or nervous. "And there *is* a Planetary Defense Center on the surface. The bastards couldn't just flatten the planet from orbit."

Not all of it, Kat thought. But the insurgents would probably tip the scales against the Commonwealth garrison. *Poor bastards*.

"Leave one platoon of Marines on the ship," Kat ordered. "You may deploy the remainder of your force to the surface."

She hoped, as she closed the channel, that she hadn't made a deadly mistake.

♦ ♦ ♦

Admiral Junayd listened absently as the cleric harangued his men, telling them of the virtues of fighting the infidel and the rewards each man could expect if he died in combat against the Theocracy's deadliest foe. Thankfully, the cleric was smart enough not to insist the men drop everything to listen, particularly as the fleet was readying itself for departure. He merely spoke through the communications network, trusting that those who had no immediate tasks would listen.

Junayd allowed himself a tight smile. They might have been caught by surprise, but the crews had responded very well. It had been barely fifty minutes since the enemy craft had vanished into hyperspace, but his ships and crews were ready to depart already. He'd sent messages to the homeworld, warning of the outbreak of war, and messages into the Commonwealth, activating sleeper cells that had been waiting for the command to move. By the time his fleet entered enemy territory, they would already have given the Commonwealth a bloody nose.

And then there would be the declaration of war . . .

The Commonwealth would have some warning, he knew. Their spy ship had made certain of that. But it wouldn't be enough to make a difference. The hammer was about to come down hard.

"Admiral," his ops officer said, "the fleet is ready to depart."

Junayd smiled again. "Then open the vortex," he ordered. There was no longer any time for doubt and uncertainty, merely victory. "And set course for Cadiz."

CHAPTER THIRTY

Lieutenant Jacob Moorland was shaking so hard as he walked into the StarCom Control Center that he was surprised the security officers didn't pull him aside for questioning. It was his fault, he knew, and he would have deserved nothing less than arrest and imprisonment for being so weak, but he didn't have the nerve to turn himself in and confess everything. Instead . . . he knew he would do as he'd been told, one final time.

He'd been bored on Cadiz. He'd moved between the giant StarCom and the spaceport, seeing nothing of the planet outside the walls and seeking what solace he could in the facilities on the ground. They'd managed to get their hooks into him there, he recalled; first, they'd helped get him into debt, then manipulated him into doing small tasks for them in exchange for payment. And then it had been too late to back out, confess all, and escape unscathed. He'd been too deeply committed for surrender.

The giant control center held over a dozen operators, each of them responsible for checking and vetting messages sent from Cadiz to Tyre and the rest of the Commonwealth. He sat down at his console, then pressed his hand against the scanner, allowing it to identify him and confirm his access permissions. There was a long pause, just long enough for him to hope the system had developed problems, then a line of messages streamed up in front of him. He couldn't help noticing that most of the messages were civilian. Military traffic was handled by another section.

He reached into his pocket and removed the datachip. It looked absurdly common, just like any other commercial datachip capable of storing a billion terabytes of data. There were trillions in existence, he knew, so many that no one would think anything of an officer carrying one or two in his pocket. It could have held anything from personal messages from home to his private collection of porn. But instead . . . it had come from his masters, from the men who had ruined his life. Whatever it held, he was sure, it wasn't something as unremarkable as porn.

"You will insert the chip into the command system," his contact had said. They'd met in one of the more extreme brothels, where the more exotic tastes were satisfied. "And then you will activate the chip."

Jacob swallowed, wondering if he dared *accidentally* lose the chip. But he knew it would result in his betrayal—or death. He'd crossed too many lines already. No one would ever look the same way at him if they knew what he'd done. He would be lucky if he was only dishonorably discharged, then dispatched to Nightmare as an involuntary exile. Bracing himself, he took the chip and pushed it into the console. A screen popped up, requesting permission to run the chip. Jacob hesitated, knowing there was no going back now, then keyed his command code into the console. The chip activated without further delay.

Nothing happened for nearly an hour as far as he could tell, then all hell broke loose. The StarCom pulsed signals across space with the assistance of a singularity, held within powerful force fields at the center of the massive structure. Now, with terrifying speed, the singularity destabilized and then fell back into the quantum foam as safety systems activated, trying to prevent a disaster. Alarms howled in the control center as datalinks to Tyre, Marigold, and the other worlds that made up the Commonwealth collapsed, isolating Cadiz from the remainder of the network. It would take weeks, Jacob realized numbly, to purge the command and control system of the rogue software and then generate another singularity. Until then, Cadiz was cut off from the network.

The authorities caught up with Jacob within an hour, but by then it was far too late.

♦ ♦ ♦

"Transmit the signal," Kat ordered as *Lightning* burst back into normal space. They'd jumped out of hyperspace far too close to the planet for comfort, but she'd seen no other choice. "And then get me a secure link to the admiral."

There was a long pause. "Captain," Ross said, "the StarCom network is down."

Kat blinked. "Locked out?"

"No, Captain," Ross said. "They've lost the singularity."

"Shit," the XO said. "It could take weeks to recreate the singularity."

Kat couldn't disagree. Everything she'd been taught about singularities said that creating one was an incredibly finicky task. First, they had to produce the gravity well itself, then set it to resonate with the rest of the interstellar communications network. The XO was right. It could take weeks of fine-tuning before Cadiz was back in touch with the rest of the Commonwealth. By then, the Theocracy would have hammered 7th Fleet into the ground.

"Find a courier boat," she ordered. There were always one or two commercial couriers in the system, even though their owners should have had access to the StarCom. Some information was just too sensitive to be placed on the network. "Hire him, then transmit a copy of our records and order him to fly directly to the next working StarCom."

The XO gave her a look. "Captain," he said slowly, "what if the entire network is down?"

Kat swallowed. It took three weeks for a starship to travel from Cadiz to Tyre. If the entire network was down, the war was within shouting distance of being lost before it had even fairly begun. The Theocracy's commanders would be able to exercise a degree of command and control the Commonwealth's officers would not be able to match. But she knew enough about the network to be fairly sure it couldn't just be taken down as easily as a commercial datanet. The system had multiple redundancies built in everywhere.

"Then we're in trouble," she said grimly. She rose. "Contact your friends and warn them of the oncoming storm. I'll speak to the admiral in my Ready Room."

"Aye, Captain," the XO said.

Kat took a breath as she stepped through the hatch and sat down at her desk, then waited for Admiral Morrison to answer the call. She'd hoped they could reach Cadiz ahead of any enemy force and it seemed likely they'd succeeded, but she hadn't anticipated losing the StarCom. And yet, in hindsight, it was the obvious move. The Theocracy could have sent their own signal ahead of *Lightning*, warning their operatives to move at once. And they'd succeeded magnificently.

She keyed her wristcom. "Patrick," she said, "the StarCom is down. Do you still want to go to the surface?"

"Yes, Captain," Davidson said. "Someone has to warn General Eastside."

Kat nodded, impatiently. The admiral *still* hadn't responded to her call.

"Then good luck," she said. Was the admiral occupied? Or was something more sinister going on? "Watch your back."

The terminal bleeped, informing her that the admiral had finally responded. Kat braced herself, then keyed the switch. Morrison's face appeared in front of her, looking tired and worn. Had they just woken him up? She checked local time and fought down the temptation to swear out loud. It *was* local night, just past midnight. She'd forgotten that detail in her desperate rush to return to Cadiz.

"Captain," the admiral said. He didn't sound happy. "I was at a party. My daughter is being introduced to Lord Percy. What is the meaning of *this*?"

"The system is about to be attacked," Kat said, flatly. She tapped a switch, transmitting the records her ship had collected. Her tactical department's analysts had been working their way through them, but hadn't drawn any useful conclusions yet. "The Theocracy has an attack fleet within range, which may be less than an hour from Cadiz."

She glanced at a message that blinked up on her display. The vast majority of the fleet's commanding officers were down on the surface, either at the spaceport or enjoying themselves at the admiral's estate. Kat had to fight to keep her face impassive. Had they learned nothing from the previous attack? The StarCom was down, the victim of sabotage, and yet they were partying? She clenched her jaw. The theory about the admiral being in the Theocracy's pay was starting to seem a great deal more plausible.

"Your ship provoked them, Captain," the admiral said.

Kat said a word she knew her mother would have slapped her for saying, at least in front of her social inferiors. But it caught the admiral's attention.

"Admiral," she said, "it doesn't matter if they thought they were provoked or not. They have already started their campaign. The loss of the StarCom cannot be coincidence. Their attack fleet is already advancing towards Cadiz. I implore you, Admiral, to sound the alert and ready 7th Fleet for action. Time is running out."

"Captain," the admiral said, "I . . ."

His image vanished from the display. Kat stared, then reached for her wristcom. It bleeped before she could touch it, just as alerts flashed up through her implants. The entire planetary command and control network had just crashed, violently. Each and every starship, orbital defense platform, and automated tracking system was now isolated from everyone else.

"Captain," the XO said, "the spaceport is under attack. So is Government House."

"Red Alert," Kat ordered. "Pat . . . ah, Davidson. Where is he?"

"His shuttle was heading towards the spaceport," the XO said.

"Recall him," Kat snapped. Newer alerts were flashing up as the command and control system struggled to rebuild itself. The spaceport wasn't the only place under attack. It looked as though insurgents were striking everywhere, from forward operating bases to medical centers and even economic assistance facilities. There were so many attacks that the garrison commander would be unable to decide which one was the key, which one to deal with first. "We need him back onboard."

She took a breath. "And try to reestablish a link to the admiral."

"That might be impossible," Roach said. The tactical officer sounded worried. "Government House is under heavy attack."

Kat shuddered. How many locals, from street sweepers to prostitutes, had worked within the security fence? They'd had years to plan their uprising, smuggling weapons into the complex while pretending to be good little collaborators. And now, they were throwing everything they had at their hated oppressors. The admiral might already be dead. He was certainly in no position to take command of the fleet.

"We can't even call in orbital strikes," the XO warned. "There's no way to separate our forces from enemy insurgents."

"Recall Davidson," Kat repeated. At least she had a full crew on her ship. God alone knew how many of the other ships had full complements. "And then try to establish links to the remainder of 7th Fleet."

She looked down at her hands, unsure of what to do. The entire situation was unraveling . . . and the enemy fleet hadn't even put in an appearance. Given time, and orbital control, the Commonwealth could restore some semblance of order, but she knew the Theocracy would know it too. Their fleet would have to arrive soon . . .

Unless they want us to slaughter the insurgents, she thought morbidly.

They're not going to leave Cadiz alone either. Better to kill off everyone who might resist first.

"Captain," Ross said, "I have lost contact with the Marine shuttles."

Kat shivered. "I'm on my way," she said. She rose. "Keep trying to reestablish contact."

♦ ♦ ♦

The high-velocity missile came out of nowhere. Davidson and his men had no time to do more than brace themselves before the missile slammed into the shuttle's drive field, sending them tumbling down towards the ground. The pilot struggled to maintain control, somehow managing to keep the craft steady long enough to make a proper crash landing. Davidson rose to his feet as soon as the craft was down, then ran for the hatch. Outside, it was calm, suspiciously calm. But in the distance, he could see smoke rising from the direction of the spaceport.

"I can't make contact with anyone," Corporal Loomis reported as the marines fanned out, weapons at the ready. Everyone was accounted for, but whoever had shot them down might be coming to finish the job. "The planetary datanet is down."

Davidson swallowed a curse. They'd landed in rough country, several miles from the spaceport, Gibraltar, or the PDC. If the smoke was any indicator, the spaceport was under attack—and he couldn't see any signs of shuttles coming or going over the land. And *that* suggested the insurgents had the spaceport locked down. For once, he found himself unsure of what to do. What *were* their orders if caught in hostile territory?

Any other world would have a large population willing to help us, he thought. *But not here.*

"We need to move away from the spaceport," he said finally. He *wanted* to run towards the installation and join the defenders, but the battle might well be over by the time the Marines arrived. He'd seen too much of the spaceport's interior to have any illusions about how long it could defend itself if it came under heavy attack. There were just too many enemies within the walls. "And find somewhere to go to ground."

None of his troops argued. Instead, they followed him as he led the way towards the capital city. Strangers would be noticed in the countryside, he suspected. It would be better to blend in with city-dwellers as much as possible. And they would probably have to ditch their uniforms and most of their weapons at some point.

He cursed the admiral under his breath. It would have been relatively simple to ensure the shit never hit the fan—or, at least, that the installations on the surface were secure. But Morrison had been too lazy—or criminally negligent—to care. Davidson silently promised himself that the admiral would not survive, no matter what else happened. He wouldn't be allowed to go home and plead his case . . .

Shaking his head, he looked towards the smoke rising from the city. It was unlikely Admiral Morrison was still alive.

♦ ♦ ♦

"I have a live feed from a drone near the spaceport," Ross reported. "The installation is under heavy attack."

Kat nodded as the images appeared on the display. The entire complex seemed devastated; fires were burning everywhere, while a number of destroyed shuttles lay on the ground. She could see hundreds of dead bodies while a handful of men armed with makeshift weapons prowled the complex, seeking survivors. The barracks, which should have housed over two thousand soldiers, were nothing more than debris. It was clear that the defenders had been overwhelmed before they'd even known they were under attack.

She bit her lip. "Do we have a link to Government House? Or the PDC?"

"General Eastside seems to have taken command of the PDC," Ross said. "But there's no contact with Government House."

Kat nodded, unsurprised. The admiral was dead. Most of the senior naval officers were dead. Or, she told herself, they were out of contact. Not that it really mattered, she suspected. The spaceport was flaming debris, while insurgents prowled the countryside with surface-to-air missiles. There was no way she could send shuttles to recover the commanding officers, even if she'd had a solid lock on their positions. They'd be shot down by the insurgents.

"Purge the communications system completely," she ordered. It would destroy any encryption codes, but right now they were worse than useless. Kat and her crew would have to send in the clear and hope the enemy wasn't able to intercept and read messages in time to make a difference. "And try to reestablish the datanet for 7th Fleet."

And then new alarms sounded, followed by red lights on the display.

Commander Fran Higgins had never considered herself prone to despair. As a mustang, she had known her promotion prospects were limited compared to officers who had followed the *proper* command track, but she had also believed her competence would see her through. But Cadiz had sapped her determination even before the shit had finally hit the fan. If she hadn't had the bare bones of a plan—and taken steps to prepare *Defiant* for operations—she might well have given up completely.

She sat on the bridge, in the captain's chair, trying to pull some sense out of the distorted reports from the planet's surface. Some of them were obvious nonsense, others far too optimistic to be believed easily. But she knew the worst when she finally saw the live feed from the spaceport. The occupation was doomed.

"The captain is dead," she said, flatly. A third of the crew was still down on the surface—if they weren't dead themselves—but at least she'd managed to keep the more competent officers and crew on the ship. "I want full operational power as soon as possible."

"We're working on it," Chief Engineer Ryan said. Thank *God* he was competent. There were at least two engineers attached to the fleet who had to have politically powerful relatives, or they would never have been promoted. "But it will take at least ten minutes to bring the ship to full power."

Fran cursed loudly enough to shock several of the younger officers. "Keep working on it," she snapped. There was nothing else she could do. "And . . ."

New icons flared into life on the display. "Vortexes," Lieutenant Robbins shouted. She sounded as though she was on the verge of panic. "Multiple vortexes."

"Divert all power to weapons, shields, and drives," Fran ordered. The enemy fleet had arrived—and the mighty superdreadnought and the rest of her squadron were practically sitting ducks. They could do without life support long enough to escape—or they'd be dead anyway. "And stand by point defense."

She gritted her teeth. The enemy ships were already launching gunboats. And 7th Fleet's gunboat crews were in disarray. It was unlikely many of them could launch in time to make a difference. The fleet was thoroughly screwed.

And there was still no word from the admiral.

CHAPTER THIRTY-ONE

"Report," Admiral Junayd ordered.

"The infidel fleet is in disarray," the sensor officer reported. "They're trying to power up their drives and weapons, but they're at a very low state of readiness."

"God is with us," the cleric said.

Admiral Junayd ignored him. "Launch gunboats," he ordered. The infidels could not be allowed more time to prepare. One icon sparkled on the display and he glowered at it. The spying battle cruiser had made it back to Cadiz, too late. They'd already lost the StarCom, ensuring they couldn't send an alert to the remainder of the Commonwealth. "Targets are the capital ships. They are not to leave this system alive."

He paused, significantly. "The battle line will advance," he added. "The troopships and their escorts will remain behind, ready to escape back into hyperspace if necessary."

The cleric turned to face him. "Admiral," he said, "must I remind you of the importance of bringing Cadiz into the fold?"

"We cannot land troops until we have defeated the enemy fleet," Junayd pointed out. It *was* important to establish a strong presence on

Cadiz, if only to hunt down the surviving Commonwealth personnel, but he was keen to keep the Janissaries and the Inquisitors away from Cadiz as long as possible. A few days under their rule and the locals would start rebelling again. "And besides, I don't care to offer the enemy a clear shot at annihilating the troops before they hit the ground."

He settled back, contemplating the task before him. His superdreadnoughts would finish the job of blowing their way through the Commonwealth's defenses and obliterating their fleet. The balance of power would swing decisively in the Theocracy's favor within an hour.

"And transmit the formal summons to surrender," he added. "We must invite them to submit to us."

It would be good if they did surrender, he knew, even though he would be cheated of a battle. But he wasn't *expecting* a surrender. The Commonwealth was no isolated single-star system, unable to police space outside its atmosphere. They had space they could trade for time and powerful fleets in reserve. It was possible they would despair so completely they wouldn't realize they could fall back, but he wasn't counting on it. They had had too much time to think since their spy ship had returned home.

"And send a general signal to the fleet," he concluded. "Today we fight for victory."

♦ ♦ ♦

Kat watched as countless vortexes opened and dispersed nemeses. Twenty-seven superdreadnoughts, forty-two smaller craft, and over five hundred gunboats, launching now from their carriers. The tiny vessels carried one hell of a sting, she knew, and a handful of them could take down a superdreadnought. The gunboat pilots of the 7th Fleet were still dawdling. It would be too late by the time they joined the fray.

"Picking up a message," Ross said. "They're beaming it all over the system."

"Put it through," Kat ordered.

The voice was strongly accented, although Kat couldn't place it. "Infidels, the hour of judgment is at hand," he said. "Accept your fate, surrender your ships, and join us in worship of the One True God, or die at our hands and be plunged into the bitterest hell. You have ten minutes to comply."

Kat glanced at the display. Ten minutes . . . just long enough for the superdreadnoughts to enter firing range. The gunboats would be on the fleet in two minutes, unless the fleet surrendered beforehand. But that was not going to happen. The officers who might have surrendered had died on Cadiz.

Outsmarted yourself, didn't you? she thought, with a moment of bitter amusement. *Your plan worked* too *well.*

But she knew it was unlikely to matter.

She looked at the XO. "Do we have any ID on the senior surviving officer?"

"I can't find anyone higher than a commander," the XO said. He sounded shocked. It was easy to believe, now, that Admiral Morrison had been an enemy agent all along. "The fleet is completely headless."

Kat drew in a breath. "Open a channel to the entire fleet," she ordered. She waited for Ross's nod, then continued. "This is Captain Kat Falcone. I am taking command of the fleet."

She pressed on before anyone could challenge her. Technically, she outranked everyone else confirmed to be alive, but they would know how little experience she had. And she wasn't part of 7th Fleet's command network. Someone might well challenge her on those grounds alone.

But, not entirely to her surprise, no one raised a challenge. They were all too focused on staying alive.

"Route the tactical fleet command net through *Lightning*," she ordered, cursing the designers under her breath. *Lightning* just wasn't designed for fleet command. If the designers hadn't been so fixated on winning the contracts for a whole new generation of command-capable heavy cruisers . . . she shook her head bitterly. It was water under the bridge now. "And get me a full status update."

She took a breath. At least some of the gunboats were finally getting out into open space. It was clear the pilots were disoriented and their flight rosters had been shot to hell, but they were out in space. She issued orders to the gunboats to engage the enemy gunboats before they attacked the fleet, then weighed the situation as best as she could. No matter how she played it in her mind, she saw nothing but defeat if they held their position and tried to fight. The enemy fleet had them firmly under their guns.

None of the reports sounded promising either. Her best superdreadnoughts required at least two weeks in the yards before they could be considered combat capable, even though the crews were doing their best to bring the ships to battle stations. Many of the smaller ships were in better condition—the rot hadn't set in so badly—but they didn't have the firepower to take on the Theocracy.

"We will cover the superdreadnoughts until they are ready to escape," she ordered. The Theocracy would go for the superdreadnoughts first, just to take them out before they could be brought back to full readiness. It would be quicker to repair any ships that escaped than build new hulls from scratch. "And as soon as they are ready to go, we will beat a hasty retreat."

She felt several of her officers glancing at her back in disbelief. The Royal Navy didn't run . . . but the Royal Navy had never faced a serious challenge before. They had never been involved in the Breakaway Wars. The only real opponent had been pirates, and none of them had posed more than a brief challenge to their might. And if 7th Fleet had been worked up and ready to go, they might have given the Theocracy a bloody nose. But she knew all they could do was run.

The Board of Inquiry might blame me for running, she thought, as the enemy gunboats raced closer. *But they won't blame anyone else.*

"The planetary defense network is still crippled," the XO said, "but some of the automated platforms have been isolated from the communications net and are responding to orders."

"Target them on the gunboats," Kat ordered. She braced herself. "And stand by point defense."

She watched grimly as the gunboats slashed into engagement range, evading with consummate skill as the superdreadnoughts opened fire with point defense. No gunboat could stand up to a single blast, but they were incredibly hard to hit. She had to admire the professionalism shown by the enemy pilots as they closed in on their targets, then opened fire with shipkiller missiles. Armed with antimatter, they would be devastating against shielded and unshielded targets alike.

"Antimatter detonations," Roach reported as four of the missiles were picked off by point defense. "They're not holding back, Captain."

Kat nodded. The gunboats had scored five direct hits on one superdreadnought, blowing the massive vessel out of formation. For a long moment, it looked as though *Hammer of Thor* had survived, then the starship vanished inside a massive fireball. Kat fought down despair as the gunboats raced away from the destroyed ship, then reformed and angled back towards their next target. The point defense crews continued firing, trying to pick off the gunboats before they could enter engagement range again. But it seemed a waste of effort.

"Message to superdreadnoughts," Kat ordered. Safety regulations warned against it, but she was so far past caring that it hardly mattered. "They are to launch shipkillers on dispersal mode."

"Aye, Captain," the XO said. He seemed to have fallen into the role of her operations officer, even though he should have taken command of the cruiser while she commanded the entire fleet. But there was no time to switch roles. "But that will damage our datanet."

Kat shrugged. "*What* datanet?"

◆ ◆ ◆

"Direct hit, starboard hull," the tactical officer snapped. "Shields held, but barely."

Fran nodded. *Defiant* had been lucky. Four of the gunboats assigned to her had been picked off before they could launch their missiles, detonating the antimatter in their warheads and wiping out several of their comrades. Only one missile had struck her shields. Fran was grimly aware that the starship's shields were held together by spit and baling wire.

She glanced at the order from *Lightning*, then smiled. "Launch shipkillers on dispersal mode," she ordered. "Target clumps of enemy ships and fire!"

She smirked as the superdreadnought launched a spread of antimatter-armed missiles aimed at the gunboat formation. There was no hope of actually scoring a hit, but it didn't matter. The warheads detonated as soon as they were within range, the giant explosions wiping out dozens of gunboats and disabling several others. It wasn't a viable tactic in the long run, but it would buy them some time. But would it be enough?

"Seven minutes until we can open a vortex," the engineer reported.

Fran cursed. It was going to be a long seven minutes.

"Clever," Admiral Junayd observed. His gunboats had been hammered by the shipkillers, far too many of them swatted out of space like flies. The remainder would have to return to their carriers to rearm before they could return to the fight. "But futile."

He smiled grimly as the fleet finally came into range. "Target missiles on the superdreadnoughts," he ordered, "and open fire."

Moments later, the Theocracy's superdreadnoughts launched the first full broadside of the war.

"The enemy superdreadnoughts have opened fire," Roach reported.

Kat nodded, unsurprised. Under normal circumstances, firing at extreme range would have been futile. There would have been plenty of time for a fleet command datanet to lock onto the missiles, calculate interception trajectories, and open fire. Hell, the missiles might have burned out their drives and gone ballistic by the time they entered the point defense envelope, making their destruction a certainty. But this time the tactic might well pay off for the Theocrats.

The point defense datanet barely exists, she thought, *and the bastards are practically holding the planet hostage. One antimatter missile on the surface and most of the population will die.*

She gritted her teeth. "The superdreadnoughts are to fall back, if they can muster the power," she ordered. She hated to do it, but preserving the fleet was her first priority. Cadiz would just have to take care of itself. "Reform the fleet; I want smaller ships between the superdreadnoughts and the incoming missiles. If we can't form a datanet, I want to put out enough firepower to prevent the missiles from getting through."

"Aye, Captain," the XO said. "And the planet?"

Kat cursed herself under her breath. She couldn't leave Cadiz completely undefended. "Reprogram the planetary defenses," she ordered. They would normally have put the planet first, but the standard command network was in tatters. "They are to concentrate on missiles that might enter the planet's atmosphere."

"Aye, Captain," the XO said. He sounded relieved. "The enemy fleet is picking up speed."

"Order our superdreadnoughts to fire a return barrage," Kat ordered. The Theocracy's fleet was advancing *towards* her ships, shortening the effective engagement range. But there would be no coordinated fire. She would just have to hope *her* fire dissuaded the enemy from pursuing too closely. "And then angle the point defense to provide as much cover as possible."

She watched grimly as the swarm of missiles rocketed towards the fleet. None of them were targeted on *Lightning*—thankfully, the limited datanet had prevented the Theocracy from realizing that a mere heavy cruiser was the linchpin of the fleet—but there were more than enough of them to do real damage. Her ship's point defense went to work, sweeping missiles out of space, yet there seemed to be no shortage racing towards her superdreadnoughts.

Then they started to strike home.

"*Kali* is gone," Roach reported. "*Agincourt* and *Bosworth* have taken heavy damage. *Bosworth* reports that her drive section is completely gone. *Butcher* and *Thundercracker* have both taken limited damage."

Kat nodded. "Keep trying to link our point defense together," she ordered. If *Bosworth* had lost her drives, there was no way she could be saved. "Order *Bosworth* to transfer all non-essential crew to her shuttles . . ."

A green icon flickered once, then vanished, to be replaced by a handful of icons representing lifepods. "*King David* is gone," Roach said, bleakly. "*Defiant* is requesting permission to launch SAR shuttles."

Kat hesitated. "Denied," she said, finally. The enemy gunboats would fire on shuttles, even though they were performing Search and Rescue duties. "The lifepods are to make their way to the planet."

Roach turned to stare at her. "Captain . . ."

"That's an order, mister," Kat snapped. "Concentrate on your duties."

She understood his feelings all too well. The Royal Navy didn't leave anyone behind. It had been hammered into them at Piker's Peak that starship crewmen and officers had to depend on one another. But she didn't dare risk allowing SAR shuttles to be engaged by enemy gunboats—or, for that matter, leaving them behind.

One more thing for the Board of Inquiry to judge, she thought. *After they've buried Morrison, perhaps they'll bury me.*

The thought was a bitter one. She hadn't been expected to assume command of the fleet . . . in hindsight, perhaps she should have made contingency plans to do just that. But she had never believed the disaster could be on so great a scale. It was a failure of imagination that would cost the Commonwealth dearly. If the Admiralty wanted a scapegoat, and Admiral Morrison was safely dead, they might turn their gaze on her.

Lightning shuddered violently. "One of the missiles engaged us," Roach snapped. "No major damage."

Kat exchanged glances with the XO. "Pull us back," she ordered. She glanced at the display, wondering if the enemy had worked out that *Lightning* was the command ship. But if they had, they would have thrown everything at her. "Time to escape?"

"Four superdreadnoughts are reporting that they've lost their drive sections," the XO said. "The remainder will be ready to open vortexes in two minutes."

Kat felt very cold, very composed. "The starships that cannot escape are to move forward and shield their fellows," she ordered, hating herself. "The remainder are to keep falling back."

There was no choice. She *knew* there was no choice. With so many weapons being fired in the same region of space, it would be impossible for one starship to open a vortex for the stragglers. And yet it smacked of sacrificing others to save herself.

"Aye, Captain," the XO said.

The fighting seemed to grow more intense as the enemy ships concentrated their fire on the lead superdreadnoughts. Their commanders switched all remaining power to shields and weapons, then fought savagely, trying to hold the line. For a long moment, Kat dared hope that they *would* manage to hold the line, but she knew it wouldn't happen. The Theocracy was already targeting those ships specifically.

"Captain," the XO said, "the superdreadnoughts are reporting that they're ready to jump."

Kat hesitated. Davidson was on Cadiz, along with thousands of Commonwealth personnel, all of whom would be at the mercy of either the Theocrats or the local insurgents. She had no idea how the Theocrats would treat their prisoners, but she suspected it wouldn't be in line with any of the post-UN conventions. She didn't want to abandon them, yet she knew all she could do was die in their defense, perhaps costing the Commonwealth its chance to win the war. They had to retreat.

"Open the vortexes," she ordered. There was no longer any time to delay. "Take us out of here."

♦ ♦ ♦

"Admiral," the sensor officer snapped, "the infidel fleet is retreating."

Junayd cursed under his breath. Four superdreadnoughts seemed determined to fight to the last, but the remainder were falling back and opening vortexes, escaping into hyperspace. He knew he couldn't give chase, not now. An engagement in hyperspace could easily go either way.

"Let them go," he ordered. There were still the few remaining superdreadnoughts in real space, fighting desperately. As he watched, one of them lost a shield and immediately rotated to avoid exposing the chink in its defenses to incoming fire. "Retarget missiles on the remaining ships."

He watched, feeling an odd glow of admiration, as the four superdreadnoughts fought and died. They couldn't stop him, they had to *know* they couldn't stop him, but they fought desperately to win their fellows time. In the end, they died, but they died bravely. It sent shivers down his spine. They'd calculated the infidels would be weak, that they would not put up a fight—and they'd been wrong. It was easy to imagine, now, that the war would be far from victorious.

They might have staved off defeat, he thought. *And who knows what that will cost us, in time?*

But he couldn't say it out loud. Who knew who might be listening?

"Clear the planet's skies," he ordered. The remaining platforms were fighting desperately, but there could only be one outcome. It was the PDC that would pose a more significant problem. "And then prepare the landing force."

CHAPTER THIRTY-TWO

"I think that was the fleet leaving," Corporal Loomis said. "We're on our own."

Davidson nodded, looking up to see flashes of light in the sky and pieces of debris falling through the atmosphere. No one had come hunting for them, as far as they could tell—perhaps the insurgents had assumed the marines had died in the crash—but the area was about to get very dangerous. The PDC would be able to engage anything it saw landing, yet that wouldn't be enough to stop the Theocracy. They'd simply land their troops outside the PDC's range and advance towards Gibraltar.

He consulted the planetary map he'd downloaded into his implants. There were a number of small farms nearby, largely ignored by both sides of the war. They might make a good place to hide. The alternative, heading further into the undeveloped regions of the planet, would take them out of the war completely. He considered it briefly, remembered his oath to the Royal Marines, and then made up his mind.

"We head towards the farms," he said. "If we can find a place to hide there, we'll hole up and wait to see what happens."

More flashes of light filled the sky as the Theocracy closed in on the undefended world. It wouldn't be long before they started landing troops, Davidson told himself, or scrutinizing orbital imagery for any sign of stragglers. He and his team needed to get under cover long before that happened, or at the very least abandon their uniforms. The marines kept moving, slipping into a forest in the hopes it would provide at least some cover as a series of thunderous explosions sounded in the distance. Davidson turned in time to see a fireball rising up from the east. It suggested the enemy fleet was softening up the planet by bombarding known Commonwealth positions from orbit.

"I'm picking up a message," Loomis said. "It's on the emergency frequency."

Davidson opened his implants and accepted the message. ". . . is Eastside," a voice said. It was so wracked with static that it was impossible to be sure, even with his implants, that it actually *was* General Eastside. "The Theocracy is landing troops. If you can disengage and hide, do so. The Navy will . . ."

The message faded as the Theocracy jammers went to work. Davidson scanned the airwaves through his implants, hoping the signal would be repeated, but there was nothing. The enemy had control of the high orbitals now and they intended to use them. Flashes of light burst out from the direction of the PDC, weapons being dropped to test the base's force field. It was clear the PDC was holding out, but not for long. The base might be able to stand off projectiles from orbit, yet it couldn't defend itself against ground troops indefinitely.

"We keep moving," he grunted. "And pray we find a way to strike back at the bastards."

It was nearly forty minutes before they came across their first farm. Davidson surveyed it from a distance, looking for signs of life, but saw nothing. The complex was really nothing more than a handful of small fields with some sheep, cows, and chickens, large enough to be productive yet small enough to be operated by a single family. He felt a sudden sense of wistfulness for the farm he'd left behind, then started to walk down towards the barn. His men followed him at a distance.

There was no sign of anyone in the barn, but his experienced eyes could see signs that the farm had been tended recently, which suggested the owners were hiding. He motioned the marines forward, then slipped up to the farmhouse. It was a wooden structure, like many early colonial buildings, but someone had added brick and stone outhouses to give the family more living space. Davidson was more impressed then he cared to admit, but froze as he heard someone talking inside. The voice was local—and sounded fearful.

He hesitated. If they asked for help, they might be betrayed—and if they took what they needed, they *would* be betrayed. The only safe options were to back away from the farm or kill the inhabitants. But he was *damned* if he was slaughtering innocent people whose only crime was being a potential liability.

And what will you do, a nasty little voice said at the back of his mind, *when the Theocracy is torturing your team because you were too nice to the locals?*

He motioned for Loomis and Private Jackson to cover him, then opened the door and stepped inside. A family—a surprisingly large family—looked up from their table and stared at him, their eyes wide with horror and fear. Like most of the locals, they had dark skin and darker eyes, but their clothes suggested a prosperity most of their compatriots didn't share. The oldest man stared, then moved to protect his five daughters. His three sons looked as though they wanted to hurl themselves at the marines, but didn't quite dare.

Davidson found his voice. "We're looking for a place to hide," he said. He hoped the locals understood Galactic Standard. Cadiz certainly *should* have included it as a second language, but he could understand why they might have resisted its introduction. "We mean you no harm."

The farmer stumbled to his feet. Davidson read his expression and felt a moment of pity. The man was scared, caught between multiple fires . . . just like everyone else trapped in the middle of the war. If he tried to send Davidson away, the marines might turn on him; if he helped, he might be branded a collaborator and killed by his own people—or the Theocracy.

"You can't stay here," he stammered, finally. "You'll be seen."

"We can hide," Davidson said as reassuringly as he could. "And we won't cause you any trouble."

He paused, then took a gamble. "And we also need to talk to the local fighters," he added. "Can you introduce us to them?"

The farmer stared at him in shock. Davidson understood all too well. At one point, admitting any connection with the insurgents would have been a death sentence. But now . . . making contact with the insurgents was a gamble, but it was one he knew they had to take. And besides, it might give their unwilling host some limited protection. The insurgents would know he'd done the best he could.

"You can wait in the barn," the farmer said after a moment. "I'll have food brought to you."

The farmer's wife eyed Davidson unpleasantly—she didn't seem any happier than her husband about having the marines anywhere near her daughters—but stood and started to gather a batch of fruit and vegetables. Davidson nodded, then slipped out of the door and led the way back to the barn. In the distance, the sound of explosions was growing louder, carried on the still air. The Theocracy was *definitely* landing troops.

He sat down in the barn and started to check his weapons, motioning for the other marines to do the same. If the insurgents attacked or called the Theocracy, they would have no choice but to fight to the death. There were just too many horror stories of what happened to prisoners who fell into Theocratic hands. He was damned if he was allowing them to take him alive.

"I'm picking up a general broadcast," Loomis said suddenly. "It's on all frequencies."

"Let me hear," Davidson said.

"It's repeating," Loomis said. "Hang on."

"This planet is now under the jurisdiction of the Theocracy," a stern voice said. "Troops are landing and will occupy strategic points of importance as soon as possible. Civilians are warned to stay off the streets. Do not carry weapons anywhere near Theocratic soldiers or you will be shot or detained. Commonwealth military personnel are ordered to make themselves known to Theocratic authorities as soon as they arrive. Monitor radio broadcasts for further orders."

"Well," Jackson said, "they're not mincing words, are they?"

"Here comes the new boss, same as the old boss," Corporal Marsha agreed. "Sir?"

Davidson looked up sharply. The farmer and two of his sons were standing in the doorway, carrying trays of food. Davidson rose to his feet, took one of the trays and thanked the men profusely. The farmer looked irked but grateful that he hadn't been shot. He motioned for Davidson to follow him outside.

"I have sent my daughter to speak to the freedom fighters," he said. "You may have a visitor."

"Let us hope so," Davidson said with the private thought that one visitor wouldn't be a problem. A whole army of visitors would be a major threat. "Have you heard the broadcast?"

"It's on all channels," the farmer said. His expression twisted. "Your people did the same when you took our planet."

Patrick lowered his eyes, ashamed.

"Wait," the farmer said. "See what the fighters have to say."

The food was tasty enough, Davidson supposed, as the marines ate and then tried to catch up on their sleep. He spent the time listening for other broadcasts, trying to identify snippets of conversation that made it through the omnipresent jamming and create a working picture of just what was actually going on. But it was impossible to draw more than a very rough idea, based on the location of enemy transmitters. It looked as though the occupation force was taking up positions round Gibraltar before moving into the city itself.

Reasonable, he thought sourly. *They'd want to try to make sure they cut all lines of supply and that no one could escape before they entered the city and secured it for themselves.*

He sighed, wondering just what had happened to Kat and her ships. None of her plans had expected the shit to hit the fan this badly, not as far as he knew. Had she made it out, he wondered, or had *Lightning* been destroyed in the battle? Were the pieces of debris falling from the sky the last remains of Kat and her ship? He shook his head firmly. Kat had an intact ship and crew. She would have made it out. But who knew where she was now?

Taking out the StarCom was brilliant, he thought. *It makes it impossible for us to coordinate our forces. Kat and the survivors wouldn't even know where to go.*

"We've got contact," Loomis snapped. "Two people making their way towards the barn. I can't see any weapons."

Davidson leaned forward. "That's the farmer's daughter," he said. He'd seen the girl when he'd entered the farmhouse. She was pretty enough, and she was almost as muscular as a female marine. But then, a farm was no place for a shrinking violet. Or a weakling. "And the person she's with . . ."

He stared. There was something *odd* about the person, something that sent alarm bells jangling at the back of his mind. He wore jeans and a shirt and a large hat that obscured his face, yet something wasn't quite right. But there was no time to think about it. Motioning for the marines to stay back, Davidson walked out of the barn and down towards the two newcomers. The farmer's daughter muttered something, then turned and walked back to the farmhouse, leaving the stranger alone.

"Greetings," the stranger said. "You seem to be a little lost."

Davidson blinked in sudden understanding. The stranger wasn't a man, but a woman—no, a girl who looked round nineteen—wearing men's clothes and doing her best to pass as a man. From what he recalled of local culture, that was unlikely to please anyone . . . although it hardly mattered in the Commonwealth, where men and women held interchangeable roles. Cadiz was nowhere near as restrictive when it came to women as the Theocracy, but a woman playing at being a man would have shocked the locals. But it was quite possible none of them had noticed. They would be too accustomed to thinking *man* when they saw someone in male clothing.

"I suppose you could put it that way," he said. He sat down on the grass, trying to seem as nonthreatening as possible. It wasn't easy. "And yourself?"

"Uncertain," the girl admitted. She sat, then held out a callused hand. "My name is Jess, by the way."

Patrick nodded. Jess as a name could be either male or female, which made sense. Had her father wanted a boy? Or had she merely called herself by a name that could apply to both sexes and allowed everyone to draw the wrong conclusion? There was no way to know without asking her, yet it wasn't something he dared ask. If she'd hidden her sex from her fellow fighters, she wouldn't take kindly to having her secret in the hands of an outsider.

"Patrick," he said, taking her hand and shaking it firmly. She definitely had a very masculine handshake. "Royal Marines."

"I'll get right to the point," Jess said. "What are you doing here?"

"Our shuttle was shot down," Davidson said. "We hiked here while the attack began. Now . . . we're hiding."

"An interesting role reversal for you," Jess said. She met his eyes. "Is there a reason I shouldn't call the Theocracy and hand you over to them?"

Davidson hesitated, composing his arguments. "I assume you've heard their broadcast," he said. "They're not here to liberate you from our clutches. They're here to take your world for themselves."

"I heard their broadcast," Jess said.

"I've heard hundreds of accounts from refugees," Davidson continued.

"They will reshape your society to suit themselves. The best you can hope for is that you will be treated as second-class citizens on your own homeworld, your religions shattered, and your population forced to follow their rules. At worst . . . you will simply be marginalized and scattered."

Jess lifted her eyebrows. "And this will be different from your occupation?"

"Oh yes," Davidson said. "It will be far worse—and permanent."

He took a breath. "Men of power and influence will be killed," he said. "People like yourself, people who can lead a fight, will be killed. Everyone from government officials and policemen to teachers and religious leaders will be killed. And then they will start reshaping your society. Women will be isolated, trapped inside their homes; men will be expected to convert or remain as second-class citizens for the rest of their lives. And many of them *will* convert.

"Give the Theocrats fifty years," he concluded, "and your society will have been completely reshaped in their image. And there will be no one left who recalls what life was like before they arrived."

"They'd have to land a huge army," Jess pointed out. "Could they afford it when they're fighting the Commonwealth at the same time?"

"They'd be able to call in planetary bombardment strikes if you got uppity," Patrick said. "I don't think they operate under restrictive ROE—Rules of Engagement."

"I see," Jess said. There was no trace of emotion in her voice. "And what can you offer us that makes concealing you from them"—she jerked a finger upwards, indicating the sky—"worth the risk?"

"We can help you fight," Davidson said. "Because I bet you anything you care to put forward that the Theocracy will have worn out its welcome within three weeks."

"I'd not take that bet," Jess said. She rose. "You will be allowed to stay here for the moment, Patrick, as long as you don't cause trouble or attract attention. Do *not* attempt to contact the PDC or any other remnants of the occupation force."

"Understood," Davidson said.

"There are other stragglers," Jess continued. "We may try and hide them, depending on what happens. But some of them won't be taken alive. Too many collaborators have already been killed in the fighting. It's hard to keep people back from murdering them all."

Patrick heard the unspoken threat in her voice and nodded.

Jess paused and then met his eyes. "If the Theocracy starts trying to control us, you can help us fight," she added slowly. "We will need your help if things become as bad as you suggest they will. But if they leave us alone, we will leave *them* alone."

"They won't," Davidson predicted.

"We will see," Jess said. "And one other thing?"

Patrick looked at her earnest eyes and nodded.

"Keep your men under tight control," Jess said. Her voice was very firm. "I had to argue for hours to convince . . . some people not to go after you at once. Some of them wanted revenge, others just wanted to eliminate you before you became a threat. I had to argue with men who don't always trust my judgment."

She took a breath. "Please don't make me regret that, Patrick."

"I won't," Davidson said. He hesitated and then asked the question that had been nagging at him since he'd realized she was a girl. "Why did you join the insurgency anyway?"

Jess smiled at him. "Isn't it obvious?" she asked. "I wanted my planet to be free."

Davidson sighed. "I'm sorry, for what it's worth," he said. "But the same factors that made you so interesting to the Commonwealth will attract the Theocracy."

He was tempted to ask what kind of life she would have had if the Commonwealth had never invaded and the Theocracy had never existed. Would she have reached a position of considerable power and influence anyway . . . or would her gender have restricted her? Would she have been allowed to choose her own husband or would her family have picked a man for her? He didn't dare disrupt their fragile agreement by asking.

"If we win the war, there shouldn't be any need to hold Cadiz against its will," he said instead. "And I believe the occupation will not be restored."

Jess met his eyes. "And if you lose?"

Davidson snorted. "I think we'll have worse problems to worry about," he said. "The Theocracy will not leave people like me alive."

CHAPTER THIRTY-THREE

There had never been a terrorist attack in Tyre City. Not one. The planet's original population had been volunteers, instead of the reluctant exiles shipped to worlds that didn't need or want them, and anyone who wanted to opt out of the corporate-based society could have done so easily. Even the handful of insurgencies the newborn Commonwealth had faced had never reached Tyre City. The locale had always known peace.

Until now, Duke Lucas thought, as his aircar flew towards the Royal Palace. Smoke rose from a dozen locations all over the city, while armed aircars and military hovercraft circled, looking for targets. Beside him, Sandra, his personal assistant, looked faintly uneasy. *No one will ever feel safe again.*

He glared down at his terminal, half wishing he could just push everything that had happened out of his mind. The attacks had seemed to come out of nowhere, starting with computer viruses striking various planetary datanets and ending with outright attacks on the political and military infrastructure. No one had expected such an assault, despite the looming threat of war, and planetary security forces had been caught flat-footed. There had already been a string of incidents caused by nervous guardsmen that had resulted in fatal shootings.

"Your Grace," Sandra said, "I have the latest report from Pinnacle."

"Go ahead," Lucas ordered. Sandra was a formidably efficient woman with East Asian features and a mind like a steel trap. He happened to know she'd pushed augmentation as far as it could go, at least for civilians. Half of her mind was permanently connected to the datanet. "What's the bad news?"

"A freighter was intercepted by the security patrols before it could break into the facility using old IFF codes," Sandra said. "The crew detonated the self-destruct before they could be taken into custody."

"Well, thank goodness for paranoia," Lucas said. The access codes had been changed only a week prior, following the reports from the border. There had been protests at the time, but he had a feeling they would be muted now. "Do we have any incident reports from the cloudscoops?"

"Not as yet," Sandra said. "They're still running round like headless chickens."

Lucas nodded, unsurprised. They'd called enough security drills over the past few weeks to leave his security teams confident they could handle anything. Evidently, they'd been wrong—or, at least, too blasé about the alert when it began. And then the shit had hit the fan. He had a feeling, when reports started to come in from the rest of the Commonwealth, that there would be more attacks. The Theocracy clearly didn't believe in doing things by halves.

But they have to make damn sure they win now, he thought as he looked at one of the plumes of smoke. *They've made us mad.*

He looked back at Sandra. "Is there any word from the Admiralty?"

"No, sir," Sandra said. "They've gone into lockdown."

Just like the rest of the planet, Lucas thought. Normally, there would be hundreds of aircars over the city and thousands of automobiles moving through the streets. Now it was eerily quiet, the only signs of life being armed soldiers as they hurried to reinforce the guards at potential targets. *I wouldn't even be here if the king hadn't called me personally.*

He sucked in a breath as the aircar dropped down and landed neatly in front of the palace. It was easy to see the Royal Marines, in full combat battle dress, pointing weapons at his vehicle as the hatch opened. One moment of panic, the morbid side of his mind noted, and his career would come to a short, sharp end. Then the Family Council would have to select his successor while the war started to rage. He stepped out of the car and submitted without an argument to the scanners the marines waved over his body. Behind him, Sandra was getting the same treatment, only more thoroughly. She rarely visited the palace.

Inside, there were armed guards everywhere, looking round as if they expected the portraits on the walls to spring to life and attack. Lucas tried not to think about new dangers as they were hurried through the corridors and up the stairs into the formal audience chamber. The king was already there, standing in front of the window and staring out over the city, his entire body tense. He'd warned of the Theocracy's threat as soon as he'd become old enough to take an interest in politics, Lucas knew. Now, his worst fears had come to pass.

"Your Majesty," Sandra said. It was the first time she'd ever spoken before her master. "Should you be standing there?"

The king turned to face her, his dark eyes glittering. "If they have a sniper with a weapon that can break through that window," he said, "I'm dead anyway. I just had to see for myself."

Sandra dropped to one knee. "I'm sorry, Your Majesty," she said. "I . . ."

"Thank nothing of it," the king said. He looked at Lucas. "Thank you for coming."

Lucas's lips twitched. "Your message didn't suggest I had a choice, Your Majesty," he said flatly. "Why did you call me here?"

"The war has begun," the king said. "We have reports from a dozen systems, each one reporting terrorist attacks on political, military, and economic targets. In some places, the damage has been quite extensive; in others, the terrorists were intercepted before they could do any real harm. These are the first shots in the war."

"Yes, Your Majesty," Lucas said. He took a breath. His daughter was on the front lines. "Has there been any word from Cadiz?"

"Contact was lost three hours ago," the king said. "I am assuming the worst."

He met Lucas's eyes. "The Theocracy's ambassador has requested permission to meet with me," he added. "I do not expect it to be a very pleasant meeting. There will probably be a declaration of war involved. Even if there isn't, Parliament is meeting in emergency session this afternoon. I have no doubt that a declaration of war will pass through both houses within an hour."

"Yes, Your Majesty," Lucas said.

"You will attend the meeting," the king said. "Your insights will be welcome. But there is another reason I called you here. In a state of war, the normal checks and balances on political power are removed. I will wield supreme power over the state."

Lucas nodded. The constitution had been designed to prevent the king riding roughshod over Parliament, but a state of war gave the monarch vast power to tackle the situation as he saw fit. It had never been tested, until now. Lucas had the nasty feeling that the years after the war would see lawyers making a great deal of money, while sensitive events were rehashed time and time again.

"I will be forming a war council," the king continued. "Someone will have to serve as Minister of War Production. That will be you."

Lucas thought, fast. His promotion would be challenged by the other dukes, he knew, although most of them were sensible enough to realize the Commonwealth *needed* a unified system of war production. It would test his diplomatic skills to the limit. Some of the other dukes would be unsuited to a role on his subordinate council but would demand one in exchange for keeping their protests to a reasonable limit.

Others would resent him taking a position over them and work to undermine him. It wouldn't be easy to deal with them.

But it has to be done, he thought. *We need to work in unison if we are to have any hope of winning this war.*

"I will be calling others over the next two days," the king said, breaking into Lucas's thoughts. "We will need to force forward programs to design and then construct new starships, then learn lessons from the opening moves of the war and incorporate them into our long-term development plans. Which weapons worked well in combat? Which ones need to be improved—or scrapped? We will be on a very steep learning curve."

"Yes, Your Majesty," Lucas said. He couldn't disagree with the logic. Besides, if he refused the post someone else would take it. "How much authority will I have?"

"Enough, I hope," the king said. "I will back you to the hilt. Just remember what will happen if we lose this war."

Lucas nodded. He would be killed, of course, along with the rest of the male aristocracy. The girls and women, including his daughters, would probably be sold into slavery—or simply raped and then killed. Kat would definitely be killed. As a trained military officer, she would be deemed too dangerous to keep alive. And the factories and industrial nodes he'd spent so long building up would be used to place the entire galaxy under the yoke of the Theocracy.

"Yes, Your Majesty," he said.

There would be other problems, he knew. The war wouldn't last forever—and when it came to an end, so would the state of emergency. Any enemies he made while gearing the Commonwealth for war would reach for their knives and try to bring him down as soon as the conflict ended. Balancing the needs of the Commonwealth with the requirements to protect his own position would be tricky. Perhaps he should just plan on stepping down as CEO as soon as the war came to an end. It might be the simplest solution.

"And we will also have to hold an inquiry into how the war actually started," Lucas added. "We need to know who put Admiral Morrison out there, in command of 7th Fleet."

"We will leave that issue until the end of the conflict," the king said. "Right now, Your Grace, pointing fingers would be far too divisive."

Lucas frowned. "Your Majesty . . ."

The king met his eyes. "We cannot risk a political catfight, not now," he said. "The charges are too serious for that to be allowed. We will leave the issue until the end of the war."

Which will give Morrison's benefactors plenty of time to bury evidence, break a few links in the chain, and remain undiscovered, Lucas thought. Anyone with the political clout to steer Admiral Morrison to Cadiz without revealing their involvement would have no trouble hiding their tracks in the confusion caused by the war. *But what if he's right?*

No one should have been able to hide their tracks from him. Lucas knew, without false modesty, that he sat at the center of a spiderweb of clients, subpatrons, and *their* clients. Almost no one should have been able to do something so thoroughly *political* as arrange Admiral Morrison's assignment without leaving tracks. And yet someone had definitely succeeded well enough to keep him baffled. That alone was worrying. It suggested that Admiral Morrison's ultimate backer was one of the dukes. No one else could have hoped to pull it off.

And a duke, if accused of something that was very close to treason, would be able to disrupt government for months before the matter was resolved.

"Yes, Your Majesty," he said grudgingly.

"I do understand your feelings," the king assured him. "But we must win first."

A dull chime echoed through the room. "That will be the ambassador," the king noted. "Please stand to the side."

Lucas obeyed, motioning for Sandra to join him. There was a short delay, then the Theocracy's ambassador was escorted into the chamber. The last time they'd met, Lucas recalled, he'd worn neat white robes and looked surprisingly dapper. This time, it was clear that he'd been thoroughly searched—and none too gently. His implants would have been deactivated before he was allowed anywhere near the Royal Palace.

And what, Lucas asked himself, *if the ambassador is carrying something we are unable to detect?*

He pushed the thought aside as the man staggered forward, escorted by two burly marines. One of them was female, Lucas noted, perhaps explaining the ambassador's clear irritation. Being manhandled was bad enough, but being manhandled by a woman would be nightmarish for a Theocrat. Lucas felt a moment of pity for the ambassador's wife, a girl who stayed in the embassy and never went out onto the streets. No doubt the diplomat would take his rage out on her.

"Ambassador Paul," the king said, with studied nonchalance, "let me guess. You've come to apologize."

Paul gave the king a furious look. "This treatment is abominable," he thundered. "A gross breach of diplomatic courtesy!"

"And so is launching a war," the king said. "Speak your piece and leave."

The ambassador drew himself to his feet. "Peace is the will of God," he said, "and the Theocracy has worked for peace since the One True Faith was brought into being by the Final Prophet. But peace has been threatened, again and again, by the actions of your illegitimate union of worlds. You have invaded our space, incited our populations to rebellion, and sought to control the spread of the One True Faith. These actions can no longer go unpunished."

He took a breath. "I am ordered to offer you one last chance to submit yourselves before the Believers of the One True Faith," he continued. "You must welcome us to your worlds, surrender your ships and industries to our custody, and prepare your people to embrace the One True Faith. Should you refuse, we will wage war until you are bowed in submission, ready to embrace God and take him into your hearts. There will be no further negotiation. It is submission or death."

Lucas wondered, absently, if Paul genuinely believed his own words. It would certainly be far more convincing if he did, he knew, but it was hard to imagine anyone who had spent time on Tyre believing the crap he was spewing out. The Commonwealth hadn't supplied anyone with weapons, let alone incited them to rebel. And they hadn't even tried to ban missionaries from spreading through Commonwealth space.

He winced inwardly. *That* would have to change. And who knew what else would be lost along with religious freedom? What would happen if all of the Commonwealth's guaranteed rights were stripped away in the name of security? How much of what his ancestors had helped build would be lost forever?

The king was leaning forward angrily. But he managed to control himself before he spoke.

"You are correct on one point," he said. His voice was icy cold. "There will be no negotiation."

He took a breath. "You have mounted an unprovoked war against my people, commencing with a series of cowardly terrorist attacks that have left upwards of nine thousand *civilians* dead. Your . . . *pathetic* attempt to give us a declaration of war, too late for us to put our forces on alert, is only the icing on the cake. There will be no further negotiation—and there will be no negotiated peace. The Commonwealth will fight until the Theocracy has been crushed, Ambassador, and it *will* be crushed.

"Your people want freedom. We will give it to them. Your conquests want independence. We will give it to them. Your sons want the right to learn more than how to recite your prayers by rote. We will give it to them. Your wives and daughters want the right to make their own choices. We will give it to them. And the entire galaxy wants to sleep peacefully, without fearing conquest by you. We will give it to them."

He met Ambassador Paul's eyes. "I promise you nothing, but war to the knife," he growled sharply. "And the next time we meet, it will be when I take your surrender in the ruins of your homeworld."

Lucas, standing to one side, sucked in a breath. It was dangerous to drive a foe into a corner, he knew, particularly when it might be more profitable to allow them a way out, but he also knew the king spoke for his people. *No one* would be interested in a negotiated peace with the Theocracy, not now. They'd want to crush the Theocratic navy, liberate its conquests, and sow the grounds of its homeworld with salt.

But the king was still speaking. "Because we are a *civilized* people, we will allow you and your embassy to leave peacefully," he concluded. "It will no longer be necessary."

He looked at the marines. "Get him out of my sight."

Lucas watched as the marines escorted the ambassador out, then turned to the king.

"Parliament will be behind you," he said. He knew it to be true, despite his doubts. The attacks on Tyre had seen to that. "But should we not offer them their lives?"

The king waved a hand towards the window, where plumes of smoke could still be seen.

"No one will want mercy, Your Grace," he said. His voice was very dark as he surveyed the scene before him. He turned to face Lucas. "Nine thousand civilians—perhaps more—are dead, killed by the vilest treachery. There can be no mercy to a government that considers such sneak attacks a legitimate way of opening the war. And I will offer none."

He looked down at the hard marble floor, then up at Lucas. "Prepare yourself for your new responsibilities," he ordered. "Our forces will need everything from starships to armored combat suits and rations. You will be charged with meeting their demands. And you will be advising me on the course of the war."

"Yes, Your Majesty," Lucas said. There was no choice. It was him or someone else, someone who might be less invested in victory. "It will be my honor."

The king nodded. "I think we shall offer the ambassador's family the chance to remain," he added. He smiled brilliantly. "And his servants too. Wouldn't *that* make their lives more interesting?"

Lucas frowned. "Why, Your Majesty?"

"The Princess Drusilla is also on her way here," the king said. "We could find a use for her, I'm sure. And we could find a use for our ambassador's family too."

CHAPTER THIRTY-FOUR

"No sign of pursuit, Captain," Roach reported. "Hyperspace is clear."

Kat let out a sigh of relief. An engagement in hyperspace might have allowed them a chance to reverse the outcome of the battle, but it might also have proven disastrous. Two or three antimatter warheads would have started an energy storm that would have seriously threatened both sides. Trying to raise a storm near the enemy fleet would have seemed a workable idea if she hadn't been certain she would risk her own ships too.

And will it seem a viable weapon of war in the future? she asked herself. *Or will both sides refrain from using it for fear of the consequences?*

"Stand down from battle stations," she ordered. The red lights dimmed. "Damage report?"

"No major damage," Lynn reported. The engineer sounded relieved. "We lost a pair of shield generators, which will need to be replaced, but the remainder are intact."

"Thank God," Kat said. She turned to the XO. "And the fleet?"

"Battered," the XO reported. "Nine superdreadnoughts are gone. Four more are almost certainly not going to be combat capable without yard time. The remainder of the superdreadnoughts have damage ranging from minor to several weeks of repair work."

Kat sighed. "Can we do any repair work in transit?"

"We'll have to shuttle engineering crews round the fleet," the XO said. "But we're still doing head counts. We don't even have an accurate idea how many people we have on the ships, Captain. And we certainly don't have an inventory of spare parts."

If Admiral Morrison isn't dead, Kat thought, *I'm going to kill him personally.*

She looked at the display for a long moment. Two squadrons of superdreadnoughts—and thirty-seven other starships—were nothing to sniff at. By any reasonable standard, she was the youngest fleet commander in history, although she knew she wouldn't be allowed to keep the fleet. She didn't have a dedicated command ship, for one thing. But it would have been a high point of her career, if the ships hadn't been so badly damaged. It would be a long time before 7th Fleet was combat capable again.

We might just break up the formation and assign the usable ships to other fleets, she thought morbidly. *I don't think anyone will care.*

"Complete the head count, then work through the engineering reports," she ordered. She wasn't trained for fleet command. What if she missed something? "Shuttle engineering crews round the fleet, concentrating on the ships that can be returned to operational status sooner rather than later. If a ship needs yard time, leave a skeleton crew and get the rest somewhere where they can be more useful."

"Aye, Captain," the XO said. "Doing it under transit will prove a challenge."

Kat nodded. "But do we have a choice?"

She thought fast. Her father's brief update had stated that Admiral Christian and 6th Fleet had been ordered to Gamma Base, a star forty light years from Cadiz. But she hadn't heard anything since then and there was no way to tell if the fleet had already reached its destination or if it was still in transit. It might not matter, she told herself. Her first duty was to report to the Admiralty and Gamma Base had a working StarCom.

Or it should have had a working StarCom, part of her mind noted. *What if the Theocracy got there too?*

She dismissed the thought, then looked at the display. "The 67th Destroyer Squadron is largely intact," she said. "Reassign two more destroyers to fill the holes in the squadron's roster, then order her CO to return to Cadiz. They are to monitor the star system at a safe distance and, if possible, attempt to open communications with forces on the ground."

"Aye, Captain," the XO said. He paused, then opened a private channel to Kat. "Captain, it is unlikely they will be able to get close enough to the planet to open a secure channel to anyone."

"I know," Kat sent back. She thought, briefly, of the millions of crowns invested in Cadiz by various corporations, including her own. The Theocracy had gained a valuable prize when it overran the system. There had been no time to rig the facilities to self-destruct. "But we have to try."

She settled back in her command chair, feeling very tired. It was her first major engagement and all she'd been able to do was run. And she was already tired of running. Part of her wanted to lurk on the edge of the system until her fleet was ready, then go on the offensive, but she knew it wasn't possible. They didn't have any supply dumps closer than Gamma Base. Admiral Morrison should have had pre-positioned stockpiles along the border. That he hadn't, Kat knew, was yet another sign of criminal incompetence.

Or outright treason, she thought. But was that really possible?

"Set course for Gamma Base," she ordered the helmsman. "Best possible speed."

"Aye, Captain," Weiberg said. "We'll be there in four days."

"Prepare to detach a destroyer to run ahead of us," Kat ordered the XO. "She can take our reports to the StarCom."

"Aye, Captain," the XO said. "But it will only shave a day off our time before we can report in."

"It doesn't matter," Kat said. By now, someone would *surely* have noticed that they'd lost contact with Cadiz. All StarCom shutdowns should be notified in advance. Someone would surely draw the correct conclusion . . . and alert the Commonwealth that it was at war with the Theocracy. But what if someone *hadn't* drawn the correct conclusion? Or what if something else had gone badly wrong? "We need to get our report out as quickly as possible."

She rose to her feet, feeling almost too tired to walk. "I'll write the report now," she said. "You have the bridge."

"Aye, Captain," the XO said. "I have the bridge."

Kat stepped into her Ready Room and closed the hatch behind her, then sagged onto the sofa and put her head in her hands. She'd failed, she told herself, as despair threatened to overcome her. Her father had expected her to gather proof the war was about to begin and galvanize the admiral into action, but she'd barely succeeded at the former and failed completely at the latter. And the end run they'd done round Morrison and his ass-kissing subordinates hadn't been enough to save the fleet. They'd had no choice but to flee.

We made it out, she told herself. The fleet might have made it out, but it had been too badly battered to be considered combat capable any longer. *We could have lost everything.*

And she *had* lost Davidson. She cursed herself angrily, first for pulling him back into her bed and then for sending him to Cadiz. He could have called General Eastside from orbit and to hell with Marine protocol. It was easy to imagine him dead now, his shuttle slammed into the ground, his body lying in a ditch . . . or him having been taken prisoner by the Theocracy. She knew what they'd do to a trained marine.

She had loved him, once. She still cared deeply for him. And she had sent him to his death.

You're too young, a voice whispered in the back of her head. *You're too unpolished to be put in command of a heavy cruiser, let alone a fleet.*

And stop whining, you stupid bitch, another voice said. *However you got it, you're in command. You have a responsibility you cannot shirk. Or are you going to cower in your Ready Room like a stupid little girl and leave the officers under your command without orders? And prove that everyone who had doubts about you was right all along?*

Angrily, she pulled herself to her feet and looked in the mirror. She looked awful, despite the genetic engineering that had gone into her body. Her hair was soaked with sweat, her uniform clung to her in awkward places, and her face looked tired and worn. She wanted to shower, then sleep for a week. Instead, she walked into the washroom, splashed water on her face, and then returned to her desk. She had a report to write.

And hope it doesn't get me shot out of hand, she thought. She *was* the fleet commander now, at least until a senior officer was assigned to the fleet. There was no way her father's influence could save her from a Board of Inquiry. And if she was found responsible for the disaster, she might well lose her career at the very least.

Shaking her head, she reached for the terminal and started to work.

"It is my duty," Doctor Braham said, as William entered the compartment, "to warn you that Sickbay is critically low on personnel."

"Duly noted, Doctor," William said. He'd ordered two-thirds of her staff reassigned to the superdreadnoughts. Over five hundred crewmen had been injured and the head count had yet to be completed. Several of them would have to be shoved into stasis until the fleet reached safe haven. "Get back to work."

"Aye, Commander," the doctor said tartly. "However, regulations clearly state . . ."

"The regulations were written in peacetime," William snapped. They *were* clear. Among other things, a vessel's senior medical officer was not to leave her ship without the captain's direct permission, while her complement of medical crew was not to be reduced by more than a third. "This is war."

He sucked in a breath. How the hell had Fran's late, unlamented commanding officer managed to get away with sending over half of his medical complement on leave at the same time? The fleet had been in orbit, with little real chance of disaster . . . but it should still have been a court-martial offense. Or had someone merely decided there was no point in trying to bring charges against one of Admiral Morrison's cronies?

"Yes," the doctor said. "But . . ."

"But *nothing*," William said. He'd expected better from her. "Those are your orders, Doctor, which you may have in writing if you wish. We do not have the medical complement on each ship to avoid breaking regulations."

He watched her storm off, then turned back to the endless stream of reports. Admiral Morrison had done a good job of suppressing initiative too, he noted. William was being asked to approve matters that should, by rights, have been handled by local officers. He should have told them to promote themselves to captains, as long as they were in command of starships, but it was unlikely they'd accept such orders. It was certainly unlikely he had authority to issue them.

But they're in command now, he thought sourly. *They should be captains.*

He pushed the thought aside as he reviewed the first after-action report. Most of 7th Fleet's deficiencies were hardly news to him, but there were a few interesting points. Notably, the shield generators had been out of harmony on several superdreadnoughts, weakening their shields under the onslaught from the gunboats. Missile hits that should have been shrugged off had done real damage to starships that not only cost *far* more than a single gunboat, but took much longer to produce.

He read the rest of the report, then dropped a copy in his private subsection of the datanet. If there was an attempt to whitewash Admiral Morrison in the wake of his presumed death, William was damned if he was going to let it succeed. A few independent media outlets would be very interested in the files.

"Commander," Roach said, "I have a detailed tactical report of our performance as a fleet command ship."

"Shit-awful," William snapped. He forced himself to calm his temper with an effort. It was hardly Roach's fault that the battle had gone so badly. Hell, it couldn't be blamed on the captain either, although she'd issued the order to retreat. "How badly did we do?"

"Not as badly as I thought," Roach said. "We did manage to organize a tactical withdrawal under fire . . ."

"Call it a *retreat*," William said. It *was* a tricky maneuver to pull off under fire, he knew, but fancy words didn't change the fact they'd lost and left the enemy in possession of their target. "Or would you like to come up with a suitably stupid term for surrender?"

He felt a moment of pain for the captain. William was far from blind and it was alarmingly clear, at least to him, that the captain and her Marine CO had been lovers, once upon a time. They'd certainly served together on an earlier ship. But they had been professional, at least in public, and she hadn't hesitated to send him to Cadiz . . . where he was missing, presumed dead. They didn't even know if he'd managed to land at the spaceport before it had been overrun and destroyed.

She's too young, he thought. The captain *didn't* have the seasoning to handle losing someone so close to her, not in a situation where she could blame herself for his death. And she certainly would. Unlike far too many aristocrats, she was aware of crewmen and officers as *people*, not things to be moved round on her own personal chess board. He stared down at his console, trying to decide what to do. But he knew there was nothing he could say.

Roach coughed. "Commander?"

William scowled. Roach had been speaking and he hadn't heard a word.

"Say that again," he said. "I was hundreds of light years away."

"Yes, sir," Roach said. "The other piece of tactical information we picked up is that their datanet *leaks*."

William leaned forward. "It *leaks*?"

"Yes, sir," Roach said. "They seem to use tight-beam radio as well as lasers to maintain the datanet. I don't think they entirely trust their laser links."

"Odd," William said. There were several reasons why maintaining laser links over a vast distance was difficult, but none of them should have applied to a fleet operating in formation. "Do you have any idea why?"

"No, sir," Roach said. "But it does give us an opportunity to ID the command ship. There will always be some backwash from the radio transmissions."

"Difficult to spot in a firefight," William pointed out. He shrugged. "See if you can devise a program for identifying their command structure, then run it through simulations and see how it might work in practice. If it works, we would know which ships to target in a major fleet engagement."

"Assuming they don't use a staggered command structure," Roach said. "*We* certainly do."

"It's a possibility," William agreed. There had been no shortage of experimental programs intended to track and decode enemy signals during a battle, but none of them had ever worked in practice. Or, at least, they hadn't provided actionable intelligence. "See what you can pull out of the records."

He watched Roach go, then turned back to his console. Maybe it would work, in practice; certainly, there had been odder theories that had actually produced workable hardware. But he knew better than to count on any silver bullet to win the war. It would be won by superdreadnoughts and battle cruisers, missiles, bullets, and beams. And the Theocracy had already scored a significant victory.

Shaking his head, he went back to work.

♦ ♦ ♦

Four days passed slowly, slowly enough for Kat to tour several of the superdreadnoughts and meet the men and women under her command. None of them looked anything other than tired; they were working double shifts, just trying to get the ships back into service before the Theocracy caught up with them. Kat did what she could to help, even to the point of cannibalizing components from the yard-bound vessels, but it wasn't enough. She was feeling the stress again by the time the fleet finally opened a series of vortexes and returned to real space in the Gamma System, well away from the naval base.

"Send an IFF signal," Kat ordered once she was satisfied there was no one waiting in ambush. The thought of the Theocracy striking so far behind the lines had kept her awake at nights. "And then link into the local StarCom. Send a copy of our report to Tyre."

"Aye, Captain," Ross said.

"I'm picking up multiple capital ships," Roach reported. "Several are definitely superdreadnoughts."

Kat felt her blood run cold. Had they been outraced by the enemy ships?

"IFF signals are Commonwealth; I say again, IFF signals are Commonwealth," Ross said. "They're the 6th Fleet!"

"Thank God," the XO said.

Kat nodded. The 6th Fleet had an admiral of its own. She wouldn't be fleet commander any longer. It was odd, but she couldn't help feeling relieved.

"Transmit a full copy of our report," Kat said. The destroyer would already have alerted 6th Fleet, but they hadn't had an up-to-date report.

"And then request a status report from their CO. If they have a fleet train handy, hit them with our shopping list. I want every ship in the fleet to draw on the facilities until they are combat capable again."

There was a long pause. "Captain," Ross said, "you are ordered to report to Admiral Christian on the *Thunderchild*."

Kat sucked in her breath. "Understood," she said. It was unfortunate that there would be no time to freshen up before she reported to the admiral. "Inform him that I am on my way."

She keyed her console, ordering her shuttle to be powered up, then rose. "Mr. XO, you have the bridge."

"Aye, Captain," the XO said. His eyes were worried. Worried for her. "I have the bridge."

Kat glanced from console to console, wondering if it was the last time she would set eyes on it, then picked up her terminal and walked through the hatch, refusing to look back. If the admiral relieved her of command . . .

You got the fleet out, she told herself firmly. *And that's all that matters.*

CHAPTER THIRTY-FIVE

The walk from the shuttle airlock to Admiral Christian's private compartment felt hundreds of miles long, as though Kat was heading to her own execution. It was a terrifyingly clear that *Thunderchild* was a happy ship, with a capable commander and crew that worked hard for their officers. Compared to the remains of 7th Fleet, she was magnificent. Kat couldn't help feeling a twinge of envy as she stopped in front of a hatch, then knocked. It opened a moment later, inviting her inside.

"Captain Falcone," Admiral Gareth Christian said. "Thank you for coming."

"Admiral," Kat said tersely.

He motioned for her to take a seat. Kat sat, studying him carefully. Compared to Admiral Morrison, he looked ugly as hell. His face resembled nothing so much as a bulldog, complete with an expression that suggested he was damned if he was letting go of anything in his mouth. Kat found it oddly reassuring. The admiral didn't seem to feel the urge to use cosmetic surgery to beautify himself. It suggested he had few doubts about his own performance.

"I read the report you sent ahead," Christian said without preamble. "Is there anything you wish to add to your report?"

"No, sir," Kat said. She'd written as cold and impersonal an account as she could. The only moment she'd allowed her feelings to show through had been when she took full responsibility for going behind Admiral Morrison's back. Commander Higgins and her fellows didn't have the political clout to escape charges of mutiny. "It is complete."

"And it seems that 7th Fleet would not have survived, were it not for you," Christian added. "You pulled two squadrons of superdreadnoughts out of a fire that could easily have consumed them."

"Yes, sir," Kat said.

"It is my considered opinion that Cadiz was beyond saving," Christian said calmly. "Do you agree with this judgment?"

"I do," Kat said simply.

"I have informed Tyre that you did the best you could, under the circumstances," Christian said. "You were not to blame for the lack of preparation, the incompetence of a number of superior officers, and the general condition of the fleet. I do not believe that anyone will seek to hold you to account for disaster."

"Thank you, sir," Kat said. She let out a long breath. Logically, she'd known she couldn't be blamed; emotionally, she knew she would always wonder if there had been something else she could have done. "I . . ."

"Self-doubt is understandable under such circumstances," Christian said, cutting her off. "I do not feel it is justified, though. You did better than anyone had any right to expect."

He straightened up, resting his hands on his lap. "And with that out the way," he said, "I need a full rundown on 7th Fleet."

Kat took a breath. "We have roughly one squadron of superdreadnoughts that can fly and fight," she said. "The remainder need heavy time in the yards before they can be recommitted to battle. Thankfully, the smaller ships took less of a beating, but several of them also require yard time."

She produced a datachip from her pocket. "This is the full report, sir," she added. "But a number of the ships used creative editing . . ."

"As always," Christian observed.

Kat felt her cheeks heat. She'd made the mistake of taking the original set of reports at face value. It had been her XO who'd pointed out that several of the officers had written the reports very carefully, suggesting their ships were ready to return to the fight even though they needed several weeks in the hands of repair crews. At least, he'd pointed out afterwards, it suggested the crews were ready to fight. The 7th Fleet couldn't allow itself to fall into despair.

"Yes, sir," she said.

"There were a number of attacks inside the Commonwealth itself," Christian continued, grimly. "Most of them were terrorist attacks, but a handful were considerably more serious, involving pre-positioned warships. Right now, we have a declaration of war and a public ready to burn the Theocracy's worlds to ash and sow the ground with salt, but the political and military leadership has yet to determine a strategy. Our morale will plummet when news of Cadiz leaks out—and it will."

He took a breath. "We cannot allow morale to fall too far," he explained. "I therefore intend to give the public a victory."

Kat hesitated. Admiral Christian's fleet was the sole intact formation for fifty light years. It would take time to move reinforcements to the front lines, which would give the Theocracy a decisive advantage if they managed to take out 6th Fleet and the remains of 7th Fleet. And the politicians would probably hesitate to ship reinforcements forward, knowing there would be public protest at the thought of being left undefended. Only a few Commonwealth worlds could hope to stave off a Theocratic offensive without support from the Royal Navy.

"A victory," she repeated. "You expect them to attack here?"

"I'm not sure they know *we're* here," Admiral Christian observed. "The 7th Fleet was meant to avoid *provocations*, after all, and reinforcing the border would definitely count as a *provocation*."

He snorted rudely. "But it does give us a limited advantage," he added. "We can take the offensive and give them a bloody nose."

Christian tapped a switch. A holographic image of the Cadiz System appeared in front of them. It split in two a moment later, one showing Cadiz, the other showing the unnamed star the Theocracy had used as a staging base. The admiral's analysts had been hard at work, Kat saw, as new icons and notes flashed up on the display. It was clear that the fleet she'd seen preparing for the assault had been the one that had attacked Cadiz.

She shook her head. As if there had been any doubt.

"This is the enemy attack fleet," Christian said. "It is powerful, no doubt about that, and it is well trained. But there's something missing."

Kat studied the display for a long moment. She'd hoped the Theocracy would be inferior to the Commonwealth, but no great deficiencies had shown themselves when the two sides had finally come to blows. And somehow she doubted the three squadrons of enemy superdreadnoughts were *all* they possessed. The Royal Navy deployed over a *hundred* superdreadnoughts.

And then she saw it. "A fleet train," she said. "They don't have any supply ships."

"Precisely," Admiral Christian said.

"But they could have remained powered down," Kat objected, playing devil's advocate. "Or they might have been hidden in hyperspace."

"By any reasonable standard," Admiral Christian observed, "the Theocracy should have begun its attacks earlier. The curiously staggered timing of the attacks deeper within the Commonwealth suggests that they were caught on the hop."

"Because of us," Kat said bitterly.

Admiral Christian pointed a long finger at her. "It was not your fault," he said. "But you probably encouraged them to launch the attack ahead of schedule. And that begs the question of precisely *why* they didn't launch the attack earlier. Could it be they don't have the fleet train to support their advance?"

Kat considered it thoughtfully. The XO's brother had been pretty clear that the smugglers were being hired to ship goods inside the Theocracy, rather than just sneaking forbidden goods past the guardships. And everything they knew about the Theocracy suggested it had a command economy. Someone in charge of shaping industrial and military growth might well have concentrated on superdreadnoughts and other warships instead of freighters, even though support craft would be vitally important if the Theocracy went on the offensive.

"It's possible," she said. But her father's warning rang through her head. There was no lie—or false conclusion—so dangerous as the one you *wanted* to believe. "But they could have just kept the freighters back, out of danger. We wouldn't fly a freighter convoy into a battle zone."

"No, we wouldn't," Admiral Christian agreed. "But did they have any reason to believe we would fly a spy ship into their staging base?"

"No," Kat said, slowly. The Theocracy hadn't had to worry about spy ships. Even if they had, none of them would have visited the unnamed system. They would have concentrated on inhabited worlds. "You're suggesting they don't have their fleet train ready to support their advance."

It sounded possible, she knew. But was that because she *wanted* to believe it?

"There are three reasons to launch a counterattack as quickly as possible," Admiral Christian said. "First, we need to give them a bloody nose, both to teach them caution and convince our own people that we can and will fight back. Second, we need to recover our personnel on Cadiz itself. And third, we need to destroy the facilities within the system. They cannot be allowed to support the Theocracy's advance."

Kat looked down at the deck. "I'm sorry," she mumbled, feeling like a schoolgirl who had been called on the carpet. "There was no time to plan their destruction . . ."

"Admiral fucking Morrison should have planned for the worst," Admiral Christian snapped. "And once the war is over I will do everything in my power to make sure his backers are rooted out and put on trial for leaving him in command of the system. It wasn't your responsibility to sabotage the facilities, Captain, and no one will blame you for not realizing it needed to be done in time. But it does leave us with a headache."

And another good reason not to discuss his plans openly with the Admiralty, Kat thought sourly. *The corporations that built the facilities might object to their destruction.*

"The 6th Fleet—and intact units from 7th Fleet—will advance to the edge of Cadiz," Admiral Christian said. "We will contact the destroyers you left watching the system—good thinking, by the way—and determine the status of the enemy fleet. If it has been rearmed and repaired, we will engage at long range and do some damage before buggering off. If not . . . we'll seek a decisive battle."

Kat swallowed. The prewar naval planners had considered destroying the enemy's fleet to be the first objective of any military operation. God knew there was no sign the Theocracy disagreed. By dangling 6th Fleet in front of the enemy commander, Admiral Christian would be offering him a chance to win the war in a single afternoon—or lose it. And if the enemy won the ensuring battle . . .

Admiral Christian altered the display, focusing—once again—on Cadiz. "We will advance towards Cadiz VII," he continued. "The facilities in orbit round the gas giant will be our main target. If possible, we will recover personnel before we blow the facilities, but those facilities *will* be blown. The enemy will have to decide between trying to stop us from attacking the facilities or leaving them to be destroyed."

He grinned at her. "You and your squadron will remain in hyperspace," he added. "If the enemy fleet advances to engage us, you will come out of hyperspace behind the enemy and attack Cadiz itself. You will destroy enemy facilities on the ground, then attempt to pick up as many of our personnel as possible, then retreat back into hyperspace."

Kat worked her way through the details, slowly. "It sounds as if there's too much that can go wrong," she said. "What if the enemy fleet doubles back to engage me?"

"Then you run," Admiral Christian said bluntly. "But I don't expect them to pass up the chance of destroying 6th Fleet. Or, for that matter, to allow us to blow the facilities without opposition, not when they need them so badly."

He shrugged. "I don't intend to try to hold Cadiz permanently," he added. "The Theocracy will already have reinforcements on the way. All I want to do is get in, smash the facilities, and then get out again. If it seems likely we can win a duel with the enemy fleet, we'll seek battle. But we cannot afford heavy losses."

Kat nodded. There was no way to know what percentage of the Theocracy's total fleet had attacked Cadiz. Twenty-nine superdreadnoughts . . . were they 10 percent of the enemy fleet, 20 percent, or 50 percent? There was no way to know. And it would be weeks, perhaps months, before additional forces were surged forward to reinforce the front lines. She couldn't argue with his logic. The Royal Navy couldn't afford catastrophic losses.

"You were wrong, sir," she mumbled. "I could have done something."

Admiral Christian quirked an eyebrow. "You could?"

"I could have killed him," Kat said. She recalled the insurgent attack on the admiral's mansion. If she'd known just how badly the battle would have gone, she would have sneaked out of the mansion and called for pickup when she was well away from the terrorists, leaving them to kill the admiral at leisure. Or she could just have shot him herself. "Sir . . ."

"Shooting one's senior officers is hardly the sort of behavior the Royal Navy wishes to encourage," Admiral Christian said mildly. "Your career would have been utterly destroyed and you would probably have spent the rest of your life in prison, if your father managed to save you from the firing squad."

"Twenty thousand officers and crew are dead," Kat pointed out bitterly. "There were hundreds of thousands of soldiers in the occupation force—they're dead. God alone knows how many civilians are dead on Cadiz—or wishing they're dead, if the Theocracy has clamped down on the locals. My life would be a small price to pay to keep them alive."

Admiral Christian reached out and rested his hand on her shoulder. "You can't change the past," he said. "All you can do is learn from it."

"Yes, sir," Kat said. "And I will personally *kill* the next incompetent officer I encounter."

"I fear war will winnow them out soon enough," Admiral Christian said. "And I would suggest you keep such sentiments to yourself in the future."

Kat nodded, reluctantly.

But she had no intention of forgetting her private vow. Her crew, her superiors . . . all of them had feared *she* was an incompetent, someone who had only gained her command through family connections. They'd probably had nightmares about her costing them their lives through a simple mistake, one a more experienced officer would have avoided. And yet . . . Admiral Morrison had been far too like her for comfort. Powerful patrons had put him in command, powerful patrons had prevented any investigation that would have led to his removal . . . she was *damned* if she was allowing it to happen again. Her career, even her life, was a small price to pay for preventing another disaster on the same scale.

"Return to your ship," Admiral Christian ordered gently, breaking into her thoughts. "I'll forward the operational plans to you as soon as possible, then assume command of the remains of 7th Fleet."

"Yes, sir," Kat said. She took a breath. "The officers in command of the ships should be formally promoted to captains."

Admiral Christian gave her a long look. "Is there a reason for that?"

Kat felt her temper flare, then forced it down. "Yes, sir," she said, instead. "They chose to work in secret to prepare the fleet to fight, despite Admiral Morrison's orders. I believe they showed considerable moral courage in accepting the risk of losing their careers if the admiral found out before it was too late. And they managed to get their ships out of the enemy trap. I do not believe they should be pushed back purely because someone else has a better pedigree than themselves."

"I see," Admiral Christian said. "And you believe I should use my authority to make the ranks they've assumed permanent?"

"Yes, sir," Kat said. She held his eyes. "I do."

"Very well," the admiral said. "There won't be a formal ceremony, of course, but they will be promoted. I'll register it in the logbook today."

Kat allowed herself a moment of relief. Commander Fran Higgins and her comrades couldn't be stripped of their ranks now, at least not without doing something to justify a court martial and formal punishment. They deserved command, far more than anyone who had sat out the battle on Cadiz. And she was confident they would make good commanding officers. They already knew what to avoid.

And besides, she thought, *no one could blame them for preparing the fleet, not now.*

Admiral Christian rose to his feet. "Return to your ship," he ordered. "I'll assign ships to your command as soon as possible. Start carrying out drills right away, Captain; we will return to Cadiz within the week."

"Yes, sir," Kat said. It wasn't long enough to do more than basic drills, but at least she would have more to work with than the superdreadnoughts. Her crews were better trained, for a start. "I won't let you down."

"And you might want to pen a private note to your father," Admiral Christian added. There was an oddly amused note to his voice. "I believe he has been worrying about you."

"Everyone will have a chance to write a private note," Kat said firmly. She wasn't going to be the only one allowed to send a message home, even though her father had enough influence to make it happen. "The StarCom can handle the traffic, sir."

The admiral smiled.

"Of course it can," he said. "But censorship rules are already in effect. You might want to warn your crews to be careful what they say."

"Yes, sir," Kat said. She looked up at the display. The Theocracy might already be sending fleets deeper into Commonwealth space. "But the folks at home will know the worst soon enough."

"I know," Admiral Christian said. "That's why I want to give them a morale-boosting victory as soon as possible. It won't be long before the full truth leaks out. And then the shit will definitely hit the fan."

CHAPTER THIRTY-SIX

The village wasn't very large, Davidson noted, as Jess led him to a place where they could watch from a safe distance. It was really nothing more than a dozen midsized houses, one large church, and a handful of shops, all surrounded by farms. He had a feeling that it had largely been ignored during the Commonwealth's occupation of Cadiz, something that would have suited the locals just fine. They had more important things to do than wage war on the occupation force.

"Several of our leaders answered calls to meet with Theocratic representatives," Jess explained as they made themselves comfortable. "None of them have been seen since."

Davidson wasn't surprised. "They probably knew precisely who to round up," he said. "If they supplied you with weapons, they knew who took them; hell, they might even have outfitted trackers in the weapons themselves."

Jess looked grim. "Several bases went silent," she added. "Mine survived. Is that because I didn't have any of their weapons in the base?"

"Perhaps," Davidson said. If the Theocracy had had agents on the surface, making contact with the insurgents, they could have been quietly gathering information for years. "Do you believe us now?"

"We haven't heard anything from inside the city," Jess admitted. "They've sealed the place off better than you bastards managed to. None of our people have managed to get in or out of the ring of steel."

Davidson gave her a long look. "That doesn't answer my question," he said. "Do you believe me now?"

"I think we have little reason to trust either of you," Jess said. She paused, then nodded as a line of vehicles came into view. "And here they come."

Davidson activated his ocular implants as the ground forces approached the village. They were led by a small tank, bristling with weapons, designed more for crowd control than armored warfare. Behind the tank were five trucks crammed with armed soldiers wearing khaki combat outfits. They all looked grimly determined—and alert. Clearly, their commander expected trouble. At the rear was another tank watching for signs of trouble. Davidson hoped that no one in the village was inclined to put up a fight.

The convoy stopped at the edge of town, the soldiers dismounting and spreading out until they had sealed the entire village. Davidson caught sight of a handful of men and women trying to flee into the countryside, only to be caught, brutally beaten with rifle butts, and then forced back into the village. As soon as the area was closed off, the soldiers entered, bellowing orders for the inhabitants to assemble. Fearfully, the locals obeyed.

Jess elbowed him. "What are they doing?"

"Looking for weapons," Davidson muttered back. The soldiers were searching the buildings, one by one. They were practiced, practiced enough to convince him they'd searched for arms many times before. A number of primitive rifles were found and tossed out onto the streets, but little else. "Once they've rendered the village defenseless, they will lay down the law."

He watched grimly as the search came to an end and the leader started to address the villagers. It was impossible to hear what the enemy commander was saying to the locals from their distance, but he could guess. They would be expected to provide a certain amount of tribute every year, to respect Theocratic law, and report on any insurgent movements within their territory. At the end of his speech, the soldiers snatched a handful of children—girls and boys—and dragged them to their vehicles. Anyone who dared object was simply knocked down by the soldiers and beaten into a bloody mass.

Hostages, Patrick thought. *They'll be taking hostages to ensure the villagers behave themselves.*

"Bastards," Jess hissed. "Now we won't be able to rely on the villagers."

"No," Patrick agreed. "And there's more."

Having restored order, the soldiers were registering the remaining villagers, entering their details into their computer network. Patrick knew what that meant, all right. If any of the villagers turned insurgent, their bodies might be recovered and their home identified. The Theocracy would then take a terrible revenge on their families. So far, everything matched what they'd been told by the refugees.

Jess looked at him. "Most of my people won't be registered," she said. "They won't be able to track down their families."

"They might," Davidson said. "If someone unregistered is run through the system, it still might be able to identify their parents or children. And then the Theocracy will hunt them down."

He watched, unsurprised, as ID cards were handed out. It was easy to guess what the soldiers were saying. Anyone caught without an ID card would be arrested, perhaps detained permanently. And anyone caught well away from their village, ID card or not, would face some tough questioning before they were released, if they *were* released. The Theocracy was fond of enslaving diehard resistance fighters and working them to death.

"They're leaving," Jess said softly. "And they're taking the hostages with them."

"We need to track down their forward operating base," Davidson said. The soldiers climbed into their vehicles and drove away without looking back. "And then we can plan a rescue."

The two slipped away as soon as the enemy vehicles were out of sight, making their way back into the forest and heading towards the insurgent base. Jess said nothing as they walked, her expression pensive. Davidson found it hard to blame her. She'd spent half her life waging war on one opponent, only to discover she and her men had been played for fools by another, far more powerful enemy, one that would seek to utterly destroy their way of life.

"I know how you feel," Davidson admitted, just to break the silence. "There were marines who worried about what the Commonwealth would do to their homeworlds."

Jess glared at him. "And what *did* you do to their homeworlds?"

"Nothing," Patrick said. "But they were afraid our influence would contaminate their way of life."

"And that's precisely what you did here," Jess said. "And now the Theocracy is doing the same."

She muttered something unpleasant under her breath and then kept walking until they reached the tiny camp. Davidson took one look—it was the first time he had visited the camp—and silently prayed it was only a satellite base rather than the main insurgent complex for the region. It didn't look very impressive, even under the forest's canopy. A handful of men were seated there, waiting for them.

"It isn't good," Jess said and briefly outlined what they'd seen. "The noose is tightening."

"It's worse," a tall, dark-skinned man said. "We got a runner from Gibraltar."

Davidson felt his eyes narrow in suspicion. "Did you search him carefully?"

"Of course we did," the speaker said. "We're not stupid."

"Bring him forward," Jess ordered. "Let us hear what he has to say."

Davidson watched grimly as the young man, his hands bound behind his back and his eyes blindfolded, was brought out. There were no obvious signs of torture, yet there was something in the way the runner held himself that suggested he knew he was damned. If he'd been exposed when the Theocracy had rounded up insurgents in Gibraltar, they might well have let him go deliberately, either in the hopes he'd lead them to the rebel base or because his mere presence might spread doubt and confusion. Davidson wasn't sure he wanted the young man to speak.

"Luis," Jess said, "tell us what happened."

"They rounded us up," Luis said. There was a gasp from one of the men behind him. "My cell . . . they took us all. They just left us in the camp for five days, then dragged me out and showed me that they had my family captive. And then they told me that I could take a message to you or watch my family die, one by one."

He broke down into sobs. "Sophia is only nine," he said. "How could I let them . . . they were going to . . ."

Davidson could guess. They'd threatened to rape his sister, forcing him to make a very hard choice.

"They sent you with a message, I presume," Jess said. Her voice was very cold. "What did they want you to say?"

"They're organizing the city to suit themselves," Luis said between sobs. "If we don't submit to them, they will crush us; if we join them, we will have rewards . . ."

"That's assuming we trust them," one of the other men said. He spat. "Why should we trust a word this traitor has to say? Cut his throat and have done with it."

"Interrogate him," Davidson urged. It had been seven days since the occupation had begun. Luis hadn't spent *all* of that time in a detention camp. But there was the very real possibility that the Theocracy had stuck a tracker on him. A nanotech implant would be undetectable, at least with the tech they had on hand, until it started to transmit. "But we can't afford to take him elsewhere."

Jess glared at Luis. "You ask him questions," she snarled. "I need to make preparations to break camp."

Davidson sat down in front of Luis, then sighed inwardly. There wouldn't be any need for drugs or torture to make Luis talk, he was sure. The young man wasn't trying to hide anything from them. It was merely a matter of asking the right questions.

"Tell me what happened when they invested the city," he said. "What happened to you?"

The story that emerged was horrific, although unsurprising. Most of the insurgents had burned themselves up attacking Government House, believing that the day of liberation was finally at hand. The survivors had fallen back when the Theocracy's forces had reached the city and surrounded it, then advanced towards the center in multiple armored prongs. They'd kept warning people to stay in their homes, and most of the population, seeing bullets flying, had done as they were told. But this had allowed the Theocracy a chance to snatch all the city's vital installations before the insurgents could react.

It had only gotten worse from then onwards, Luis admitted. The Theocracy had been everywhere, taking over schools as barracks and knocking down places of worship with a fervor born of fanaticism. The destruction of one church, the oldest on the planet, had brought worshippers out in protest . . . and they'd been met with armed troops, who'd opened fire. And then the survivors had been put to work clearing rubble from the streets.

"By the time I was caught, restrictions were tightening on everyone," he said. "My sisters were told never to go outside without a male escort; kids were told they wouldn't be going back to school until the educational system was revised. Anyone who tried to hide a priest or a government official was shot. I don't know what happened to the priests."

"I can guess," Davidson said.

He sighed. Terror, it seemed, would be the driving force behind the occupation. The locals would be terrorized until they submitted, having been taught the futility of resistance. Some would always break and accept the new order, changing their religion to blend in with their new masters. And then they would serve as puppets for the Theocracy.

The social controls weaken the society they overwhelm, he thought. It would be easy to restrict women from all public roles if going outside alone brought threats of rape or death. How long would it be, he asked himself, before such separation of the sexes seemed natural and right? *And it also serves as incentive for women to convert, perhaps leading their husbands with them.*

"I wonder," he said. "Is the PDC still intact?"

"I don't know," Luis said. "I heard nothing."

Davidson scowled. The PDC was immune to orbital bombardment, at least from weapons that wouldn't render the planet uninhabitable. But the base could be surrounded, isolated, and then stormed by forces on the ground. And, with jamming still pervading the airwaves, there was no way to know what had happened to General Eastside. All Davidson could do was assume the worst.

Jess walked back to face him. "I think we can't stay here any longer," she said. She produced a knife from her belt and held it out towards Luis. "And . . ."

"Don't," Davidson said. "He didn't ask to come here."

Luis tensed. An unpleasant smell filled the air as he voided his bowels.

"He chose to carry their message," Jess snapped. "That makes him a traitor."

"But not a willing one," Davidson said. If the insurgency became increasingly desperate—and ruthless—the locals caught in the middle would turn to the Theocracy out of sheer self-preservation. "Leave him here. He can make his own way home if he wants."

"They'll kill me," Luis said. "I . . ."

"It's your only hope," Jess said. She pushed him to the ground, then used her knife to saw through his bonds. "Count to a thousand before you look up, then go wherever you want."

She turned and caught Davidson's hand, then led him back into the darkening forest. Davidson had to admit to the sharpness of her skills as she walked through the woods; even with his implants, it was growing increasingly difficult to see in the dark. He glanced up and saw flickers of fire high overhead as pieces of debris continued to fall out of orbit and burn up in the planet's atmosphere. The Theocracy, it seemed, hadn't bothered to sweep the orbitals after winning the battle.

"We had someone in a village that got visited by the new occupation," Jess said very softly. "He said they'd been told that any resistance would result in the destruction of their village—and that any sightings of resistance fighters had to be reported at once. And if they weren't, the village would be destroyed, after the hostages had been brutally murdered right in front of them."

Davidson winced. It wasn't fair to expect parents to keep their mouths shut when their children were at risk—and no one would take the chance the Theocracy was bluffing when it threatened to hurt the children. The villagers would be caught between two fires; they could serve the insurgency and risk losing everything when the Theocracy caught them, or serve the Theocracy and risk losing everything when they were punished for collaboration.

Jess caught his arm, then spun him round to face her. In the darkness, her face seemed surprisingly pale. "Tell me," she said. Her voice was very low, as if she was afraid of being overheard. "Do we have a chance?"

"Not on your own," Davidson admitted. There was no avoiding *that* conclusion. "The Commonwealth never wanted to rip your society apart, let alone take hostages and hold others accountable for what their brothers did. But the Theocracy has the tools to do just that, Jess. Given time, they will have your entire planet locked down tighter than Earth."

He shuddered. It was hard to know how many of the horror stories about UN-ruled Earth were actually true, but it was well known that no one had had any privacy, and freedom of speech was largely a joke. No one could do anything on Earth without leaving a trace behind, one that could be followed by the police and used as evidence against them. The entire planetary society had been falling apart even before the Breakaway Wars.

"Shit," Jess said. She let go of his arm, then started to pace frantically. "Should we just surrender, then? Walk up to them and offer the bastards our throats, so they can cut them as efficiently as possible?"

"Hell, no," Davidson said. "The Commonwealth is still out there, Jess. They will organize a rescue mission, given time, or simply win the war outright. And when the system is attacked for the second time, you and your people can strike against the bastards on the ground. You can bide your time until then."

"And how many horrors," Jess asked, "will go unchallenged until then?"

"Far too many," Davidson said. He paused, weighing his words carefully. He could understand how despair might be working its way through the insurgency, now that they saw their new enemy far too clearly. Somehow he had to try to encourage her. "And we will be staying to help."

Jess snorted. "How much can a handful of marines like you do for us?"

"Train you," Davidson said. It was true. Marines had a great deal of training in insurgent warfare, although they'd generally been trying to defeat insurgencies rather than actually encourage them. "And coordinate with the relief force, when it finally arrives."

He took a breath. "But we need to know if the PDC is still active," he added. A thought had occurred to him. There had been heavy armaments stockpiled in the PDC as well as shield generators and planetary defense weapons. "If so, we might have other options."

"Oh," Jess said. "To die bravely?"

"Maybe," Davidson said. He gave her a sharp look. Part of him wanted to ask her story: why she'd become an insurgent. He wasn't sure he wanted to know, though. She was a girl doing a job most of the planet would have said was a *man's* job. But she'd survived when others, more trusting, had gone like lambs to the slaughter. "We will see."

Jess eyed him for a long moment, then turned and led the way into the darkening forest.

CHAPTER THIRTY-SEVEN

"The PDC is still holding out," the cleric observed. "*Why* is it still holding out?"

"Because the Janissaries have failed to capture it?" Admiral Junayd asked smoothly. "Or because the Inquisition has made it clear that prisoners of war cannot expect good treatment?"

It was all he could do to smile rather than scream in rage. The battle had gone well, but the war was not yet won! There was absolutely nothing to be gained from mistreating prisoners, even if they were infidels who would never be allowed to return home, let alone imposing Theocratic rule on the locals. There would be time to convert the infidels after the war was over. But the Inquisitors had refused to delay their work. They *needed* a success to bolster their position when the Speaker died and the next power struggle began.

"You should flatten the base from orbit," the cleric said. "Stamp on it with a hammer."

"Anything we use powerful enough to crack the base's force field will devastate the local environment," Junayd pointed out, for what felt like the thousandth time. "An antimatter bomb would depopulate all of Cadiz. I hardly think the Speaker will thank you for exterminating an entire planet of potential converts."

He took a breath. "And the Commonwealth would certainly retaliate in kind," he added sharply. "We would see the entire Theocracy turned into nothing more than dead worlds."

The cleric snorted, but said nothing. Junayd turned his attention back to the latest update, cursing Princess Drusilla under his breath. Her father should have beaten her into submission or had her brain rewired from the moment it had become clear she was far from the ideal wife for a Theocratic officer. But he'd been merciful and *this* was the result. The Commonwealth had detected his fleet, the attack had been launched ahead of schedule, and a carefully prepared plan lay in tatters. Half of the attack fleets that should have swept into Commonwealth space were still on their way, while there was no way to know—yet—just what had happened to the fleets that had already reached their targets. And his goddamned fleet train was overdue.

Junayd cursed the planners under his breath. Surely they could have assigned more freighters to his fleet before he assembled it, but no; they'd insisted the fleet train would be assembled later and forwarded to him. As he should have expected, he was fifty light years from his base, waiting for the freighters to catch up with him. There was no way he could go on the offensive again until he had reloaded his ships.

At least we captured a few thousand workers, he thought. The Inquisitors had wanted to round up the space workers along with everyone else, but he'd managed to snatch the infidel engineers for himself and put them to work. *But converting their weapons to launch from our ships is impossible.*

"The infidels are still out there," Junayd observed. "They're watching and waiting."

He scowled. At least five starships were watching the system, sneaking in until they were detected and then escaping at high speed rather than sticking round to fight. It was hard to blame them—they were only destroyers, after all—but it was a constant headache. As it was, he didn't dare draw down the forces defending Cadiz or Cadiz VII. It left the other inhabited worlds in the system largely uncovered.

The cleric turned to face him. "Admiral," he said, "are you having doubts about the ultimate success of our operation?"

And if you knew more, Junayd thought, *you'd be having doubts too*.

"God never promised us an easy victory," he said instead. "But we cannot go back on the offensive until our fleet train arrives."

He triggered the display, then studied the star chart thoughtfully. Where would the infidel fleet go? It was tempting to believe they'd flee all the way to Tyre, but he knew better than to believe it, no matter what he told the cleric and the Inquisitors. The infidels had been caught by surprise, crippled by their own leaders, yet they'd managed to escape under heavy fire. They were no cowards, he told himself firmly, nor were they incompetent. And if they weren't caught by surprise, they would be a dangerous foe.

Ten days, he asked himself. *Where could they have gone in ten days?*

"Then we will wait until it arrives," the cleric said. "By then, we will know about the other assaults, will we not?"

"Perhaps," Junayd said. He hoped the attacking fleets could capture StarCom units, but he knew better than to count on it. The infidels would definitely destroy them if they had the chance, just to make it harder for the Theocracy to coordinate its offensive. "But we will still know nothing about how the infidels are reacting."

"That extra squadron of superdreadnoughts is doing nothing," Lieutenant Lindsey Harrison reported. "They're just sitting in orbit."

Commander Pete Hellman frowned. HMS *Primrose* had been playing catch-as-catch-can with the Theocracy's patrols ever since she had returned to Cadiz with the remainder of her squadron. To be fair, apart from the odd patrol through the asteroids, the Theocracy seemed to be focusing their attention on Cadiz itself and Cadiz VII. But it made no sense. The asteroid miners had had plenty of time to rig their facilities to blow, then hide in uncharted asteroid habitats. Logically, the Theocracy should have swept them up in the first few hours of the occupation.

"It could be a set of drones and nothing else," he suggested. "Do you think they're solid contacts?"

"They definitely came out of a vortex," Lindsey objected. She'd been a sensor officer long enough to gain plenty of experience. "I don't think they could fake that, sir."

Pete nodded, reluctantly. Four squadrons of superdreadnoughts, several battered; fifty-two smaller ships . . . the Theocracy had assigned a surprising amount of firepower to the system. It had made sense when they'd intended to trap and destroy 7th Fleet, but not now. There was little in the system worth taking, let alone tying up so much firepower in holding. He wasn't sure if it was a reflection of the enemy's power—they *could* afford to spare four squadrons of superdreadnoughts for Cadiz—or something else was at play. Were they waiting to hear from other attack forces that had entered Commonwealth space?

"Keep a sharp eye on the bastards," he ordered. He turned to face the helmsman. "Alter our course randomly, then take us away from the planet."

"Aye, sir," Lieutenant Shawn Dorsey said. "I don't *think* there's anything in our way."

Pete snorted. They were cloaked, and any hunting Theocracy starships would *also* be cloaked. It was unlikely they'd accidentally *collide* with an enemy ship, but they might well completely miss one another with their respective invisibility. He settled back in his command chair as *Primrose* put some distance between herself and Cadiz, then tried not to think about what the enemy might be doing. It was quite possible they'd already started hitting worlds far closer to Tyre than Cadiz.

They wouldn't have risked such a disaster, he told himself. An operation of that magnitude would be such a violent breach of the KISS principle that it would almost certainly be guaranteed disaster for anyone stupid enough to try. *If their attacks failed, they'd cripple themselves in an afternoon.*

"Captain," Midshipwoman Han said. "We're nearing the remote platform."

"Query it," Pete ordered. "Tactical, stand by all weapons."

"Aye, sir," Lieutenant Commander David White said. "Weapons ready . . ."

Pete braced himself. The platforms were—in theory—undetectable, unless someone literally stumbled over one of them. The spy probes were also meant to be undetectable, though, and the Theocracy had managed to detect one of *them*. If someone had managed to detect the platform, they might have staked it out rather than simply destroying it, watching and waiting for a Commonwealth starship to come along. And if the ship was engaged completely without warning, there would be no time to escape before it was blown into debris.

"Captain," Han said, "the platform is requesting a full data dump. Every last scrap of tactical data we have."

"Send it," Pete ordered. Was someone planning to *attack* the system? It didn't seem likely. The 7th Fleet was far too degraded to take the offensive. And yet there was no need for the data unless someone was planning to attack the system. "And then hold us steady."

"Aye, Captain," Davidson said.

There was a long pause. "The data dump has been sent," Han then reported. "There's no saved response."

Pete nodded. "Take us away from the platform," he ordered. By now, the signal would be racing across the system, where . . . *someone* was waiting for it. "And then sneak back towards the planet."

Davidson looked up. "Sir?"

"Someone needs tactical data," Pete said. "Let us see what we can provide."

♦ ♦ ♦

Admiral Christian was so much more efficient than Admiral Morrison that it wasn't even remotely funny, Kat decided as she sipped her tea. Apart from their first private meeting, he'd insisted that all meetings be held electronically, allowing all of his senior officers to attend. Admiral Morrison, she knew, would have insisted on his officers meeting him on the planet. Ironically, that might just have worked in 7th Fleet's favor.

"The data collected by the destroyers suggests the enemy are guarding Cadiz extensively," an analyst said. "One squadron of superdreadnoughts has apparently reinforced the fleet—we must assume those ships have full magazines—but there does not appear to be a fleet train in the system. We dare not take that for granted, of course."

Kat nodded in agreement. Cadiz was largely valueless now the war had begun, save for the facilities orbiting Cadiz VII. If those superdreadnoughts had been able to take the offensive, she was sure they would have attacked Gamma Base by now. The base was only meant as a stopgap, but it was the most likely target. Instead, the superdreadnoughts had sat on their butts and done nothing.

"A smaller formation, composed largely of battle cruisers, is covering Cadiz VII," the analyst continued. "We must assume that the industrial platforms have been occupied and their crews have been captured. The enemy has clearly decided they are vitally important."

She took a breath. "I believe the plan remains sound," she concluded. "They are more likely to defend Cadiz VII than Cadiz itself."

"Good," Admiral Christian said. "Are there any questions?"

Kat keyed a switch. "What about ground forces?"

"As far as we can tell, the PDC is still in our hands," the analyst said. "Her force field is definitely still active and Theocratic warships seem to be avoiding entering weapons range. However, it has proven impossible to activate a communications link so we have no way of knowing the situation on the ground. Nor do we have any links with anyone else on the surface."

Patrick, Kat thought, feeling a twinge of guilt. He wasn't dead. He couldn't be dead. And yet part of her was convinced she'd *sent* him to his death. *I'm sorry*.

Admiral Christian waited to see if anyone else had a question, then pressed forward. "There is no need to alter our basic operational plan," he said. "Force One will jump into the system in thirty minutes, once we are in position near Cadiz VII. Force Two will wait until hearing from Force One"—he glanced at Kat's image, sharply—"then jump out near Cadiz, sweep orbital space of any unexpected surprises, and then send down shuttles to rescue our personnel."

He took a breath. "It is possible the Theocracy won't take the bait," he added. "In that case, Force One will destroy the facilities orbiting Cadiz VII and then withdraw."

Kat couldn't imagine the Theocrats *not* taking the bait. The extra squadron of superdreadnoughts had been a nasty surprise. Combined with what they already knew about enemy superdreadnoughts, the Theocrats would have a pronounced firepower advantage . . . and Admiral Christian would be tempting them with the prospect of catching 6th Fleet in a gravitational well. A fleet couldn't open enough vortexes to escape so close to a gas giant. Even one ship would be pushing her luck if she tried to escape . . .

And yet they might well have shot their bolt, she thought. *If only we knew for certain . . .*

She shook her head. The cadets had been told, often enough, that there were no certainties in war. War was a democracy. The enemy got a vote too. Whatever choices the enemy CO made could be relied upon to screw up or limit the choices available to his opponents.

"We could always go after their superdreadnoughts," a captain she didn't recognize said. Her data console identified him as CAPTAIN YU. "They would be a tempting target."

"We may do so," Admiral Christian said. "But our first priority is destroying the facilities and trying to recover our people." He looked down at his wristcom, making a show of it. "Are there any final issues to discuss?"

There were none. Kat was silently relieved. A handful of officers from 6th Fleet had complained about *her* being given command of Force Two, even though it was composed of starships from 7th Fleet. The admiral had pointed out that Kat was the only commanding officer they knew and there was no time to get the ships and crews used to a newcomer, while 6th Fleet had drilled as a unit. They would be a match, she had told herself after watching one of their exercises, for a superior number of Theocratic superdreadnoughts. And they had the training and discipline to stand off gunboats.

"Very well," Admiral Christian said. "Force One will begin the offensive in thirty minutes."

He paused, then looked from image to image. "The war began in the most treacherous manner possible," he said. "They struck directly at Tyre itself and countless other worlds, leaving thousands of dead civilians in their wake. This isn't a localized border dispute, nor is it a rebellion against tyrannical central authority. This is all-out war aimed at shaping the future of the entire galaxy. If we lose, the worlds we have sworn to defend will fall under the rule of a religious society intent on crushing all its rivals. We dare not lose.

"We *will* not lose.

"We will fight," he continued. "We will fight them at Cadiz. We will fight them at Gamma Base. We will fight them at Cottbus, Hebrides, and Iceland. We will fight until they are pushed out of our space, then carry the offensive into their territory. We will keep fighting until we are standing in the ruins of Ahura Mazda, dictating peace terms to the so-called believers. For who can dare claim to believe in God when they slaughter civilians merely to gain a slight advantage?"

He took a long breath. “We will win this war,” he concluded. “And when we are done, the galaxy will be a better place.

“Dismissed.”

Kat cut the channel and watched as the images of her fellow commanding officers popped like soap bubbles. Thirty minutes. Thirty minutes before they would know if Force Two would have its chance to redeem itself or if they would just fall back into hyperspace and wait for the admiral. She sat for a long moment, then rose to her feet and headed for the bridge. Whatever happened, she told herself as she walked through the hatch, she would meet it squarely.

“Captain on the bridge,” the XO said.

“I have the bridge,” Kat said. She sat in her chair and surveyed the display. “Do we have direct datalinks established with Force Two?”

“Aye, Captain,” the XO said. He sounded confident. They’d improved the command and control system considerably during their flight from Cadiz. “They’re reporting that they’re ready to move.”

Kat nodded, although she had her doubts. They’d only had two days outside hyperspace to exercise the nine warships and five troop transports the admiral had placed under her command. If she’d had more time . . . she smiled, tightly. If there had been more time, the admiral might have put someone else in command, reasoning that the new commander would have enough time to meet his subordinates and learn how they thought. She knew she wouldn’t be allowed to retain command once the front lines settled, but for the moment she would enjoy it.

And give the Theocracy one hell of a bloody nose, she thought.

“Then take us to the first waypoint,” she ordered. On the display, Force One was already heading towards its target. It looked invincible . . . and yet she knew the Theocracy had more raw firepower. “Try to keep us away from any potential guardships.”

She thought briefly of the message her father had sent to her. It had been short and sweet, sweeter than she’d expected. He’d told her about his new job, at least in vague terms, yet thankfully, he hadn't tried to pressure her to return to Tyre. Even in wartime, her father could presumably have influenced her commanding officers to order her home. Kat was relieved, more than she cared to admit.

I will see this out to the end, she thought, coldly. *And I will not leave anyone behind this time.*

"We're approaching the first waypoint," Weiberg reported.

"No sign of any guardships," Roach reported. He sounded perplexed. They'd trained to avoid any starships near the planet. "Local hyperspace near Cadiz appears clear."

Kat and the XO exchanged a look. Standard procedure *was* to keep a guardship in hyperspace near a planet, particularly in a war zone. Who knew when the enemy might be sneaking up on an unsuspecting target? But the Theocracy might have concluded there would be no immediate counterattack . . .

. . . or they might have something else up their sleeve.

"Hold us here," she ordered. There was no time for worrying, not now. "We'll wait for the admiral's signal."

And then go on the offensive, her own thoughts added. *Let the dice fly high*!

CHAPTER THIRTY-EIGHT

"Admiral, I'm picking up vortexes—multiple vortexes," the sensor officer snapped, as alarms howled through the *Sword of God*. "They're opening near Cadiz VII."

"Show me," Admiral Junayd ordered. "And then bring the fleet to battle stations!"

He looked up at the display, thinking hard. Commonwealth's 7th Fleet was in no state for a counterattack—unless, of course, the current fleet commander preferred to die heroically rather than report home and face the Commonwealth's judgment for losing a battle. And there were more superdreadnought-sized vortexes than there should have been, if it were 7th Fleet alone. It suggested the Commonwealth had moved reinforcements into the sector quicker than he would have believed possible.

The display cleared as the vortexes closed. There was no way to track the intruding starships in real-time, not now. They'd have to take the fleet a great deal closer to have a hope of tracking, then engaging the enemy. He thought fast. Cadiz was important, but right now the facilities orbiting Cadiz VII were far *more* important. Losing them and their crews to enemy fire would make his deployment's supply problems, already bad, far worse. The facilities had to be defended.

And yet, the enemy would know he had to cover Cadiz VII. They could be setting a trap.

"Set course for Cadiz VII," Junayd ordered. The forces on the ground could take care of themselves now that his fleet had deployed the orbital bombardment platforms, which would hammer any traces of opposition from high overhead. "Open vortexes on my mark, then plot exit coordinates *here*."

He tapped a point on the display, well outside Cadiz VII's gravity well. If this was a trap, if the enemy outgunned him significantly, he could retreat back into hyperspace rather than fight a losing battle. Theocratic intelligence had already failed once. If there were more than three squadrons of superdreadnoughts waiting for him, he wasn't too proud to retreat.

"That's quite some distance from the planet," the cleric observed. "Are you sure you don't want to come out closer to the facilities?"

"We need room to maneuver," Junayd pointed out. The hell of it was that the infidels could devastate the platforms before his fleet arrived if they hurled themselves straight into the gravity well. There was simply no way to rewrite the laws of interstellar travel to get the fleet there any faster. "And we can try to trap them against the planet."

Assuming they don't outgun us, he added, in the privacy of his head.

"Vortex generators online," the helmsman said.

"Take us out," Junayd ordered.

Moments later, they slipped through the vortex and headed into hyperspace.

♦ ♦ ♦

"Captain," Roach said, "I am picking up enemy ships entering hyperspace."

Kat nodded. Hyperspace rolled and boiled as superdreadnought after superdreadnought plunged through the vortexes and slid into hyperspace, then set course for Cadiz VII. She had to admire their determination, although she knew it was driven by fear of losing what they'd captured. Normally, navigating through hyperspace within a star system was a tricky proposition, even though it was safer than trying to fly through an energy storm. But they didn't really have a choice if they wanted to protect their facilities.

She looked at her console, frowning. "Have they seen us?"

"I don't think so, Captain," Roach said. "But it's impossible to be sure."

"They would have closed to engage, surely," the XO pointed out. "Or simply launched a few missiles in our direction and fled."

Kat nodded. Hyperspace was always oddly twisted near a gravity well. Few officers would have dared to lurk so close to a planet's hyperspace shadow, knowing their sensors and communications would be utterly unreliable. If the fleet they were seeing hadn't matched the known configuration of the Theocratic fleet they'd observed earlier, she would have feared that it was another series of sensor ghosts.

"Give them five minutes," she ordered, "and then prepare to take us out of hyperspace."

"Aye, aye, Captain," Weiberg said.

"I did a head count," the XO said. "They left behind five destroyers, at least."

"Then we'll deal with them," Kat said firmly.

She sucked in her breath as the minutes ticked away. The destroyers alone posed no real problem, but the real danger was enemy gunboats—or one of their ships jumping out in time to alert the main fleet that Cadiz was under attack. She had no illusions about the balance of firepower. If the enemy fleet doubled back, she would have no option but immediate retreat, leaving the people on the ground to an uncertain—probably unpleasant—fate.

"Prepare to raise shields as soon as we exit hyperspace," she ordered as the seconds ticked down to zero. "Take us out . . . *now*."

Her stomach clenched as the vortex flowered to life in front of her, then *Lightning* surged forward and burst out into real space. The display flickered, then updated; a handful of red icons circled the planet in high orbit. Destroyers, she noted, and a handful of captured freighters, all Commonwealth designs. It looked as though there were no Theocratic freighters at all.

They must have wanted to capture freighters too, she thought, with grim amusement. *They can't fight a war without bullets and beans.*

"Target the enemy ships," she ordered, as the makeshift squadron spread out round *Lightning*. "Fire at will."

The destroyers had their shields up, she noted, but they clearly hadn't seriously expected an attack. Cadiz was largely worthless, after all, compared to the facilities. Kat watched with grim satisfaction as her starships belched missiles, launching far more than strictly necessary to smash the enemy ships. The destroyers, their vortex generators powered down, didn't have a hope of escaping. One by one, they were overwhelmed and destroyed. The freighters died moments later.

"All targets destroyed," Roach reported. He paused. "Automated weapons platforms are swinging to target us."

"Take them out," Kat ordered. They didn't seem designed to engage starships, judging from the surveillance records, but that didn't stop them from being dangerous. And, more practically, they might well have orders to bombard the planet indiscriminately if they believed they were about to lose control. "Then attempt to raise the PDC."

"Aye, Captain," Roach said.

"Standard communication links are down," Ross added. "I'm attempting to make contact through laser now."

Kat wasn't surprised. The Theocracy had blanketed the planet in jamming, according to the surveillance reports. It would be a nuisance to their operations, but absolutely nightmarish to any surviving Commonwealth forces. She had the strong feeling that anyone who'd remained alive would have gone into hiding, convinced they were the only surviving Commonwealth personnel on Cadiz. Or they might have been wiped out by the insurgents or the Theocracy.

"See if you can locate the sources of the jamming," the XO suggested. "We would make much faster progress if we could use radios."

"Aye, sir," Ross said.

"Captain," Roach snapped as the display washed red. "We were just swept by an active tactical sensor."

Kat blinked in surprise. There were no other enemy starships in orbit and the orbital platforms were being smashed, one by one. They didn't even have a *chance* to shoot back, not with weapons intended to bombard a planet rather than engage starships. But why bother with an active sensor sweep, running the risk of revealing one's position, if there was no way the information could be used? She didn't like the potential implications.

"Find the source," she snapped. "And then bring up long-range sensors and sweep the entire orbital sphere."

"Aye, Captain," Roach said. He started to work his console, then swore. "Captain, I'm picking up missile emissions in orbit."

Kat stared as new icons appeared on the display. The Theocracy hadn't managed to get a supply convoy into the system since they'd booted the Commonwealth out of it, unless the observing destroyers had missed something. But if they were critically low on missile stocks—she knew how many they'd fired during First Cadiz—they wouldn't have unloaded so many into orbit just to help defend the planet. It would have rendered their superdreadnoughts largely defenseless . . .

And then, as the display identified the missiles, she knew the truth.

"They took our missile stockpiles," she said, mentally cursing Admiral Morrison. The stockpiles that should have been used to prepare 7th Fleet for battle had been captured by the Theocrats. They hadn't been able to transfer them into their starships, but that hadn't stopped their commander from finding a use for them. "Order the transports to fall back, then brace for missile attack."

"Suggest we use our IFFs too," the XO added, as the missiles came to life. "We might manage to disarm them."

Kat nodded. "See to it," she added. "And use our own shipkillers to thin the herd."

She braced herself as a tidal wave of missiles roared towards her tiny squadron. If they'd had time to jump out . . . she checked the display and realized they had another five minutes to wait before they could make their escape, no matter the danger. Her shipkillers detonated ahead of *Lightning*, blowing holes in the enemy missile formation, but there were hundreds of missiles inbound. She gritted her teeth, knowing she might be about to lose her ship, her life—and the entire squadron. They should have anticipated such a trick from an enemy commander who had proved himself alarmingly wily.

"Deploy decoys," she ordered. If there was one silver lining to the dark cloud, it was that her personnel knew their missiles intimately. Spoofing them would be easier than spoofing a missile of unknown design. "And stand by point defense."

"Missiles entering terminal attack phase now," Roach said. "Point defense going active . . . *now*."

Kat watched, helplessly, as missile after missile raced into attack range. Thankfully, they'd had several days to test their point defense datanet—they weren't caught by surprise, not like 7th Fleet—but there were just too many missiles for them *all* to be blown out of space. Hundreds died, others fell to the decoys and expended themselves harmlessly, but dozens made it through the point defense network and rammed home.

Lightning rang like a bell, twice in quick succession. Kat grabbed hold of her chairs as the compensators fought to keep her ship and crew intact. She saw hundreds of red icons flash up on the ship's status display. Most of them vanished within seconds, but the remainder glared at her accusingly. Her ship had taken one hell of a battering . . . and yet she'd survived.

"*Graceful* and *Princess Royal* have been destroyed," the XO reported. "*Cornwall* and *Jackie Fisher* have been badly damaged."

Kat cursed under her breath. The missiles had specifically targeted the battle cruisers, the largest ships in the squadron. It was probably the only thing that had spared *Lightning* from destruction. And each of them had had over a thousand officers and crew . . .

She pushed the guilt aside, promising herself she would pray for them later. There was no time to waste.

She keyed the console. "Damage report?"

"Five shield generators are gone," Lynn reported. The chief engineer sounded harassed. "Major damage to . . ."

Kat cut him off. "Carry out repairs as quickly as possible," she ordered. It looked as though they'd been lucky. *Lightning*'s shields had been weakened, but her drives and most of her weapons remained intact. They could still fight. "We don't have time to withdraw."

She turned and looked at the tactical display. It looked as though they'd swept the planet's orbitals clear of anything threatening, but it was impossible to be sure. And yet she knew it didn't really matter. They had to move fast before the Theocratic fleet returned and caught them in the act.

"Check with the Marines," she ordered. "Have they located the enemy bases?"

"Aye, Captain," Roach said. "They've established a number of facilities in and around the planet's major cities."

She took a moment to study her squadron's status, then nodded to herself. "*Cornwall* and *Jackie Fisher* are to withdraw into hyperspace," she ordered. *Cornwall* didn't have a working vortex generator, but now that the missiles had stopped exploding, *Jackie Fisher* could take both ships into hyperspace. "They are to head directly to Gamma Base."

"Aye, Captain," the XO said.

"The remainder of the fleet is to close in on the planet and start destroying the bases on the ground," Kat added. "Do we have a link with the PDC yet?"

"No, Captain," Ross reported.

Kat grimaced. If the PDC was monitoring near-orbital space, they should know that the Theocracy's ships and orbital installations had taken a pounding, but what if they couldn't tell the difference between friend and enemy? What if they fired on her ships, on the assumption the Royal Navy wouldn't be able to mount a relief mission so soon? Still, there was no time to delay any longer.

"Engage the bases on the planet as soon as possible," Kat ordered. She glanced at the planetary display. It was dark near Gibraltar, just after midnight. Hopefully, most of the civilians would be in bed, away from the occupation forces. "And then warn the troop transports to prepare to launch shuttles."

She watched, grimly, as bases on the planet started to die. It looked so simple on the display, as if it was nothing more than a computer game, yet she knew the reality behind each icon as it flared, then darkened. People were dying—and not all of them enemies. There was no escaping the fact that a number of civilians—and perhaps captured Commonwealth personnel—would be caught in the blasts and killed, but there was no alternative. She had no time to land Marines who would eliminate the hostiles while preserving the civilians—and besides, she knew the Theocracy couldn't be allowed to develop a habit of using human shields. It was easy to imagine them using human shields everywhere if they thought it would deter the Commonwealth from attacking.

And yet, she told herself, the simple survival of the PDC *was* reassuring. The Theocracy had refrained from using weapons that would take out its shields, knowing it would devastate the entire planet.

But they thought they had all the time in the world, she thought. *They didn't know we would take the offensive so rapidly.*

"Captain," Roach said, "the Marines have identified a number of POW camps."

"Mark them down for attention from the shuttles," Kat ordered. She looked up and noted their positions on the display. Thankfully, most of them were well away from the cities. "And tell the Marines they can proceed with deployment . . ."

"Captain," Ross said, "the jamming is gone!"

Kat let out a sigh of relief. They must have taken out the generators when they'd bombarded the enemy bases on the ground. There was no longer any need to rely on the PDC.

"Transmit the prerecorded message," she ordered. Davidson would be down there, somewhere. She refused to believe he could be dead. "And ready the second flight of shuttles for immediate departure."

"Aye, Captain," Ross said.

The XO grinned at her. "All bases on the planet, apart from POW camps, have been destroyed," he said. "Their forces are in disarray."

Kat grinned back. Even if they had to beat an immediate retreat, they'd given the Theocracy a bloody nose as hoped. Its occupation force had been smashed. The Theocracy would have to put together another force for Cadiz, one designed to hold down a civilian population that had learned just how nasty occupation by the Theocracy could be. And the Theocracy couldn't afford to look weak, not now. The war had barely begun.

"The insurgents will take most of them out, I hope," Kat ordered. "Do we have any of our own forces reporting in?"

"Several," Ross said. "They're requesting immediate pickup."

"Detail shuttles to recover them," Kat ordered. "And warn the pilots to watch for ground-based fire. We can't assume the bombardment took out all of their SAMs."

The XO opened a private channel. "The Marines know their job, Captain," he said. "Trust them."

Kat flushed. She'd been micromanaging. "Understood," she sent back. "And thank you."

She forced herself to sit calmly in her chair, thinking hard. Assuming there wasn't a prowling starship watching her squadron, and none had been detected, it would take forty-five minutes for a signal to reach

Cadiz VII from Cadiz. They would have that long before the enemy commander realized the planet was under attack. And then . . . what?

They'd war-gamed the battle as best as they could, but they'd already been surprised at least once. Would the enemy commander turn and engage Kat's squadron or would he persist in trying to engage Admiral Christian? Given the Theocracy's advantage in firepower, Admiral Christian had planned a long-range duel rather than closing to energy range. But plans could go wrong . . .

"Shuttles are on their way, Captain," the XO reported. "The POW camp has been targeted for careful attention."

Kat winced. If the Theocracy had time, they might blow up the camp rather than allow the prisoners to be recovered. They knew better than to expect mercy from the planet's population, not now. She'd offered to uplift any of them who wanted to go, hoping to encourage a few defectors, but no one had replied so far. It was quite possible they wouldn't believe her message. The refugees had said that enemy soldiers were warned to expect nothing but suffering from the Commonwealth.

"Good," she said.

And now all she could do was wait.

CHAPTER THIRTY-NINE

Davidson jerked awake when his implants started to bleep.

"Wake up," he hissed as he sat upright. "They're here!"

Jess rolled over and stared at him. "So quickly?"

Davidson accessed the data download and blinked in surprise. "They're recovering personnel from the PDC and detention camps," he said. "This isn't a full-scale invasion."

Jess sat upright. It crossed Davidson's mind to wonder, briefly, how she posed as a man in such close contact with men, but he decided he didn't want to know. She got to her feet and looked upwards, peering through the canopy of leaves high overhead. Once again, pieces of debris were falling through the atmosphere, leaving trails of fire in their wake.

"So," she said, "are you going to leave?"

Davidson considered it briefly. Part of him wanted to stay and help prepare the locals to fight for their freedom. But he knew his duty. His orders were to call for pickup, then return to the Commonwealth to join the war. One marine wouldn't make much difference, he tried to tell himself, but Kat would need him.

"We need to call a shuttle," he said. "Come with us."

Jess glared at him. "Are you suggesting I just abandon my homeworld?"

"No," Davidson said. "I'm suggesting you come with us now, help build up a force to recover your world, and then return when the Royal Navy retakes the system for good."

He took a breath. "They're going to be mad when they return," he added. Flashes of light in the distance suggested that nearby enemy bases were under attack. "They'll sweep the countryside for anyone who might have helped the resistance. Come with us and you can survive . . ."

"I am going to stay," Jess said. She turned and addressed the marines. "Any of you who wish to stay too will be welcome. If not, we wish you the very best of luck."

Davidson winced. He understood, all too well. If his homeworld had been occupied, he would have wanted to stay and fight too, even though he knew it would be futile. He was damned if he was surrendering to the Theocrats. But he also knew that he had his duty.

"If any of you wish to stay," he said, "I'll put you on detached duty. But it may be years before Cadiz is liberated."

He looked at Jess, deliberately not looking at his men. "Go underground, stay out of sight, and build up your forces," he said. "Keep our radios—we've already shown you how to use them. When we return to the system, we will contact you and coordinate our activities with your forces. But don't engage the enemy too openly."

"It depends on what they do," Jess said. "Call your shuttle, Patrick."

"Captain," Corporal Loomis said, "I'd like to stay."

Davidson sighed. Loomis had been talking to the farm girl . . . perhaps he should have had a word with him before he became too attached. But there had seemed no point in interfering with something that might have helped, if they had remained stuck on Cadiz. Marrying into local families was a common insurgent trick, creating ties that made it harder for their new relatives to betray them.

"Then make sure you do not fall into their hands," Davidson ordered.

He wanted to scream at his subordinate, to point out that their duty lay elsewhere, but it would do no good. Instead, he nodded shortly at the younger man. "And watch yourself on this planet."

Turning, he led the way towards the nearest suitable landing zone, using his implants to signal for pickup. Moments later, he had a reply. The shuttle was on the way.

♦ ♦ ♦

"The enemy are holding the range open," Admiral Junayd observed. He couldn't fault the Commonwealth warships for their tactics, but it was irritating as hell. Both sides were launching missiles, yet only a handful of hits—none of them fatal—had been scored. "And our gunboats are equally matched."

"So it would seem," the cleric agreed.

Junayd kept his face blank. They'd managed to prevent the enemy superdreadnoughts from recovering their workers or destroying the facilities, but the enemy commander was clearly settling in for a long, stern chase. It was a losing game, Junayd knew; he had far fewer missiles to expend than his opponent. Judging by his opponent's decisions, it was clear his enemy was well aware of his weaknesses.

I should break contact, he thought bitterly. *But it will make me seem a coward.*

"Admiral," the communications officer snapped, "the planet is under attack!"

Junayd whirled. "They attacked the planet too?"

"The destroyers got off a message," the communications officer said. "It cut off before it could be completed."

Destroyed, Junayd thought.

Losing the destroyers was annoying—and losing the planet would make him enemies among the Inquisition. But it would be far from fatal. There was no shortage of ill-educated young men willing to serve as the hammers of the True Faith, not when the rewards were so great and oversight almost nonexistent. And yet . . . he took a breath. It might just work in his favor if he used the report as an excuse to break contact. They couldn't accuse him of fleeing in the face of the enemy if he was attempting to save the occupation force.

"Prepare to reverse course and enter hyperspace," he ordered. "Take us back to the planet, best possible speed."

♦ ♦ ♦

"Captain, POW Camp One has been liberated," the XO said. "We're loading the former POWs onto the shuttles now."

"Have the medics standing by," Kat ordered. They'd located every medic on Gamma Base and transferred almost all of them to the troop transports, but she was bracing herself for a humanitarian disaster. No one believed the Theocracy would take good care of its prisoners, not when they had shown a frightening lack of concern for their own lives. "And the remainder of the shuttles?"

"They're picking up stragglers now," the XO reported. "But there are fewer than we might have hoped."

They might think it's a trick, Kat thought grimly. There were interstellar agreements against broadcasting certain kinds of false signals, but the Theocracy hadn't signed any of them, any more than it had signed navigational or POW conventions. It was quite possible that thousands of Commonwealth personnel would keep their heads down until Cadiz was liberated, once and for all. There was nothing she could do about it.

"Have them returned to the ships as quickly as possible," Kat ordered. She wanted to ask if Davidson had been among the people recovered, but she didn't dare say it out loud, not even through a private channel. It would probably take weeks to sort out everyone who had been in an enemy camp. Many of them would probably be locals snatched up along with Commonwealth personnel. "And the PDC?"

"General Eastside has expressed an interest in remaining with a volunteer skeleton crew," the XO reported. "The remainder are being loaded onto the shuttles now."

Kat wondered just what the General was thinking. The PDC was tough, but it would be stormed eventually, particularly if some of the ground troops were withdrawn. Did he think he could force the Theocracy to tie up its troops or was he just reluctant to return to Tyre with such a disgrace hanging over his career? Admiral Morrison hadn't been the only senior officer in the system, after all.

There was nothing she could do about that either.

"Wish him luck," she said as the shuttles started to rise off the planet's surface and begin the climb back to the troop transports. "And get me a head count as soon as possible."

"Captain," Roach snapped, "I'm picking up a vortex—*multiple* vortexes!"

Kat swung round and stared at the display. Fifty-five minutes. Fifty-five minutes since the attack had begun. By her most optimistic calculation, it had taken the enemy commander little more than five minutes to swing his fleet round and return to Cadiz. She would have been impressed if four squadrons of superdreadnoughts weren't bearing down on her tiny squadron. There was no way her seven remaining warships would be able to slow down a single superdreadnought, let alone four entire squadrons . . .

"Order the remaining shuttles to lift off now," Kat ordered. At least they had a contingency plan for this, although not one she'd ever wanted to use. "If there are any POWs left on the ground, they'll have to take their chances."

"Aye, Captain," Ross said.

"Order the transports to start Operation Breakaway," Kat ordered. She ran through the situation in her head, but saw nothing apart from certain disaster. The sheer weight of firepower bearing down on her made any tricks utterly immaterial. There was no way she could just stand and fight. "And they are to prepare to open vortexes."

She shook her head, cursing the enemy's timing. If they'd come ten minutes later, she would have been able to get most of her people out. As it was, she had to pull off *another* tactical withdrawal under fire, only worse. They wouldn't let her open vortexes for the shuttles . . . or would they? She considered trying to open one close to the planet, but she knew what the enemy would do. A few antimatter explosions would force her ships to close the portal before more than a handful of shuttles could make it into hyperspace.

"Aye, Captain," the XO said.

"Move us to cover the transports," Kat ordered. "We'll cover them as long as possible."

"Captain," Roach said, "there are *additional* vortexes forming!"

The 6th Fleet, Kat realized. But they were too late.

"Stand by point defense," she ordered. A thought struck her. "Can you ID the enemy flagship?"

"Not without probes," Roach said. "Request permission to deploy probes."

The bean counters will hate it, Kat thought with a flicker of dark amusement. It really didn't matter. They'd lose the probes along with *Lightning* herself if the ship was destroyed.

"Launch probes," she ordered. "And pass the information to 6th Fleet."

Admiral Junayd bit down a curse as he saw the tiny squadron that had devastated his occupation force. Seven warships, a number clearly damaged, had hammered the forces on the ground so badly that even his most urgent calls couldn't provoke a response. Beyond them, their transports were already on the move, followed by streams of fleeing shuttles.

They didn't want to recover the planet, merely their people, he thought, coldly. Maybe they knew about the other attack fleets, maybe they were just playing it cool, but in the end it didn't matter. *They want a cheap victory they can use against us.*

"Open fire," he ordered.

"Admiral," the tactical officer said, "we only have a hundred missiles left."

Junayd clenched his teeth. "Then fire them," he snapped. It was imperative to deny the Commonwealth a propaganda victory. "Target the transports and open fire!"

♦ ♦ ♦

"Captain, the enemy fleet has opened fire," the XO said. "They've targeted the transports."

Kat nodded, watching as the missile swarm rocketed towards their targets. And yet . . . she looked at the display, silently calculating everything they knew about the enemy superdreadnoughts. They should have been able to fire enough missiles in one salvo to vaporize Kat's entire force. But they hadn't. Indeed, she had a suspicion that she would be able to swat almost all of the missiles out of space before they even reached their targets.

Understanding clicked. "They've run out of missiles," she said. "They'll have to close to energy range if they want to press the offensive."

"So it would seem," the XO agreed. "There's nothing to be gained by being *subtle*."

"True," Kat agreed. The irony was chilling. There wasn't a ship in her squadron that couldn't outrun the enemy superdreadnoughts if they hadn't had to coddle the transports and shield them from incoming fire. And that meant disaster when the superdreadnoughts finally lumbered into energy range. "Order the transports to expedite the recovery of the shuttles."

She ran through it again, calculating vectors in her head. The 6th Fleet had come out of hyperspace close enough to batter the enemy fleet, but if the enemy remained fixated on her squadron it wasn't likely to matter. In their place, Kat would have broken off and ordered a retreat, yet the Theocracy didn't seem to know the meaning of the word. Instead . . .

Missiles lanced towards her ships, only to be blown out of space or decoyed aside. But three of them slipped through the defenses and slammed into the rear transport. Kat watched helplessly as the starship died, taking over three thousand men and women with it. The remaining transports altered course slightly, ordering the shuttles that would have docked with the destroyed starship to dock with them instead. But there were just too many limits on the loading.

"Enemy ships launching gunboats," the XO reported. "The 6th Fleet is launching its own gunboats."

"Align the point defense," Kat ordered. At least they had hard data on gunboat performance from First Cadiz. This time, the enemy gunboats were facing interlinked shield generators, a working datanet, and computers that had a better idea of just how well they could perform. "Engage as soon as they enter range."

"Aye, Captain," the XO said.

"Captain," Roach said, "I believe I have identified the enemy flagship."

Kat looked at the display. A single red icon was flashing on and off. "Are you sure?"

"No, Captain," Roach said. "But she does seem to be serving as the communications hub for a superdreadnought squadron at the very least."

"Then target her with everything we have," Kat ordered. If they *did* kill the enemy commander, there would be some confusion in the ranks until the next commander took charge of the fleet. Even if they didn't, at least they'd give their opponent a fright. "And fire at will."

She watched as missiles launched from her ships, passing the gunboats as they swooped in to attack. Several gunboats died as point defense picked them off, but a number survived long enough to launch their missiles before falling back. They'd targeted the cripples first, Kat noted, cursing the bastards under her breath. *Amherst* fell out of formation as her drive nodes failed, leaving her to be overrun by the oncoming superdreadnoughts. She kept firing, her weapons raking at their shields, but it was futile. One of the enemy superdreadnoughts blew the battle cruiser apart with contemptuous ease.

"Ablative armor is not as effective as we had been led to believe," Roach noted.

"At that range, it wouldn't matter," the XO countered. "She was just blown to bits."

Kat looked down at the display. "Time to finish embarking the men?"

"Two minutes, if the remaining shuttles parasite on the hulls," the XO said. "The enemy will enter attack range in one minute."

"Evasive action, deploy decoys," Kat ordered. The minute rapidly ticked down to zero. "Fire at will; I say again, fire at will."

She braced herself as the enemy opened fire. Even at extreme range, even with decoys, her ship took hit after hit. If they'd been firing at closer range, she knew all too well, *Lightning* would have been atomized as quickly as *Amherst.*

"Shields are taking a pounding," Roach reported. The entire ship started to quiver, as if raindrops were falling on the hull. "They're breaking through . . ."

"Reroute all nonessential power to rear shields," Kat ordered. It might keep them alive a few seconds longer. The enemy commander was ignoring 6th Fleet in his determination to catch the fleeing refugees. "Continue firing."

"*Sultan* is gone," the XO reported. On the display, there was nothing more than an expanding cloud of debris where a light cruiser had been seconds ago. "They're retargeting their weapons . . ."

"The transports are ready to leave," Ross snapped.

"Open a vortex," Kat ordered. "Get us out of . . ."

The entire ship bucked like a maddened horse. Kat clung desperately to her command chair as the lights flickered, then came slowly back to life. The display vanished and then slowly booted up again, covered in red icons. The entire lower rear section of the ship seemed to be completely pulverized. If the vortex generator was gone . . .

"The generator is fluctuating, but still online," Lynn reported. "Recommend we get the hell out of here!"

"Open a vortex," Kat ordered. *Lightning* was losing speed as her drive field started to fail. It wouldn't be long before she was blown into atoms. "Get us out of here!"

The lights dimmed again, then the vortex shimmered into life on the display and they plunged forward into hyperspace. Moments later, the portal snapped closed behind them.

They had escaped—but only barely. And her ship was too badly damaged to be considered combat capable any longer.

"Set course for Gamma Base," she ordered. She shook her head, wiping sweat off her brow. Force Two had started the battle with nine ships, but only three of them had survived, all badly damaged. If the enemy gave chase now, they were doomed. "Best possible speed; 6th Fleet can catch us up later."

"Aye, Captain," the XO said.

Kat rose to her feet. They'd won, for a certain value of *won.* The mission had been a success, but it had cost them dearly. She couldn't help feeling that they hadn't won anything in the long run. But they had given the Theocracy a bloody nose.

Perhaps that's all we need right now, she thought. *Proof the Theocracy can actually be beaten.*

She shook her head. It wasn't reassuring at all.

And civilians will still see Cadiz in enemy hands, she thought. *They might see it as a defeat.*

"Order engineering to start repair work as soon as possible," she said. It was possible that they wouldn't be able to make it back to Gamma Base without help. "And signal the remaining transports. I want a full head count as soon as possible."

And then, she added to herself, *we might know if the battle was worth it after all.*

♦ ♦ ♦

Admiral Christian stared at the display, silently calculating the odds.

He could press the offensive, he knew. The enemy superdreadnoughts had to have emptied their missile magazines completely. There might not be a better chance to smash four squadrons of superdreadnoughts with long-range fire, hammering the enemy ships from outside their energy range. And yet . . . he could win the battle, but not the war.

No one knew how many superdreadnoughts the Theocracy possessed. Four squadrons might be a large fraction of their military—or it might be tiny, a drop in the ocean of their naval might. No matter how he looked at the problem, he knew he didn't dare risk prolonging the engagement and overplaying his hand. His 6th Fleet was the sole intact Commonwealth naval squadron for seventy light years. It had to be preserved.

And they'll be sending more attack fleets than just this one into our territory, he thought. *I'll have to oppose them elsewhere.*

"Signal all ships," he ordered. "It's time to take our leave."

CHAPTER FORTY

Admiral Junayd sat in his cabin, staring down at the knife in his hand.

He'd lost. He knew he'd lost. The enemy had reentered the system, devastated the forces on the ground, then escaped with a number of former POWs . . . and they'd taken out the facilities orbiting Cadiz VII. By trying to avoid a futile engagement, he'd accidentally ensured that the battle, although a tactical success, was a strategic defeat. And he'd shot his ships completely dry in the process.

And worst of all, he knew, was the simple fact he owed his mere survival to the enemy commander. If their fleet had pushed the offensive after their transports had retreated into hyperspace, he would have had to retreat himself and flee through hyperspace, knowing that he couldn't even fight back if they came after him. He owed his life to an enemy officer . . .

He lifted the knife, admiring the light glinting off the blade. He'd done everything right, he told himself; he had prayed, he had served the Theocratic Navy well . . . and he'd thought he'd been rewarded with his command. But everything had turned to ash. His defeat would mean certain disgrace, now that he looked to have lost the favor of God. Enemies would turn on him, friends would shy away from him, and even his wives would eye him doubtfully. He'd lost a battle he should have won. Was there a *reason* God no longer favored him?

But I did nothing wrong, he protested, mentally. *I did everything right!*

The thought was a bitter one, but it had to be faced. Were they doing the right thing?

It wasn't something he had ever questioned, not really. The True Faith's history had taught the foolishness of turning the other cheek to those who would destroy them. They had once been pacifists, intent on developing themselves and serving as a beacon of hope to others. No more. Those who had mocked and attacked them were dead, while the True Faith lived on. Their mere survival seemed a sign of God's blessing . . .

Yet he'd lost a battle.

Could it be that they were wrong? Could it be that all their other conquests were the result of invading worlds too poor or idealistic or stupid to raise the forces to defend themselves? He had always seen *that* as a sign of God's favor. But might it have been a temptation instead?

He pushed the thought aside, bitterly. It no longer mattered. All that mattered was expatiating his failure before it was too late. His wives and children wouldn't suffer if he admitted his guilt through suicide. He would no longer fail his people . . .

The hatch sprang open. Three men in red robes ran into the cabin. Junayd had only a moment to recognize them as Inquisitors before the first one knocked the knife out of his hand, then sent him flying to the deck. His hands were wrenched behind his back and secured with heavy chains, followed by his feet. And then he was rolled over and forced to look up into the eyes of his cleric.

"Admiral," the cleric said, his voice very flat, "you will be taken back to face the Speaker for your failure."

Of course, Junayd thought bitterly. *The cleric will be blamed for my failure unless he manages to put all the blame on me.*

But if he was put on trial, his wives and children would be held to account for his failures too . . .

He opened his mouth to argue, but it was already too late. Something touched his neck and he plunged into darkness.

"I'm sorry for taking you away from your work, Commander," Major Rogers said. He was a typical intelligence officer, wearing a uniform without any rank markings or other insignia, his face so bland as to be completely unnoticeable. "But we do have to talk to you."

"It's fine," William said numbly. They'd returned to Gamma Base only to hear that three more attack fleets had crossed the border. Hebrides, his homeworld, was under enemy occupation. He had no idea what had happened to his remaining family. Their great victory now seemed like a sham. "What can I do for you?"

"Your captain recommended you for promotion and your own command," Rogers said. "But we need you—and your connections—for something else."

William nodded, unsurprised. He'd expected his links to a smuggler gang to be either exploited or used against him. Now that the war had broken out, it was quite possible that someone in intelligence thought they could make use of his family connections, with threats of dishonorable discharges if he refused to cooperate. He *had* left it out of his file, after all.

"Yes," he said. He was damned if he was calling this young officer *sir*. "What do you want me to do for you?"

"We have an operation in the planning stages, with the intent to launch once the war front settles down," Rogers said. "Your brother may be able to assist us."

"You'll have to pay him through the nose," William warned. The captain had massively overpaid Scott for what he'd offered, although he had to admit it had paid off for her. "He doesn't have any sense of loyalty to anyone."

Rogers lifted his eyebrows in pretend shock. "Even his own brother?"

"He's a *smuggler*," Williams pointed out tartly. "Family loyalty is not considered something to sell or buy, thus he wants nothing to do with it."

"I see," Rogers said. "And he won't help you for free?"

William shook his head.

"Then we will find something to offer him," Rogers said. "A reward to match the risk we expect him to take. His crimes wiped, perhaps; the chance to go legit after the war. Does that sound worthwhile?"

"Yes," William said flatly. "But you will need to be careful. Scott is not a very trusting person."

"Understood," Rogers said. He stood. "We'll contact you when ready, Commander. And good luck with your ship."

He walked out of the compartment, leaving William alone.

It was clear what he wanted from Scott, William considered. Navigational data for Theocratic space, perhaps even assistance in linking up with underground movements already within the Theocracy. And then . . . William knew better than to expect Scott to put his life on the line for the Commonwealth. Rogers would probably have to arrange for starships to enter Theocratic space and start raiding behind the lines. They might tie down some local defenders and give the Theocracy some major supply problems.

Shaking his head, William rose to his feet. That was all in the future, if anything came of it at all. Until then, he had work to do.

"This seems very exposed," Kat said as she sat down facing her father's seat. Her implants reported more than a hundred privacy fields in the dining hall. "Is this a good place to meet?"

Her father was staring out of the window, peering out over Tyre City.

After a long moment, he turned to face her. Kat was struck by the change in his appearance in the five months since they'd last met, before she'd assumed command of *Lightning*. He looked older, although she couldn't have said why. Perhaps it was something in his bearing, she told herself. He'd been over sixty when his wife had given birth to his youngest daughter.

"It's important to show people we're not worried," Lucas Falcone said finally. "And we are far from alone."

Kat glanced round the dining hall, catching sight of two more dukes, several minor aristocracy, the third space lord, a number of society reporters and . . .

"Is that the *king*?"

"Indeed it is," her father said. His voice was very grave. "And I believe you will recognize the woman with him."

Kat felt her eyes narrow. "Princess Drusilla," she said. "What the *hell* is *she* doing here?"

"Officially, His Majesty intends to use her as a tool when the Theocracy is finally defeated," her father informed her. "Unofficially . . . she's taken up residence in the Royal Palace and they've been spending a lot of time together."

Kat shook her head in disbelief. "The security issues alone . . ."

"His Majesty has always been a stubborn man," her father said. "And, as far as anyone can tell, she's clean. No implants, no direct conditioning, no brainwashing . . . she's quite ignorant in many ways, but she doesn't seem dangerous."

Kat frowned, then turned back to her father. "Why did you ask me to come here?"

"You're quite the hero," her father said. "Your presence here will be as reassuring as *his*."

"Oh," Kat said.

The media had been harassing her since *Lightning* had returned to Tyre, the ship so badly damaged that it would need at least two months in the yards before she was fit to return to active service. Kat had been told she was considered young, beautiful, glamorous, competent, and valiant. But she also knew that none of those things staved off missile fire.

She took a breath, forcing herself to calm down. "And is there another reason for us to meet here?"

Her father smiled. "We could always discuss your romantic life," he said. "I note that you and young Davidson have been sharing an apartment . . ."

Kat flushed. After Second Cadiz, all the objections to having a relationship no longer seemed even remotely valid. They could both die at any moment. She'd taken him into her cabin as soon as he'd returned to *Lightning*, then moved into an apartment on Tyre with him. It wasn't a relationship she knew her family would approve of—Davidson had nothing to offer the Falcone Consortium—but she didn't care. She had her own career now.

And it was none of her father's business.

"No," she snapped. "I *don't* want to talk about my romantic life."

"As you wish," her father said without taking offense. "There is another issue, then."

He leaned forward, as if he wished to whisper despite the privacy fields. "I still don't know who was backing Admiral Morrison."

Kat shook her head. "Who could hide his manipulations from *you*?"

"Someone with as much power and influence as myself," her father said grimly. "I believe someone wanted to ensure that there was no chance of a war—or further expansion by force—and chose Admiral Morrison to serve as his agent. He could be relied upon to do nothing more than party on Cadiz. Politically, it's understandable."

"They crossed the line into outright treason," Kat muttered. "Even if their first piece of reasoning was sound, the whole scheme was failing as war came closer and closer, no matter what we did."

"Indeed," her father agreed. "But that also gives them a great deal of incentive to bury their tracks."

Kat couldn't disagree. Political manipulation for tactical advantage was common within the aristocracy, but this had almost cost the Commonwealth the war in its opening stages. If the people behind Admiral Morrison had *intended* to commit treason—and she couldn't imagine how they benefited—they would have covered their tracks very well. But they would have done the same if the war had been a horrendous accident. Hundreds of thousands dead, four worlds under enemy occupation, nearly sixty starships destroyed . . . someone would have to take the blame. And even for a duke, it would be catastrophic.

She turned and looked round the dining hall. Was she sitting in the same room as the traitor—or the useful idiot? There was no way to know.

"The war will continue," her father said. "The declaration of war has seen to that, I believe."

Kat nodded. The king's speech to his people had been magnificent. He'd warned there would be hardships ahead, that there would be many dark days to come, but concluded by informing his subjects that there was no doubt the Commonwealth would eventually emerge victorious from the fires of war. The Theocracy was powerful and dangerous, yet it was far from invincible. Second Cadiz had proved that beyond a doubt.

"We will win," she said. "Their system wasn't designed for a major war."

"Neither was ours," her father pointed out. "But I believe we have a larger workforce, a greater technological base, and a far larger merchant marine. We have advantages we should be able to use to win."

Assuming our theories about the Theocracy are correct, Kat thought silently. Few of the defectors or POWs from Cadiz had been able to tell the interrogators anything useful. *But nothing we've seen suggests the Theocracy is geared up to fight a long war.*

"And we can hardly back away," she added. "They won't let us come to any agreement, other than outright submission."

"True," her father agreed.

He leaned back in his chair, then met her eyes. "I'm proud of you, Katherine."

"But not proud enough to call me by my chosen name," Kat said. Still, she couldn't help feeling warm inside at his obvious pride. "Or to avoid using me to do your dirty work."

Her father nodded, then waved to the waitress. "Order whatever you want," he said. "Tomorrow . . . I'm afraid Candy wants you."

Kat sighed. Her sister had been holding society balls to encourage aristocrats to support the war since the lockdown on Tyre had come to an end. Kat wasn't sure who her sister thought she was fooling, but she doubted the Theocracy was remotely intimidated. The Commonwealth had already made a massive commitment to support the war.

"I have work to do," she said quickly.

"Tough," her father said. "The party itself will be worthless, of course, but there will be some . . . private discussion in the back rooms. Your advice would be welcome."

"Yes, Father," Kat said. She took the menu the waitress handed her, then skimmed through it, rolling her eyes. Everything on the list seemed to have been renamed with a victory theme, as if it was a vital contribution towards winning the war. "I'll have the Victorious Curry with Starship Rice."

Her father laughed. "Some people are trying to help," he said. "But . . ."

"It isn't very helpful," Kat said.

"Keeping people calm is our first priority," her father said. He nodded towards the giant window. "Panic down there will make it harder to fight the war."

He took a breath. "I wish you weren't fighting the war," he said. He pointed to the medal on her chest. "You've proved yourself, Katherine. You thoroughly deserved the Royal Lion. And you don't have to go back to the front lines . . ."

"Yes, I do," Kat said. She knew her father could pull strings to put her at a desk instead of a command chair, but she was damned if she was going to let him. "It's my duty."

END OF BOOK ONE

APPENDIX: TIMELINE

2030–2050—Return to the moon. Establishment of American, Japanese, European, Chinese, and Russian mining bases. Fusion power enters widespread service on Earth. Long-range missions are dispatched to Mars, Titan, and Jupiter. Collapse of Middle East, third world as resources start flowing in from space. Development of quasi-fascist governments in US/EU.

2051–2053—NATO-Chinese War over settlements on the moon. War ends with the collapse of China and NATO hegemony in orbit and beyond.

2054–2108—Large-scale settlement across the solar system. Hundreds of asteroids are settled, some independent, others closely linked to founding corporations, religious bodies, or governments. Fascist states evolve, but still see mass emigration of young and smart people who want to live free. UN grows in power, slowly bringing more and more failed states back into the global mainstream.

2109–2112—Professor Richard Anderson develops the first prototype hyperdrive. Exploration starships set out at once, only to discover that navigating hyperspace is far from easy. Eventually, very limited beacons are devised to allow navigation from Earth and an eventual safe transit to a new star.

2113–2180—Discovery of nineteen life-bearing worlds within range of Earth. First Expansion Era begins, with national power blocks claiming and settling worlds. UN creates first large-scale navigational service, constantly monitoring the storms and freak shifts in hyperspace that could make the difference between a successful transit or disaster.

2181–2358—UN Survey Service locates an additional five hundred worlds within months or years of Earth. (Hyperspace travel times are picking up as the monitoring service is expanded and technology for FTL communications is improved.) Worlds are settled by corporate-backed development companies, religious groups, artificial societies, and ethnic groups keen to preserve some element of their pre-space nature. UN assumes full responsibility for governing Earth and the Sol System, then starts expanding its claims over the first settled worlds.

2250—Tyre is settled by Tyre Development Corporation.

2291—Tyre Development Corporation folds into the Kingdom of Tyre (actually, a veneer over a state dominated by multiple corporations). Tyre rapidly establishes its own shipbuilding industry, intending to cash in on the growing demand for colony starships of all shapes and sizes. King Thomas is crowned; establishment of House of Lords and House of Commons. The Royal Tyre Navy is founded.

2359–2367—The Breakaway Wars/Breakdown. The UN attempts to assert control over various more productive colony worlds, claiming an overall right to rule mankind. Unsurprisingly, the colonies do not accept this argument and eight years of increasingly bitter fighting breaks out. In the end, rebel factions bombard Earth, only to see their homeworlds bombarded in turn. UN authority effectively ends; navigational service terminates, either through war damage or as part of the general collapse.

2366—Tyre formally declares independence from Earth. This is largely a formality, as Tyre was never in serious danger during the Breakaway Wars.

2369—The Royal Tyre Navy provides assistance to Gamma Orion, a nearby colony world, against raiders. With the concurrence of the monarchy, the Lords, and the Commons, the RTN starts rebuilding parts of the navigational network, patrolling local hyperspace, suppressing raiders, and reopening contact with other colony worlds. Local business people soon follow, intent on building up new trading networks to replace those destroyed by the war.

2370—Gamma Orion formally requests annexation by Tyre.

2372—After a bitter debate, Tyre founds the Commonwealth of Tyre. Gamma Orion is the first out-system member state.

2373–2390—The Commonwealth expands to claim fifty-seven star systems, most of which are grateful to join the Commonwealth. Those that aren't are kept outside the Commonwealth's Free Trade Zone.

2389—Hadrian, Prince of Tyre, is born.

2391—Kat Falcone is born on Tyre. She is the youngest daughter of Duke Lucas Falcone.

2397—Cadiz is rediscovered by the Commonwealth. Its rulers choose to decline the offer of membership.

2399—The Commonwealth's traders make first contact with Ahura Mazda, another multisystem successor state. Worryingly, it rapidly becomes clear that Ahura Mazda is a theocracy—and expanding rapidly towards the Commonwealth. Worlds are being forced into its grasp without being offered a chance to resist. Prince Hadrian (more accurately, the courtiers surrounding him) is one of the strongest voices demanding preparations for war.

2402—After a long debate, the Commonwealth determines that Cadiz is in a position of vital importance for any possible war. The War Hawks insist that Cadiz be annexed by the Commonwealth, even though it is a breach of the Commonwealth's previous determination never to force anyone into its fold. Eventually, after much horse-trading, Cadiz is formally annexed on a very flimsy basis. Unsurprisingly, despite sincere offers of technical support, an insurgency breaks out on the surface within months.

2408—Kat Falcone attends Piker's Peak, the RTN Academy.

2409—There are a number of "incidents" along the border with Ahura Mazda. Although the diplomats eventually sort out a workable border, intelligence believes that the insurgents on Cadiz are receiving assistance from Ahura Mazda.

2412—Kat Falcone graduates from Piker's Peak as a lieutenant. She is assigned to CL HMS *Thomas*.

2413—King Travis dies. Prince Hadrian assumes the throne.

2414—CL HMS *Thomas* is attacked by raiders of unknown origin while patrolling the border. Kat Falcone distinguishes herself in combat and is promoted to lieutenant commander.

2415—The Putney Debates. King Hadrian remains firm in his support of the War Hawks, but the Leader of the Opposition—Israel Harrison—moves against the ongoing occupation of Cadiz, pointing out that the locals are still resisting the Commonwealth, despite all the benefits of Commonwealth membership. Eventually, after much point scoring on both sides, the government remains in control and Cadiz remains occupied. However, the king becomes more determined to press the issue of war as soon as possible, particularly as the stream of refugees crossing the border has become a major problem.

2416—Kat Falcone is promoted to commander and assigned to HMS BC *Thunderous* as XO.

2418—Admiral Morrison is assigned to Cadiz Naval Base, following the assassination of his predecessor by a local insurgent. Readiness reports start to sink alarmingly.

2420—Kat Falcone is assigned to command HMS CA *Lightning*.

ABOUT THE AUTHOR

Christopher G. Nuttall has been planning sci-fi books since he learned to read. Born and raised in Edinburgh, Chris created an alternate history website and eventually graduated to writing full-sized novels. Studying history independently allowed him to develop worlds that hung together and provided a base for storytelling. After graduating from university, Chris started writing full-time. As an indie author, he has published eighteen novels and one novella (so far) through Amazon Kindle Direct Publishing. Professionally, he has published *The Royal Sorceress*, *Bookworm*, *A Life Less Ordinary*, *Sufficiently Advanced Technology*, *The Royal Sorceress II: The Great Game* and *Bookworm II: The Very Ugly Duckling* with Elsewhen Press, and *Schooled in Magic* through Twilight Times Books.

As a matter of principle, all of Chris's self-published Kindle books are DRM-free.

Chris has a blog where he publishes updates, snippets, and world-building notes at http://chrishanger.wordpress.com/, and a website at http://www.chrishanger.net.

Chris is currently living in Edinburgh with his partner, muse, and critic Aisha.